A MURDER
MOST FRENCH

Kensington books by
Colleen Cambridge

The Phyllida Bright mystery series

Murder at Mallowan Hall

A Trace of Poison

Murder by Invitation Only

Murder Takes the Stage

An American in Paris mystery series

Mastering the Art of French Murder

A Murder Most French

A MURDER
MOST FRENCH

COLLEEN
CAMBRIDGE

KENSINGTON
PUBLISHING CORP.
www.kensingtonbooks.com

KENSINGTON BOOKS are published by

Kensington Publishing Corp.
900 Third Avenue
New York, NY 10022

All Kensington titles, imprints, and distributed lines are available at special quantity discounts for bulk purchases for sales promotion, premiums, fundraising, educational or institutional use. Special book excerpts or customized printings can also be created to fit specific needs. For details, write or phone the office of the Kensington Special Sales Manager: Kensington Publishing Corp., 900 Third Avenue, New York, NY, 10022. Attn. Special Sales Department. Phone: 1-800-221-2647.

The K with book logo Reg. U.S. Pat. & TM Off.

Library of Congress Control Number: 2023951794

ISBN: 978-1-4967-3962-9

First Kensington Hardcover Edition: May 2024

978-1-4967-3964-3 (ebook)

10 9 8 7 6 5 4 3 2 1

Printed in the United States of America

A Note from the Author

Although Julia and Paul Child lived at 81 rue de l'Université in Paris in 1950, and she most certainly attended classes taught by Chef Bugnard—as well as afternoon cooking demonstrations—at L'Ecole de Cordon Bleu, Julia Child never witnessed or was involved in a murder at one of those classes . . . or anywhere, as far as the author knows. Thus, Tabitha Knight, her "messieurs," and the deadly occurrences in this book are complete figments of the author's imagination.

CHAPTER 1

Paris
January 23, 1950

I WAS JUST ABOUT TO CRACK THE SECOND OF TWO EGGS INTO A BOWL when I hesitated.

Now, what had Julia told me about scrambling eggs?

I sighed, frowning, summoning the memory of my good friend and neighbor Julia Child and her enthusiastic description of the best way—the *very* best way—to make scrambled eggs, because apparently, we Americans had been doing it all wrong, and she'd learned the correct process at Le Cordon Bleu, the prestigious cooking school here in Paris.

I squinted, trying to remember. . . . Did I add butter to the pan or to the eggs? And what about the milk or cream? Did I whisk it into the eggs or into the pan? And when did I put in the tarragon?

I sipped my well-sugared black coffee and was still vacillating on the next step after the basic one of cracking an egg when someone banged the front door knocker.

I fumbled the second egg, saved it, then hurried to answer the knocking before it—or our little dog, who was a champion barker—woke my *grand-père* and Oncle Rafe. My messieurs, as I affectionately referred to them, along with Oscar Wilde, the dog, were still sleeping on the floor above and weren't due to rise for at least another hour. Madame X, the cat, might awaken, but at least she wouldn't make any noise. She'd simply sneer.

"Julia!" I cried in surprise when I opened the door to my friend. "Aren't you supposed to be in class?"

She was enrolled at Le Cordon Bleu and normally spent her mornings tucked away in the basement of that building with eleven former American GIs and the kind but exacting Chef Bugnard. She was the only woman in the class and, according to her, the one who took it the most seriously.

"There's a problem with the ovens today, and *monsieur le chef* canceled our classes this morning," Julia explained. She was beaming, as she usually was, a barely leashed font of energy and enthusiasm about life, new experiences and, most of all, *food.*

Somewhere over six feet, two inches tall—she tended to underestimate her height when asked—Julia swept into the house with her muffler and coat flowing, dragging the hat off her curling brown hair. She plopped two canvas tote bags onto a chair.

"Are you going to the market? I need to go, and I thought I would see—What are you cooking?" she asked, sniffing, as she unwound herself from the muffler and coat.

Could she actually smell the raw egg from the foyer?

"How did you know?" Instead of hanging them in the closet, I slung her coat and scarf over the banister.

"I smell tarragon . . . and, besides, you're holding an egg." Her eyes danced with humor.

"Oh!" I laughed. Of course she would smell the freshly chopped herb. "I was trying to make scrambled eggs, because I wanted something different than an omelette. But I couldn't remember when to add the butter. And the cream," I added with a weak laugh. "And . . . actually how to do it."

Julia had taught me how to make omelettes, and I could usually muddle through the process and produce something quite delicious—to the relief of Grand-père and Oncle Rafe—but this morning I'd thought I'd try scrambled eggs. After all, you can only eat so many omelettes.

(I don't feel that way about cheese and baguettes, however. I could eat cheese with a torn piece of crusty bread every day for the rest of my life and not mind it at all. Especially if it was accompanied by a nice red wine.)

"Oh! *Les oeufs brouillés* with fresh tarragon! *Magnifique!*" Julia said, breezing toward the kitchen. "Let's have a lesson, then, Tabitha, since I'm unwillingly playing hooky. I'll supervise."

Darn. I was hoping she'd just offer to make them herself.

"Chef Bugnard called me out in front of the entire class one day," Julia said as she pulled on an apron and handed one to me. "Lordy, how I love your kitchen! Mine is so dratted tiny. Like a postage stamp! Anyway, monsieur le chef asked for volunteers to make scrambled eggs, and I figured I could do it. How can you mess up scrambled eggs? *Well . . .* you can!" She peered at the bowl with my single broken egg, then looked at me. "You didn't get too far, did you?"

I giggled. "No . . . I couldn't remember when to add the butter—to the pan or the eggs."

"To the pan. Just slick it all over the pan—no, no, this is not the time to be reticent, Tabs, you've got to *bathe* the eggs in butter. Let it melt all over the bottom and sides of the pan, and while it's heating, go ahead and crack the second egg in the bowl—you're only making two? What about your messieurs?"

"They're still sleeping," I told her. "And Bet and Blythe will be here in an hour or so and will bring coffee and croissants up to them in the salon when they get up."

"All right. Now—ye gods, don't beat them to death!" she said quickly as I started to vigorously whisk the two eggs with a fork. "Nice and easy; you're not trying to mutilate the poor darlings. Just enough to blend them, like you do for an omelette. Ah . . . good. Nice. Just—whoa, that's enough. That's it. Now *les oeufs* can slide into the buttery pan, like . . . so . . ." She watched me with an eagle eye as I poured in the eggs. "No, no . . . don't do *anything* to them for a few minutes . . . just watch . . ."

I watched and watched, glanced at Julia, who was also watching the pan of creamy bright yellow goo, then watched some more. I wasn't sure what she was waiting for.

"Ah, *now* . . . now, see how they're beginning to get a little custardy in the center there? Now, with the fork, you can stir them . . . Oh, turn down the heat! It should be very low . . . right. Now just keep stirring. Take it off the heat for a sec, Tabs," she said suddenly. "Let it rest—now put it back. We are cooking these little *oeufs* very nice and slowly . . . like a seduction in the pan. No rush here."

I listened and did my best, stirring with the fork—egged on (ha!) until I was doing so rather vigorously—removing the pan from the heat, then putting it back again, even as I was stirring. I had no idea scrambled eggs were so complicated!

"Now, now, take them off the heat . . . See how they're still loose? Do you see? *Oh la la!* That is *perfection! Now* you add the milk or cream, or even butter if you like—it stops the cooking there, right where we want it! There will be no rubbery eggs in La Maison de Saint-Léger! Yes, yes, a good splash of milk for sure," she said when I hesitated with the jar of milk.

"Mix it up, and then the tarragon. Just sprinkle it over the top, *et voilà!* Creaminess and lush goodness!" She smiled, as proud as if I'd built an airplane right in front of her. "Now, go ahead and eat. I've already had my croissant and *café* this morning. I got all the way to the school before I found out the classes were canceled. That's what I get for being there so early."

She retrieved a mug and filled it with coffee from the kettle, then sat on a chair next to the small kitchen table. I joined her with my creamy, custardy, tarragony eggs and the rest of my coffee. The toast I'd made before cooking the eggs was cold, but I was going to eat that, too.

"Oh my God," I said as I tasted the eggs. I felt my eyes go wide. "These are *so* good. You don't expect scrambled eggs to be anything that special, but these are *delicious.*"

"You see? You don't know what you are missing until you have food that is cooked *well.*" Julia was still smiling as she sipped from her coffee. "Chef Bugnard says that even the simplest, most basic of dishes must be given the same attention and care as the most complicated ones. Every little step, every ingredient must be attended to. And you must taste, taste, *taste!*"

I was nodding in agreement while still working my way through the eggs. I was torn between eating them quickly while they were hot—they were so good!—or savoring them. I chose eating them quickly.

Since I'd moved to Paris last April, I'd become accustomed to French cooking—so much better than the sliced Spam, Campbell's soups, and overdone roasts I'd grown up on. Despite being French, my mother is unequivocally *not* a cook.

And I'm not even going to mention the food they fed us while I was working as a riveter at the Willow Run Bomber Plant during the war. Julia would have been appalled—or, more likely, she would have sympathized.

After all, she had met her husband, Paul, while working with him at the Office of Strategic Services (which was now called the Central Intelligence Agency) during the war, and I'm not certain the fare served to them was much better than ours at the bomber plant.

A year or nine months ago, I wouldn't have even noticed whether the eggs were bland and boring—but that was before the change that had happened when I moved here to Paris. Food was no longer simply a substance to fuel my body; it was an *experience* . . . and I was learning to appreciate it.

"Come to the market with me, Tabs!" said Julia as I finished the last of my eggs and cold, dry toast.

I sighed as I put the dishes on the counter. Bet and Blythe, our day maids, who were identical twins and impossible to tell apart, would attend to them. I had been taught back home to always clean up after myself, but when Bet (or Blythe) had found me washing my breakfast dishes one morning, she'd been horrified and chased me out of the kitchen. And so now I left everything for them.

Who was I to argue?

"I do have to find something to make for dinner tonight," I told Julia.

"Oh, wonderful! We'll see what they have and find something

for you to make. Are your gentlemen getting tired of *poulet rôti?*" she said with a grin.

I laughed. Thanks to Julia's tutelage, over the past few weeks I had mastered the simplicity and deliciousness of roasted chicken—complete with crusty brown skin and delectably moist interior. "I made it twice already this week," I confessed. "Grand-père and Oncle Rafe ate it happily, but . . . I suppose I should try something else. I tried to make a chicken fricassee last night with the leftover chicken, and it ended up a mess. Watery and tasteless. And last week we had to resort to cold sliced sausage and cheese for dinner *twice* because I ruined everything. I didn't realize you could overcook sole."

That was the only thing about living here in Paris that wasn't perfectly glorious: the cooking for dinner fell to me. Just after I'd arrived in April, Grand-père's housekeeper/cook had left to stay with her ailing sister down in Provence. I had no idea when or even whether she would return.

I didn't *mind* cooking for my messieurs—not in the least. It's just that I wasn't that good at it, and what I did know how to cook was very . . . *American*. Which would not suit my very Parisian gentlemen, as I learned the time I made them spaghetti with canned sauce. I winced at the memory.

"Then let's be off," Julia said, sweeping to her feet.

I gulped down the rest of my coffee—Parisian *café* was worlds better than the Maxwell House instant coffee I was used to—and began to pull on my boots and coat.

Moments later, we slipped out the front door of the large, fancy home in the seventh arrondissement where I lived with Grand-père and Oncle Rafe. Most people, including me, would call it a mansion. Some would call it luxurious. It was a miracle it had survived the German Occupation intact. The only remnant of that deplorable time was a single bullet hole in the front wall of the house.

There were marble floors and high ceilings and tall windows and spacious rooms with walls papered in silk. There were three bathrooms—one on each floor!—and a tiny greenhouse built on top of the portico in the private gated courtyard, where I parked my cherry-red Renault, which had been a recent gift from Grand-père. The ground floor contained the kitchen, or *cuisine*, as well as a parlor, a sitting room—I wasn't certain of the difference—and quarters for live-in servants, which we didn't have. The first floor (which in America would be considered the second floor) offered access to the greenhouse through the salon, where my messieurs spent most of their days, along with bedrooms and a bathroom.

I was ecstatic to have the entire second floor, which was the top floor and almost like an attic, to myself. With its rows of dormer windows and a peaked ceiling—plus my own bathroom—the space was more generous than anywhere I'd ever lived before.

I pinched myself nearly every day, for I could hardly believe I was living there, rent free, within sight of the tour Eiffel and across rue de l'Université from Julia.

I stepped outside into the cold winter's day, but I didn't mind the crisp fresh air brushing across my cheeks and pointy nose. After all, I was *in Paris*, and today the sun was out. It was glorious to see the bright light spill over the distinctly Parisian buildings of creamy Lutetian limestone like a pale honey glaze, then dance over the lightly snowed trees and bushes.

It still felt like a dream, coming to live here with my maternal grandfather in such a beautiful, fascinating city—especially after the dark days of the war. I had been at a loss back home, and coming here had given me the chance to find something *unusual* to do with my life.

I hadn't yet figured out what that was, but I was enjoying trying to find out!

"I'm sorry your classes were canceled today," I said as we started down the street toward rue de Bourgogne and its outdoor market. "But I'm not sorry you're going to the market with me. It's always easier to find something to make with your guidance."

"Oh, me too, Tabs. I really hope the ovens are fixed by tomorrow!" Julia said. "I'd hate to miss another day. You're still coming to the demonstration at school this afternoon, aren't you? The chef is a wine aficionado, too, so he's going to be talking a lot about the proper way to serve and cook with wine."

"Sure . . . but how can there be a demonstration if the oven isn't working?" I didn't really expect to learn that much from watching someone cook, but it was always fun going to things with Julia. I was curious about her school, too. Besides, from what she'd told me, everyone who came to the demonstration got to taste the food that was cooked, so I was enthusiastic about that.

"The ovens in the classroom dungeon aren't working, but the one in the demonstration hall is," Julia told me patiently as we waited to cross the *rue*. "So you can come over to the school with me after lunch—do you have a tutoring appointment this morning? What time are you done?—and then we can make sure to get seats. There are only thirty spots, so we don't want to be late. It's three hundred francs for the class—is that okay?"

Three hundred francs was just over a dollar, so that was no problem for my pocketbook. "I should be finished with my tutoring by noon," I told her.

Thanks to Paul Child, who worked for the United States Information Service out of the American embassy, I'd taken on a number of expat students—most of them the children or wives of his coworkers—to help them with their French. Having been raised in America by my maternal grandmother and mother, both of whom were Parisian, I was fluent in the language. Back home, I had gone to school to be a teacher, because that was what women did—became teachers, nurses, secretaries, or wives—and so that credential made my services even more valuable.

I hadn't really *wanted* to be a mathematics and science teacher, but doing private tutoring in Paris was a dream come true—and the perfect way to use my degree.

"Wonderful. I'll pick you up at one thirty. You can ride over with me in the Flash," Julia said, linking her hand through the crook of my arm and bumping gently against me with affection.

The Flash was the Childs' beat-up blue station wagon, and I was mostly not terrorized when I rode with my boisterous friend through the narrow, dogleg streets of the Left Bank.

By now, we'd reached the market. It was early enough in the day that it was busy but not too crowded. Many of the students and bohemian residents were still sleeping off the previous night's debauchery, and the serious shoppers, like Julia and me, were free to go about our business.

This block of the *rue*—dedicated to the market—was filled with vendor carts and stands, pedestrians, leashed dogs, and bicyclists. Only a very narrow pathway down the center of the cobblestone street would allow a motorized vehicle to pass—and they rarely did, except early in the morning and late in the day to bring and remove stock and supplies. Some of the vendors had stalls or tents that spilled from the sidewalk onto the cobblestone street. Others, like the *crémerie* and the *poissonnier*, offered their wares from inside storefronts.

"Bonjour, madame!" boomed Julia as we approached one of the most popular merchants.

"And bonjour to my favorite mesdames!" Marie des Quatre Saisons beamed at us as we approached. Famous in the market at rue de Bourgogne for her produce, she was known as Marie of the Four Seasons because she always had the best produce offerings for each season. She was also a font of gossip and information.

A tiny, plump woman with an extensive network of wrinkles—and who seemed to have been around since the beginning of time—she usually had a cigarette in her hand or mouth. Madame Marie had baskets of the best potatoes, shallots, turnips, radishes, and apples at this time of year. We all bemoaned the lack of the more varied and delicate offerings that would be plentifully available in the spring—bright green fava beans, perky lettuces, strawberries, tomatoes, plump spring peas, asparagus wrapped in bright red paper—but for now, we would scrounge among Madame Marie's stock for the best unrooted potatoes, the firmest and reddest radishes, and any unwrinkled beets we could find.

"Bonjour, madame," I said with a smile. "And what do you recommend for me today?"

To my mild embarrassment, I had become well known in the neighborhood market for two reasons: First, because I was a young, unwed American woman who was half Parisian, which meant that everyone on the block was determined to find me a French husband . . . or at least a lover. And second, because I was the granddaughter of Maurice Saint-Léger, who seemed to be an object of fascination all on his own.

"Ah, but, Mademoiselle Tabitha . . . that will depend upon what you mean to cook tonight for your messieurs. A stew? A roast? Or will it be a savory pie? But first, tell me, how is it for you today, eh?" Madame asked, her gleaming brown eyes watching me as her gnarled hands moved over the baskets of produce, hovering over a stash of carrots, then moving on. She selected a bald white turnip with its pink-lavender cap and hefted it in her palm as if to assess its weight, then tsked and dropped it back into its basket.

"Today? Why, it is very much the same as yesterday, madame," I replied with a smile. "I come to the market, I buy food that I try to cook for my messieurs, I muddle about in the kitchen, and then I have a large glass of wine, and I take myself off to bed." I'd learned that when Madame—or nearly anyone at the market— asked how things were for me that day, it was a coded way of asking whether I'd met any interesting men.

"Taking to bed alone every night is not the way for a pretty young woman like you," tsked Madame as she offered me a different turnip, this one with a darker purple cap.

"I keep telling her that," Julia said, examining potatoes, then dropping her selections, one by one, into a small basket in front of Madame. "And I keep trying to introduce her to some of the nice men Paul works with or the brothers of our friends, but she doesn't listen." She, too, tsked pityingly at me, even as a grin twitched the corners of her mouth and her eyes danced.

"She's always too tired or wants to stay in with her grand-père and uncle, and so on. Why, I've been insisting she come to a special tasting event and lecture with Paul's wine club tomorrow night, and it's as if I'd asked her to cut off an arm! And there are sure to be some eligible men there," Julia went on.

Laughing, I shook my head and set the turnip in a basket that would contain the selections I would pay for. This exchange was the routine, and I'd become accustomed to it. It was part of going to the market in Paris, which was so very different than rushing into a grocery store back home, grabbing the items I needed, paying for them, and then zipping out to the car—having spoken to no one except an impersonal "thank you" to the check-out girl.

Here in Paris there was a process, an expectation—even a sort of artistry—around a visit to the market. It was never merely a transaction, but a kind of fellowship, a participation in a community. Going to the market and partaking of its ensuing gossip would not be rushed, nor would it be stifled. And everyone was unfailingly polite. No matter who you met or how often you'd spoken to them, everyone was monsieur or madame. The number of bonjours and handshakes you'd experience with everyone you encountered during a day in Paris was astonishing. It was a completely different, vibrant, and eclectic experience from my life in a suburb of Detroit.

And so I went along with the gossip and interference regarding my love life because I found it amusing and charming—if not mortifying at times.

What made it more amusing than annoying, however, was that Julia truly understood my desire not to settle down and simply be a "good little wife." She was so happy and so in love with Paul—and he with her—that she wanted me to find that same fulfilling experience. But even so, she and I both knew we each wanted something *more* from life than being a wife.

Julia had found her calling—cooking!—along with a husband who supported her in that endeavor (mostly by eating her creations and writing home about her triumphs in the kitchen), but I was still looking for mine.

"What shall I make with the turnip, Madame?" I asked, ready

to move on from the discussion of my nonexistent love life. It was nonexistent mostly by my choice. I was certain if I wanted to, I could meet a man who interested me. But it wasn't a priority.

"I think Tabitha might be holding out for that Inspecteur Merveille with the ocean-gray eyes," Julia added conspiratorially, winking at Madame Marie as she dropped several carrots into her basket.

I felt the heat of shock and embarrassment rush from beneath my muffler and up over my face. "Inspecteur Merveille? Where on earth did you get that idea?"

"And who is this *monsieur l'inspecteur*? Ah, I see . . . It is the policeman who helped to catch the murderer those few weeks ago!" Madame Marie leaned forward, her eyes wide with excitement. Everyone in the market knew that Julia and I had been involved in a murder investigation over Thérèse Lognon, a woman who'd been found dead in Julia's apartment building. "Oh, now, that is a new development, *non*?" She gave Julia a sly, knowing look.

"Julia, I have no interest in Inspecteur Merveille," I said firmly, knowing I had better nip this "new development" in the bud before the entire market climbed on board that train. I noticed that Mademoiselle Yvette, the flower seller (whose wares were obviously limited this time of year, but who still offered pretty fir and holly branches), was looking over from her stall with great interest. I could almost see her ears perking up beneath the stretchy red hat she'd pulled down over them. "And even if I did, he's got a picture of a woman on his desk, so he's obviously not available."

I had encountered Inspecteur Étienne Merveille more than once during his investigation of the dead woman found with Julia's chef's knife next to her—an investigation in which I had also become involved, thanks to Julia's encouragement and my own adventurous internal sprite, which had always gotten me into trouble.

Regardless, I certainly had no interest in seeing Merveille again.

"And the fact that she *noticed* the picture of the woman on the *inspecteur*'s desk . . ." Julia gave a little shrug as she smiled at Madame Marie *and* Mademoiselle Yvette.

"There's no reason I'll ever see *l'inspecteur* again, anyway," I said, feeling the gossip train leaving the station as both merchants nodded sagely and with glittering interest in their eyes. "At least, I certainly hope not! But what I really need is to figure out what to make for dinner tonight," I added firmly and desperately.

"A veal roast," said Julia, surprising me with not only her promptness but her seeming willingness to abandon a topic she'd mercilessly pursued. "I've just learned the simplest, most delectable way to make it—not that I think you need to be simple *en cuisine*, Tabs, dearie, not at all, but it *is* divine, and it's impossible to mess up."

"A veal roast sounds perfect," I said happily. "Especially if it's simple."

"It is! Simple and easy. You'll need—"

"Oh, oh, Madame Marie! Have you heard?"

We all turned to look as a short, dumpy man barreled toward us. His coat flapped around his ankles, and his nose was red beneath a heavy wool cap. I recognized him as Monsieur Jean, the knife and scissors sharpener from the far end of the block. As I didn't have the sort of collection of knives that needed careful sharpening—a fact that Julia often bemoaned—I rarely had the need to patronize his shop.

"What is it?" asked Madame, suddenly serious and alert. As one of the oldest and most respected merchants in the market, she was the de facto matriarch of the informal society.

"There was another of the incidents this morning," said Monsieur Jean, panting. His mustache needed a trim so badly it curled down over his upper lip.

Madame's mouth flattened, creating a network of new wrinkles around it. "And who was it this time? And why am I only hearing about this now, eh?" She squinted at him as she spewed out a stream of smoke from her cigarette.

By now, Mademoiselle Yvette had left her bundles of greenery and twigs, dried eucalyptus, and anemic roses to join the conversation. I could see Mademoiselle Fidelia, the egg merchant, looking over in our direction, as well.

"It was Gérard, and he was late today," puffed Jean. "And so he's only just arrived to find several bottles of his mead smashed on the ground, along with some jars of honey. The roof of his stall was torn away. The back brace has been splintered, too."

Madame swore gustily and without shame as Julia and I exchanged worried glances. As if reading our minds, Madame explained. "There have been now three instances like so in the last week. Overnight, a place which has always been left safe and unharmed has now become a target for thieves and vandals." She made a face and spat on the ground, but her expression was one of worry.

"Aren't there any constables that patrol the area at night?" asked Julia.

"Eh." Madame shrugged, appearing ready to spit again at the mention of the authorities. "*Oui*, but, of course, there are many other places for them to keep watch than here. The students, the philosophers, the *artistes*! Even the Communists! They're all much more of interest to *la police judiciaire* than a few poor market stalls."

"That's terrible," I said, looking around at the friendly, lively market. Even on this wintry day, it was awake and busy, and the street was filled with conversation, laughter, and calls. The merchants worked so hard to eke out a living, and to be targeted like this was unconscionable. "Has anyone been hurt?"

"No one has been hurt in the body, but there has been damage to our goods, and damage to the carts and stalls. Our livelihood has been injured. Our hearts. And there is damage now almost every morning, is it?" Madame squinted at Jean and Yvette, and they nodded in sober agreement.

"Have you filed a report with the police?" Julia asked, but the others burst into derisive laughter. Even the delicate and mild Fidelia, who'd covered her baskets of eggs with a canvas so she could join the conversation, scoffed in disgust.

"I guess that answers that," I said to Julia in English. I had suspected that there was still a sense of distrust between Parisians and their police force, since during the Occupation the authorities in general had been corrupt collaborators with the occupiers.

Returning to speaking French, I said, "Do you have any suspicions as to who might be doing it? A gang of kids? Rival merchants?"

Was there such a thing as rival merchants? I had no idea; back home we didn't have anything like these markets, so I had no idea whether there was any reason for one mead seller to want to sabotage another mead seller. I didn't even know what mead was until I came to Paris, anyway. Fermented honey. Who would have thought it?

Madame was shaking her head, and I wasn't certain which of my questions she was responding to. "No, we don't know. But something must be done. It was like this when the Germans were here, but, of course, it was them—*les Boches!*—who were causing the problems and taking our stocks and breaking things. *Pah.* Now it is *Parisians* doing the same to Parisians."

CHAPTER 2

*T*HE BAD NEWS ABOUT THE VANDALISM IN THE MARKET PUT A damper on the rest of our shopping trip.

However, we did perk up a little when we made our last stop at the wine shop, or *cave à vins*, of Monsieur Nicolas, for it was impossible to remain subdued in his presence.

"Madame Child!" he cried when we crossed the threshold, as if it was some sort of stupendous miracle that she'd appeared. He pronounced her name as most French people did—like "Scheeld." "And *la charmante* Mademoiselle Knight! To what do I owe this greatest of honors, madame and mademoiselle?" His hand gestures were as effusive as his words, and the thick gold rings he wore glinted with every movement. A trail of cigarette smoke followed from the stub he held between two fingers.

"Bonjour, Monsieur Nicolas," said Julia, beaming. "We are in search of the perfect bottle of wine for a veal roast"—she gestured at me—"and for the *filets de sole à l'américaine* that I intend to make."

"*Oh la!* What a pleasure it will be for me to help you, Madame." He gave a little bow. Monsieur Nicolas was slender and elegant, with sleek black hair, a long, slender mustache, and olive skin. As his *cave* was an actual store, and we were inside, instead of in the bitter January weather, he was coatless. His sleeves were rolled up to his elbows, and he wore a bright red necktie and a fat silk poppy of the same color pinned to the front of his black sweater vest. His shop smelled like cigarette smoke and whatever grooming products he used on his hair and mustache.

"Now, then . . . first, we must find the perfect wine for Monsieur Child, *non*? He has become one of my best customers over these past months." Beaming, he turned and began to peruse the shelves behind him.

"That's the truth," Julia muttered to me. "Paul's been building up quite a wine cellar. Thank goodness we've got extra money from my trust, or we'd be *broke* over how much we spend on food and drink! It's a good thing we mostly eat at two-forker restaurants." Two-forker restaurants were those in the *Michelin Guide* with a rating of two crossed forks, meaning they were of medium cost and quality.

Julia laughed joyously, practically dancing on her tiptoes. "We're *so* lucky, Tabs. I just want you to be lucky, too! And I'm so looking forward to tomorrow night's wine club meeting. It's not just the club. They can bring guests, too, and that's why you *have* to come."

Not long after Paul had been introduced to Monsieur Nicolas, he'd been invited to join a group of wine aficionados that met weekly to taste and discuss wine, often with special guest speakers. He joked that he was a Cordon Bleu widower and that he'd had to find some way of filling his time while Julia was busy practicing her cooking and taking classes. Of course, he was always around to happily eat whatever she prepared.

"And here we are . . . a most exceptional Maire et Fils Côte de Beaune for Madame Child and her esteemed monsieur to accompany the sole. And perhaps you might bring this one home for him, as well, madame. It would make a fine addition to his collection. A Chambertin-Clos de Bèze, nineteen twenty-nine . . . for a mere seven hundred francs, madame, and the monsieur will be very pleased." Monsieur Nicolas set two bottles of wine on the counter, giving me a wink.

As Julia examined his selections, Monsieur Nicolas turned his attention to me. "Now, then, Mademoiselle Knight, we must find you a most excellent vintage. A Médoc, I think, *non*, for the veal? One that will make your Monsieur Saint-Léger sigh with delight at her bouquet and swoon in bliss when she rolls over his tongue. And, of course, something the esteemed Monsieur Fautrier will appreciate, as well. To make the monsieur giddy with pleasure at the very nose of *une bouteille de vin* . . . Ah, I would love to see that." His eyes danced, and I could see how much he enjoyed the idea of impressing Oncle Rafe.

I hadn't realized until I'd been living here for a while that Rafe Fautrier was from *the* Fautriers from the left bank area of the Loire valley, one of the preeminent vintner families of the Sancerre region. Fautrier et Fils produced small and exclusive bins of wine. Although Oncle Rafe wasn't directly involved in the family business any longer, he was still a Fautrier and possessed a highly discerning nose and a sophisticated palate when it came to the national libation of France. From what I could tell, his connection to the wealthy and renowned Maurice Saint-Léger only made him more interesting and perhaps a little mysterious.

Of course, there were other reasons Oncle Rafe and Grand-père were considered interesting, as well—reasons I was only just beginning to understand.

"I've been trying to convince Tabitha to join Paul's group tomorrow for the wine club meeting," Julia said. "But she's being stubborn."

"But of course you must attend, Mademoiselle Knight!" cried Monsieur Nicolas. "Why, don't you know that the great Monsieur Loyer will be there? He has only just arrived back from London for the first time since the war! He was the proprietor of Maison de Verre, one of the most famous and exclusive restaurants in Paris, which, sadly, was overrun and destroyed by the Germans." He swore under his breath and spat to the side, his normally gregarious expression becoming dark and hard.

But the disgust faded almost immediately as he turned back to me. "They must be very fortunate to have arranged for the great monsieur to speak about his wines. Surely you can break the heart of your young man tomorrow night and tell him you will join Monsieur Child's club instead, *non*, mademoiselle?"

I laughed, brushing him off. "No, no, there is no young man, monsieur. But I—"

He stopped and stared at me. "But how can that be? How is that possible? No young man for the lovely mademoiselle with the chestnut curls and the intriguing smile and the flashing brown eyes? Where are these men who are not banging down your door? Do they not have eyes? Do they not have ears? I do not begin to understand the young men these days!" He tsked and shook his head sadly, for, despite the dramatics, he appeared deadly serious. "But at least you will go tomorrow night, then, *non*? Perhaps some young man will have the eyes to see and the ears to hear then, and the heart to appreciate. If he does not, well, then, I shall have to court you myself, Mademoiselle Knight." He said this with great finality, punctuated by a sharp nod.

By now I was giggling. After all, Monsieur Nicolas was surely sixty if he was a day, and I had just turned thirty. "All right, all right, you've convinced me. I'll attend—but not for any young man, but because you asked so prettily *and* because of this great Monsieur Loyer," I said.

"Oh, you won't regret it, mademoiselle," Monsieur promised as he set a bottle of wine on the counter. "No, no, no, it will be the most interesting and exciting night of your life."

Little did we know how right he would prove to be.

"Did you happen to bring your Swiss Army knife?" Julia asked as she navigated the Flash to rue du Faubourg Saint-Honoré, where Le Cordon Bleu was located. "Maybe if the ovens haven't been fixed, you could take a look."

"Of course I have it. You know I never go anywhere without my knife, especially since it saved my life," I told her.

"It sure did. Maybe I should start carrying a Swiss Army knife around in my purse, too—not that I'd have the faintest idea what to do with it." She chuckled. "But at least there's a cork-screw on it, which you know I'd put to use!"

I laughed. My multi-tool knife actually stayed in my dress or skirt pocket instead of my purse, which was why it had been handy when I used it to jam a door closed between me and a killer. It had, quite literally, saved my life.

Unfortunately, the tool had been destroyed in the process. However, Inspecteur Merveille had given me a replacement, which was a fact I wasn't about to mention to Julia. I wasn't certain she knew, and she didn't need any fuel to add to the fire of her harebrained idea that I was interested in Merveille.

"So, *will* you look at the ovens, Tabs, dearie? I wouldn't like to miss *another* day of class again tomorrow," Julia said, then crowed suddenly when she saw a parking place on the street.

I jolted a little as she swerved to grab the parking place, even as I laughed at her insistence. "I've never worked on an electric oven before, but I'll take a look if you want me to. I mean, if they aren't already fixed."

"Half of them don't work on any given day, anyway," she said with a grimace. "But apparently, they are *all* out of commission today. Hence the class canceling."

Julia seemed to think I was a combination of Henry Ford and Thomas Edison—an inventor who could fix anything—simply because the first day we met, I'd fixed her radio. And only last week I'd adjusted the Childs' new radiator, which had been acting up. And she'd happened to be there when I was fixing Grand-père's mantel clock last week—one of the cogs had been out of joint. I wasn't an expert by any means, but I did like to tinker with mechanical things, especially things that had moving parts, like clocks.

"Besides, how hard could it be?" Julia said as she concentrated on fitting the Flash into a parking space that might have been a bit too tight. "You *made* airplanes!"

"Well, I riveted pieces of metal in place," I told her modestly. "Anyone could do that, really, if they could handle holding up the nine-pound rivet gun for hours on end." That was why my arms were toned and smooth, each with a gentle bump of bicep, which, five years later, I still managed to keep in shape. But boy oh boy . . . that first week or two had been hell. My muscles had screamed at the end of the day, and I had hardly been able to move the next morning.

"If you fix the ovens, maybe Madame Brassart won't be so snide and rude to me all the time. That woman owns the school, and she does *not* like me. Well, she doesn't like *any* Americans." Julia huffed a laugh as she put the car in park and turned off the ignition. "So be forewarned."

We got out and walked a block.

"Here it is! L'École du Cordon Bleu, in the flesh—or the brick, so to speak. It certainly doesn't look like the world's most prestigious school of cookery, does it?" She laughed and pushed open the door.

I could see what she meant. The school was housed in an unassuming gray building on a corner of rue du Faubourg Saint-Honoré, and its blue and white sign was old and a bit faded. Inside, the foyer was tiny and plain, with peeling paint and a single battered chair. I peered down the hall and saw doors to four rooms or offices, but before I could start in that direction, Julia stopped me.

"Down to the dungeon first," she said, pointing to the stairs that led to the basement. "I want to show you my classroom, since we're early. And you can check out the ovens. Let's hope we don't run into that dragon Madame Brassart," she added in an undertone.

The place felt more like a hospital than a culinary school, the difference being I could smell the residue of aromas that had been baked into the walls and ceilings from years of cooking. The hallway was plain, cold, and sterile, and worn. And the basement—the dungeon, as Julia called it—was worse.

Low ceilinged, with old appliances—which apparently only worked when they felt like it—the classroom space was at least well lit. The scents of fried, roasted, simmered, and baked dishes lingered. Counters and tables were white and sparkling clean, and every utensil, knife, board, pot, and pan was lined up in its respective place.

"This is it. This is where all the magic takes place with me and the boys," Julia said, sliding her palm affectionately over a table. "I think I've made crêpes Suzette about a dozen times at this table." She laughed happily. "These are the two ovens that usually work. Do you want to look at them, Tabs?"

I went over and began to poke around, opening and closing the oven doors and turning the knobs to see if the insides would heat. One of the doors was off-kilter, too, not quite fitting into place.

It would be easy enough to fix; I just had to realign the hinge and tighten it up. I had finished that with a few turns of the screwdriver on my multi-tool knife and was waiting to see if either oven would heat when we heard footsteps coming down the hall. Julia and I exchanged glances, and I could see that she— my bold and ever-adventurous friend—was a little nervous about who might be arriving on the threshold.

But when the newcomer came into the room, Julia's eyes lit up. "Chef Bugnard!"

"Madame Child! How good to see you." Chef Max Bugnard spoke in English, which was how his classes were taught, as all the students in that particular course were American. He was about seventy, with a short, slightly round body and a bristling walrus mustache stained with tobacco. He wore thick round glasses and an easy but sober expression. His eyebrows were bushy and looked as if they had a mind of their own. "And who is this, here, eh? Another potential student?" He was, of course, referring to me. "*Bonjour*, mademoiselle." He gave a brief, charming bow.

"This is my friend Tabitha Knight, Chef." Julia completed the introductions and explained why I was there.

"Oh, that is so very kind of you, mademoiselle, to see to our contrary ovens," said Chef Bugnard, smiling. His eyes crinkled delightfully, and I could see why Julia adored him. "But they have already been fixed and should be working properly now, *non?*" He came over just as one of the ovens dinged that it had reached its temperature.

"*Trés bien.* I fixed one of the doors, as well," I told Chef Bugnard, demonstrating that it would fit tightly now, keeping the heat from escaping.

"I'm *so* glad to hear that! I couldn't bear to miss another day of class," Julia said, looming over our shoulders as we checked the door. "Oh, and Tabitha and I are staying for the demonstration. I wanted to show her where we have class."

"Of course, of course," replied *monsieur le chef*, still smiling. He seemed to truly like Julia—well, who wouldn't?—and he didn't appear the least bit put out that we were in the classroom. "It is anticipated to be an excellent demonstration with Chef Beauchêne. He is an old colleague of mine, you see, from my time after Escoffier."

"Oh damn," I said suddenly, looking at my sleeve. I'd been poking around in the oven, and now I had a streak of soot or grease on my arm, and it had smudged the edge of the sleeve of my pale blue sweater, a new one that drew out the little blue flecks in my brown eyes. "I'd better see if I can get this out before it sets. Where's the toilet, Julia?"

She told me—it was upstairs, out of the dungeon—and I hurried off. I realized I probably could have tried to wash off the streak at the sink in the classroom, but I needed to use the facilities, too, so off I went.

I couldn't have known how that simple decision would turn out.

After only one wrong turn, I found the bathroom on the main floor of the school and managed to get most of the stain out of my sleeve by scrubbing it with soap. I'd removed my hat inside the school, and as expected, my thick and unruly chestnut hair left much to be desired.

I'd given up on ever having the sleek, refined look of Lauren Bacall, but at least I could run a brush through and adjust the barrette that kept a heavy curl from falling in my face. I might carry a Swiss Army knife in my pocket, but I never left home without my lipstick and a brush in my purse. I refreshed my pink lip color and left the bathroom.

But somehow, I got turned around or took a wrong turn, because I ended up walking down a hallway that didn't look familiar at all. No classrooms, but two small offices and a storage room. When I ended up at a T intersection of a hallway streaked with smoke residue that I definitely hadn't seen before, I knew I was on the wrong track.

It was frustrating. The building wasn't that big, but somehow, I'd managed to lose myself in its depths. I was about to retrace my steps when I heard footsteps hurrying down the hallway perpendicular to me, and I looked over.

A young man—hardly more than a boy, really—was running toward me. He wore a cap and a ratty wool coat and holey gloves and looked as if he'd just come in from the outside.

"Is everything all right?" I asked, alarmed by his agitated expression.

"*Oui*, mademoiselle, but this must be delivered *today*, now, right away, to *monsieur le chef*," he said, his feet slapping to a halt on the bare tiled floor.

"Chef Bugnard? What is it you have to deliver? I can take it to him," I said, looking at the basket he was carrying.

"Oh, no, mademoiselle, not Chef Bugnard. It is for Monsieur . . . er . . . Ah, *oui*, it was Beauchêne. Chef Beauchêne." He was panting a little, and he gestured with the basket. Something heavy rolled inside it. "This is for him, and it must be delivered to monsieur *immédiatement, s'il vous plaît.*"

Before I could protest, he thrust the basket at me. I took it without thinking, and he thanked me effusively, then dashed back down the hall. The encounter was over nearly as quickly as it had begun, and there I stood in the hall with a basket slung over my arm.

It wasn't terribly heavy, and I could tell it probably contained a bottle of wine and perhaps something else. I peeked beneath its cloth covering and confirmed I was correct. Nestled inside was a single bottle of wine or some type of spirits; I couldn't tell exactly, for its body was swathed in midnight-blue and emerald-green silk damask. A jaunty red bow was tied around the neck of the bottle, holding its fancy wrapping in place, and I saw a gift tag hanging from its ribbon. I resisted the urge to read the tag, even though my impudent internal sprite thought it was perfectly fine for me to be nosy.

I supposed I'd better try and find this chef Beauchêne, wherever he might be.

I started back down the hall, reasoning that if I could at least find my way back to the basement, I could ask Max Bugnard where the other chef might be.

I was hurrying along when I turned a corner and nearly slammed into someone. I caught the basket before it tipped, but the wine bottle spilled out, anyway. I snatched it before it hit the floor, my fingers closing over the smooth glass of its neck; then I looked up.

A slender, brittle woman in her fifties was glaring at me with a thin-lipped expression. "And *who* might you be, mademoiselle?"

From Julia's descriptions, I realized immediately this must be the dragon herself: Madame Brassart.

I thrust forward the basket, now with the wine safely back inside. "I have a delivery for Chef Beauchêne, and I couldn't find the demonstration room, madame. If you could . . . um . . . show me?" I dared not suggest she might want to take the delivery herself, and I thought it best to keep Julia's name out of the situation for now. She already had a contentious relationship with the school's owner.

Madame lifted her bladelike nose and sniffed, looking suspiciously at the basket. The neck of the wine bottle poked out from beneath the disrupted wrapping. Apparently, that was all she needed to see to confirm I had a legitimate purpose. She jerked her chin in the opposite direction I'd been walking. "There. The room has a sign that reads L'EXPLICATION on its door," she said, looking at me as if I were an imbecile.

It couldn't be because I was an American; she couldn't know that, for I looked Parisian and spoke French like a native. I decided she must only be an unhappy or anxious woman in general, trying to keep the last vestiges of her school's prestige alive.

I hoped I didn't end up like her someday: cold, impatient, condescending.

"Merci beaucoup, madame," I said, then made my escape, the wine bottle bumping against the sides of the basket as I hurried off.

The demonstration room was exactly where Madame said it would be, and down a corridor I had not yet traveled. (By now, I felt as if I'd had a tour of the entire school.) It was a small space, with thirty seats arranged in a rising half circle that looked down upon the stage. It reminded me of a medical surgery for student observers. From what I could tell, the equipment here—oven, stove, icebox, mixer, and so on—was far more updated and well kept than that in the dungeon.

The room was empty, but there were signs that it hadn't been so for long. Supplies for the demonstration had already been carted in, and I smelled the scent of raw meat and fresh fish. There was also the underlying scent of stale cigarette smoke.

I wasn't certain whether I should just leave the basket with the other supplies or attempt to find Chef Beauchêne and deliver it in person. But then I heard voices. They were coming from behind the door at the back of the dais-like cooking stage.

I wove my way between the semicircular rows of chairs that were arranged like choir risers down to the platform. As I drew closer, I could hear the voices better and realized they sounded angry.

Whoever it was—it sounded like two men—they were shouting at each other. The French are expressive and dramatic, raising their voices with passion and alacrity over any topic, so I wasn't alarmed.

One of them said, "But I will *never* . . ."

And the response was, "Die first!"

I still wasn't alarmed, having indulged in such hyperbole myself, but I did hesitate before the door, which wasn't completely closed. I couldn't see who was beyond the narrow crack, but their words continued to filter out, remaining heated and antagonistic.

There was a sharp expletive from one of the men; then the door flew open. I was just far enough away that it didn't slam into me, but I certainly felt the rush of air from the motion.

The man, who was dressed in chef's whites, jolted a little when he saw me. His face appeared red with anger or distress, but he immediately attempted to contain his emotions.

"Mademoiselle . . . may I help you?" he said, shutting the door behind him without looking.

But to the delight of my curious internal imp, I had managed to get a good look at the man with whom he'd been arguing. I had seen lots of white hair, along with a strawberry-blond beard and mustache, on a stocky, red-faced man before the door closed.

"Oh, *oui*, Monsieur . . . Beauchêne? Is it you, *monsieur le chef*?" I smiled, and when he nodded in affirmation, I gestured with the basket. "This was delivered for you. I was asked to bring it right away. Perhaps it's something you need for the demonstration?"

He took the basket, a mystified and curious look on his face. Beauchêne was about the same age as the man with whom he'd been arguing, as well as Chef Bugnard—that is to say, around seventy. He was also slightly round but taller than Bugnard. His unruly beard and mustache seemed to be more the result of simply not caring to shave than any fashion statement. The distinct waft of alcohol drifted from his person, as if he'd just finished a large glass of wine or whisky.

"Ah, merci beaucoup, mademoiselle," he said, flipping up the cloth covering. When he saw the contents, he set down the basket and pulled out the silk-wrapped bottle, murmuring something I couldn't hear.

There was no need for me to stay, but of course, I was curious about it all, and so I lingered as he read the tag.

His eyebrows rose, and his face changed from the sober, tense expression that had remained from his altercation to one of pure delight and pleasure. "*Non!*" he exclaimed, glancing at me, then returning his avid attention to the wrapped wine. "*Qu'est-ce que c'est?*"

He tore off the ribbon and pulled away the silk to reveal a dark bottle that, even to my amateur eyes, appeared quite old. Its label was worn and battered, as if the bottle had been stored somewhere in primitive conditions.

"*Mon Dieu,*" he murmured. "*C'est pas vrai,*" he went on, but this time in a whisper. His eyes had gone wide, and he stared at the bottle as if it were a treasure chest filled with gems.

Perhaps it was to him. After all, to the French, wine was just as vital and important and valuable as food and oxygen. And an excellent bottle could be as revered and treasured as a string of diamonds.

He beamed at me; whatever travails he'd experienced previously were obviously forgotten for the moment. "Thank you again, mademoiselle," he said, very nearly hugging the bottle to his chest. "I will most certainly put it to use . . . and very soon. You are staying for the demonstration, *non?*" he asked.

"Yes, I am," I replied just as the door through which I'd originally come opened. Julia surged in.

"Tabitha! There you are! I couldn't imagine where you'd gone off to, and then I found Madame Brassart"—she winced a bit—"and she told me where you were—oh, *pardonnez-moi, monsieur le chef,*" Julia said, belatedly realizing we weren't alone.

But Chef Beauchêne didn't seem to be offended or even to notice Julia's brash entry. He was still looking at the bottle of wine as if he couldn't believe he was holding it. "But it is no matter, madame," he said vaguely.

Julia raised her brows, then said, "Let's get seats, Tabitha. We'll be able to sit in the front row and have a good view."

We'd just sat down and I was beginning to fill her in on what had happened when the door behind the chairs opened again and people began to filter in. I realized I hadn't paid my three hundred francs for the demonstration, and was about to rectify the situation when Julia stopped me.

"No, that's all right. I paid for you. You can owe me. Finish the rest of your story."

As long as Madame Brassart wasn't going to be hunting me down for my fee, I was happy to do so.

I finished telling her what had happened and gestured to the wine bottle, which now sat on a table on the stage.

"I wonder what sort of wine it is." Julia peered at the table a few feet away, but the bottle's label was obscured by a stack of bowls, and she couldn't read it. "It must be something *incroyable* to get Chef Beauchêne so excited." She strained in her seat but still couldn't see the label.

By now, the demonstration room was filled with people and most of the chairs were filled. Madame Brassart came in and called everyone to attention, then introduced the esteemed chef, and the demonstration began.

Julia dug out a notebook from her purse and immediately began to take notes. "Oh! *Sole a la lorgnette!*" she whispered with a sigh as the chef ran through the menu of items he was going to prepare. "And clafoutis! Oh, Tabitha, I'm so glad you came to this one! *Ye gods*, it's going to be *spectacular!*"

The man sitting next to her gave Julia a quelling look when her voice rose a little, but my friend ignored him in favor of Chef Beauchêne.

To be honest, I didn't expect to get much out of the demonstration. I knew that whatever was being prepared here was so far beyond my capability that I simply sat back and watched. It was mind-boggling to see how fast the chef's knife moved, flashing expertly and smoothly over onions and garlic, and how skillfully he used a different, slender and very sharp knife to cut the backbone from each fish and lift it out, leaving the body soft and pliable.

Chef then skinned the sole, leaving the head intact, then rolled up each small *poisson* before arranging them neatly in a pyramid stack in preparation for being deep-fried. My mouth was watering by the time he began to slip each lightly floured roll into the oil and butter, and when the smells of delicately fry-ing fish reached my nose, I had to suppress a moan. I'd grown up on rainbow trout and walleye from the Great Lakes of Michigan, and I could imagine having our local pink-fleshed trout prepared the same way.

I had seen Julia work in her kitchen and had been amazed by her fluid and professional skills, the way she moved from oven to stove, cutting, chopping, kneading, rolling, forming, basting; but Chef Beauchêne was a man who'd been wielding a knife and preparing food for decades . . . and despite whatever he'd imbibed before the class, his expertise showed.

Watching him in action was like viewing a symphony in the kitchen, all the coordinated movements and practiced techniques accompanied by the glorious scents of raw fresh herbs, vegetables, spices, and more, followed by the aromas of fried, baked, basted, and sautéed dishes.

The chef prepared a complete meal in just a little more than two hours, and the smells were divine. The demonstration was so energetic and fast that I could hardly believe so much time had gone by. I hoped Julia was right that we each got to sample the prepared food.

I hadn't asked her, for she'd been scribbling nonstop in her notebook, eyes fixed intently on Chef Beauchêne the entire time. I knew that she would leave this class with the information fresh in her head and would go directly to the market to buy all the ingredients so she could duplicate the meal at home. Paul Child was going to be one lucky man tonight!

As the chef finished plating the meal he'd prepared, his attention turned to the bottle of wine sitting on the table. There were two other bottles there, as well, but it was the one I'd delivered that he picked up when he spoke to us.

"And now for a special treat," he said, his eyes soft with affection. "Only a short while ago, I was gifted with this beautiful and magnificent bottle of Volnay Clos de la Rougeotte, eighteen ninety-three."

There was a low murmur of surprise from the back of the room, to which *monsieur le chef* responded with a gentle nod and a small smile. *"Oui. Il est vrai."* He looked around the room, holding up the bottle. "She is a miracle, *non*, this bottle? Such a glorious year, eighteen ninety-three . . . and to have been protected from the Germans all this time and only now resurrected . . ." His voice trailed off dramatically.

The quiet murmur from the back of the room now spread through the rest of the audience. I felt the shimmer of interest and excitement grow, and I understood why.

During their Occupation of France, the Germans forced the vignerons—the winemakers—to sell them the bulk of their stock for unfairly low prices, raided the *caves* of vintners, restaurants, and private homes, and drank whatever they liked or simply destroyed bottles upon bottles of wine. Train cars filled with wine were shipped off to German warehouses not because Hitler liked to drink it, but because he disliked wine, and he knew how important it was to the French.

For any prestige wines—and I knew enough to know that 1893 had been one of the most extraordinary years for wine production in France—to have survived the Occupation was indeed a miracle. Frenchmen had died attempting to protect their cellars and stocks from being razed or looted by the Germans.

"And so, in honor of Saint Vincent, who has protected our vignerons over these years of wars," Chef Beauchêne went on, still with that beatific smile, "and in gratitude for *le bon Dieu*, I shall taste this *vin miraculeux*."

The room seemed to hold its collective breath as he carefully twisted a corkscrew into the old bottle, then just as carefully pulled out the stopper.

Still smiling, his eyes glinting with pleasure and perhaps even tears of joy, he poured a short stream of pale red vintage into a waiting wineglass.

He lifted the glass, held it up to the light, and swirled it to watch the legs—the rivulets of wine that dripped down the inside of the vessel—and smiled.

His aged brown eyes were bright with anticipation as he pushed his nose deep into the glass to draw in the scent. It was the long, steady, slow inhale of an oenophile so that he could appreciate and differentiate whatever elements there were to the "nose," or smell, of the wine.

I thought I saw his smile slip a little, a little flicker of surprise in his eyes, but I wasn't certain what would cause that . . . unless this *vin miraculeux* had gone bad.

What a disappointment that would be!

He sniffed again, long and slow, and I saw a little crinkle between his brows. The anticipatory light had faded a bit from his eyes.

"The wine's gone bad, I think," I whispered to Julia as Chef Beauchêne brought the glass up a third time and this time took in a healthy mouthful of the beautiful pink-red liquid.

The chef swished the sample in his mouth, allowed it to sit on his tongue in order to smell it from inside his mouth.

Then he swallowed, paused for a moment. . . . The suspense was *killing* us!

At last, he smiled, warmly, beatifically, the corners of his eyes crinkling, as he looked around the room at everyone. I got the impression he was relieved.

"And . . . she is beautiful. *Magnifique!* Only as I had expected . . . and anticipated." Tears of pleasure glittered in his eyes as he lifted the glass once more. He took another healthy swallow as someone in the room began to clap.

Everyone joined in, showing their appreciation and respect not only for the quality and rarity of the wine but also for his erudite demonstration.

Chef bowed, smiling, still holding the glass.

And then all at once, his face changed. He dropped the glass, clutching the edge of the table. His eyes widened, and he began to gasp for breath. His face flushed red and his eyes were wide with pain as he fought for air . . . and then, as a nasty white froth appeared at the corners of his mouth, he collapsed.

CHAPTER 3

*E*VERYONE STARED IN SHOCK FOR AN INSTANT; THEN ALL AT ONCE people shoved to their feet and rushed to the dais.

Julia dropped her pencil and grabbed my arm. "Oh my God," she said under her breath as the room descended into a sudden, horrified silence, broken only by the terrible sounds coming from Monsieur Beauchêne. She was craning her head, leaning forward to try to see what was happening, but even her generous height didn't seem to give her an advantage.

Neither of us rose to push our way forward out of practicality— there were enough people crowding around the fallen man, and we weren't medical personnel.

"Someone call a doctor!" a man shouted, and I lunged to my feet. That I could do.

But despite it being only seconds before I reached the door, it was too late.

"He's—he's dead," someone said in a shocked voice that cut through the taut silence in the room. I heard a quiet gasp from someone. "He's *dead.*"

I hesitated, then went through the doorway anyhow. *Someone* had to be called. I nearly ran into Madame Brassart again, but this time I didn't give her the chance to react.

"It's Chef Beauchêne. He's . . . well, he's died," I said breathlessly. "We must call . . . someone."

She stared at me uncomprehendingly for an instant, then

surged into action. "I will call." She spun and hurried down the hall.

I turned more slowly and went back to the demonstration room.

Most everyone was sitting around, either silent and stunned or murmuring softly to each other.

I couldn't take my eyes from the dais as I navigated back to my seat next to Julia. Chef Beauchêne's lifeless feet, enclosed in worn but polished shoes, were visible from behind the counter where he'd worked. They were positioned awkwardly, sagging in a way that looked so unnatural it seemed to scream tragedy.

My heart panged with a rush of sadness, and my belly felt strange—tight and ill.

I took my seat, still staring at the stage and those poor, pathetic feet in their shoes.

I'd read plenty of murder mysteries . . . most recently, a book by Agatha Christie titled *Remembered Death*. In it, two people died almost instantly after drinking from their glasses of champagne.

The drinks had been poisoned with cyanide.

And once it lodged in my mind, I simply couldn't dismiss the idea that someone had poisoned Chef Beauchêne. . . .

I told myself it was my internal sprite, my little adventurous imp, who for some reason was insisting it must be poison that had so quickly and painfully felled the older man. Not a heart attack or a stroke—far more common in a man of his age—but poison.

Which meant *murder*.

Julia nudged me, her usually lit-up eyes sober and shocked. We exchanged looks. We were both thinking the same thing.

Maybe it was because we'd been caught up in a murder investigation ourselves only a few weeks ago. It had become so very real, the elements of crime scenes and investigations I had read about in the detective novels I devoured. . . .

Since I'd experienced a homicide for real, was murder now to be *expected* in my life? Anticipated? Simply because I'd once been involved in more than the periphery of a case?

But mostly, I admitted, it was because of the *way* Chef Beau-chêne had died—the sudden convulsing and pain, the red flush over his face . . . and, most tellingly, the white foam that had appeared at his mouth.

I didn't think those were symptoms of anything natural. And they had come on so very suddenly.

But when and how had the poison been administered? Could it have been in the bottle of wine?

But how? Chef Beauchêne had removed the cork right in front of us all!

Still . . . I couldn't help but remember his small, hardly noticeable reaction when he stuck his nose deep into the wineglass and sniffed. Something had been wrong.

Perhaps he'd smelled that something was off, and assumed it was the wine possibly having gone bad.

Didn't cyanide have a smell? Like bitter almonds?

And cyanide worked quickly—at least according to Agatha Christie.

The hair on the back of my neck prickled.

We didn't have to wait long before the door opened again, and I was surprised to see a young, mustachioed *agent de police* hurry in, his distinctive képi hat with its slanted top tucked under his arm. Madame Brassart followed. She must have found him on the street nearby for him to have arrived so quickly.

"*Mesdames et messieurs,*" the agent said to the room at large.

No one seemed to hear him, and he twice cleared his throat loudly before finally resorting to using his whistle to get everyone's attention. "I ask that you please remain here and seated for the moment until it is determined what has happened. More help will soon arrive."

Madame Brassart, who appeared even more prune-like and irritated than ever, took up a position, leaning against the wall, arms crossed over her middle. Her gaze darted around the room, her eyes small, dark, and cold.

I felt a pang of sympathy for her; after all, she was only trying to keep the school running. And now she had, possibly, a *mur-*

der, which might close the place down or, at the very least, create some terrible publicity.

I looked around the rest of the small auditorium. Many of the thirty spectators were men, but there were perhaps ten smartly dressed women—housewives, according to Julia—occupying seats, as well. We were all witnesses to what had happened . . . but was anyone here also a suspect?

"Do you know any of the other people?" I murmured to Julia.

She looked at me, maybe a little confused. . . . Then I saw comprehension rush over her face. "Why? Do you think one of them did it?" she whispered. For the first time since Chef Beauchêne had collapsed, there was a glint of light in her eyes.

"If it *is* poison, *someone* had to do it," I whispered back. As usual, when it was just the two of us, we were conversing in English, for Julia wasn't nearly as comfortable with French as I was. That was good, for there was less of a chance of anyone understanding than if we were talking, even quietly, in French. "And wouldn't they want to witness the fruits of their labor, so to speak?"

Julia was nodding as I spoke. "Definitely." She eased away from where she'd leaned closer to me, and looked around the room. "I've seen most of these people here before. They come all the time. Two of them are American GIs from my class— hmmm, I wonder how much they understood from the lesson in French," she mused, still speaking quietly to me. "That group of six women come together often, too. The ones in the back row. I think they're in a bridge club."

I nodded. I had shifted slightly in my seat in order to look around as she spoke.

"Oh, the man with the V-shaped beard and the perfect mustache—I've seen him before. I think he's a chef at a local *bistrot.* And the man he's with, I think he's his brother and works at the *bistrot,* too."

The door opened once more, and Julia and I both looked over.

A dark-haired man strode in with great purpose and efficiency. He was wearing a stone-gray overcoat with a black and blue knit muffler and a charcoal-colored fedora, and he was followed by two more police agents.

It was Inspecteur Merveille.

Julia elbowed me sharply, and I'm not sure whether it was her sudden movement or my squeak of pain that drew his attention, but he looked in our direction.

His stride didn't so much as hitch when he saw us, but I felt my face heat. Not because of him, but because of my friend's reaction. I could feel her practically straining at the bit to say something, practically *quivering* as she sat next to me. It was all I could do not to elbow her in return.

Merveille gave no indication of surprise, pleasure, irritation, or any other emotion related to our presence. There was that quick glance; then his attention returned immediately to the scene in front of him. He removed his fedora, revealing miraculously unmussed hair, then crouched beside Chef Beauchêne's lifeless body.

"What are the *chances*?" Julia hissed near my ear. "We were *just* talking about him this morning."

"*You* were talking about him this morning," I muttered back, feeling very contrary. "I certainly wasn't."

We both subsided into sober silence. After all, it *was* a murder scene.

By now, I was sure of it.

I watched Merveille as he examined the scene. What else was there to do?

There was an air of efficiency and care, along with reverence, in his actions. Most of the chef's body was obstructed by the workstation, but I could see the careful, thoughtful way the inspecteur went about his business. Even if I couldn't exactly discern what he was doing, I could imagine it. Lift each arm, check the pockets, observe the dead man's face, perhaps even lean forward to sniff at his mouth and nose.

Would he smell bitter almonds?

The other people in the audience were becoming restless and

were audibly (though quietly) wondering when they could leave. I empathized a little, for it was after five thirty and the demonstration should have ended twenty minutes ago.

There were housewives who needed to get home to make dinner for their husbands. There were cooks who needed to get to their restaurants and *bistrots*, brasseries, and cafés. And the rest . . . I didn't know. Would the GIs go to a dance club or a music hall when they left here?

"Mesdames et messieurs . . . s'il vous-plaît." Merveille's calm, commanding voice drew the attention of everyone in the room in a way the first, mustachioed agent's had not. "If you please. I understand this is an inconvenience, this delay, but it is far more of an inconvenience for poor Richard Beauchêne, *non*? Now, we will take the names and addresses of each of you." His ocean-gray eyes skimmed the room and caught mine very briefly before moving on. Obviously, he already had that information from me and Julia. "And a brief statement. And then you will be on your way. If you please." He gestured to his two assistants, who'd been standing respectfully, waiting for direction. Obviously, we were each to speak to one of them, then leave. The third agent, the mustachioed one who'd first come on the scene, remained at the door.

The tension in the room seemed to relax just a little, now that everyone knew freedom was imminent. And when, a few moments later, Chef Beauchêne's body—swathed in a sheet—was removed by the coroner's assistants, the anxiety among the spectators eased even more.

I rose, more than happy to give my statement to whoever wanted to take it and make my way home, but before I could do so, I saw Madame Brassart approach Merveille. She was speaking rapidly with great, impassioned hand movements, which concluded with her pointing directly and peremptorily at *me*.

I sighed.

Inspecteur Merveille's shoulders shifted in a movement that could only be described as a bracing up. He was not happy.

Well, that made two of us.

He spoke to the mustachioed agent who'd been the first on the scene, and this agent glanced at me, then nodded. He seemed ready to come over and take my statement, but the inspecteur shook his head and sent him off on another task.

After that, I expected Merveille to take the junior agent's place and talk to me, but instead, he went over to the workstation.

The bottle of 1893 wine was still sitting on the work table and the inspecteur crouched down so that it was at eye level and examined it without picking it up. Then he pulled on a pair of gloves that had been stuffed in his pocket, took up the wineglass Chef Beauchêne had been drinking from, and examined what was left of its contents (for it had fallen over when he dropped it) before putting it down and turning his attention back to the wine bottle.

This entire time, I sat there waiting, with my belly churning and my annoyance growing.

He *knew* me. Surely, he *knew* I wanted to get home. He *knew* I had information. But he let me sit there! Everyone else was filing out of the room, and there I sat.

Even Julia had been beckoned to by one of the *agents de police* and had given her statement. When she would have returned to her seat next to me, the agent shook his head politely and gestured to the door. Apparently, she was to leave.

I waved her off. I didn't see that I had any choice, but I certainly wasn't going to make a big deal about it with Merveille there. I could find my way home by cab or the *métro*—or maybe I'd insist one of the police agents drive me back since they'd forced my ride to abandon me.

Julia hesitated but then shrugged and went out the door. But not before I saw the tiniest of smiles playing over her mouth.

"Mademoiselle Knight."

I looked up into a pair of cool eyes.

Merveille was probably in his early or midthirties—an age I'd thought was a little young to be a police inspector. But he'd conducted himself very well during the first murder investigation (it felt odd knowing that it *was* only the *first* murder investigation I would be involved in, because here I sat, entangled in a second one!) and certainly hadn't been the bumbling type of detective that is often portrayed in fiction. I had been the one to put a lot of the pieces together, but that had mainly been a big dose of luck . . . along with outsized curiosity and a nagging sense of adventure.

The inspecteur had strong features—a prominent nose, square chin, deep-set eyes, high cheekbones—set in olive skin. Every time I'd seen him, his hair had been parted ruthlessly straight, slightly off-center, and was perfectly combed—as it was now. Not one lock *dared* curl up at the ends or even suggest a wave. He was smoothly clean-shaven, as if he'd just used a razor, and his collar and tie were expertly aligned. I caught a waft of damp wool and something citrusy and fresh, which might have been hair pomade or aftershave.

"Inspecteur Merveille." I resisted the urge to reach up and touch my own hair to see what sort of mess it had turned into since my moment in the restroom. I winced internally, realizing if I had just cleaned off my sleeve at the sink in the dungeon, I never would have encountered the delivery boy and would not be in the position I was now in.

"I understand it was you who delivered a bottle of wine to Richard Beauchêne only just before the class."

"Do you think it was poisoned?" I asked in a low voice.

Not an iota of emotion flickered in his eyes. "Mademoiselle, if you could please answer the question."

"Yes, that is correct, Inspecteur." Before he could ask something else—or perhaps he didn't even intend to, as Merveille, I'd learned, was proficient in using gaps of silence to prompt answers—I explained exactly what had happened, including nearly dropping the bottle on the floor when I ran into Madame Brassart. I finished by saying, "So you'll need to take elimination prints."

One eyebrow shifted briefly, so slightly that I wasn't even certain I'd seen that display of surprise or acknowledgment. "Elimination prints," he repeated.

"So you know which fingerprints are mine," I explained.

His eyes widened a fraction, and he coughed softly, as if to cover up some other reaction. "Yes, mademoiselle, I am quite aware of the purpose of elimination prints. Thank you for offering so readily. If you'll be so kind as to present yourself at the *police judiciaire* tomorrow, we can attend to it then. Now, what can you tell me about the boy who gave you the wine?"

I'd known this question was coming, so I'd been thinking about it for the past thirty minutes, trying to resurrect a picture of the boy in my mind. Thus, I didn't hesitate. "He was perhaps fourteen, fifteen. Pale skin, light brown hair, dark blue cap. His clothing was rather worn, so I suspect he might have been a street urchin looking to make a sou or two. He is trying quite desperately to grow a mustache—and not succeeding much more than your police agent is," I said, trying to crack the tension of the moment. It didn't work, and I probably shouldn't have tried. This was, after all, a murder investigation.

"Let me see . . . He had a noticeably large nose. Taller than me . . . but not so tall as you." I was still sitting, but I knew how tall Merveille was. "Very slender. He, um, was wearing a sort of shabby dark coat—black or very dark blue—and had fingerless gloves with a few holes. Knitted."

"All of that, but he did not give you his name or address, then, mademoiselle? How could that be?"

For a moment, I thought he was serious. Then I realized that he was very possibly joking—Merveille joking?—and that his response was a wry, appreciative reflection on my detailed description of the delivery boy. Apparently, a hint of levity *was* permissible, even while at the scene of a homicide.

I merely gave him a look that indicated my displeasure over his little jest.

The glint of humor ebbed from his eyes. "Thank you very much, mademoiselle. That will be very helpful. Is there anything else you can tell me?"

Was he asking simply out of habit or because he expected more from me, considering my exploits last time?

"There was a gift tag on the bottle. I didn't read it," I said without bothering to hide my chagrin. I used my hands to show him the approximate size of the note. "There might have been the letter *L* on it, but I couldn't swear to it. And the bottle was wrapped in that piece of fabric. Do you see it there? That dark blue and green damask silk? It was like a gift."

"Yes, thank you, mademoiselle." His attention settled on the piece of cloth that lay in a small heap on the workstation. "A tag?" He moved swiftly back to the table and began to look around.

Without an invitation, I joined him, reasoning that I, at least, knew what I was looking for. And that he had very nearly confirmed my suspicion that the bottle of wine had been poisoned.

"I don't see it," I said, frowning.

"Nor do I."

"There's no other place it could be," I said, crouching behind the workstation to make certain the tag hadn't fluttered to the floor. There was no sign of it. "Unless it's in the pocket of the killer." I rose as I said this, and discovered that Merveille's expression had gone very stern and sober.

"That is possible," he replied. Was he aware that he was confirming my suspicions that we were dealing with a poisoned bottle of wine? "Or . . . perhaps it is only in Chef Beauchêne's pocket."

I didn't believe that for one minute, and I guessed he didn't, either. After all, hadn't Merveille done a thorough examination of the man's body? Surely, he would have checked his pockets. More than likely, his comment was the inspecteur's way of attempting to waylay me from becoming involved in the case.

"I highly doubt that. You needn't worry that I'm going to be snooping around this investigation," I told him bluntly. "I almost died the last time. I've no interest in repeating the experience." But even as I spoke, I felt a little internal nagging that said, *But it could be interesting . . . and you'll be really careful this time.*

The look Merveille gave me suggested he knew exactly what was going on inside my head. Even so, I just smiled blithely at him and changed the subject. "If I could get a ride back home from one of the agents . . . ? Since you sent Madame Child off without me."

I'm not sure whether he believed my easy acquiescence; *I'm* not sure I would have believed it.

But at the time, I truly had no intention of getting involved in another murder investigation.

CHAPTER 4

*B*Y THE TIME I ARRIVED HOME, IT WAS AFTER SEVEN O'CLOCK, VERY late to begin making dinner, even if it was going to be "*the most simple and delicious thing ever!*" according to Julia.

The agent who'd given me a ride—the same mustachioed one who had arrived first on the scene and hadn't quite been able to collect everyone's attention—had been polite and even talkative. Maybe that gregariousness would go away as he became more jaded; he seemed younger than my age of thirty and was probably only a few years out of training.

He asked if I was a cooking student, and I laughed and, shaking my head, explained why I'd been at Le Cordon Bleu.

Then he asked me how it was I'd come from America and my French was so perfect, and I told him. He seemed impressed that I was the granddaughter of Maurice Saint-Léger, for apparently, Inspecteur Merveille had not mentioned it to him.

I was curious about Merveille's reputation among his peers . . . and other things, but despite our chatty interaction, I resisted the urge to question Agent Grisart about him. Instead, I limited my comments to what I hoped was an enticing "The inspecteur seems to be quite a serious man."

"*Oh, oui, en effet il est, m'moiselle,*" he replied with a nod nearly as sober as Merveille's. "He has quite the reputation at the 36."

But what sort of reputation he was referring to, he didn't make clear. And by then, we had arrived at my house, so I couldn't probe further. I thanked him for the ride, even though he'd only been following orders, then opened the car door as he explained cheerfully that it was no inconvenience—he lived not very far away at all.

"Not so far from Sainte Clotilde, with my mother," he said even as I was climbing out, as if eager to continue the conversation as long as possible, "because *mon père* died recently, and she has no one else."

"That is very kind of you," I replied, thinking how much Grand-père and Oncle Rafe seemed to appreciate me living with them—even though *I* was the one who should be grateful to them. *"Bonsoir, monsieur l'agent, et merci beaucoup."*

As I closed the door of the car, I suddenly realized I'd forgotten to tell Merveille about the argument Chef Beauchêne was having when I arrived in the demonstration room. The inspecteur had asked about the delivery boy, and then I'd remembered about the tag on the bottle, which we had searched in vain for—and by then, I had been distracted and had forgotten about the argument.

Ah, well . . . I was to see Merveille tomorrow morning at the 36—which was the nickname for the station of the *police judiciaire* located at 36 quai des Orfèvres on Île de la Cité—and I could tell him about it then.

I put that problem out of my mind for the moment as I hurried up the walkway to the mansion. I needed to work out how to make dinner in time for Grand-père and Oncle Rafe. I'd become accustomed to Parisian dinners being served around eight o'clock, instead of six or six thirty, which was usual back in Michigan, but it was still too late for me to have the meal prepared by that time.

Julia would be in the middle of cooking for Paul, so she wouldn't be able to take the time to help me. Our original plan had been for her to give me the instructions when we got home from the cooking demonstration, and then I would call her if I had any questions. But that was obviously not going to work.

I burst through the front door, prepared to rush up to the

salon and explain to Grand-père and Oncle Rafe what had happened, but I stopped dead when I smelled something *amazing* coming from the kitchen.

Maybe Bet and Blythe had stayed late tonight to cook for my messieurs. Or, possibly, Oncle Rafe had decided to try his hand at cooking something . . . perhaps warming up a soup from the *bistrot* around the block. That seemed unlikely, but I had no other explanation.

Before I had the chance to poke into the kitchen to find out who was cooking what, Oscar Wilde appeared at the top of the stairs, barking his head off.

He was a tiny dog—no more than seven or eight pounds—with disproportionately large butterfly-wing ears and flowing silky hair, which I, with the wild, curling, and sometimes frizzy tresses, couldn't help but envy. Mostly white in color, he had a few splotches of brown and black on his face and trunk. But his ears were completely brown, and the long hair that grew from them was tipped in black.

He was technically Oncle Rafe's dog, although he was loved and spoiled by everyone and, in turn, was a profligate when it came to sleeping in anyone's lap. Today he was dressed casually in a snazzy sky-blue bow tie.

"Monsieur Wilde, hush!" I said as the little sweetie continued to herald the announcement of a new arrival, as if trying to notify the entire neighborhood. With Oscar Wilde on guard, there was no chance of ever coming in the house unnoticed.

It was a good thing I didn't have any reason to sneak in (or out) at night.

By now, Madame X, Grand-père's elegant black cat, had sauntered to the landing at the top of the stairs in order to ascertain what the fuss was all about. Madame X had been named after the woman in the famous portrait by John Singer Sargent and always wore a collar of diamonds, which echoed the straps on the slinky black evening gown worn by the subject of the portrait.

Madame chat wouldn't deign to express any emotion other

than disdain, and certainly not the curiosity her feline counter-
parts were known for. Instead, she more often pretended to simply have come across a new arrival or some other event of interest,
rather than seeking it out like Monsieur Wilde would do. But I
wasn't fooled. She might pretend disinterest, allowing Oscar Wilde
to sound the alarm in his raucous manner, but Madame was always right on his heels when he did so.

Sometimes I wondered if she actually sensed the newcomers
first and somehow instigated Oscar Wilde to do the hard work
of announcing it.

"Tabi! *Ma chère*, is it you at last? Do come up here, won't you?"
Oncle Rafe, lured from what surely had been his comfortable
chair and blanket next to the salon's radiator, stood at the top of
the stairs. He was wearing his customary black knit cap—to keep
his bald head and ears warm in the winter—and a heavy sweater
over a shirt, along with worn, comfortable trousers that he
would never have worn in public.

Oncle Rafe (who was not any sort of blood relation to me at
all) still had an almost pure black mustache and beard, both
trimmed closely and neatly, despite the fact that he was well over
seventy. He had a dusky olive complexion and a wickedly handsome face that had hardly begun to show his age. His close-fitting
cap was pulled down almost to his bushy black brows. "Madame
Child is here, and she has told us all about the excitement tonight."

Immediately, I relaxed. That explained so many things—the
least of which was the magnificent smells coming from the
kitchen. Julia had told my messieurs why I was delayed (and
therefore, they hadn't been worried), and she must have started
to cook the veal roast for us. Not only had dinner been saved,
but I didn't have to cook it!

I dashed up the stairs, stopping to pat Oscar Wilde on the
head as I passed by. He bounded after me, still barking but now
also leaping and sproinging against my calves in an attempt to
get my attention, which he hoped would result in a tiny treat.

"I'm so sorry I'm late," I said, sliding into Oncle Rafe's embrace for a hug and a kiss on each bristly cheek. He smelled faintly of spirits and the spicy and expensive black cigarettes he enjoyed.

"Oh, no, no, no, but Madame Child has been telling us all about it, Tabi," said my grandfather with a wave of his elegant hand. He was sitting in his chair, as close as possible to the radiator situated on one side of the room, a thick wool blanket on his lap and a cigarette in his veiny, long-fingered hand. A fire roared in the fireplace, as well.

While I wasn't certain of his age, I guessed Grand-père was older than Rafe by several years. Maybe he was even eighty. He was a little more frail than I would like, and his hand tremored on occasion, but Grand-père was still quite active—mostly managing the tiny greenhouse, where he grew his herbs, and, when the weather was nice, walking along the broad Grands Boulevards with Oncle Rafe.

Taller than his partner, Grand-père had lighter skin and a full head of hair that was a gleaming silver white. He was cleanshaven, with a handsome face that was so smooth and supple I wondered if hair even *dared* to grow on his chin or cheeks any longer. He held his cigarette away as I leaned in for a hug and more kisses. He smelled, as always, of tobacco, the Armagnac he favored, and some pleasing masculine scent that was either a lotion or cologne.

I'd known him and Oncle Rafe only since April—not even a year—and I already loved both men deeply. They were fascinating, amusing, affectionate, and generous people, and I would have adored them even if I wasn't sharing their lovely mansion.

"Oh, Tabs, finally! I've been *dying* for you to get back here." Julia was sitting on a chair, with a short, fat glass that contained a healthy pour of whisky. "The cops made me leave before I could get any more information from you or anyone."

The salon was easily the coziest and most inviting room in the house. A large circular Aubusson rug filled the center of the high-ceilinged room, which was normally drenched in light from the tall, narrow windows. Now the heavy aubergine velvet drapes had been drawn against the cold night air, and the wall sconces and table lamps were lit up with a soft golden glow. The crackling fire added a cozy spill of light and warmth.

A sparkling chandelier, which was lit with candle-shaped lights, hung from an ornate plaster medallion above the circular rug, and carved wainscoting adorned the lower third of the tall walls.

There were two large armchairs for the messieurs pulled up next to the radiator, which sat on a small tiled area about four feet from the wall. Two more chairs and a small sofa uphol-stered in rich cobalt brocade created a semicircle in front of a low, ornate table of carved mahogany. Silk in a pale blue, laven-der, and gold chinoiserie pattern covered the walls in huge wood-framed rectangles above the wainscoting. A life-sized re-production of the original version of *Portrait of Madame X*—where one of the gown's straps had slipped suggestively off Madame's shoulder—hung above the fireplace, opposite the ra-diator. A fire blazed within, making the room even more toasty warm.

"What's cooking in the kitchen?" I asked, nodding gratefully when Oncle Rafe wordlessly lifted the carafe of whisky toward me in a questioning gesture.

"Why, your veal roast, of course," Julia replied. "I've promised Monsieurs Saint-Léger and Fautrier that it's going to be simply . . . *mwah!*" She kissed her fingertips dramatically. "Luscious and juicy and *delicious!* We'll go down and finish it as soon as you tell us all the news. At the moment, Monsieur Rôti de Veau is wrapped in his delicious, cozy salt pork blanket with a smattering—just a *smattering*—of seasonings. But you'd better talk fast, Tabs, be-cause it's almost time to *baste* the life out of that sweet and ten-der hunk of meat."

I smiled as I shook my head affectionately. Julia, when talking about food—eating it, preparing it, shopping for it, imagining it—was always deliciously dramatic. How could you *not* want to rush to the kitchen to cook when she told you all about it—and especially when you were already smelling it? Even I felt a rush of anticipation about basting that "tender hunk of meat"—and I barely knew what basting was.

"But what about Paul's dinner?" I asked Julia.

"Oh, he called from the office and said a dinner meeting came up, and would I mind if he went?" she replied. "I told him not at all, because then I could come here and get all the information from you! *Sole en lorgnette* can wait until tomorrow." Her eyes danced, then sobered. "It *was* murder, wasn't it?"

Oncle Rafe handed me a small glass of whisky, then settled back into his chair as I finally sank into my own.

"Well, then, *ma mie*?" Grand-père said expectantly. "Madame Child has told us some of what has happened, but surely you know more."

"Not very much more," I told him, then took a sip of whisky. It burned deliciously, and immediately I relaxed even more. I explained how I'd come to deliver the suspected poisoned wine to Chef Beauchêne—and this time, remembered to describe the brief argument I'd witnessed—and I ended with how I'd confounded Merveille with my unexpectedly detailed description of the delivery boy.

"Ah, I see you are in fact taking after your father, then, *chère*," said Grand-père with a gleam in his eye. "The careful observer, the mind of the policeman, the fitter of puzzle pieces."

This flattering comment surprised me a little, for I had never been certain how my grandfather felt about the man who'd fallen in love with my mother during the Great War and lured her—along with *her* mother, Grand-père's wife—to America. I'd been under the impression that my grandparents' separation had been nothing but amicable, and I had the letters between them from over the years to prove it, but it was still a balm to hear such a direct compliment to my father.

"The inspecteur certainly seemed impressed," I replied. "Not that he would actually *say* so. And you should have seen his face when I told him he'd need to take elimination prints." I chuckled at the memory.

"This is the fine inspecteur Étienne Merveille you are speaking of, *non*?" asked Oncle Rafe.

"Oh, yes, it is," Julia put in. "The *fine* inspecteur indeed. And you should have seen his face when he saw Tabitha—and me—sitting there!"

I gave her a look, then shook my head with a scoff. There had been no discernible reaction on Merveille's face when he saw us, and she knew it. Julia certainly liked to stir the pot—both literally and figuratively.

"And so it is believed *le vin* was poisoned?" said Oncle Rafe. "But it is an *insult* to desecrate a gorgeous bottle of wine such as that. An eighteen ninety-three Volnay? Indeed, it is a *profanity* to do such a thing! Who would be so imbecilic?"

"And from where would he *obtain* such a rare vintage?" Grand-père said thoughtfully.

"But there's another interesting thing," I said. "There was a gift tag on the bottle when I gave it to Chef Beauchêne. The bottle was wrapped in a silk covering with a ribbon around it, and the note was tied with the ribbon. But neither Inspecteur Merveille nor I could find the tag."

I was pleased when three sets of eyes widened with interest and surprise.

"But someone must have taken it!" said Oncle Rafe, sitting straighter in his chair. His dark eyes gleamed with delight. "And that is *proof* that there was a murder! And that someone who took the tag must have been . . ."

"The murderer," Grand-père finished for him. "For who else would have taken it?" They smiled at each other.

"Exactly what I said," I replied after sipping more of my whisky. "But Merveille suggested it could also be in the pocket of Chef Beauchêne, whose body had already been removed from the room."

I scoffed with them as the others shook their heads in equally strong negation.

"Exactly," I went on. "Inspecteur Merveille would have already examined Richard Beauchêne's pockets, and if there had been a tag, he would have noticed it and removed it. I think he was only trying to discourage me from getting involved—which

I have no desire to do, anyway," I said quickly when I saw how Julia's eyes lit up.

"But, Tabs—"

"No, I'm not getting involved this time," I told her firmly.

"But how would that discourage you from getting involved? Oh, ah, I see, I see it now," said Grand-père, his eyes glittering with pleasure. "The good inspecteur seems to think that if the killer was present in the room so he could take the tag before anyone could find it, then you would be interested in determining which of those people was the killer. It would be a lead, *non?*"

I nodded. "*Exactement.* If someone took the tag—which it seems someone did—then it must have been the poisoner . . . and that means the poisoner was there at the demonstration. Which means . . . we probably saw him. Or her."

"That makes sense," Julia said. "If *I* were going to poison someone, I'd want to be there to watch and make sure it worked. If you were going to murder someone, you'd want to watch them *die*, right?"

I laughed. Julia Child was the last person I could imagine poisoning someone. Feeding them to death (and what a glorious way to die that would be!) maybe, but not homicide by poison.

"Now, what is this about this elimination printing?" said Grand-père.

"Oh, yes," I replied, realizing that hardly anyone besides a police inspector would know about such a thing. I was more familiar with the steps and processes a detective would perform than most people because I was interested in them, and I had quizzed my father about such things.

And since my own recent involvement with the murder of Thérèse Lognon a few weeks ago, my interest had been even more piqued. I'd even written to my father, asking him to send me articles or publications about detective work and criminal investigations.

Was it a morbid interest? A useless one? Perhaps. But it was logical, given my penchant for mystery novels, my father's occupation, and my recent personal experience.

I explained that the authorities needed to have copies of my fingerprints so they could eliminate them from consideration from any other prints, which, presumably, would be from the person who'd sent the wine as well as those of Chef Beauchêne.

"Oh!" Julia bolted from her chair as if her derrière was on fire, which set Oscar Wilde scrambling up from Oncle Rafe's lap to bark wildly. "Monsieur Veau! Tabs, we've got to finish him up. I'm going to show you how to make the most *delectable* gravy for him. He'll *bathe* in it, and it'll be so *magnifique,* you will want to, as well!"

We left Grand-père and Oncle Rafe chuckling as we hurried from the salon and down into the kitchen. The delicious scents had grown even stronger since I'd been upstairs, and I stood there for a moment, inhaling the aromas.

"Tabs, don't just stand there—this is your monsieur, and he's waiting for you! Now, open the oven—do you see?"

I did and was rewarded by a rush of moist, steamy heat and even more gorgeous smells.

"I've rolled him all up in the salt pork . . . and do you see all of that magnificent juice on the bottom? Now just take this spoon—I can't believe you don't have a baster, Tabs, we're going to have to get you one—and just pour the juices over him lovingly."

I crouched at the open door and carefully pulled the rack out a bit so I could spoon up the drippings without burning myself. The veal roast was as large as my two hands together, and as Julia had said, she'd smothered him with thick white slabs of salt pork. By now that delicious, glistening swath had begun to crisp up, releasing its juices into the pan below. There was also a bunch of skinny-cut—I think the term was "julienned"—carrots and onions strewn over the bottom of the pan. I assumed they were basking in the juices, too, while adding their own unique flavoring.

"*Lovingly,* Tabs, like you're tucking him into bed with a drizzle of love, you see? Don't be shy—just *drench* him with the drippings—can you see the fat circles, how they're forming in the gravy? *That* is beauty, dearie. Oh, *yes*, that is gorgeous," she said, crouched next to me and watching like a hawk as I "lovingly" "drenched" the little veal roast with the salt pork drippings in the pan.

"Excellent. Now we let him roast for a bit longer, and we mash up the potatoes," Julia said. "And then we will make the sauce, once monsieur comes out."

Make a sauce? I didn't make sauces. They were much too complicated.

I started to demur, but Julia was already directing me to a pot of potatoes that had been cooking on the stove. I drained them, added gobs of butter and milk per her direction, and began to smash them. I was going to have to forgo my Renault for a couple of days and walk or bike instead to make up for all this goodness.

"I used to put about a hundred herbs and spices on my veal roast," Julia was saying as she watched me work. "And then Chef Bugnard taught me that sometimes simple is better. So now I just salt and pepper him—the veal roast, not Chef!—and wrap him up with salt pork and tuck him in the oven."

"But what about a sauce?" I said nervously. "I can't make a sauce, Julia. You know I can't."

"Of course you can! I'll show you. It's *so easy*," she gushed.

I scoffed. Easy for her, maybe, but not for me.

"So . . . did Merveille say anything to you?" Julia said as I put the top back on the pot of mashed potatoes to keep them warm.

"About what?" I knew what she meant, but I was being stubborn.

"About anything. Did *he* drive you home?"

"No," I said. "And he didn't say anything to me that wasn't related to my statement. Julia, you don't need to play matchmaker. I don't need a man, and I—"

"Oh, I know, I *really do*, but, Tabitha, I'm just *so* happy with Paul I only want you to be happy, too! He's just so *smart* and *interesting*—but best of all, he *understands* me. He knows I don't want to be only a housewife and sit around waiting for him at home. I want to do something more—and he agrees with me!

He wants me to find my *thing.* And I only want you to have something like that, too."

I waved her off. "That's all true, and maybe someday I'll find 'my' Paul, but I'm not in a hurry. I'm still trying to figure out what *I* want to do, and you are, too, aren't you?"

"I know I want to *cook.* I know that *now.* But I don't know where or in what way . . . Maybe I'll work in a restaurant. I'd really like to open a restaurant with Paul's twin's wife. Have I told you about her?"

She had, but I didn't mind hearing it again. "That's going to be awfully hard with you here and Freddie back in America," I said with a chuckle. "Maybe you should teach people how to cook, like you're doing for me."

"Someone else just said the same thing to me," Julia said, her eyes wide and sparkling. "There are a few women at the embassy who'd like to learn to cook French food. I've been thinking about it. Ooh! It's time to baste monsieur again!"

I dutifully basted "monsieur," and we chatted a little longer while he finished cooking. Then it was time to remove him from the oven and make the sauce.

Julia was right. It *was* easy! I could hardly believe it. All I did was add a big dollop of butter, along with some broth she'd brought with her, and mixed it all up with the drippings in the pan after removing the carrots and onions. We added some tarragon and parsley, too. Of course, if Julia hadn't been there guiding me along, I'm certain it would have been a tasteless, goopy mess instead of a gorgeous brown stream, glistening with fat circles and speckled with fresh-chopped herbs.

Moments later, I proudly carried up to the salon a platter of veal roast surrounded by the julienned carrots and onions, with a mound of mashed potatoes next to it. Julia brought the sauce in a gravy boat, along with plates and flatware.

We had a *feast,* all of us crowded up close to the radiator in the cozy salon. And it was, indeed, *magnifique.*

Best of all, I had made it.

Well, most of it.

* * *

I skipped out of joining Julia at the market the next morning, using the excuse that I had to go up to the 36 to give my fingerprints.

I usually enjoyed our visits to the food market and the gossip that ensued, but I didn't want to be there when Julia told Madame Marie and everyone else about our encounter with Merveille yesterday. I did wonder, though, whether there would be any new vandalism events.

I had a tutoring appointment, and so it was after that—with a fresh payment in my pocketbook, along with a sandwich of ham, mustard, and Brie on crusty bread that my student's mother had pressed upon me—that I drove my peppy little Renault along the *quai haut* to the Pont au Change, one of several bridges to the Île de la Cité that spanned the Seine.

Only a few weeks ago, I'd nearly been run down by a murderer while I was on my bicycle in this exact location. (That was part of the reason Grand-père and Oncle Rafe had bought me the car. That and the fact that they were scandalized when I wore trousers to ride on my bike. Good thing they hadn't seen me wearing denims or overalls every day at the bomber plant.)

As I drove, I couldn't help but look for the tattered street cat who'd been my savior that day. If I hadn't slowed to look at him and his poor mangled tail, the killer would have run me down. As it was, my bicycle had been destroyed beyond saving, and I had small scars on my knee and elbow.

To my surprise, there he was!

Looking like a haughty miniature gray tiger, the cat lounged atop a snow-frosted stone bench. His tail—the top third of which hung, broken, from its base—seemed not to bother him in the least, for he twitched it gently as he eyed passersby. No doubt he was looking for an opportunity to pounce on a small bird or rodent or to lunge for a bit of paper-wrapped food that had been discarded.

I swerved to the side of the street, to the loud and angry dismay of two other drivers. Ignoring the furious honking, I parked, then jumped out of my car. I don't really know why I did it; I just did. I had never thanked him for saving my life, so I suppose it seemed like the right time.

"Hello, kitty," I said, crouching a little as I drew near. I didn't know whether he was skittish or not, but the impression I got from his cool, unimpressed gaze was not one of shyness.

But neither was it particularly welcoming. Perhaps it was my gauche Americanized greeting.

Suddenly, I had a brilliant idea. I swung back to my car and grabbed the last bite of sandwich. At least I could offer *monsieur le chat de gouttière* a tasty treat as a thank-you for his unwitting heroism.

I was just approaching him when I heard a deep, amused voice from behind me.

"Feeding the gutter cats now, are we, mademoiselle?"

I straightened and whirled, taken completely off guard by Inspecteur Merveille's appearance.

"Yes," I replied stoutly, wondering what he was doing there, and on foot.

As if reading my mind, he gave me a small smile, his eyes unreadable beneath the brim of his fedora. "I saw your car swerve out of traffic so suddenly and supposed I would make certain whoever was the driver wasn't in jeopardy." He glanced casually over his shoulder, and I saw the dark, nondescript police-issue car pulled up behind my hasty parking job, where one tire was on the curb. "Imagine my surprise when I discovered it was you, Mademoiselle Knight."

"Ah," I replied, fighting back a blush. I wondered if he would be so obnoxious as to give me a traffic ticket. I probably deserved one, but still. . . . "It's only that I saw the cat here, and I had a bit of sandwich I thought I'd offer him. After all, it was he who saved my life a few weeks ago."

"Ah, yes, the hero cat," he replied, then made a gesture as if to encourage me to continue my task. "We often see him with his half-mast tail here or over on the *île.*"

"Were you on the way to your office?" I asked as I offered a scrap of ham to the cat.

"*Oui*, mademoiselle."

As was to be expected, *monsieur le chat* showed no interest in the tasty morsel. He barely deigned to look at it. Even so, I would leave it on the bench next to him, knowing he'd eventually do me the favor of tasting it, acting like a martyr the whole time.

Up close, I discovered that he had a very handsome triangular pink nose and penetrating eyes the color of a deep, dark lake on a winter's day—not unlike those of the police inspecteur who seemed to turn up like a bad penny every time I looked around. But the feline monsieur was also flea bitten and scruffy beneath his haughty gaze, and I couldn't control a giggle as to what Madame X would think if she set her eyes on him.

"Something is amusing, mademoiselle?"

"No, no, not really." I offered the last piece of bread to the cat, who looked at it, looked at me as if offended that I should even suggest he needed to be fed, then swung his head to eye a bird fluttering on a branch above his head, as if to say, "I'd much rather catch my own dinner, foolish mademoiselle."

I turned back to Merveille, knowing that the minute I left, my savior cat would gobble down the food. "I was on my way to your office."

"As I suspected," he replied. "Elimination prints, of course." Was there a bit of a dry humor in his tone?

"And there is something else I forgot to tell you yesterday," I said as I climbed into my car. I closed the door before he could ask what it was; after all, we were both going to the same place, and I was certain he'd want a formal statement, anyway.

I smiled and waved at him as I pulled out into the traffic.

CHAPTER 5

GOING THROUGH THE PROCESS OF BEING FINGERPRINTED WAS NOT what I had expected.

I'd assumed I'd put my fingertip against a pad of ink and then press it onto a piece of paper or cardboard, and I'd be done.

That was not how it went.

First, I had to take a seat so that my arms would rest on the table at the proper angle for the prints. Then I had to clean my hands with a bit of rubbing alcohol applied with a soft cloth.

Then, to my surprise and consternation, Merveille came to stand behind me. From over my shoulder, he took my left hand and said, "Relax, if you please, mademoiselle, and allow me to do the work. This will ensure clear, complete prints."

Relax?

I felt supremely self-conscious as his large, warm fingers closed firmly around the top of my index finger, curling my other four digits into a gentle fist in my palm. My heart thudded in my chest, and I hoped I wasn't blushing. And I was glad that I had dabbed a little bit of perfume behind my ears this morning.

I was *not* going to tell Julia about this.

He didn't seem to notice my self-consciousness (or my perfume, for that matter) as he gently and efficiently pressed the side of my finger onto the ink pad of shiny ink, then rolled the rest of my finger smoothly across the pad once, from one side to the other. Not only was the tip of my finger covered with ink, but the entirety of the sides and bottom along the length of my first knuckle were also wet and black.

Then, without hesitation, he drew my inked finger to a piece of heavy, shiny paper, like photograph paper. It had an empty rectangular block printed on it for each finger. My name, along with my birth date, had already been written at the top of the record in his neat masculine writing.

Merveille repeated the same motion there on the card. Keeping my finger in the same position, he rolled it with a gentle, firm motion from one side to the other quickly and smoothly, and without pressing very hard at all. My finger left a print in the block marked LEFT INDEX that looked nothing like what I'd imagined.

It was not the pretty oval-shaped impression as I'd envisioned, but an oblong splotch wider than my finger so as to capture the patterns on my finger's sides as well as that at its center. I realized that made great sense, for if someone was to leave a fingerprint on an object, it could be from any angle and any part of the finger—not just the flat pad at its center.

I was fascinated by the sight of my fingerprint—the whorls and arches and all the complicated ridges so starkly displayed on that photograph paper. It was one thing to look at my fingers and see the ridges there in the flesh or to read about fingerprints, but to see the marks so delineated in black and white made me shiver a little at the knowledge that no one else on earth had the same design on their fingers as I did.

Merveille repeated this process with my other nine digits, standing behind me and moving one by one through each of my fingers and thumbs, curling the unused ones into my palm with his larger hand.

I was acutely aware not only of how close he was standing behind me, and the scent of whatever cologne or hair product he used, along with those of damp wool and coffee, but also of the way his sure long-fingered hands—warm and callused, darker and much larger than my smaller pale ones—touched mine, moving them through the process with the ease of long practice.

It was strangely intimate, yet at the same time strictly impersonal, as I sat there, allowing him to manipulate my hands like he was a puppeteer.

When he finished, I had ten very inky digits, and he had produced ten perfect prints, which he looked over with a sound of satisfaction.

"If you would like to wash your hands, mademoiselle, I can show you to the ladies' lounge," he said, handing me another cloth that had been dampened with alcohol. I noticed that there wasn't even a smudge of ink on his hands.

"I remember where it is," I told him.

"Of course, but perhaps you would allow me to open the door for you." He gave me a small smile and gestured to the door, as if he hadn't just had his hands all over mine in a weirdly intimate way.

"Oh, right," I replied, looking down at my fingers, which were still smeared with ink and would have left a residue on any doorknob I touched.

I was quick in the ladies' lounge and made my way back to Merveille's office. To my surprise, he wasn't there, probably having been waylaid by someone while I was washing up.

That meant I could be nosy.

With one eye on the door and my ear cocked toward the entrance, listening for voices or footsteps, I walked over to stand in front of the wall where the inspecteur had begun to post information about the murder of Richard Beauchêne.

The dead man's photograph, clearly having been taken at the crime scene, was in the center of the space. Pictures of the wine bottle, its cork, its silk wrapping, the glass, and even the ribbon that had tied the missing gift tag to the bottle were all posted next to it, along with photographs of the workstation where he'd been cooking and the front of Le Cordon Bleu.

None of that was anything new, and there were no notations near the pictures . . . which meant my attention strayed to Merveille's desk.

Neat as a pin and as spare as an army barrack, the surface

held only one file folder, a jar of pencils and a pad of paper, a mug for coffee, a desk blotter . . . and the framed photograph.

My attention darted to the door, which was still mostly closed, and I listened. There was no sound of anyone coming, so I edged around to the other side of the desk a position that would allow me to look at the photo but also lunge back toward my chair the moment I heard his approach.

The frame held the same photograph that had piqued my curiosity before (not that I had expected it to change): a young woman dressed and coiffed in prewar fashion who would probably be my age now. The same thing that had sparked my interest previously—besides the simple fact that there was a woman's picture on the equable Merveille's desk—was the light of mischief in her eyes. If she was his wife or girlfriend, it simply fascinated me that someone like Inspecteur Merveille would be attracted to a woman who seemed to have her own unapologetic internal imp. Someone who had a sense of humor and who liked to have fun.

There was a soft scuff in the corridor, and I spun as the door opened wide . . . just a little too late not to be caught. *Damn.*

Merveille's eyes settled on me, went to his desk, tracked to the photo, then flickered back to me.

There was no sense in hiding the fact that I'd been snooping, so I supposed I might just as well own up to it.

"Who is she?" I asked.

His face turned even more stony than it normally was. "Marguerite. My fiancée."

"She's lovely," I said, feeling a sudden and strange sinking in my middle. Which really irked me, because I wasn't at all interested in Merveille romantically, so it didn't matter that he was engaged.

"Sit, please, mademoiselle," he said with a surprisingly graceful gesture, considering his forbidding expression. "You had something to add to your statement from yesterday, *non?*"

Chastised but not allowing myself to be embarrassed for my curiosity—after all, the photo was *on his desk*, where anyone might see it and comment on it, never mind that his office likely wasn't one with much comings and goings—I told him about the argument I'd heard before the demonstration yesterday.

"I couldn't really hear what they were saying," I finished. "They sounded impassioned, but then again, who doesn't sound impassioned at times?" I gave him a little smile. No reaction. "It might have been over something as important as which cheese to serve with the *sole en lorgnette*—although I don't know that cheese and fish go together very well, do they?" I'd have to ask Julia about that. "Or something as unimportant as what shade of blue the plates were. But I did see the man Chef Beauchêne was arguing with."

"And what did he look like, mademoiselle?" Sitting, Merveille had jotted a few brief notes during my speech, but now his pencil was poised, as if he was prepared to write an epistle.

"I only caught a glimpse of him through the doorway, but he had a lot of white hair—it reminded me of Dr. Einstein a little," I said, smiling again. "But he had a reddish-blond beard and mustache. As if his hair had gone white with age but his facial hair had not grayed yet."

"And so he was about what age?"

"Sixty-five or seventy maybe. Around the same age as Chef Beauchêne. And average height, thinner than Beauchêne. I didn't really notice anything else. It was so quick."

"Very well. Thank you, mademoiselle." He put down his pencil with an air of finality and rose.

With my own air—of reluctance—I stood, as well.

"Why would anyone want to kill Chef Beauchêne?" I asked. I was unwilling to leave without feeding some of my curiosity, even though I suspected I was fighting a losing battle. Merveille was as impervious as a tank.

"We have not yet determined that it was murder, mademoiselle," he replied. "And have certainly made no statement to that effect."

It was all I could do not to roll my eyes. That might be his official stance and what had been put out to the press and even to

Monsieur Beauchêne's family, but I knew better than that. "Do you have any leads? Any suspects?"

"Mademoiselle Knight," he said with more than a hint of exasperation, "you know that I cannot share that information with you. Despite the fact that you seem to be surprisingly aware of things such as elimination fingerprints and how to describe a suspect, you are not involved in this investigation."

"My father is a detective," I said, working hard to delay my departure by answering his implicit question. "Back home, I mean."

"Ah." His wry, pained expression said it all: *And now I have a young woman who thinks she is a detective only because her father is one.* He shook his head. "Mademoiselle . . . I do not need to remind you what happened the last time you, er, inserted yourself into a murder investigation. Monsieur le chat—or your handy tool knife—may not be enough to save your life the next time."

The wine tasting being hosted by Paul Child's group of friends was to take place at the grand and spacious home of Monsieur and Madame Deschamps.

I had almost begged off going with Julia, but since I had nothing better to do—and she'd sweetened the deal by offering left-over *sole en lorgnette* and clafoutis, which she'd made for Paul's luncheon earlier today, for Grand-père and Oncle Rafe's dinner—I'd decided not to cancel.

Instead, I made it an evening out, just in case there *was* an eligible man who caught my attention. I wouldn't mind having someone to go on dates with, even if I wasn't looking for anything serious.

I tamed my hair as well as I could, using a sparkling blue barrette to anchor my long bangs to one side, and dressed in a new frock that I'd recently purchased from a shop on the Champs-Élysées. It wasn't a Dior, but it was very flattering, if I do say so, in cobalt blue silk, with a fitted waist and a deliciously full skirt.

After the scarcity of materials during the war years, fashion designers had started using lots of fabric—in some cases, an exorbitant amount—in their latest creations. Not only that, but nylons were plentiful again (no more drawing a fake seam down the backs of my calves after painting on liquid stockings!). My shoes were dark blue, open-toed, with fabulous French heels, and I wore white dinner gloves and a sable-trimmed chocolate wool coat that had belonged to my *grand-mère.*

I knew I looked particularly good when I came into the salon and my messieurs actually looked up from their meal to gape with pleasure, not shock.

"*Magnifique!*" cried Grand-père, half rising from his seat. "Tabi, you are *une déesse!*"

I laughed and waved him back into his chair. I wasn't anywhere near being a goddess, and it was only a simple evening frock—it was not as if I was dressed in haute couture or wearing a Dior evening gown. But I didn't mind their reactions at all. I might carry a multi-tool knife and like to wear trousers, but I also appreciated compliments to my femininity.

It was sometimes difficult to be a woman—wanting to be appreciated for my sex while also not being *limited* by it.

"And whose head are you going to turn tonight, eh, *chère?*" asked Oncle Rafe with a sly smile. "Or shall I say, *heads?*"

"Oh, none at all. I just wanted to wear something new." I was speaking the truth, despite Julia's insistence that there would be at least one eligible bachelor at the tasting.

The "eligible bachelor" turned out to be a nice, freckle-faced American boy who was staying at the Deschampses' home because he was working on expanding his father's very successful wine business, selecting and purchasing wines to import to the United States from France. Monsieur Deschamps was apparently an old friend of Bryant Howard's father, and he was obviously well connected in the world of *le vin.* To be fair, Bryant wasn't really a boy—in fact, he was probably older than me—but he had a roundish baby face, on which he was attempting to grow a mustache. And he was very talkative.

I was relieved when the Deschampses corralled all of us from the salon, where everyone had been chatting, smoking, and sipping vodka martinis or gin and tonics (the latter of which I strictly avoided, thanks to an extremely unpleasant experience

when I was sixteen), into the dining room. I managed to extricate myself from Bryant and his easy but nonstop chatter—he
was definitely cut out to be a salesperson—as we flowed into the
other room.

The dining room was spacious enough to hold the two dozen
of us guests, plus a long dining table filled with an array of wineglasses. On one wall was a buffet loaded with platters of cheese,
cured meats, olives, pickles, breads, spreads, and more—obviously to sop up the various wines we would be sampling. As I had
not had much dinner (having saved it for my messieurs), I was
relieved to see the repast.

At one end of the long room was a large table filled with a
dozen bottles of wine and a dozen wineglasses—presumably for
the celebrated chef Loyer, wherever he was.

I was just about to ask Julia if she knew which of the men in
the room was the famous restaurant owner when Monsieur
Deschamps clapped his hands to gather our attention.

The room quieted as we looked at him and his wife, who were
both wearing proud smiles.

"Bienvenue," he said, welcoming us officially as he slid an affectionate arm around his wife's waist. "Sadie and I are delighted to host the great chef Louis Loyer to our home tonight.
He is recently returned from London, his first time back in our
beautiful city since the war, and he has elected to grace us with
his presence and his incomparable knowledge about the
lifeblood of our beloved country . . . le vin. Please welcome Chef
Loyer." He turned, gesturing to the pair of French doors that
stood behind him.

As we applauded, the doors swung open and a man with a
self-important air flowed into the room.

I gaped, smothering a gasp and very nearly spilling my martini as I elbowed Julia.

The man—Louis Loyer—was the one who'd been arguing
with Chef Beauchêne yesterday!

CHAPTER 6

JULIA WAS LOOKING AT ME STRANGELY, AND PAUL—WHO WAS STIFFER and more formal than either she or I—gave me a pointed look. I tamped down my surprise and shock and returned my somewhat distracted attention to the celebrated chef.

I couldn't wait to tell Merveille I'd found out who Monsieur Beauchêne had been arguing with. The best part was that the inspecteur couldn't even be annoyed with me, because it had been completely by accident!

"Before we begin," Monsieur Loyer was saying as he looked around at the small group of us, "I must raise a toast to my old friend and partner, a brilliant chef in his own right, Richard Beauchêne, who was suddenly taken from us only yesterday."

He appeared sober and thoughtful as he picked up one of the bottles. "A gift from my friend Richard," he said, gesturing with the wine. "Sent to me before he died."

A murmur rustled through the small crowd, mingled with a few gasps, as the attendees saw the label on the bottle. I was too far away and far too ignorant about wine—at least in comparison to those present—to know why there was such an expectant hush, but I guessed it was a special vintage.

"He suggested it was meant to be opened in honor of our blessed Saint Vincent, whose feast day is today, of course," Monsieur Loyer went on. "And so we will drink and we will toast *mon ami* and we will ask for Saint Vincent to intercede as my friend goes on to the other life that awaits us all."

I felt a strange prickle over the back of my neck. Partly because of the heartfelt speech, but also because I was having a sense of déjà vu from yesterday. It was the mention of Saint Vincent that really made me uncomfortable. That sense of disquiet heightened as Monsieur Loyer expertly opened the bottle of wine.

"An eighteen seventy-one Sauternes," he said, looking around at us. His excitement was palpable, and his eyes danced with delight as he poured a healthy portion into a slender wineglass. "Normally saved for the end of the evening, *non?* But tonight, as I said, we will honor Richard Beauchêne and begin with his selection. This vintage is from the impeccable Château d'Yquem, of course, and it has somehow survived all these years intact. Even with the Nazis and their filthy hands grubbing about."

This just all seemed so familiar. I was beginning to feel very anxious now, and I looked over at Julia. She was leaning companionably against Paul, the side of her chin resting against his temple as they watched, arms slipped around each other's waists here at the back of the room, where no one would notice.

I cleared my throat, trying to get her attention, but she didn't respond. She must not be having the same déjà vu as I was.

Was I crazy, reading too much into the similarities between this moment and yesterday? My palms were damp inside my gloves, and I gripped my martini glass tighter.

Maybe I shouldn't have had the cocktail on an almost empty stomach.

Monsieur Loyer lifted the glass and put his nose deep inside, sniffing deeply. Still nervous, I watched closely for any sort of strange reaction or surprised response but saw neither. He smiled from behind the glass, then lowered it, obviously delighted with the nose on the vintage.

He swirled the glass's contents, then sniffed again, deeply. Again, he seemed pleased.

Didn't he know how strange this was—that his friend had died the day before, after drinking from a rare vintage? Didn't he have the same sense of foreboding I did?

But Monsieur Loyer didn't seem to find anything amiss. Still, as he lifted the glass in a toast to Chef Beauchêne, then brought it to his mouth, I had the sudden urge to cry out, "*Stop!*"

I could hardly breathe as my heart pounded in my chest. It was as if everything slowed down, and I watched in silent terror as he tipped the glass to allow the wine to slide into his mouth. I felt myself gathering up inside; it wasn't my mischievous imp nagging at me this time, but a strong and horrific sense of foreboding.

I should say something.

I *needed* to say something.

But what if I was wrong? It would be an awful, embarrassing scene.

I *had* to be wrong.

But what if I wasn't?

Just as Loyer was about to take in a mouthful of wine, the martini glass slipped from my fingers and fell to the floor, hitting the table next to me on its way down. The sound of it crashing, then shattering had everyone turning to look at me, and I felt a rush of heat swarm up my throat and over my cheeks.

A servant was there immediately with a hand broom and dustpan to clean up the mess, and I returned my attention to Monsieur Loyer. . . .

Just in time to see him swallow the mouthful of wine.

My heart lurched and my stomach twisted, and Julia looked at me with a strange expression, as if to ask if I was all right and would I settle down? I ignored her, staring at Monsieur Loyer, watching him fearfully, waiting for something to happen. . . .

But it didn't. He'd swallowed the wine and given a bow to the room, saying, "Quite excellent. *C'est magnifique,* this last gift from my friend." Some of the people in the room responded with a quiet smattering of applause. "Perhaps I will even share some with you when we are finished, *non?*" he added, drawing a ripple of a chuckle from the small crowd.

Nothing happened. He was fine.

My body relaxed, and I could breathe once more. Julia looked at me again, and I shrugged, giving her an embarrassed smile. I was glad now that I'd said and done nothing except drop my glass.

Everything was fine.

Monsieur Loyer took up a new bottle of wine and gestured for everyone to select a glass from the dining table as he began to describe the vintage.

"You will all taste each of these after I have told you about them," said Loyer with a broad smile. "Although I cannot promise that the d'Yquem will be—" He stopped suddenly, his words cutting off sharply.

My stomach dropped, and I reached over to clutch Julia's hand, gaping. She turned to look at me in shock, then horror, as Monsieur Loyer began to make terrible choking and gasping noises as he clutched the table. His face was flushing dark red, and he sounded as if he couldn't breathe.

I felt faint—clammy, light-headed, sick to my stomach.

"I'm a doctor!" cried one of the men near the front of the room, pushing his way to Monsieur Loyer's side. "Move back!"

But I knew it was too late, and by the look on Julia's face, she did, too. The horror on my face was reflected in her own, and she murmured something to Paul. His face turned to stone; his eyes widened with shock.

Julia and I stood there silently, gripping each other's gloved hand, and watched as Monsieur Loyer collapsed on the floor, still struggling to breathe, still flushing red, with the doctor unable to do anything to save him.

Moments later, it was over.

Louis Loyer was dead.

CHAPTER 7

I PUSHED MY WAY THROUGH THE STUNNED CROWD. EARLIER, I HAD noticed something on the table, by the wine bottles, something that had caught my attention, and I wanted to see whether I was right about it before anything was disturbed.

No one seemed to care as I approached the table that held the bottles of wine—including the one that surely had been poisoned.

But how? How had it been poisoned?

I'd seen the corks removed both times. Could someone have taken out the cork, poured in potassium cyanide—or whatever it was—and replaced the cork? But surely one of the two wine experts would have noticed it wasn't the original cork.

I put that thought away for the moment as I reached the table.

It was there—the piece of dark fabric I had noticed earlier but hadn't thought anything of until now.

Until it was too late.

Dammit. Why hadn't I listened to my instincts? Why hadn't I said something? Why hadn't I stopped Monsieur Loyer from drinking that wine?

I could have prevented this.

My stomach felt like there was a stone in it but at the same time, I felt an ugly internal sloshing and churning that was a combination of the vodka martini and extreme discord within.

I drew in a deep breath and blinked back the sting of tears. There was nothing I could do about Monsieur Loyer's death except wallow in my guilt.

And help find out who'd done such a thing.

I looked back down at the piece of fabric lying in a small crumpled heap. I didn't have to pick it up or smooth it out to recognize it. To *know.*

It was the same dark blue and green silk damask that Chef Beauchêne's wine had been wrapped in yesterday. The same red ribbon lay on the table next to it.

But this time, the gift tag was still there, as if Monsieur Loyer had opened the bottle right at the table.

I hesitated, then reached for the small rectangular piece of cardboard that had been tied to the bottle. I was wearing my dinner gloves, so I wouldn't leave prints. This time, I read the tag.

> *For the day of Saint Vincent! A most special gift for an old friend.*
> *—Beauchêne*

Frowning—how could Chef Beauchêne send a poisoned bottle of wine to Monsieur Loyer the day after he'd been poisoned . . . in the very same manner?—I tucked the tag into my pocketbook. I wondered if that was really Richard Beauchêne's handwriting on the tag or if our killer was only trying to confuse us.

I would give it to Merveille as soon as possible.

The thought of Merveille had me spinning around, as if he might be stalking up behind me at any moment. I'd heard someone cry, "*Appelez les flics!*" but the authorities wouldn't have arrived so quickly unless a police agent had happened to be patrolling nearby.

Someone ought to contact Merveille directly, but I didn't want to abandon the table with the wine on it. I didn't want to take the chance of something—a clue—disappearing like the gift tag had yesterday.

There was a small paper bag on the floor behind the table, and I picked it up. It was empty, as I'd hoped. The bottle of wine would fit in it, along with Monsieur Loyer's glass and the piece of silk. At least I could save that for Merveille.

He wouldn't like it, but he would have to deal with it.

Merveille did not like it at all.

He didn't even try to hide his exasperation when he saw me from across the room. I just gave him a look of resignation and shrugged a little.

I knew he'd speak to me only when he was good and ready, so there was nothing left to do but wait. I turned away, feeling listless and sick to my stomach with guilt and regret.

Why hadn't I said something?

Monsieur Loyer was still lying on the floor. Someone had covered him with a tablecloth, but not very well, and one tightly curled hand was visible. No one went near the shrouded figure until Merveille went over to crouch next to him.

The rest of the guests were sitting in chairs around the dining room, speaking quietly and drinking martinis and whisky. Julia and Paul were in a huddle with another couple I didn't know, and I was glad they were occupied. I didn't feel like talking to anyone.

I had just sunk onto a chair in the corner when Bryant Howard approached. I drew in a bracing breath and gave him a weak smile.

"Pretty awful, huh?" he said and offered me a glass of something dark gold in color. "Here. You look like you could use it. I promise it's not from one of the wine bottles." At least he wasn't trying to make a joke; his expression was sober and serious. "Some people are saying that it—the wine—was poisoned!"

"Thanks." Even though the contents of my stomach were still sloshing around, I took the glass. I probably wouldn't drink whatever was in it, but at least I had something to hold.

He looked as if he was about to pull up a chair and sit down, and I just couldn't bear the idea of having to make conversation—even though he'd probably handle most of it. In the fifteen minutes we'd conversed earlier, I'd learned nearly his entire life story, including the name of his fifth grade teacher, Mrs. Gurzo, and the fact that his cat, Socks, had had eight kittens when he was ten. Three of them had had socks of their own.

I managed a smile and said, "Excuse me a minute? I have to use the ladies'. I'll be right back." I set down the glass of whisky and rose before he could reply, gathering up my pocketbook and the paper bag containing what I believed was evidence of murder.

My actions were borderline rude, and I hoped he would attribute my abruptness to the events of the evening, not himself. I had no intention of hurting him. In order to take any sting away, I patted him on the arm and summoned up a warm smile. "Save my seat?"

I spent longer than necessary in the bathroom without managing to make much improvement to my pale face, although my hair was relatively in control, thanks to the sparkling barrette I'd slipped into place. I did freshen my bright pink lipstick, which only made my cheeks look even paler.

I came down the hall to find Inspecteur Merveille speaking with Agent Grisart—who had apparently arrived with him—at the entrance to the dining room. Merveille held up a hand to stop me, then sent the younger man into the dining room.

"Mademoiselle Knight." That was all Merveille said, but his expression spoke volumes.

I silently handed him the paper bag containing the wine bottle, the glass, and the silken gift wrapping. I had added the cardboard gift tag to the collection, as well.

"It happened the same way," I told him as he peeked inside the bag. When he looked up, his gaze unreadable, I held up my gloved hand. "No prints this time."

"*Oui*, mademoiselle." He looked like he was about to say something else, then paused, looking at me closely. "Mademoiselle?"

"It's my fault," I said suddenly, in a rush. I hadn't intended to say anything—and certainly not to Merveille—but I couldn't stop myself. "I didn't stop him. I should have said something, but I didn't." My eyes stung, but at least my voice didn't choke up and break.

"Do you mean to say . . . you knew the wine was poisoned?"

We were standing in the hall of this magnificently large home—even more luxurious and spacious than Grand-père's. It was a large gallery boasting a tall ceiling, with gold-painted relief molding and gilt everywhere. If I spoke too loudly, my voice would echo in the long, high space, and it did a little when I responded.

"Well, I didn't *know* for certain." Then I lowered my voice. "I told you, it was the same way. It was so similar to what happened yesterday, and Monsieur Beauchêne seems to have sent the wine to Monsieur Loyer. It *felt* the same—the whole situation. He even mentioned Saint Vincent. I could almost feel it happening . . . before it did." I suppressed a shudder.

"I see." Merveille's expression was grave. "But you did not know for certain."

"Of course not," I snapped. "But I should have said something."

"And if you had, what do you think would have happened, mademoiselle? Do you truly think that a warning from a . . . a young woman would have kept the infallible Louis Loyer from tasting a bottle of eighteen seventy-one Château d'Yquem?"

I shrugged. "At least I would have tried."

Merveille was silent for a moment. Then he said, "You say that Richard Beauchêne sent this bottle of wine to Louis Loyer?"

"That is what Monsieur Loyer said during his talk. I don't know how it could be true—maybe the killer faked it. The note, I mean. It's in the bag with the bottle. I took it before someone else could. You can't deny there's a killer on the loose now, Inspecteur."

"No, mademoiselle. It seems there is no sense in denying it."

"This wine was wrapped the same, as you can see."

"Yes," he murmured, glancing in the bag again. "And there is the gift tag." He looked up. "*Merci*, mademoiselle. You and Madame Child and Monsieur Child may leave now if you like."

I was relieved. "Oh, there's one more thing. I recognized

Monsieur Loyer. He was the man Chef Beauchêne was arguing with yesterday."

That got the most reaction I'd ever seen on Merveille's face. His dark brows shot up, creasing his forehead, and his eyes widened a little. *"Non. Est-ce vrai?"*

I nodded. "Yes, it's true."

"And so they were arguing together yesterday," he murmured, almost as if he'd forgotten I was there. "And now they are both dead . . . in the very same manner. *Vraiment très interessant.*"

"Champignons!" Julia proclaimed, sliding her arm companionably through mine. Her nose was tipped with red, and her eyes sparkled with delight. "We shall find mushrooms and make a delicious *sauté à la crème* . . . and pour it over something magnificent!"

I knew she was trying to cheer me up, to distract me from last night's debacle. I was willing to let her, to be honest—after all, there was nothing I could do about it now. I'd told Grand-père and Oncle Rafe about it this morning, and they, too, had tried to talk me out of feeling responsible for Louis Loyer's death.

"After all, it was not you who put the poison in the wine, was it, *ma mie?*" Grand-père had said, before pulling me down to tenderly kiss my cheek before I went down the stairs. "You cannot blame yourself, *petite.*"

But I still felt a heavy guilt over doing and saying nothing before Monsieur Loyer drank that wine.

Julia pointed out that I *had* tried to do something—that dropping my glass had been my way of interrupting the tasting. "You needed more time to gather your courage, so your brain made you drop the glass. Everyone turned to look at you, remember? Unfortunately, Monsieur Loyer didn't wait, and he went on with the tasting. The man obviously couldn't bear to be upstaged."

I began to argue, but she went on, "Tabs, you couldn't have stopped him. You didn't even *know* for sure. How could you have? We were both there when Chef Beauchêne died, and it didn't even occur to me that it might be the same thing. Why would it be? Who on earth would suspect it?"

I had suspected it. Or, at least, I'd wondered.

I appreciated Julia's passionate words and, even more so, her attempts to distract me by dragging me to the market so we could find something to cook.

And so, for the moment, I put it all aside. I was still alive, and maybe somehow I could help right the wrong I hadn't prevented. I breathed in the cold, crisp January air, and along with the biting chill came the aromas of fresh-baked pastries and tobacco, punctuated by coal smoke. The sun was shining, and the sky was perfectly clear and blue. The sun frosted the snow with gold and gilded the creamy stone of the Haussmann-style buildings. Looking like little terra-cotta soldiers, orange chimney pots rose in collections of two, three, four, or more on the tops of slab chimneys on the roofs. Smoke poured from them on this chilly day.

It was Paris, and today she was sparkling.

When we got to the market, Madame Marie waved to us, and we made a quick stop for onions, shallots, and garlic from her baskets. Thankfully, she had another customer, with whom she was arguing the merits of red beets versus golden beets and what to do with their greens, which allowed me to escape without having to report on the events of last night.

"We'll do *suprêmes* with a sauce of mushrooms and cream," Julia announced suddenly as we paid for our onions. "*Suprêmes de volaille aux champignons.* You'll want to slather yourself with it, Tabs, I promise you. The sauce is going to be richer than Croesus and much better tasting. Oh, and with your grand-père's herbs . . . it's going to be *over the moon!*"

"*Suprêmes?*"

"*Oh la,* dearie, but they are zee best part of zee sheecken, of course!" she replied in her most French-like English, which always made me laugh. That was probably her intent. "The plumpest, choicest, *meatiest* parts of the breast—and that is why they are called supreme! We'll debone them and ignore even the wing parts, you see, and it will all be *delectable*, swimming in a gorgeous herby, *creamy* sauce chock-full of handsome white mushrooms. Come, now, let's speak to Monsieur Michel about those champignons!"

I'd met Monsieur Michel only a few times before. He was a mushroom grower, a champignon seller who offered, among other varieties, the small and tasty Paris mushrooms that looked like chunky white buttons.

Not much older than me, Monsieur Michel was a quiet, polite, and diminutive man who always had a subtle but pleasant aroma of earthiness and compost clinging to his person. His seller's stand was at the far end of the market, tucked just inside a narrow dead-end alley. He claimed he liked being there, off the main road and in the shadows, for it was a bit dark and damp and quiet—very like the environment he claimed, where his beloved mushrooms grew.

But we found Monsieur Michel in an awful state.

"Do you see? Do you see what they have done?" He was standing at his small merchant stand, looking at it with fury in his stance and the glisten of tears in his small, dark eyes.

"Good heavens," Julia said, looking at the broken shelf and the torn awning that hung hopelessly over it. Two wood-slat baskets had also been crushed.

"Who would do this?" I said, my heart sinking at the sight of the vandalism. I felt the same rush of fury as Madame Marie—that some Parisian would do such a thing to his own countryman, especially after having been so repressed by the Germans. It was sad and terrible.

"I don't know!" Monsieur Michel stood with his hands on his hips and glowered at the situation. "But it is *intolérable.*"

The stand was still usable, fortunately, but it was the principle of the thing. The damage would have to be repaired and could be costly for someone like the farmer, who likely barely eked by growing and selling mushrooms.

"Were any champignons ruined?" I asked, looking at the broken shelf. It would be easy to repair—all I needed were two screws and a piece of wood. And the awning . . . Well, a good patch would fix it up. The baskets, however, were beyond help.

I set down my purse and began to dig through it. I thought I had a few extra screws in there from when I'd fixed a drawer pull at Julia's.

"I did not harvest yet this morning," he said, watching me curiously as I removed my wallet, a compact, a comb, lipstick, two matchbooks, a handkerchief, three tiny nails, a metal bracket, a small chain, the keys to my car and Grand-père's house, and, at last—from the very bottom—the screws I'd remembered.

"I came and I found this, and then I talked to everyone, and no one has seen anything," he said, still eyeing my pile of odds and ends. "But now everyone is watching even more closely. First, the bootblack, then the mead merchant, and now the *producteur de champignons*! We will have to stand guard overnight, now, eh?" He spat at the ground, and I didn't think he'd been chewing tobacco.

"I am so very sorry, monsieur," Julia said, patting him on the arm as she looked worriedly over the destruction. "I hope that you find the vandals soon. Tabitha is going to fix your shelf, I think." She smiled at me as I opened up my Swiss Army knife to the tool that fit the screws I had.

"Oui, merci beaucoup, mademoiselle!" he said, pulling off his knit cap to scratch his head as he watched me.

It took me only a few minutes to fix the shelf, splinting it with a piece of wood from an old crate he'd used to ferry mushrooms. "At least it is partly fixed," I said, looking at my handiwork.

"*Oui*, and I will get a patch from the good Tana, who repairs the canvas and sells the linens," Monsieur Michel said with a smile. Then he looked at us expectantly. "Ah, now, mesdames . . . enough about my troubles . . . How may I help you?"

"Is it possible to buy some mushrooms?" Julia asked hesitantly.

"Oh, *oui, oui*, but of course! I must go and retrieve them first from their growing patches, you see."

"Oh, could we go with you?" Julia asked, her eyes lighting up.

"I've always wanted to see a mushroom farm. Chef Bugnard has impressed upon us that it's important to understand how our ingredients come to our kitchens," she added, glancing at me. "When we do that, we understand—and appreciate—the ingredients even more."

Monsieur Michel looked at her in surprise; then his eyebrows rose, and he smiled. "But of course you may see it if you like. You, as well, mademoiselle?"

"Most definitely," I replied. I didn't know anything about mushroom farming, but it sounded interesting.

This seemed to be the right thing to say, for his eyes lit up even more and his smile widened, revealing a missing tooth on one side, near the back. "And you are dressed in the boots and gloves that can get a bit dirty, *non?*"

I looked down at my trusty boots, currently crusted with slush, gestured with my heavy wool gloves, and grinned. *"Oui!"*

"Then let us be off." Monsieur Michel seemed energized by our interest, and I was happy for that at least. We all needed a distraction after bad things happened, did we not?

To my surprise, instead of walking out of the alley onto rue de Bourgogne and into the busy market, he turned into the depths of the narrow passage. I glanced at Julia, who shrugged, and we followed him.

At the back of the narrow, zigzag alley, Monsieur Michel stopped by a rickety wooden shack that seemed simply to lean against the cobbled brick (decidedly *not* Haussmannian) on the back side of an old, decrepit building with tiny windows, many missing their glass panes and boarded up against the winter. It was shadowy in here, for the buildings were so close, they nearly leaned into each other. The bricks here were dark with age and smoke, uneven and crumbling in places, and looked as if they'd been here since the time of Jeanne d'Arc.

I'd assumed the shack was an outhouse, but to my surprise, Monsieur Michel opened a door on the side of the primitive little building.

"This way, mesdames," he said with a smile.

I peered in behind him and watched as he lifted an oil lantern—one of several—hanging on the wall inside the shack. He lit the lantern, and it sent a warm golden glow inside the dank, leaning building—which was definitely not an outhouse. It didn't smell, for one thing, and there was nowhere to sit and do one's business, for another. There were rags on the floor, and a pile of sacks—some paper, some canvas—the latter of which would make an excellent patch for Monsieur Michel's stall roof.

No, the shack wasn't an outhouse—although there was a large hole in the center of the floor. It was covered by a metal disk, like a manhole cover, and Julia and I watched as Monsieur Michel moved it away to reveal a dark shaft that dropped into nothingness. A column of metal rungs was set into the side of the tunnel. Immediately, my fascination was piqued, and my curious internal sprite leaned over my shoulder to look with me down into the recess, breathless with anticipation.

For me, secret passages, hidden doorways, and dark tunnels were exciting and tempting. I had, after all, grown up on a continuous inhalation of Nancy Drew, the Hardy Boys, Tom Swift, and Dick Tracy.

"The mushroom farm is down *there?*" Julia said, a combination of shock and curiosity in her voice. She peered down into the dark.

"*Oui! Dans les catacombes,*" replied Monsieur Michel with great pride. "They are the perfect place to grow *les champignons de Paris.*"

I was itching to climb down the metal rungs. It never occurred to me for even an instant that Monsieur Michel had any sort of nefarious purpose for taking us down into the passages under the city. I felt no apprehension, only excitement and intrigue.

Of course I'd heard about the Paris catacombs, but I had never been inside them. They'd been built, this macabre warren of tunnels under the city, during the 1780s in order to house the hundreds of thousands of skeletons of Paris's deceased from over the centuries. At that time, the largest and most central cemetery in the city, le cimetière des Innocents, was overflowing, unsanitary, and smelly, with bodies layered upon bodies, thousands of skeletons stacked inside its walls, and fetid odors emanating from the newer remains, which were, of necessity, buried shallowly or layered on top of others.

The solution was to move the remains underground, into the quarries where stone had been harvested to build the city above, and so the catacombs were constructed. Every night for two years, beginning in 1785, bodies were exhumed from des Innocents and brought—with the appropriate solemnity and accompanied by priest or monk—into the subterranean tunnels and chambers. In effect, the catacombs were a vast, labyrinthine ossuary located beneath the *rues* and buildings of the Left Bank.

"Shall I take a lantern, too?" I asked. Not because I was afraid of the dark, but because I wanted the opportunity to lead the way—or at least to be able to look down an intersecting tunnel or more closely at anything down there if I wanted.

Monsieur happily equipped me with a lantern. Julia declined, deciding she'd rather have both hands available for climbing down the metal rungs.

"You can make a sandwich of me," she declared, setting down her bag of market purchases. "One of you on each side with a light."

I think Monsieur Michel could see how enthusiastic I was, so he offered me to descend first. Either that or he was just being gentlemanly by not putting himself in a position where he could look up our skirts as we climbed down.

"Take care not to bump the glass against the wall," he said as I maneuvered myself to the opening in the ground. "Start down and I will hand it to you," he added, taking the lantern from me as I positioned myself to climb down the ladder, backward over the hole.

It was at that moment that I decided I should start to carry a small flashlight in my purse at all times. As handy as my Swiss Army knife was, it was missing the very useful tool of a portable light.

I readily started down the rungs. When my head was just at ground level, I took the lantern back from Monsieur Michel, and holding it carefully in one hand, I continued my descent.

I went down, down, down. . . . I counted the rungs. Fifty-five of them before the light I was carrying spilled onto the dirt just below me. A total of sixty-three before my foot touched the ground.

I stepped back from the ladder and looked around. The space was twice as large in diameter as the earthen silo that I'd climbed down. The walls were roughly hewn but fairly smooth and empty of any markings or design. If I had expected to see femurs and knobby vertebrae and smooth skulls protruding from the walls, I was disappointed. The floor was smooth packed dirt, barely damp, with the exception of a dark, wet patch near the wall on one side of the space. The air was thick and damp with moisture.

There was a surprisingly broad tunnel that led off into the shadows; its ceiling was high enough that I wouldn't have to stoop, but I wasn't certain about Julia.

As I waited for my companions, I couldn't help but wonder how on earth the workers and priests had transported so many bodies down into the depths. Had they used pulleys and baskets? It must have taken forever.

It *had* taken forever—years of nightly work.

"Whew!" said Julia when she set foot on the ground. She looked around. "Ye gods, it's *dark* down here. And damp. And creepy." But she didn't sound frightened; she sounded nearly as intrigued as I felt. "I wonder where all the bodies are buried," she said.

"I think we will see some of them," I replied as Michel climbed down as nimbly as a monkey, his lantern attached to his belt near one hip.

"And here we are," he said, giving us that pleased smile, leaving me to wonder how often anyone accompanied him to his subterranean garden. "This way, if you will, and I will show you my mushroom farm. And you can have your pick of the freshest of *les champignons!*"

It wasn't nearly as cold down here as I had expected it to be. In fact, it felt a little warmer than the wintry air above.

The air was still, though, and carried a scent that was of old, musty earth . . . damp rot . . . , and whether I imagined it or not, I also smelled death.

CHAPTER 8

*A*S WE MADE OUR WAY ALONG THE TUNNEL, MONSIEUR MICHEL IN front with his lantern and I at the rear with mine, I noticed evidence of other passersby, which sort of answered my question as to whether anyone ever accompanied the *producteur de champignons* to these depths.

Watching the ground to make certain I didn't trip, I saw cigarette butts and crumpled, empty packs—the vibrant blue of Gitanes, the lighter blue of Gauloises, even a Lucky Strike pack with its red circle logo—empty paper wrappings for food; bubble gum wrappers; used matchbooks; even a single leather glove; and, most surprisingly, given how much Parisians were suspicious of the beverage, an empty bottle of Coca-Cola.

It wasn't as if the place was littered with trash—not at all. These items were few and far between, scattered randomly along the way. There were also one or two dark, smelly piles of something I didn't want to get too close to, along with a few carcasses of dead rodents and something large enough to have been a cat.

I winced at the thought, but none of this was enough to put me off. Instead, I followed Monsieur Michel eagerly, lifting my lantern to read an occasional (and surprising) street sign. I saw ones for rue de Bourgogne, rue Las Cases, and even rue de Martignac, along with markings for passages I didn't recognize. Many were stone or metal plaques, and they were actually embedded in the wall on occasion, usually where the tunnel split off or came to an intersection. Some were carved into or painted on the stone wall. The signs referred to the streets above, not to the passages below, which helped me to orient myself and determine approximately where we were relative to the food market.

The sense that we were truly in a city beneath a city became more profound when the tunnel suddenly opened into a large space—almost as big as the first floor of Grand-père's house or a cozy café. The ceiling was high and curved, carved into the stone that created the foundation of Paris. There were archways that reminded me of those in a church—which was fitting, *non*, with this being the final resting place of many people?—and columns that flanked each side.

Several tunnels went off in different directions from this spacious chamber, and I was itching to follow any or all of them. One was so tiny in circumference that I would have to crawl—and Julia, who was a tall, sturdy woman, might not fit, even on her hands and knees.

There were lanterns hanging from hooks embedded in the walls; two were lit already, leaving me to wonder by whom and when. I'd heard somewhere that a lit lantern underground was an indicator of whether oxygen remained. As long as the light was shining, it was safe to remain.

The fact that the lanterns burned smooth and strong gave me an added sense of security.

"Aren't there supposed to be bones down here?" whispered Julia as we paused in the large chamber while Monsieur Michel added oil to the wall lanterns and lit more of them.

"Yes. Somewhere," I replied, holding up my lantern to look down one of the tunnels that spoked off from this chamber "Like there."

Her attention followed my gaze and the spill of my light. "Oh my God," she said as we both started toward the tunnel as if pulled by an invisible string.

A few feet into the passage—which was about six feet wide and seven feet tall—we saw the bones.

I cannot describe what an incredibly eerie and shocking sight it is to be faced with a wall literally made from human bones. Macabre and fascinating and horrible all at once.

Rather than being haphazardly piled, the skeletal parts were organized into bands. A foot or two of similarly sized and shaped long bones created the bottommost layer . . . then there was another section made up of skulls. Only skulls. They were lined up facing the tunnel, positioned on top of each other in a band a foot high. Then more long bones, this time a taller layer; then another section of smaller, rounder and some irregular bones—vertebrae, I thought, and maybe some patellas. Then followed another row of long bones, then more skulls, piled neatly, like a honeycomb of crania . . . and so on, alternating thus, to the ceiling on both sides of the tunnel.

To this day, I can remember the visceral visual impact of all those vacant eye sockets gaping at me, of the long aged femurs and the circular knobs reflecting the spill of illumination from my lantern . . . and the sense of *something*.

Something else . . . something spiritual.

Something otherworldly.

And even though I knew these poor souls had been dead for centuries, I *smelled* death and decay . . . and I mourned those people, that they should have come to this: a place where anyone could see them in their most vulnerable and final state, jumbled and naked.

It was stunning.

A quiet cough from Monsieur Michel drew our attention.

We turned to see him waiting, but to his credit, he didn't rush us.

"It is sad, *non?*" he said with the hush of reverence. ". . . And beautiful and terrible all at once."

I nodded.

Julia stared a moment longer, then reached out gently and with care, brushing lightly through the air but not quite touching any of the bones. When she turned, I thought I saw her swipe a hand over her eyes.

As we started off down a different tunnel—one that wasn't

lined with bones—Monsieur Michel said, "*Les catacombes* were a meeting place for some in the Resistance, you see. And also a hiding place for the Germans. They built bunkers down here, but the Resistance had their own safe places away from them. And there are other secrets here, too . . ."

His voice trailed off a little, and if I was prone to superstition, I might have been spooked by that ambiguous comment. But I was still more fascinated—while also being appalled—than apprehensive or anxious.

As morbid as it felt, as ugly as the thought was of bodies mixed randomly together to create walls, there was yet a sense of veneration and serenity that permeated the strange ossuary.

"No one knows all of the tunnels and passages," our guide said as we continued to follow him. "It is impossible to do so. Although some have made maps—or tried to. There are the many, many passages with so many entrances and exits. But it is enough that I know the way to my own *champignonnière, non?*" His low laugh was flat in the tunnel, absorbed by the stone walls as quickly as if someone had lifted the needle from a record album. "And that I pass on the way the most excellent mead room of Monsieur Gérard."

He gestured to the right, and with my lantern's beam, I caught sight, down a short tunnel, of an alcove filled with barrels, all lying on their sides.

We walked on a little farther and then turned off into another alcove. I noticed a marking on the wall—a symbol carved into the stone—and asked Monsieur Michel about it. I had seen other carvings during our walk.

"Ah, *oui*, those are the signs or notices of where we are and who is the user of the space—the address, you see. It was once that a rent would have to be paid to the quarry workers for use of the space . . . but that is long over, for hardly any of us work and grow down here any longer after the building of the *métro*, and the quarriers no longer maintain the safety of the place. Back then, one paid the rent to them for the maintenance, you see. But that is not the case any longer. So that is my symbol, and this is my mushroom farm." He smiled, showing his missing tooth once more, as he swept an arm, inviting us into the alcove.

I stepped in first, holding my lantern high.

It was a good-sized space, though not nearly as large as the first hollowed-out chamber we'd seen. The ceiling was lower here, but still tall enough for even Julia to walk through without ducking.

Several lanterns hung on the walls and were flickering with light that cast large circles of gold over long, dark, mound-like rows, three times as long as a man and twice as wide. I smelled something new here—not rot or decay, but the unique and specific smell of a barnyard.

Manure?

In the catacombs?

I wandered through the space, using my lantern to spill light over the dark mounded rows. They were studded randomly with little white bumps. The mushrooms.

They grew like warts, protruding from the mounds on the tops and sides. When I bent closer to see, I realized the long, raised rows were piles of manure and deep, rich soil.

"You see, the Paris mushrooms, they like the damp and the dark," said Monsieur Michel. He had hung his lantern on a hook and had picked up a basket. "They grow in the countryside only in the spring and autumn, after the big rains. Not in the forest. Never in the forest, like other mushrooms!

"But here, underground, they grow all year round because of the damp and the temperature—it is not too cold and not too warm. Of course, I will help them with some water at times, but they grow very well on their own with the assistance of cow shit and some extra soil." Again, he smiled, then bent to pluck several mushrooms from one of the rows.

He held one up. It was a small whitish thing with a thick round cap about the size of an American quarter. It reminded me of a button.

"These are the Paris mushrooms. There are others who try to produce them in all the different soils underground, but *here*, below Paris, is where they grow the best and taste with the most flavor. You wanted to know about your ingredients, Madame Child . . . You cannot have a *champignon de Paris* that is not grown in Paris. Not in Marseilles, not in Lyon, not in Anjou, and certainly not in Japan or Holland." He spat, clearly expressing his opinion. "It is the *terroir*, you see."

I glanced at Julia, unsure of what he meant.

She nodded. "*Terroir*, yes, it is the belief—no, I think the *knowledge*," she added quickly, "that the climate and the soil, even the topography, directly and uniquely affects a crop—whatever it might be. It is a very, very French aspect regarding food and wine."

I was nodding. "Like champagne?"

"Exactly. No sparkling wine can be labeled or called *le champagne* unless it is from grapes grown and fermented in the Champagne region—and that is because of its *terroir*. Everything produced there will have the AOC on its label—*l'appellation d'origine contrôlée*—to prove that it is the real McCoy, you see. That it was produced in that *terroir*." She glanced over at Monsieur Michel, who was still plucking mushrooms from their moorings and dropping them in his basket. "Another one is Roquefort cheese."

"*Oui*," said Monsieur Michel, glancing up. "And we have tried to claim an AOC for our mushrooms here in Paris, but it has not happened. There are not so many of us any longer, as I said, and so the voices are not loud enough, even though the *terroir* . . . it is most obvious." He gestured sharply to the surrounding catacombs.

"And you see how these little ones are white?" he said, picking one and brandishing it. "These are the babies. And if we let them grow longer—eh, three months—and so I do for only a small harvest—they grow larger and become brown, and they are *les champignons cremini*.

"And for an even smaller crop, I will let them grow for six months, you see, and they will be *les champignons portobello*. But, *oh, la*, the babies, the white buttons, they are the *champignons de Paris*, and they are the ones I grow the most."

Julia mouthed, *"Fascinating!"* at me, her eyes dancing in the dim light.

She and I helped Monsieur Michel fill three baskets with *champignons de Paris* before it was time to leave. He piled the baskets in a small wooden wheelbarrow and hung his lantern from a stick that rose from the front of the cart.

I led the way, partly to test myself as to whether I remembered the path, and partly because of the wheelbarrow being difficult to navigate through the winding and sometimes narrow tunnels.

I had noticed not only the street name plaques (and some that were carved or painted on the walls), but also now that I knew Monsieur Michel's symbol, when I saw it, I knew it was an indicator of which direction to go.

Only once did monsieur need to tell me where to turn, and that was as we approached Monsieur Gérard's cache of mead barrels.

Maybe it was because I was in the front this time, or maybe it was because of the different angle of approach, but as we drew near, I noticed something strange in the back, by the barrels.

I stopped suddenly, and Julia squeaked in surprise, barely catching herself before she mowed me over. The wheelbarrow clattered to a halt behind as Monsieur Michel called up to me.

But I had left the path and was hurrying toward the shadows of the barrels . . . because one of them seemed wrong.

I was only a yard or so into the alcove when I realized why it was wrong. . . .

Two booted feet protruded from behind the low stack of barrels. And they weren't moving.

CHAPTER 9

I DROPPED MY LANTERN WITH A CLATTER AND WAS BARELY AWARE (and thankful) that it didn't break as I rushed to the collapsed body.

There was enough light from the lantern that I could see it was a man lying on the ground. By the time I got to him, Julia had picked up the lantern. She brought it over to me, then shined it over the prostrate person.

I recognized him right away—Monsieur Gérard. The moment I touched him, I gave a sigh of relief.

His body wasn't cold, and it wasn't stiff. In fact, as I gently shook his arm, he moaned and stirred.

"Monsieur Gérard," I said. "Where are you hurt?"

By now, Monsieur Michel had joined me and Julia with his lantern.

"Gérard!" he cried, pushing past me to kneel by the man, whom he certainly considered a colleague but also quite possibly a friend. "What has happened? *Mon Dieu*, Gérard!"

Monsieur Gérard's eyes fluttered, and he moaned again. His head moved over the ground, and he cried out, then turned away. When I reached to gently touch the back of his head, I found a wet, sticky mass.

"He's bleeding, and it feels like a bad wound to the back of his head. Water and or a cloth or something to wash it away might help, but he needs to see a doctor." I had no idea how long he'd been lying here, but at least he was conscious.

"Gérard, can you speak to me?" Monsieur Michel helped me and Julia to carefully move the mead maker out from behind the stack of barrels.

Fortunately, the injured man was able to help a little; it seemed his only injury was at the back of his head.

"Can you see me? Do you know my name? How many fingers am I holding up to you, Gérard?" Monsieur Michel demanded as we helped his friend to a half-sitting position against the wall.

Julia had unwound her scarf and was pressing it to the back of Monsieur Gérard's head as he forced open his eyes. There was a bucket of water on the floor, but I didn't trust it to be clean enough to wash an open wound, so I ignored it. Instead, I picked up one of the lanterns.

Something—probably my Nancy Drew fantasies—prompted me to examine the area where we'd found Monsieur Gérard unconscious. He had to have hit his head on something, but I couldn't imagine what it was. The ceiling was high enough that even Julia didn't have to crouch. The barrels seemed undisturbed, so none of them had fallen and caused him to trip and hit his head. What else was there?

I brought the lantern over and streamed the light over the ground where Monsieur Gérard had been. It didn't take me long to see it.

A brick.

Not one that matched the walls or ceilings of these catacombs, but one that looked more like those outside, in the back alley.

There was a brick, and it had a dark stain on it. Blood.

Monsieur Gérard had not fallen and bumped his head.

Someone had come up from behind and hit him.

"And so how did you get the poor monsieur out of the catacombs?" said Oncle Rafe, who'd been leaning forward in his chair with rapt attention as I'd explained why I was so disheveled and dusty. "And he will recover, I hope?"

"I don't know for certain what his prognosis is, but Monsieur Gérard was awake and aware when we were pulling him up and out of the tunnel," I said after taking a healthy sip of sweet hot chocolate that had been well flavored with cognac and cream. I felt I deserved a decadent treat after the events of the past thirty-six hours. Two murders, a visit to the catacombs, and the discovery of an assault. "We had to pull him up with a rope."

"You and Madame Child? And the mushroom farmer?" Grand-père's eyes widened. "But you are only a little thing, *ma mie*! Although Madame Child, she is the lovely Amazon, is she not?" he added. "Oh, the legs on that woman . . . !"

"Oh, we had a lot of help," I told him, smiling. "There were others from the market who were there, and even a police agent who lives nearby—the one who drove me home after Le Cordon Bleu. And by the time we carted him through the tunnels to the ladder in a wheelbarrow, Monsieur Gérard was awake enough to help a bit, going up the rungs." My smile faded. "I feel terrible for him. First, his market stand was vandalized, and now he has been seriously injured. I hope he can return to selling his mead very soon."

"And so do I," replied Oncle Rafe. Oscar Wilde was being particularly adorable, lying in his master's lap and allowing Oncle Rafe to scratch his belly while one delicate little leg kicked gently in ecstasy. His beady black eyes were half-closed, and his head was tilted back, the long hair from his ears clinging to my uncle's wool blanket.

"It is a shame I am not such a lover of the fermented honey drink, or I would buy a large quantity from him. Ah, I should do it, anyway, *non*? You will drink it sometimes, won't you, *cher*?" Oncle Rafe looked at Grand-père, who was smiling at him with soft affection. "And perhaps Madame Child can cook up something with it, too."

"Always with the soft heart," Grand-père murmured, reaching out a veiny hand to pat Rafe on the hand. "Of course we will buy some of it. You say he ferments it *in* the catacombs, Tabi?" Grand-père seemed delighted by this idea. "In barrels, like *le vin*?"

"He does. Monsieur Michel told me that it is the same as for his mushrooms—that the environment—the *terroir*—is exactly right for the fermenting of mead." The hot chocolate was so good, I was considering making another one. But I had a tutoring appointment in an hour, and I didn't want to be full, sleepy, or tipsy, so I had to resist. And later, Julia was coming over to help me make the *suprêmes* with Monsieur Michel's champignons.

"And so what did you think of *les catacombes?*" asked Oncle Rafe. "They are morbid and unpleasant, *non?*"

I shrugged. "Yes, a bit, but away from all of the bones, it wasn't so bad. But I swear I *felt* the souls of those poor people surrounding me." I gave a little shiver, and Grand-père looked at me with concern.

"And I am certain you did, *ma douce fille*," he said. "They linger, there, do they not? The souls . . . I have not been down there for some years, but I remember." He tucked the blanket around his legs, as if he, too, was chilled.

"But not that long ago, *non?*" Oncle Rafe said, giving him a look. "Not so very long ago were we there."

"When you were working with the Resistance?" I asked.

Oncle Rafe gave me an inscrutable look. "Perhaps."

Grand-père chuckled low and rough and took a sip from his cognac. "It is long past those days . . . Surely, there is no need to still be so very mysterious, *cher.*"

But Oncle Rafe merely smiled and shook his head. "Some secrets are meant to be kept. As you well know."

I had finished my hot chocolate and now looked down into my cup with regret. I should have savored it a bit longer.

"And so there is no new information about the two poisoned wine murders, Tabi?" said Oncle Rafe. "What an abomination that someone would ruin such beautiful vintages! It is *blasphemy.*"

Grand-père nodded. "*C'est révoltant.* If one could think of any way to attack the Frenchman, contaminating such a national treasure is the worst. The most hideous! And surely it could not be one of our countrymen who is putting poison into such rare wines. It must be a Russian."

"Or a damned Nazi," growled Oncle Rafe. "Ah, *non*, I don't

care what you say, they are still lurking about, *cher*, you know that." He flapped an angry hand at Grand-père. "It wasn't enough that they lived here and defecated in our streets and breathed our air and hung their *German signs* over our buildings— as if they were *theirs!*—but they hurt and killed our friends, humiliated all of us. They took all of the pride from our city. Those terrible black spider symbols hanging everywhere. On our *streets! Over our buildings!* Outlawing our tricolor and replacing it with those abhorrent black and red banners. Everywhere. They hung them *everywhere!* No matter that it has been four years! Their stink still remains, just as do their bullet holes."

I didn't have anything to say. I had never seen such blazing anger and raw loathing in Oncle Rafe's eyes.

I couldn't imagine what it must have been like for them, living under the Nazi regime in their own beautiful city.

"They delighted in taking the heart of France from us," Oncle Rafe went on with great bitterness. "Did you know that, Tabi? The heart of France, our national treasures . . . the lifeblood of our country. I speak not so much of the artwork and the buildings—and, *oui*, they desecrated and destroyed those, too . . . but they delighted the *most* in taking our *wine*. They stole it, you see. They stole it or ruined it and forced us to serve it to them. To *sell* it to them—*pah!*—it was not *buying* what they did. It was *theft*. It was *destruction*."

I exchanged glances with Grand-père, and he nodded sadly, then reached over to pat Rafe's arm again.

"The point of it all was the humiliation of the French," said Grand-père in a low, raw voice, as if he were reliving it. "Hitler didn't even like wine. He loathed it. But he knew how important it is to us—to our national pride, to our republic's identity. And so he took it and destroyed it or hid it away." His mouth was twisted with distaste.

I had heard some of this before—about the *Weinführers*, as they'd been called: the Nazi appointees who were responsible for the management and procurement of French wines during the Occupation—but it never truly sank in how that must have affected the French as a nation . . . until now, when I heard the long, impassioned speeches of my messieurs.

Before I came to Paris, I hadn't fully understood how deeply important to the French was their wine—how it was their pride and joy, the basis of their national identity. It wasn't merely a product but a symbol of who they *were* as a country.

I knew that this capitalistic sort of suppression must have been particularly raw and devastating for Oncle Rafe, who was from the family Fautrier, who operated a *premier cru* vineyard in Sancerre. If wine was the lifeblood of France, then it was part of Oncle Rafe's heart and soul and was ingrained deep in his own genetics and ancestry.

"They took all the wine?" I asked.

"Not *all* of it. But much of it, at prices that were robbery," said Oncle Rafe bitterly. "And they came into the vineyards and the restaurants, and they took the stock from the cellars. What they didn't drink, they stole or broke."

"What was not hidden away, they took," Grand-père said with a wry smile.

"Hidden away?" My internal sprite sprang to attention at this bit of information.

This brought a twitch to Oncle Rafe's lips, for which I was grateful. "*Vraiment.* There was much illicit activity before the Nazis came, Tabi. And some of the best wines were hidden away from those greedy bastards."

"*Oui,*" said Grand-père. "The vignerons did this, you see. They moved some—not all, of course, for they knew the Germans were not stupid—of their best wines deep into the caves in the mountains of Bordeaux and the cellars of Champagne and elsewhere. The Fautriers and the Drouhins and the Miailhes—many of the famous domaines did this. They secreted their wines in tunnels in the mountains where they could, and they also built walls in the cellars to hide some of the wines, too—down in their own *caves* at the very vineyards, right beneath the noses of the *Weinführers.*"

"Did the Nazis find them?" I asked.

"Not very often," replied Oncle Rafe. "On occasion, *oui*. It was unfortunate that perhaps the brick wall looked too new or the *Weinführer* knew the terrain too well and suspected the hiding. For, you see, most of those sent by the Germans to oversee the *vin* production and sale already knew the vignerons and perhaps had already been the sales agent between the territory and Germany before the war. And so they knew enough how many bottles should have been there, how much stock there was—and where it might be hidden.

"But there were many, many bottles that the Nazis did not find, and I am grateful for every last one of them that did not find its way into those filthy Gestapo hands," he spat, his eyes filming with fury once again.

"And even here in Paris there was some sleight of hand, *non?*" Grand-père said in an obvious attempt to soothe Rafe's emotions. "La Tour d'Argent—the old, very old restaurant that is known throughout the world for its collection of very old and very rare wines, many from the eighteen sixty-seven vintage— why, they hurried to build a wall in the cellar to hide *les vins* from those Nazis. More than one hundred thousand bottles in their collection!"

"Did they hide them *all?*" I asked, trying to imagine how large a space one would need to hold so many bottles of wine—even without needing to hide them. It was mind-boggling.

"No, no, no—sadly, they could not. But they saved twenty thousand of the best bottles—all of those famous ones from eighteen sixty-seven and some select others. They had only hours to do it before the Germans came, and they moved those wines out of the *cave* and bricked them up behind a brand-new wall. And when the Nazis came, they demanded to have some of those eighteen sixty-seven wines. La Tour d'Argent was so very famous for its collection, you see, and so the Germans knew to ask for them," said Grand-père.

"They asked for the eighteen sixty-seven wines, but the son of the owner had already planned for this, and he told the Germans they were all gone. They'd already been drunk," said

Oncle Rafe, his eyes crinkling at the corners. "And when those bastards went down to the wine cellar to see for themselves, they found none of those wines, only eighty thousand *other* bottles. But then they took all of those with them," he said, the smile fading from his eyes. "Eighty thousand bottles of wine—they simply *took* them. A collection that had taken decades to build. Ah . . . poor Terrail. He was the owner. He was devastated."

"But the most important ones were safe behind a brick wall covered with cobwebs," said Grand-père.

"The brick wall they'd just built?" I asked, fascinated by the story.

"Indeed." Grand-père leaned forward, his eyes twinkling now, too. "You see, I suspect there were spiders captured and brought in, too, with plenty of time to spin their webs against the wall. And thus and so, La Tour d'Argent—and there were others, too . . . they kept at least some of their wines safe from the Nazis."

"There was a winemaker who moved all his wines into a room and placed a very large and heavy armoire in front of the door and arranged it such that it appeared to be built into the wall," Oncle Rafe said, a faint smile returning. "The Germans might have suspected it hid something—for surely they knew that many bottles had been tucked away—but they didn't have the time or energy to look *everywhere* and to tear down every wall or suspicious door, thank *le bon Dieu*."

"Would you like to hear another secret, *ma mie*?" Grand-père said.

"Yes!" I was leaning forward, too.

He chuckled and settled back into his chair. Madame X decided this was the perfect opportunity for a scratch, and she jumped gracefully onto his lap, and Grand-père complied. "There is a carpet company here in Paris called Chevalier. And they take all the beautiful and expensive Persian and Aubusson rugs and clean or repair them. They have such the reputation that when the rugs from even a museum must be cleaned—the very old and ancient ones—it is only Chevalier who is trusted to do this.

"And someone at this carpet company decided that it was a great shame to allow all that ancient, aged dust to go to waste . . . and so they saved it. They bottled it up! And they gave it to the restaurants like d'Argent and Maison de Verre and Véfour."

"So they could camouflage their new brick walls?" I exclaimed in delight.

"Ah, perhaps they did—of that I do not know. But I do know that the restaurants, they covered some bottles of wine—the perhaps not so very good ones, perhaps a nineteen thirty-nine Burgundy or even a nineteen thirty-seven Bordeaux—with this very old dust from Chevalier's in order to fool the Germans into thinking they were drinking very old and rare wines," Grand-père replied with a little chuckle.

"That was very clever and devious," I said, smiling back at him.

"One had to fight back however one could do," said Oncle Rafe, refilling his glass yet again. "And even then, one could be found out and jailed or beaten—or both." His face was grave, and I exchanged glances with Grand-père.

"Some of the vintners were found out when they changed labels on the wines to make them appear to be better vintages than they were, or when they secretly drained the barrels from right off the train when it stopped in a station, leaving empty barrels to be delivered all the way to Germany," said Oncle Rafe, his eyes distant. "They were found out, and some were made an example of. Friends were jailed or killed—here in Paris and elsewhere, for these efforts of resistance. And more."

On those words, we fell silent. Oncle Rafe brooded over his whisky, no longer stroking Oscar Wilde's tummy. Instead, the little dog seemed to understand his master's pain, and he licked his hand twice with a delicate pink tongue, then simply watched him, as if waiting for an opportunity to soothe even more.

Grand-père looked at Rafe, sadness limning his eyes—sadness and concern.

I knew both men had somehow been involved with the Resistance, but neither had been willing to tell me much about their activities. I supposed, even though it had been four years since the war ended, it was still too raw and ugly for them to think about. Especially if friends had been hurt or killed at the hands of the Nazis.

The French who had been collaborators—ones who willingly worked with the Germans—were still ostracized by many of those who'd resisted or otherwise fought against the Occupation. Many were still in jail. I knew there was a bill currently moving through the government that, if passed, would give amnesty to about eight thousand of those collaborators, ones who had not been responsible for murder or any actual crime during their liaisons with the occupiers.

I didn't know if passing that law that would help matters or hinder them. Not very long ago, a group of women had had their heads publicly shaved because they'd consorted willingly with German soldiers.

The French had lived through a great hell—something I, who'd been cocooned safely in the Midwest, away from the realities of the war even as I helped build machines of death, couldn't even fathom—and it was an impossible memory for them to put aside. It must be even more difficult to forgive fellow countrymen who'd assisted the occupiers, no matter what their reason.

It was no wonder there was such an overt sense of suspicion toward police authority even now, for the institution itself had been put under the control of the governing Germans to use as they wished. Thus, Parisian police had been required to help round up and arrest French Jews as well as enforce German law. Although some of the agents had joined the Resistance, the vast majority had not.

Filled with these thoughts and faced by Grand-père and Oncle Rafe's grief, I didn't know what to say. There was nothing I *could* say to alleviate their pain and memories. So I stood and went to Grand-père and then Oncle Rafe and gave them each a long, strong hug and a kiss on the cheek and told them I loved them.

That was all I could do.

* * *

Later, during my tutoring appointment, while I was helping ten-year-old Elizabeth Meade from Connecticut learn some basic French, I was also trying to think of an excuse to go to the 36 afterward.

I wanted to find out if Inspecteur Merveille had any clues or leads about who'd been poisoning the wine. Obviously, I couldn't just appear at his desk and ask; that would get me nowhere and probably thrown out of his office.

But by the time I finished with Elizabeth and assured her mother that the young girl was doing extremely well with her vocabulary and pronunciation, I had come up with an excuse. It was a flimsy one, but it would get me to the *police judiciaire*, and possibly even to Merveille's office.

When I arrived and came into the police station, I couldn't believe my luck, for there he was, standing there in the corridor, talking with Agent Grisart. Agent Grisart was the basis of my flimsy excuse for coming to the 36, and to find both of them together was more than I'd hoped for. I wondered if that was because the junior policeman had been assigned to assist the inspecteur in the murder cases.

"Mademoiselle Knight!" Agent Grisart saw me first. My first impression of him had not changed since he tried to collect the attention of the audience at the Cordon Bleu demonstration: he seemed inexperienced yet earnest, and perhaps a little too open and chatty to be a police officer. I thought of him as young, but I didn't think he was much younger than me. It was his demeanor that gave that impression. His greeting to me was so enthusiastic, I almost blushed.

I hoped he wasn't getting the wrong idea. He *had* been very talkative when he drove me home after Le Cordon Bleu, and he'd been even more familiar when he helped us with Monsieur Gérard this morning.

Merveille looked over and saw me. His sturdy shoulders moved in a shift of resignation. As usual, not one dark hair was out of place. Today he was dressed in a slate-gray suit coat with dark trousers and a dark tie. Since he wasn't wearing an overcoat or carrying a hat, I assumed he wasn't in the process of leaving.

Trés bien.

"Bonjour, mademoiselle. I understand you had a bit of excitement at the market this morning. *Monsieur l'agent* has been telling me about how you helped retrieve a man from *les catacombes.*" Merveille tilted his head as if he actually wanted to hear my story, but I suspected I knew better.

Even so, I couldn't have asked for a better lead-in. "Indeed, Inspecteur. In fact, that's why I'm here. Agent Grisart was there to assist with Monsieur Gérard, and I realized he—or someone— would probably want my full statement." I smiled wide and innocently, hoping there wasn't lipstick on my teeth. I had just refreshed it before coming inside and had forgot to check.

Merveille's expression didn't change, but somehow, I had the feeling he was rolling his eyes. He gestured grandly to his companion. "The mademoiselle wishes to make a statement, then, Agent Grisart. Please, proceed."

But I wasn't letting Merveille off that easy. I could see he was ready to make a break for it—his office was down the hall behind me—so I had to do something to keep his attention, or how else was I going to quiz him about the wine murders?

"It was an *assault,*" I said dramatically, edging in front of Merveille so he couldn't easily pass by me. "Someone assaulted Monsieur Gérard by hitting him on the back of the head with a brick. And this was after two or three—I'm not certain how many—incidents of vandalism there on rue de Bourgogne. Perhaps you have heard about them, *monsieur l'agent?*"

"Oh, *oui,* mademoiselle. They did tell me about it," replied Grisart, squaring his shoulders importantly. "And I was just speaking to the inspecteur regarding these problems."

I could hardly control a smile. "Ah, so is this a case you will be working on now, Inspecteur Merveille? The vandalism and assault at the rue de Bourgogne market?"

"Sadly, *non,* mademoiselle," he replied with great gravity and the tiniest of bows. "I find I am far too busy with the other incidents—as I'm certain you're aware—and I'm confident it is something Grisart—er, Agent Grisart—will be quite capable of handling. Particularly now that you have arrived to give your statement, which I am certain will be quite helpful."

Good grief—were those crinkles at the corners of his eyes from a suppressed chuckle? I forgot myself for a minute, surprised by the possible sign of levity and the way it made his ocean-cold eyes seem almost pleasant for a moment.

"I always try to be helpful, Inspecteur," I replied.

This time, he didn't even try to suppress his bark of laughter. "Very well, then, mademoiselle, do not allow me to delay you and your *statement* any longer. *Bonne journée.*"

CHAPTER 10

I HAD NO CHOICE BUT TO LET MERVEILLE PASS BY ME; I COULDN'T think of anything else to delay his exit, and I knew better than to jump right in with questions about the case.

Damn.

And now I had to go with the very careful and solicitous Agent Grisart into a small, spare, windowless room. We sat across from each other at a table, and I rapidly went over everything I had already told him earlier today, after he'd helped extricate Monsieur Gérard.

Unfortunately, I found myself having to repeat certain details, because he wrote far more slowly than I spoke, and he was very, very detailed.

When we were finally finished, I rose and gathered up my purse. "I hope you'll find the culprit very soon," I said. "It's so very terrible for the sellers in the market."

"*Oui*, m'moiselle," he replied. "But of course I am on the case! It is the same market where my *maman* goes, and she will be sad to hear about Monsieur Gérard, too. And I have been assisting *le bon inspecteur*, as well. It is very busy being a police officer now." He smiled proudly.

But his words had given me an opportunity. "So you are working with Inspecteur Merveille on the murders of Chef Beauchêne and Monsieur Loyer?" I sounded fascinated—which, of course, I was—but if Merveille were there, he would have discerned that perhaps there was a little *too* much fascination in my voice and that my eyes were maybe a little *too* wide with ingenuous interest.

"Oh, *oui*! It is a case most challenging, you see, m'moiselle. There are no suspects! No clues! Nothing to point *l'inspecteur* down the right path."

I was disappointed. I had expected Merveille to be well into the investigation by now, with numerous suspects and a number of interrogations and perhaps even someone in custody. I had to remind myself this was only the morning after the second death, and this was real life—not an Agatha Christie novel, where all of the suspects were right up front and obvious, all neatly collected in the same mansion or on the same train, boat, or plane. In real life, as I knew from my father, the detective followed clues to identify the suspect, trying to determine who would have a motive.

"But the wife of Monsieur Loyer, she was here this morning," Grisart went on. "And the inspecteur had her in the interrogation room for some time. She did not appear happy when she left."

My curiosity perked up at this bit of information. So Monsieur Loyer had a wife, did he? And she'd been interrogated for some time? I knew from my father—as well as from all the crime novels I'd read—that the spouse was always the best suspect and, more often than not, the culprit.

But this wasn't enough information to satisfy my impertinent internal imp. "Who else has Inspecteur Merveille had in for questioning?" I asked as Grisart opened the door to the room.

"Oh, well, there has been the owner of the culinary school, of course, and the Deschampses. It was at their home that Monsieur Loyer was staying, you see, as he had just arrived from London, and the bottle of wine from Monsieur Beauchêne was delivered there, you see."

I hadn't known that Monsieur Loyer had been staying at the Deschampses' home. Maybe I should call Bryant and see if he'd like to go for coffee. He might know something. "Did he find the delivery boy who brought the basket to the school?" I asked.

"*Non*, m'moiselle, I do not believe so," replied Grisart sadly as he gestured me into the corridor. "That would be most helpful, would it not? Perhaps he would remember something about the person who gave it to him."

"Does Merveille have *any* idea *why* someone would have killed two people in two days? Any motive?" I decided I'd get as many questions in as possible as we started down the hall.

Grisart shook his head, still sad, and I realized I was going to get no further information from him. I also noticed the ladies' bathroom door right there, and I said, "Thank you so much, *monsieur l'agent*. I'll go in here for a minute, and I can find my way out. I know you have much work to do."

I waited in the bathroom for a good five minutes to ensure he was out of sight. After I washed up, I took the time to confirm that I wasn't wearing any lipstick on my teeth, and to see that my hair was still relatively controlled by my hat. Not for the first time, I thought maybe I should just cut it very short. I'd been seeing Frenchwomen in fashion magazines (and a few on the street) wearing the shingle-style haircut lately, and it looked very chic along with their long, lean clothing lines, which harkened back to the twenties. I wasn't tall enough to have long, lean lines, and I was curvier than the old flapper style, but the idea of not having to fight with my curls all the time really appealed.

Finally, I felt that enough time had elapsed, and I poked my head out of the doorway. Neither Merveille nor Grisart was in sight.

I hesitated, not sure exactly what I was going to do, then bit the bullet and turned in the direction of Merveille's office. I truly didn't have any intention of snooping around in there, but if I could see anything from the doorway . . .

Unfortunately (or maybe it was fortunate), when I reached the doorway, I found the inspecteur sitting on the edge of his desk. His arms were propped behind him, palms on the surface of the desk, his long legs stretched out in front and crossed at the ankles. He was staring at the wall where I knew he hung the photographs from the poisonings; I couldn't see them from where I stood on the threshold.

He looked over and saw me. "Yes, mademoiselle? Have you lost yourself on the way out of the building?" It was obvious he didn't believe that was the case; after all, I'd been here at least three times now.

"I . . . um . . . got a little turned around," I said, stepping inside the room.

Merveille sighed, crossing his arms over his chest, as he stood from his perch on the desk. "What is it you want, mademoiselle?"

I was looking at the pictures on the wall. There were more of them now—one of Louis Loyer, of course, and there were also photographs of the Deschampses and their guest Bryant Howard, and Madame Brassart from Le Cordon Bleu, along with some people I recognized who'd been at the wine tasting. Even Chef Bugnard was on there, which I found surprising, but, after all, he did work at the cooking school.

"Is that Madame Loyer?" I asked, walking boldly over to the wall. The photograph in question was in the center of the space, just below the two poisoning victims. She was an attractive woman in her fifties. Madame Loyer—I could see her name now, Émelie Loyer—wasn't dressed expensively, but she was wearing clothing that was of postwar fashion. She didn't look very happy in the picture, and I wondered if that was her normal expression, based on what Agent Grisart had said.

"*Cherchez la femme, mm?*" I said, giving him a sidewise glance.

"Mademoiselle Knight," Merveille said in a mildly threatening tone. "You have been reading too many novels."

"Did Émelie Loyer know Chef Beauchêne, too?"

Merveille merely shook his head. I didn't take that as a negative answer as much as an expression of his irritation.

"It was cyanide, wasn't it? At least tell me that, Inspecteur."

"Potassium cyanide was found in both bottles of wine," he replied formally after a brief hesitation. "And in traces in the glasses."

"All right. At least it's confirmed that it was poison. But that won't help much, will it? You can find cyanide in so many places, it would be hard to track down where the killer got it.

It's in apple pips and apricot seeds, it's in pesticides, they use it in photography—"

"That is ferricyanide, mademoiselle, that is used in photography, and it is not toxic enough to have killed Richard Beauchêne or Louis Loyer."

I blinked, startled out of my speech. "But it—Prussian blue, that version of cyanide—can be mixed with something . . . I don't remember what . . . to create hydrogen cyanide," I said, wishing that maybe I had decided to teach chemistry after all. "Which is extremely toxic."

"That is true. But that is not what was found in the wine."

"And," I went on without pause, "potassium cyanide was also in the suicide pills they gave to spies during the war. They bit down on them, released the poison, and *boom*. Almost instant death."

Merveille didn't respond to that, which I found interesting. He merely pursed his lips and looked at me silently.

I took that as an invitation to proceed. "Do you at least have a motive? Did you get any fingerprints off the wine bottles?"

He shook his head. He wasn't going to tell me anything else. But I kept on.

"Why would someone want to kill a chef who hasn't been in Paris for ten years? Two chefs in two days, murdered in the same way . . . Surely, there is a connection," I pressed. He *had* to tell me *something*!

No, he didn't.

"Is that all, mademoiselle? I have work to do." He started toward me, gesturing to the door.

I had no choice but to leave, for I wouldn't put it past him to remove me bodily from the premises.

"*Bonne journée, Inspecteur,*" I said brightly, stepping across the threshold and out into the corridor.

The door closed firmly in my face.

"So Merveille doesn't have any real suspects," said Julia.

"And no motive for either murder—at least that I can tell," I told her.

It was later in the day, and Julia had come over to show me how to cook dinner. We were in the kitchen at Grand-père's house. Julia loved to cook in there because it was larger and better equipped than her tiny little *cuisine,* for it had an icebox and regular hot running water, which her kitchen did not.

I'd told her about my interactions with Grisart and Merveille as we sipped cups of *café,* sitting at the table, with bags from the market and their contents strewn all over its surface. Mushrooms, onions, shallots, chicken breasts, cream, butter, potatoes and haricots verts, which Julia had found on her second visit to the market today, along with some clippings of tarragon and chervil fresh from Grand-père's little rooftop garden.

"But Merveille did confirm that there was cyanide in the bottles of wine as well as in the glasses," I said.

"So how did the cyanide *get* there?" Julia said. "We watched them uncork the bottles."

"I've been thinking about it," I said slowly. "Since the poison had to be in the bottles before they were poured, I wonder if somehow the killer injected it through the cork into the wine."

"Do you mean stuck a hypodermic needle through the cork, like a shot?" Julia seemed enthused by this idea.

"I can't think of any other way to get the poison in there without uncorking the bottles—and surely Chef Beauchêne or Monsieur Loyer would have noticed if the cork had been removed and replaced."

"It sounds plausible to me," said Julia. "But that still doesn't bring us any closer to figuring out who did it."

"Us?" I said, grinning, then sipped from my cup of well-sugared coffee.

Julia laughed. "You *know* you're trying to solve the murders, Tabs. I know it, you know it—and Inspecteur Merveille knows it."

I laughed, too. "Well, I'm really not *trying* to do anything. I just think it's an interesting puzzle. I can't help but be curious. How did the poison get in the wine? And who did it?"

"And *why?*" Julia said, poking me with a finger. "You're on the case, Tabs, I know you are."

I waved her off. "Shouldn't we start cooking dinner if you want to be home in time to make something for Paul?"

She shoved to her feet, pushing the chair back with a little rasp over the floor. "You're right—we need to get started. But don't think I'm going to drop the subject. You're interested and involved in this case, Tabitha, and there's no reason you can't put your brain to work while you're in *la cuisine*!"

I slugged the last bit of my coffee and rose, as well. "All right. Where do we begin?"

"With *les champignons*, of course! Now, you don't just *dump* them into the butter and fry their little selves all willy-nilly like most people do. You have to have a little care with them, and they have to be *perfectly* dry.

"Let's cut the really big ones into quarters, but first, take off the stems on any of them where you can see the gills. That way we can clean out any dirt that might have gotten in there. I'll take the stems home and make duxelles with them and sprinkle that over an omelette for my dear Paul tonight." She brought over two knives and two cutting boards for us.

I sat and set to cutting the largest mushrooms into quarters, leaving the smaller ones intact. Julia chopped two shallots and a clove of garlic with rat-a-tat speed, while I clopped my way like a plow horse through the mushrooms.

"I can't stop thinking about the fact that the gift tag on Chef Beauchêne's bottle of wine was missing from the crime scene," I said as I finished the last few champignons on my pile and pushed them over to Julia's side of the table, next to the shallots and garlic. "*Someone* had to take it."

She was cutting out a circle of waxed paper and looked up. "Agreed. But *who*? Can you fill a large bowl with cold water, Tabs?"

I nodded and stood to do so. The chopped shallots and garlic smelled *so good*, and my stomach rumbled a little. I had a feeling I was going to be eating very well this evening. "I don't know. But it's really bothering me. Whoever took it has to be the killer, right? Why else would anyone take a little note card? It wasn't in the trash can or anywhere to be found. Merveille and I looked. Several people were gathered around Chef Beauchêne when he first collapsed, and then people came closer to gawk after . . . well, after. So it could have been any of them who took it. It was probably sitting right on top of the workstation where he'd opened the silk wrapping. My guess would be that the killer made a point of going up to the worktable for that purpose."

Julia, who was spreading a thick layer of butter over one side of the circle of waxed paper, nudged her elbow toward the stove, where she'd set a large cooking dish on one of the burners. "Drop a big chunk of butter in the casserole there, Tabs. I really do need to take you to Dehillerin to get copper-bottomed pots and pans for you. That shop is like a candy store for cooks!"

She peered over my shoulder. "Don't be shy about it, now— you need at least two tablespoons! And half as much oil. Now, let me give these chubby little *bébés* a bath." She stood and dumped the mushrooms into the bowl of cold water, then began to rub them vigorously between her hands. "This will get any little bits of dirt out."

She removed the pretty white mushrooms and pieces from the water and poured them onto a towel; then we began to dry them with more towels.

"They have to be *completely* and utterly bone-dry, Tabs," she warned me. "And the butter has to be *hot, hot, hot!* That way they actually sauté and turn a little brown and don't just steam themselves. Steaming makes them release their juices—and we don't want that!" She looked over at the casserole, where I was again working. "The butter looks ready. See how the foam has gone away now? Dump them in. Careful now. Don't splash!"

Apparently, I was doing the cooking, while Julia was supervising. I didn't mind, but I was always a little nervous under her watchful eye, because I didn't really know what I was doing.

"Now you shake the pot around a little—be careful not to splash too much. Let those babies roll around in there like little greased pigs. You can't put too many in the pan, or they'll get all crowded, and then they lose all their goodness! So if the killer took the tag," Julia went on, watching as I shook the heavy casse-role dish probably far more gently than she would have, "why didn't they take the other tag at the Deschampses' last night?"

"Maybe they didn't have the chance. Maybe they weren't even *there* last night. Or maybe," I went on, talking a little louder over the noise of the heavy pan scraping back and forth over the burner's grate, "they didn't care, because the message was writ-ten out from Richard Beauchêne—who was already dead and obviously *couldn't* have sent the poisoned wine."

"That's *right*! And I don't understand how a bottle of poi-soned wine could be sent by a dead man—but it probably wasn't really him who sent it, was it? Keep shaking, Tabs. You want those little darlings to absorb all that luscious butter! Ye gods, look how they're just *rolling* around in it!" Julia sounded as ec-static as if she'd found a two-carat diamond. "You're going to love them!"

I couldn't *wait* to taste one. They were starting to get a little bit brown. "I'm betting it wasn't Chef Beauchêne who sent the wine. But whoever did must have made it somehow look as if he had. Maybe it was delivered early in the day, before Monsieur Loyer heard about his friend dying. Or maybe he was just sup-posed to believe it took a day for it to be delivered. That's cer-tainly possible."

"All right, now, do you see that?" Julia crowded me at the stove, pointing at the mushrooms. They glistened deliciously, and I had to resist the urge to pop one in my mouth right then. "All that gorgeous, juicy fat showing on *les champignons?* They ab-sorbed it—and now, *now* it's coming out. That means they'll start to get a little more brown, and then we will add the shallots and garlic. No, no, not the tarragon and chervil—not yet. We wait until the end, you see, so your grand-père's *bébés délicieux* don't get overcooked. Go ahead, put in the shallots and garlic, but turn down the heat. Burned garlic is *not* what we want.

"Try one of the mushrooms, too, Tabs. You need to *taste*! Al-ways to *taste*! That's what Chef Bugnard always says. '*Taste, taste, taste! Goûtez, goûtez, goûtez!*'" She brandished a spoon at me, which

I took in order to scoop up a mushroom. "But why wouldn't Louis Loyer at least be suspicious about getting a bottle of wine after the friend who supposedly sent it was poisoned, drinking from one the day before?"

I gathered up a mushroom and popped it in my mouth. It was hot, but I moaned in delight at how good it tasted.

"See?" Julia used a fresh spoon to slide one into her mouth. Her eyes widened as she bit into it, and she grinned. "*Ye gods,* do you *taste* that? *Magnifique!* And we picked them ourselves! That's why they're so damned *perfect!*"

As I stirred the shallots and garlic and inhaled their delicious aromas, I had to resist eating another mushroom, because I knew it would lead to trying another and another and another. . . .

I wondered how long until we would eat. Surely, it would be a while, for the chicken hadn't even been touched. I sighed internally. My hot chocolate had been too many hours ago, and although I'd had a hunk of bread with mustard and a slab of ham before I left for my tutoring appointment, it hadn't been enough.

"Monsieur Loyer didn't know about Beauchêne's wine being poisoned, so he wouldn't necessarily be suspicious," I said, picking up our conversation again. "The police weren't saying anything about it—I suppose they didn't want a panic or to let the killer know they were on to him. And they wanted to make certain before making any statement to that effect. Besides, the newspaper only reported that Chef Beauchêne had died suddenly, but not how. Oncle Rafe showed me the notice."

"Right. That makes sense. You can turn off the burner, Tabs, for now it's time for *les suprêmes!*" announced Julia. I did and turned from the stove. She was holding up two pinkish chicken breasts, one in each hand, flopping them around with enthusiasm. "It's no accident they're the same shape as falsies, is it?"

I giggled, shaking my head. Julia in any situation was energetic and fun; Julia *en cuisine* was a delightful oxymoron of irreverence and reverence at the same time.

"Take note, Tabs—these are *suprêmes*, not *côtelettes*—they don't have any part of the wing still attached, see?" She flapped them again. "They're pure *breast!*"

"I see," I said, trying not to laugh.

"All right, now we are going to make some magic here, Tabs. We put all these sassy, sexy *suprêmes* into the pan with the mushrooms and shallots, see? Roll them around in the butter so they're sweet and glistening, now, see?" She slipped in next to me and watched as I rolled the four chicken breasts in the butter. Then she placed the piece of waxed paper over them, butter side down. "Now put the cover on and pop those dearies into the oven!"

I hadn't even realized she'd turned on the oven. That was one of the reasons I was barely capable in the kitchen. Had I been working without supervision, I would have forgotten to turn on the oven, and then I would have to wait while it heated up.

"Now, while they loll about in those mushroom juices, we will see to *les haricots verts*," said Julia, gesturing for me to sit at the table. "Snap off the end and pull off that string right along the side of the bean," she told me, already doing so herself. "See? And then take the little curling pig's tail on the other end and do the same on the other side. We'll blanch them now, and then they can rest until we're ready to finish everything."

I'd grown up picking green string beans in a small garden at home. *Every day* in the summer. And when I wasn't picking the beans, I was weeding around their plants.

Because of that, I wasn't particularly fond of green beans . . . until I came to Paris and was served haricots verts. They were long and very skinny and always bright green when they were served—unlike the thicker, darker, almost mushy ones we'd eaten at home.

"I wonder if the killer was in disguise," Julia said suddenly.

I looked up from the pile of skinny, elegant beans. "What do you mean?"

"Well, I was just thinking. We're pretty sure the killer was at Le Cordon Bleu, because he—"

"Or she. Poison is often a woman's weapon, because it's so

easy," I told her, with the benefit of my having read so many mystery novels.

"Right! It doesn't take any strength to poison a man's drink, does it? But it does take planning and cunning." Julia's eyes sparkled. "Anyway, the killer took the tag at the demonstration, so he—*or she*—had to be there. But you and I were the only people who were both at Le Cordon Bleu *and* at the Deschampses'—"

"Unless the killer was in disguise at the demonstration!" I exclaimed.

"Right!"

"Because they didn't want Chef Beauchêne to recognize them!"

We looked at each other, the possibilities bounding through our minds. Julia's eyes gleamed, and I was certain mine did, too.

"And it's possible whoever it was slipped out during the confusion," she said. "After picking up the tag, of course. Everyone was gathered around Chef Beauchêne. He or she wouldn't have been noticed."

"I went to find a telephone to call the police, and I didn't see anyone in the halls," I pointed out. "But I didn't get very far, because I ran into Madame Brassart, and the killer might have already sneaked out before that—or even through the door behind the workstation. Although I'm sure someone would have noticed that."

"Maybe not. Everyone was in an uproar," Julia said. "And no one was thinking *murder* at that point—at least, not right away."

I nodded. She was right. It would have been risky, but if the person slipping away was caught, he or she could just say they were going to get help. And if they were in disguise . . .

"It is weird that you and I were the only people at both events," I said.

"It's a good thing Merveille likes you, or we'd probably be his number one suspects. *Again.*" She laughed.

I snorted and tossed the curling string from a bean at her. "Merveille does not like me. He tolerates me—barely—because I've helped him a little bit, that's all. Besides, he's got a fiancée."

"Oh, bah!" Julia brushed off poor Marguerite with a flap of her hand. "Fiancée, schmee-on-cée. I'll believe it when I see it."

"I wonder . . . ," I said, still thinking before I tried to put my idea into words.

"What?"

"Well, it's always the spouse who's the number one suspect, right? And I know that Merveille had Madame Loyer in for questioning today, so maybe he's really looking at her. What if *she* was at the demonstration, but in disguise? Because Chef Beauchêne would probably recognize her, wouldn't he? The two men obviously knew each other."

Julia's eyes widened. "That's true. I was talking to Chef Bugnard today after class, and I told him about Monsieur Loyer and what happened. He had already heard about Chef Beauchêne. *He* told me that Beauchêne and Loyer used to be business partners in a restaurant before Loyer went off to open Maison de Verre. Two chefs in one restaurant—that might have been a little touchy, do you think?"

"So they definitely knew each other well. Did Chef Bugnard say whether they parted on good terms?"

Julia shook her head. "I can try to find out more in class tomorrow."

I sighed. "But even if they parted on bad terms, that doesn't tell us why someone killed them both. Monsieur Loyer only just returned to Paris . . . He'd been gone since the Germans took over. And then he's killed only a few days after he returns." I told her I'd learned Loyer had been staying temporarily at the Deschampses'. I wondered if Madame Loyer had been staying there, too, and if not, why not? And whether Madame Loyer had been in exile with her husband these past eight years or not.

If she hadn't . . . if they were estranged . . . and he finally returned to Paris, maybe there *was* a motive in there somewhere. Had she been waiting for him to return so she could kill him? Or had she *not* wanted him to return, and so she got rid of him when he did?

"It's probably important that he was killed so soon after returning," Julia said, almost reading my mind. "He comes back and *boom!* Someone kills him."

"But why Chef Beauchêne, too? He never left Paris—at least I don't know whether he left. Merveille probably knows. Would Chef Bugnard know?"

"He might. I'll ask him that, too, tomorrow," said Julia. "Let me write both of these questions down so I don't forget."

She made her notes; then we continued to prepare the beans. Or at least, I did, while Julia deftly peeled and sliced some potatoes very thin. "I have decided *les champignons sautés à la crème* will be *magnificent* over roasted potato slices!" she said, her eyes shining. "These won't take long, since they're so thin, and they'll be crispy and delicious. Your messieurs are going to think they died and went to heaven!"

"And so will I." I had finished the beans and stood to pace the kitchen, feeling restless.

"What is it?" asked Julia as she poked around to find a baking dish for the potatoes.

"It just occurred to me . . . Where did the killer get these very rare and unique wines that he poisoned? It's not as if you can just go buy them at a *cave à vins*, right?"

Julia stared at me from her seat at the table. "Well, shoot, Tabitha, you're right. That's a really good point."

I was pacing faster now, my hands moving wildly as I spoke. "Instead of tracing where he or she got the poison, we—I mean, Merveille—should be tracing where the killer got the *wine!*" I went on to explain about how the Nazis had either taken all the good wines, drunk them, destroyed them—or they'd been hidden away. "These must be bottles of wine that were hidden away, right? They're so old. And somehow, they've been either found or brought out."

"But *who* would destroy such valuable wine? Those bottles are worth a lot of money," Julia said, shaking her head. "It just doesn't seem . . . *French* . . . to bastardize something so precious."

"That's what Oncle Rafe and Grand-père have been saying," I replied.

Just then, Julia sprang to her feet. "*Merde!* The *suprêmes*! It's been six minutes already! Quick, Tabs! Open the oven and lift off the top of the casserole. Now press one of those saucy little breasts with your finger. Does it bounce back a little? Kind of springy?"

"Ye-es," I said, my face warm from the steaming oven. How springy was too springy or not springy enough? "It's bouncing back a little."

"Excellent. Now let's just take them out—leave the mushrooms in the casserole—and you can put *les petites dames* on a platter while we make the sauce!"

Julia stuck a baking dish with the potato slices, which had been tossed in oil, in the very hot oven, then walked me through the making of the sauce, which was shockingly simple. I added chicken broth (which she had brought with her, thank goodness) along with some Madeira to the mushrooms and the juices left from cooking the chicken breasts and let it cook on the stove. While I did that, she dunked the haricots verts into boiling salt water.

When my concoction started to get thick like syrup, she handed me a cup of heavy cream, and I poured it in and stirred some more.

"Now for *les herbes*," she said.

I added the tarragon and chervil, stirring them into the sauce as Julia removed the green beans from their hot water.

Moments later she was gleefully arranging the *suprêmes* on an oval serving platter and placing the lightly browned and crispy potato slices around them. The green beans glistened with butter and made a neat little pile at each end of the platter. And then she insisted I be the one to pour the mushroom and shallot cream sauce over the chicken.

"I can't believe we made that," I said, gaping at it as my mouth watered. "In less than an hour!"

"*We* didn't make it," Julia said. "*You* made it. *Trés bien*, Tabitha! Now let's get it upstairs to your messieurs. They are probably *dying* over the smells coming up to them!"

* * *

The next morning, I was still feeling sated and happy over the gorgeous meal. And Grand-père and Oncle Rafe's reactions had made it even more delightful. I really owed Julia Child a lot of gratitude, with her spending so much time helping me muddle my way through the kitchen.

I was drinking my morning *café* in Grand-père's cozy and sunny little greenhouse when the telephone rang. I bolted up quickly, nearly knocking over my drink, in an effort to stop the ringing before it woke my messieurs.

Fortunately, there was a telephone on both the ground floor and the first floor, and so I didn't have to go farther than into the salon from the greenhouse.

"Hello?" I said.

"Tabitha! You have to come to the school! Now!" It was Julia.

"What is it? What's wrong?" Was someone else dead?

"It's Chef Bugnard! They think he did it!"

CHAPTER 11

I ARRIVED AT L'ÉCOLE DU CORDON BLEU IN WHAT I CONSIDERED record time, considering that when Julia called me, I had been dressed in a robe and my hair was a wild rat's nest.

I parked my little Renault down the street and hurried to the front doors of the school, grateful I'd been here before and knew where to go, all while hoping I didn't encounter Madame Brassart.

I bounded down the stairs to the "dungeon" classroom, coat flapping around my ankles, purse bumping my side, and rushed through the doors.

"Oh . . ." I said when I found Julia and Chef Bugnard sitting there calmly, each with a cup of coffee, plus a croissant in front of my friend. "I thought . . . from what you said, Julia . . . I thought he'd been arrested. Er . . . bonjour, Chef Bugnard," I added quickly, with a little bow in his direction.

He smiled beneath his yellowish walrus mustache as he stabbed out a cigarette. "Bonjour, Mademoiselle Knight. I am afraid Madame Child is a bit concerned, and I . . . well . . ." He gave a Gallic-type shrug of "It shall be what it shall be." Although he was dressed in his chef's whites, he wasn't wearing the matching hat, and there were dark circles under his eyes that I didn't remember seeing before.

"Merveille had him at *le police judiciaire* for two hours yesterday, Tabitha," Julia said. She bristled with affront, her eyes flashing and her mouth uncharacteristically flat.

I took a seat, wishing I'd had time to finish my coffee. I'd rushed because I thought Chef Bugnard was being dragged off to the 36, and I'd thought I'd be able to talk to Merveille about it—or him out of it. (Both of which were, granted, ridiculous thoughts.)

"Where are the rest of the students?" I asked, realizing that Julia should have been in the middle of class.

"We sent them home," Julia said, glancing at her teacher. "*Monsieur le chef* was too distracted to teach about pie crusts and deboning a goose today."

Bugnard shrugged again, but this time he didn't smile. "It is not the most pleasant experience to be questioned by the police."

How well I knew *that*.

"What did they want to know?" I asked. Unlike Julia, I didn't automatically dismiss Max Bugnard as a suspect, although I certainly didn't have him near the top—or even *on*—my list.

. . . But that was because I didn't have a list of suspects at all. Other than the possibility of Émelie Loyer—and she was on my nonexistent list only because of what Agent Grisart had told me and because of her photograph on Inspecteur Merveille's wall—I had no suspects at all. It was frustrating.

"*Oh, la*, he wanted all of the gossip about Beauchêne and Loyer, of course," replied Chef Bugnard with a dismissive wave. "About their history, you see, and when they worked together and why they did not any longer. And if I knew of any enemies of either of them."

All right. That was good. Merveille was trying to uncover a motive. Which, my internal adventure seeker pointed out, meant I could get the same information from Chef Bugnard and do the same.

I didn't even try to argue with myself. *Of course* I was going to be inquisitive and interested in trying to solve *two murders that had happened right in front of me*. I wouldn't be *me* if I wasn't.

In no way did I think I'd do it on my own or try to "beat" Merveille to the punch or anything like that. Just like before, when I was caught up in the investigation into Thérèse Lognon's murder last month, I would tell the inspecteur everything that I had learned so *he* could do the dangerous stuff.

That's exactly what I told myself, and I really, truly meant it. I couldn't help how things actually turned out.

"What did you tell Merveille?" I prompted . . . and then I smelled fresh coffee. Julia had taken to the stove and was making some. Hallelujah!

"Ah, well, I told him Beauchêne and Loyer owned a restaurant together in the nineteen thirties. It was very nice, very successful, excellent haute cuisine, and they were quite happy. It wasn't La Tour d'Argent or Le Grand Véfour, of course, but there was a wait for a table every night, and the food was *magnifique*." He kissed the tips of his fingers and smiled, his eyes crinkling at the corners. "Although I did not think they did a sole meunière as well as they could have done, you see. And . . . well, their *confit de canard* was a bit below par, but, *eh*, what did it matter when the rest of it all was so good? And I certainly did not tell *them* what I thought, for Beauchêne—he has the temper."

"Was his temper part of the reason he and Monsieur Loyer parted ways at their restaurant?" I asked.

Chef Bugnard's eyes widened, and he looked at Julia again, astonished. "But *l'inspecteur*, he asked me the very same thing."

I stifled a smile. He seemed surprised that a young woman would have the same astuteness as a seasoned police inspector. I had asked an obvious question, but still, I was pleased to confirm that I was following the same trail of questioning as Merveille. I didn't say anything but waited until Bugnard picked up his story.

He did so after Julia brought over two steaming cups of coffee and placed them in front of us. Mine was dark and, I was certain, well sweetened, while his was lighter from cream. She took away his used cup as we continued to talk.

"Ah, well, they would never *say* that his temper was the reason, but one did hear the gossips. But two chefs in the same *cuisine?*" Bugnard tsked and shook a finger. "It is like a bad marriage, *non?* The couple, they love each other at first, but then they fight, and . . ." He shrugged. "And sometimes they make the love passionate, and other times they throw the pots and pans, *non?*" He sipped his coffee. "But I do remember hearing that Beauchêne was perhaps to come to Maison de Verre and to cook with Loyer once again."

"Really?"

"*C'est vrai,*" said Bugnard with a decisive nod. "This was before the war, of course. Before the Germans." His face darkened, and he paused to light another cigarette. I waited patiently as he took a deep drag and exhaled, his eyes far away.

At last, he continued. "You see . . . Beauchêne was *le chef suprême.* And Loyer . . . why, he was very, very, *very* good . . . but he was not Le Beauchêne. Loyer, he knew *le vin* . . . and he was . . . Well, as I say, he was very, very, *very* good *en cuisine.* And so the two made good partners."

"And what about Madame Loyer?" I asked.

Bugnard looked at me, astonished once more. "It is almost as if you were there when the inspecteur was asking me the questions—they are all the same!"

I nodded complacently and waited. Maybe I really did have a Nancy Drew or Sam Spade sort of knack for investigation.

"Émelie, er, Madame Loyer." He sighed. "She is *la femme difficile,* you see. One cannot please her, you see, although for some reason, one is compelled to attempt it. And many have tried." Bugnard shook his head, with a small smile, dragging on his cigarette again. "She has the . . . the je ne sais quoi and the smile and . . . *oh, la,* even now the figure . . . !" His voice trailed off, and I got the distinct impression that perhaps even Chef Bugnard had been compelled, at some time, to attempt to woo Émelie Loyer.

"You know her well," I said, understanding, I thought, why Merveille seemed interested in Max Bugnard in the murder investigation.

"Oh, but of course. We all know each other from years ago," Bugnard replied easily. "Loyer, Beauchêne, Émelie, Terrail—he is from d'Argent, you know—and so on. It is, as they say, a small world, those of us who create the masterpieces in the kitchen, who have studied and improved and become masters of *la haute cuisine*. I do not wish ever to return to the work of the fine restaurants, but I well remember the life. It was exciting and exacting and exhausting."

"How did Madame Loyer figure in? Is she a chef, as well?"

"Oh, no, no, not a chef . . . but she . . . she knows the *vin* as well or better than Loyer. It is her family, you see—she is from the Beaujolais—and she often advised Beauchêne and Loyer on their cellar. She was the sommelier—the expert of the wine, if you will. It is," he said with a moue of distaste, "what one does when one is not *quite* accomplished enough to be the chef. One takes the—er—the consolation prize as the sommelier."

"Was Monsieur Loyer a sommelier as well?"

"*Merde, non!* Of course he was not! He was *l'excellent cuisinier*, but Émelie, she taught him much about the *vin*. But he has—had—a good nose and knew how to taste and how to select."

"She didn't go into exile with him when the Germans came," I said, thinking of how much younger than her husband Madame Loyer was. "Why? And why did he leave? Did Chef Beauchêne leave, as well?"

"Ah, so many questions, and all familiar ones," he replied wryly. "No, Émelie and Loyer, they have not lived together since before the war. I think . . . Well, at one time, I thought perhaps she had returned her affections to Beauchêne. He had been her lover before Loyer. But their relationship ended before Louis Loyer met her. And so there was no difficulty between the two men when they started their restaurant."

I wondered if that was really true. "And so Madame Loyer was already estranged from her husband when he went away during the war?"

"Yes. He left when the Germans insisted on taking over Maison de Verre. Loyer would not serve them, he would not cook for them, and he would not suffer their stink in his restaurant. And so, in the dead of night, he fled rather than being jailed.

He was welcomed in London, where he opened a celebrated restaurant and did very well."

"And so why did he come back if he had a successful restaurant in London?"

Bugnard looked at me in surprise. "But . . . this is *Paris*. Of course he wanted to come back." He stabbed out his cigarette and took another long drink of coffee. "It is his home. And Maison de Verre—it was very fine. The glass, it was everywhere—a large and beautiful window, many, many chandeliers, and hanging from the walls in places, with dark fabric coverings framed in between. It was beautiful. Like being inside a crystal. And the *food*!"

"Did he intend to reopen the restaurant, do you think, when he came back?" I asked.

"I think so," said Bugnard. "I think he did. But . . ." His expression saddened, and he shrugged again. "That will not happen now."

I wondered suddenly if that was a motive. Someone didn't want the famous chef to reopen his restaurant, and so they killed him before he did so.

"But what about Chef Beauchêne? If he was such a brilliant chef—better than Loyer—and he stayed here in Paris during the war, wouldn't his restaurant be more famous?"

"One would think so, *non*? But Richard Beauchêne, he . . . well, he was the brilliant chef *here*"—he tapped his temple—"but he was not so brilliant when it came to the work and the management and the other people. He liked to drink, you see, and he had that temper, and . . . well . . ." He threw up his hands, leaving me to fill in the blanks. Which I did.

"He drank too much and didn't know how to run a restaurant," I said, remembering the strong waft of spirits that I'd smelled from Chef Beauchêne. He likely hadn't changed his habits much in the past eight years. "But he could cook."

"*Oui*, he could cook! But Loyer, he knew how to manage him—until he became tired of doing so, you see? And then he opened his own place, Maison de Verre."

"I saw Chef Beauchêne and Monsieur Loyer arguing right before the cooking demonstration here at Le Cordon Bleu," I said. "They were both here at the school. Do you have any idea what they might have been arguing about?"

Chef Bugnard seemed astonished by this information. "Loyer was here? Before the demonstration? But, no, I did not even see him—and such a pity, for I had not spoken to him since his return, and now I never will. I do not know why they might have been arguing. But, mademoiselle, remember what I said. The two, they were like old lovers who shared a kitchen. Their argument could have been over the most simple of things. It was their nature."

I nodded. That was what I'd thought. "Can you think of any reason someone would want to kill both Chef Beauchêne and Monsieur Loyer?"

Max Bugnard shook his head. "No. *L'inspecteur* asked me the same question, and I told him the same. I can think of no reason anyone would want to murder either of them. It seems foolish! But it is a great loss for the world—and for *les gastronomes* in it."

Before I left Le Cordon Bleu, I asked Chef Bugnard if he knew where Madame Loyer lived. To my surprise and delight, he gave me her actual address, which was back over on the Left Bank, closer to home.

But I had a tutoring appointment here on the Right Bank, not too far from Le Cordon Bleu, which gave me time to think about what, if anything, I was going to do next.

I drove to my tutoring appointment, and then, since I'd rushed out of the house without breakfast, I found a café where I could have a galette and a glass of wine and mull over things a little more.

I had been in Paris nearly ten months and still found it strange— and indulgent, almost hedonistic—that the French drank wine with nearly every meal. Even, sometimes, with breakfast! As I ate my galette sitting at a table in the window of the little eatery, I thought about what I'd learned from Chef Bugnard. . . .

How the two chefs had worked together, but not without problems. How they'd both loved the same woman—albeit at different times, if Bugnard was correct. And how Madame Loyer was estranged from her husband and had not gone into exile with him.

What had she been doing in Paris while he was gone?

Another fact that stood out to me was that Émelie Loyer was an expert on wine. The killer was using wine to kill—exclusive and rare vintages. If anyone would know how to obtain such rarities, Madame Loyer would.

But if she was such a lover of wine, why would she bastardize those priceless treasures? I wasn't certain it made sense, and besides, I still couldn't think of a motive. Bugnard hadn't had one, either.

Yet . . . two of Émelie Loyer's former lovers were dead from poisoned wine. Both had worked together and might have planned to do so again. Surely, it couldn't be a coincidence.

I sighed. I was stymied, and I wondered if Merveille was feeling the same way. Of course, he had far more resources than I did. Which reminded me . . . Had he found the delivery boy yet?

Maybe I'd have better luck spotting him, since I'd actually met the kid.

I finished my little meal and decided a brisk walk in the area of Le Cordon Bleu, where I might see the delivery boy, might clear my head while I thought about whether I should actually go to Madame Loyer's house, which would be almost on my way home. (Even at that time, deep inside, I suspected I *would* go there, but I told myself I hadn't actually made the decision yet.)

Having my car was a godsend, but I'd previously enjoyed biking or walking around Paris not only for the exercise but also because it brought me closer to the beauty of the city: the creamy buildings, the jaunty terra-cotta chimney pots, the broad streets, the wrought-iron decor, the smells of food and coffee and tobacco, the people . . . the cats.

There were cats everywhere in Paris. Fancy, fluffy cats, sitting in the windows, swathed in filmy curtains, watching the activity below with arrogant eyes. Pet cats, carried by their owners in their arms or in large handbags, peering out at the world, pink noses just visible over the edge of the carrier. There were cats in cafés. In cars. In bicycle baskets. Alley cats, lurking in the narrow, shadowy passageways, eyes gleaming in the dim light. Strays—like the one who'd saved my life—scrawny, fierce, and always on the lookout for sustenance . . . or a brawl.

After my early luncheon, I drove back toward rue du Faubourg Saint-Honoré and parked three blocks from the cooking school. As I walked, I breathed in the crisp January air, along with a whiff of baking bread and the aroma of cigarettes, and once again reminded myself that *I lived in Paris.* What a different life from my home in Michigan, where I'd planned to marry Henry McKinnon and teach school and likely have children. . . .

There were so many more possibilities here, where I was unfettered by familial and societal expectations. So much more adventure! I was eternally grateful to my grand-père for inviting me to the City of Light—and to my mother for insisting I go.

I still wondered about that—why my mother was so enthusiastic about me, her eldest daughter, moving so far away for an indeterminate length of time.

I was certain her unbridled enthusiasm about me going overseas—and getting out of the house—didn't have *anything* to do with the fact that I was a bookish sort of girl who nonetheless climbed trees and liked to take mechanical things apart (and put them back together, most of the time correctly) . . . and who, during high school—well, and college, too—occasionally set up booby traps in the desks of teachers who gave me Bs when I deserved As . . . or occasionally sneaked to clubs in downtown Detroit to listen to jazz music . . . or poured flour all over the car of the guy who dumped my best friend—on a night that it rained.

Certainly *those* couldn't have been the reasons my very proper, very feminine, and elegant French mother (who was married to a just as correct police officer) suggested I visit her father here in Paris.

Surely, it was only because I was moping around the house, with nothing interesting to do.

I was sure of it.

I grinned and laughed out loud. *Everyone* was glad I'd flown the coop, so to speak. We'd all been ready for a change, and I'd felt lost and trapped and needed to spread my wings. Plus, my sisters had been ecstatic, because one of them could move into my bedroom. For whatever reason, Mama had sent me here, and here I would stay as long as possible.

In spite of the cold, I walked for at least an hour, enjoying the sights and smells of the city that had become my own. And even though I kept my eyes peeled, I didn't see the shabby-looking boy who'd delivered the wine for Chef Beauchêne.

I was just about to give up and climb back into my Renault when I saw a scruffy, slightly unkempt young man—a boy, really, and about the same age as the delivery boy—loitering on the corner. He smoked a cigarette that might just as easily have come, stubbed out, from an ashtray or found on the street, fallen from a pocket, as from a fresh pack in his pocket.

He gave off the impression that he was waiting for something: something to do, some way to make a few sous, something interesting to happen, someone to walk on past who might need assistance. I started toward him, then made a quick turn into a pâtisserie and purchased a fresh chocolate croissant. I wasn't certain which would be a better bribe: food or a pack of Gauloises, but I'd opted for the food simply because there was no *tabac* in sight.

"Bonjour," I said as I approached the boy.

"Bonjour, m'selle." He eyed me curiously as he sucked deeply— and far too expertly for his young age—on the last bit of the cigarette, but his attention fell on the paper-wrapped croissant.

"Do you work around here?" I asked. "Have you been here for a while?"

"*Oui*, m'selle," he replied, leaning against the wall in a manner I suspected he thought made him look cool and insouciant. It probably did, to girls of twelve or thirteen. "Four years, it's been." Which put him at about age ten when he started . . . and just after the Liberation. I shuddered at the thought of what he might have seen in his young life.

"What is it you need, m'selle?" he asked, standing upright now that the possibility of money was in the air. "A package delivered? Send a message? Pick up a parcel? I'm fast and cheap."

"Information," I replied. I shifted the croissant so the paper crinkled, and his attention slid to the flaky pastry.

But he edged back a little and took a big drag from the cigarette, as if to use it as a shield. "What sort of information, m'selle?"

"There was a young man here. It was Tuesday," I said. "He brought a delivery to Le Cordon Bleu. Do you know it?" I pointed in the general direction of Faubourg Saint-Honoré. "It was a basket with a bottle of wine in it."

His eyes narrowed suspiciously, and he edged back farther, but his eyes kept drifting to the croissant. *"Peut-être."*

"Do you know the messenger? I only want to speak to him for a minute. You see, he gave me the delivery at the school, and I didn't pay him for it."

The boy's eyes widened a little. "But he was already paid—" Now his eyes goggled as he snapped his mouth shut, chagrin washing over his face.

"So you do know about it," I said. I waggled the croissant at eye level. "This is yours if you tell me about him, all right? Or where I can find him."

The boy hesitated, but it seemed that even a cigarette was no match for a young man's empty belly. That, along with the fact that I was *not* the police, and therefore inherently more trustworthy. And possibly even better looking.

"Pierre," he said. "But he's gone. Hasn't come back. I did. No one's going to run me off my street corner." He puffed his chest proudly. "And I won't talk to *les flics*, you see. Don't trust them."

It wasn't a surprise to me that he didn't like the cops. And that likely explained why Merveille hadn't made any progress finding this Pierre, although I would expect the police to have some streetwise informants.

"Do you know where Pierre is?"

The boy shrugged. *"Gaar . . .* I don't know. *Le poulet,* he run us all off, you see. Three of us, we worked these streets over the years—since the German pigs!—and *le policier* runs us off. Said we're nuisances, and if we keep loitering about, he'll give us a night in a cell." He flicked what was left of his cigarette to the ground to demonstrate his opinion. "But this is *my* corner, my block, and I came back, eh? Even *les Boches* couldn't scare me off."

"But where's Pierre?"

The boy shrugged. "Last I saw him, we—him and Thomas and I—we tried to find work at la Vendôme. But there wasn't enough business for us, you see. Too many other messengers. And so I came back."

"You don't know where he's working now?"

"*Gaar*, m'selle, it's a big city," he replied in disgust. "He could be anywheres, couldn't he? Maybe in rue de Castiglione, maybe somewhere else." He put his hands on his hips and looked at the croissant. "You going to pay me now or not?"

"Yes, but I have one more question," I said, handing him the croissant in its wrapping. "Were you there when Pierre got the delivery? Did you see the person who gave it to him?"

He lifted his face from the pastry, chocolate streaking the corner of his mouth, and swallowed heavily. "Oh, *oui*, of course. We were all three standing there, and the monsieur comes up and he calls over to us. Pierre was quickest," he said in self-disgust. "I was lighting a fag and didn't see him until it was too late."

"So it was a man." I felt a little bump of disappointment but shoved it away. It was a clue, even if it didn't point to Émelie Loyer as I'd hoped. "What do you remember about the man?" I tried not to sound too excited—or desperate—sensing I didn't have much longer before I'd lose my informer's attention. I should have waited to give him the croissant. "Are you certain it was a man?"

The boy looked at me as if I was crazy. "He was wearing trousers, and he had on a big, heavy coat, you see. And a big, bristly mustache. Light. Oh, and he was wearing glasses. For the sun, you see? Like the pilots?" He used his hands—including the one holding the pastry, sending flakes wafting to the ground—up by his eyes to make the shape of the aviator sunglasses that had become popular during the war.

I nodded. A big, bristly mustache and dark-tinted glasses, with a bulky coat. A great way to disguise oneself—whether it was a man or a woman. "And what about his hat?" I asked. If it had been Madame Loyer, she could have worn a hat and put on a false mustache and worn Ray-Bans and pants and passed for a man.

The boy was shifting from one foot to the other, and I had the impression he was about to make a break for it. "*Gaar*... he wasn't even wearing a hat," he said, shaking his head. "Funny, that was—the glasses and a big coat, but no hat on a day like that, cold and wet."

"No hat." I found that strange, too. No one went about without a hat on—a fedora, a homburg, a flat cap or beret, a wool pull-down, *something*—especially in the winter. "Have you seen that man around here since?"

The boy shook his head and crumpled the empty pastry paper. I could tell he was about to bolt.

"One more question," I said quickly. "Was the man tall or short or fat or thin?"

"*Gaar*, m'selle . . . he was the same as anyone. Not tall, not short, not fat, not thin . . . just the same."

"All right. Thank you," I said. "What is your name? Just in case I ever need a messenger."

He flashed a smile punctuated by the streak of chocolate at his lip. His teeth were unbelievably crooked and stained with tobacco use. "Théo. *Merci*, m'selle," he said, then, with a wave, he darted off across the street before I could ask him to contact me if he saw Pierre.

I sighed, watching him go as he wove through the traffic and then darted around pedestrians, bicycles, and dogs on the sidewalk. I started walking back to my car, reflecting on what little I'd learned.

It hadn't been a waste of time: I'd gotten some fresh air, spent some money on a croissant that I *hadn't* eaten, and maybe discovered a clue.

It sounded as if whoever had given the basket for Chef Beauchêne to Pierre had been in disguise, with a bristly light-colored mustache and dark glasses. I hadn't asked whether the man's hair was light, as well, but it seemed logical.

However, I couldn't recall seeing anyone at the cooking demonstration meeting that description. So either he or she—it was *possible* it had been a tall woman—had removed the disguise before going into the school or had even adopted a different disguise for the demonstration . . . or hadn't been there at all.

But the killer *must* have been inside the school, in the demonstration room, in order to remove the gift tag.

And what was so important on the gift tag that it had to be taken? Probably fingerprints, handwriting, and maybe even the contents of the note.

I got in my car and navigated out onto the *rue*. It was after one o'clock. I didn't have anything else I *had* to do today except decide what I was going to make for dinner.

I had plenty of time to drive by Émilie Loyer's apartment.

CHAPTER 12

*T*RAFFIC WAS SURPRISINGLY LIGHT AND COOPERATIVE AS I TOOLED over the Pont au Change, crossing from the Right to the Left Bank. As I did so, I could see the twin Gothic towers of Notre-Dame from where they rose on Île de la Cité, the long, elliptical island in the middle of the Seine, where both the famous church and *la police judiciaire* were located.

I briefly considered stopping there to leave word for Merveille about what I'd learned regarding Pierre the messenger boy, but decided it wasn't important enough to bother him in person—even though I wanted to nose around and peek more at the pictures he'd posted on his "crime wall." I could telephone him later with that information.

The address Chef Bugnard had given me put Émelie Loyer in the part of Paris known as the Latin Quarter, a mile or so (I still thought in American terms of measurement) east of rue de l'Université, where Julia and I lived, and just east of the avant-garde neighborhood of Saint-Germain-des-Prés.

Here in the Quartier Latin, the streets remained mostly untouched by the omnipresent hand of Haussmann and its uniform stonework, and the buildings were a myriad of styles, heights, breadths, and depths. Crumbling brick, blackened from centuries of age and smoke, tiny windows, skinny balconies barely the size of a hand, and deep overhangs gave the neighborhood a close, almost claustrophobic feeling. You could even see places where a building had been taken down from one side of a shared brick wall, leaving different colored patches that showed the paths of what had been fireplace flues.

The *rues* were narrow and tangled, having gone unchanged since medieval times, when students at La Sorbonne were required to speak Latin. The cobblestones were old and uneven, and the streets so narrow that sunlight had to fight to find its way down between the buildings to warm and dry the bricks beneath our feet and tires. One of the streets was so ancient, it was the road the Romans took to Italy when they ruled the Mediterranean.

Although the Latin Quarter was a stunningly huge departure from the broad, elegant avenues and Grands Boulevards of the renovated city center, I found the neighborhood just as intriguing and consummately Parisian as the perfect lines of Lutetian limestone on expansive, tree-lined boulevards.

There were cafés, *bistrots*, *tabacs*, bookstores, and shops selling everything from leather products to clothing to devotional articles lining every street. People—many of them students and most in their twenties or early thirties, like me—filled the sidewalks and rambled into the *rue*, heedless of the motorized traffic, which was forced to creep along the narrow passages in order to avoid hitting people or other vehicles. These pedestrians—many of the men with straggly bohemian beards, and both sexes wearing slouching berets and loose black trousers—talked, shouted from street to window, laughed, walked their dogs, drank coffee and cognac, smoked tobacco and marijuana.

They made out in alcoves or on street corners, over their wine or coffee at café tables, on omnibuses and the *métro*, and anywhere else that suited their fancy. The openness of the younger French generation when it came to sex—not just talking about it, as we all did back home, but actually *doing* it, wildly and with abandon—had been a little shocking to me at first. It was still surprising to come around a corner and find a couple in the middle of some serious mashing on a public street corner. And yet the sight of such young, passionate love often elicited a little lonely, envious twinge inside me.

I didn't want to get married anytime soon; I didn't even know if I wanted a serious boyfriend, who'd probably be pushing me in the direction of matrimony. But I did miss male companionship and the pleasure that came with it.

I slid my car into the first parking place I saw, which was two blocks from Émelie Loyer's address. When I got out, I just missed stepping in a pile of dog leavings right next to my car door. Whew.

Just as Paris was bursting at the seams with cats, she was nearly as rich with dogs—and what they left behind. I heaved a sigh of relief and made a mental note to pay attention to the ground when I climbed back in the car.

A young man, bearded and dressed all in black, stood on the corner with his guitar and its optimistically open case, which sat on a small mound of gray snow he'd likely arranged for that purpose. A fair number of coins glinted against its red velvet interior, and I dropped in two of my own. He winked and smiled at me but didn't stop strumming or singing about some enchanted evening.

I didn't hurry to the address Chef Bugnard had given me. I still wasn't certain how I was going to proceed when I got to the Grand Hôtel La Harpe, where Émelie Loyer rented a room. I supposed I hoped I might even run into her on the street.

But by the time I reached the address, I hadn't seen anyone who looked like the photo I'd seen on Merveille's wall. I stopped in front of the building and looked up at it. Despite its grandiose name, the building was hardly even "grand." However, it seemed like a decent place to live; the windows had shutters and were relatively clean, and there was an actual intact fire escape down the side facing a small alley.

A woman carrying a long-haired dog—a Lhasa apso, I thought—came out the front door as I stood there, but she was too brunette and too broad to be Émelie Loyer. She eyed me curiously as she let the fancy dog, who wore blue bows in the hair that hung over the ears and torso, down to do its business.

"Bonjour," I said, walking over as the dog lifted his leg to pee against the corner of the building. From the stains thereon, I suspected it was a daily habit. "What a sweet little dog. May I say hello?"

"Bonjour, mademoiselle. Of course you may say hello to Robey. Now, Robey, be nice to the good mademoiselle!" she admonished, tugging on the leash when the little dog bristled as I approached.

Whereas Monsieur Wilde merely barked in announcement and greed, and didn't have a suspicious (or vicious) bone in his little body, Robey seemed to be prepared to take off the hand of anyone who came near him—whether they were a villain or friend. Even so, I crouched near him, moving my coat hem out of the slush, and held out my gloved fingers for him to sniff. I wasn't certain whether the smell of Oscar Wilde and Madame X would reassure the little combatant or upset him, but I had to try.

His beady black eyes glistened with threat as he growled low in the back of his throat, his back legs wide and taut, as if ready to spring at the slightest provocation, but I waited patiently with my hand out. The little beast couldn't be more than fifteen pounds—larger than Oscar Wilde, but hardly frightening. Still, those tiny teeth were sharp and could definitely do some damage, even through my gloves.

"Look at all his pretty hair," I said, glancing up at the woman. "You must have to brush it every day."

"Oh, *oui*, but he sits so pretty on my lap and eats his biscuits while I do so," she said as proudly as if Robey were her own off-spring.

"What a good boy you are, Robey! Do you happen to know Émelie Loyer, madame?" I remained crouched by her dog. At least Robey had stopped growling, and he seemed as if he was thinking about whether to sniff me. I carefully edged closer, still with my hand out and doing my best not to lose my balance and land on my behind in a patch of slushy snow. "She lives here, *non*?"

"Émelie? Yes, of course. She rents from me." The lady looked at me with suspicion for the first time. While the French liked to gossip just like everyone else, they also had a strong sense of privacy. "Why do you want to know that?"

"I wanted to speak to her. I heard about what happened to her husband," I said, wishing I'd thought to buy a bouquet of flowers as a prop for my story. "I wanted to offer my condolences."

"Ah, yes, what a tragedy! Robey, *non!*"

He'd suddenly lunged, snarling and yipping and fighting the leash, as if to throw himself at me.

I gave up and rose, deciding that my presence was probably upsetting him. Besides, now that I had the landlady talking, I didn't need to make nice to her dog—as cute as he might have appeared.

"I . . . I wasn't certain whether it would be appropriate, considering . . . well, her husband had been abroad all these years, and she was here without him . . ." I let my voice trail off and gave the woman a suggestive look.

She nodded in understanding. "*Oui, oui,* she hadn't seen him for years. And then he came back, and, *la,* it was as if there was no problem!" She shook her head, as if disappointed.

"Oh, so he was living here with her?" I tried to sound relieved.

"Oh, no, no, no, Louis wasn't here, no, no, but she was talking about him opening the restaurant again, you see. And so I thought, well, the lovers have mended the rift, after more than nine years"—she snorted—"and now Émelie will move out of here, and I can rent her room to someone else—but not an existentialist. Or a student," she said, leaning closer and looking up and down the street, as if to see one of those offensive creatures. "All of them—they're loud and dirty and they have sex in the stairwells and they leave ashes everywhere! Robey doesn't like them, does he?"

"They were going to reopen Maison de Verre?" I said, as if astonished and pleased. "That would be wonderful!"

Not for the first time, I was thankful for my native fluency in French; I was certain that if I had come across as an American, the landlady would be far more suspicious and far less forthcoming.

"Eh, perhaps." She shrugged. "But what Émelie was going to do with the young man now that her husband has returned is another question, *non*?" She leaned closer, her voice lowering conspiratorially as her eyes gleamed. "I said she ought to keep a *cinq à sept* with the young one and take what she likes from Louis—him leaving her all those years."

A *cinq à sept* referred to the hours of five to seven in the evening, which in Paris was traditionally reserved for adulterous meetups. Dinner with one's spouse would follow after, at eight o'clock or so. The French are very organized when it comes to sex.

"Young man?" It wasn't difficult for me to sound surprised as well as admiring. Émelie had to be at least in her early fifties. Although "young" was a relative term, for the woman in front of me was probably in her sixties or so.

"Eh, well, Émelie has always been like honey to the bees," said my companion with a wicked grin. "The men, they can't help but flock to her, and she . . . well, she flicks them off whenever she is done with them."

"Is that what happened with her husband?" I asked. "He left when the Germans came, and she flicked him off, and so he went to London?"

"Eh, I don't know about that so much, but I do know she didn't miss him a lot. And when she first heard he was coming back, she was *not* a very happy madame, eh?"

"I wonder why that was," I replied.

"Eh, I—Robey, *non!*" She gave the leash a firm yank, for her little dog had done the rest of his business while we were talking and was sniffing the malodorous lump experimentally, as if considering whether to taste it as well.

Robey gave his mistress a dark look, then gave me one, then turned away to sniff at some interesting stains on the cobblestones.

"I don't know why she wasn't happy to have him back, if he was going to open the restaurant. She worked there and liked it, you see. Ah, and she knows *le vin*, she does. Came from a family in Bordeaux, I think it was. The restaurant made good money and had a reputation, and then the *Boches* came along." She spat, and Robey eagerly pounced on this new development, his long hair dragging over the cobbles.

"I'd've taken a knife to any of them if they came to my place and tried to run it." She glanced meaningfully at the doorway to the *hôtel*. "But Louis—he just gave it up and ran away. And she came here."

"This young man," I said. "He is definitely her lover?"

The woman shrugged, but there was a gleam in her eye. "What else would she have him for?"

"What does he look like?"

But that was a question too far, and now Madame Loyer's landlady narrowed her eyes at me. "I don't pay any mind to those comings and goings, you see. None of my business, is it, if she's angry at him for not coming around when he says he will?"

"I can't help but wonder who wanted Louis Loyer dead," I said, hoping that the change of topic to murder would alleviate her suspicion.

"Ah! He was *murdered*, then?" Her eyes glistened with delight at the nugget of gossip. "You hear the rumors, but . . ."

Here was a way for me to repair the bump of suspicion. "Most definitely, he was murdered. It was cyanide. In the *wine*."

"*Dans le vin?*" Madame's eyes goggled with morbid delight. "What a notion!"

"*Oui*," I agreed. "Someone wanted him dead. And Richard Beauchêne, as well—you know him?"

"Beauchêne?" She screwed up her face in thought. "The chef? They were partners, were they not? Loyer and Beauchêne?"

"They were. Someone murdered both of them." I took a chance and leaned closer to her. "You don't think . . . ?" I waggled my eyebrows meaningfully and rolled my eyes toward the *hôtel*.

"Émelie?" Madame reared back in shock, but I was certain

there was a light of interest and delight in her eyes. She wasn't completely convinced of Madame Loyer's innocence, and that was all I needed.

I shrugged. "She loved them both at one time, and now, the moment Loyer returns, they are both dead. From *poisoned wine.* Can it be a coincidence?"

"But *non!*" Yet Madame's eyes said, *C'est possible!*

Just then, Robey began to bark wildly, straining at the leash so frantically I thought he might pull his madame into the *rue.* We looked over to see another dog trotting along with its master across the street. It was a large poodle, and the only word to describe its careful stepping through the slush was mincing.

Robey was not about to quiet, even under the admonishment of his mistress, and so I bid the landlady adieu. She gave me one last assessing look and allowed her dog to tow her across the street.

I looked at my watch and sighed, then started back to my car. It was nearly three o'clock, and I hadn't even thought about what I was going to make for dinner. I'd missed my daily trip to the market, too.

As I got in my car (after successfully having avoided the dog crap once again), I decided to call Julia when I got home to see whether she had any ideas for something simple I could make. There were always croque monsieurs, I thought with a sudden spur of interest. I'd become infatuated with the creamy, cheesy ham sandwiches since my arrival. Unlike Julia, who'd been served sole meunière at a fine restaurant, my first meal in France had been the simple yet luscious sandwich at a tiny *bistrot.*

Surely, a croque monsieur couldn't be difficult to make, and I knew we had some ham left over as well as cheese. And Bet and Blythe always brought fresh bread every day. . . .

When I came into the house, I heard voices up in the salon. It sounded as if Grand-père and Oncle Rafe had guests. Male guests, from the sound of it.

As usual, Oscar Wilde greeted me with his excited barking from the top of the stairs. I ignored him as I hung up my coat and scarf; then I slipped into the kitchen with the wild hope that something would already be cooking, thanks to Bet or Blythe.

But the oven was empty, and the stove was cold except for the ever-present kettle of water for coffee.

I guessed I would be cooking tonight. *Damn.*

I made a cup of coffee and started up the steps to the salon, skirting Oscar Wilde, who'd bounded halfway down the stairs. He paused to sniff suspiciously at me, but since I hadn't actually petted Robey, he probably didn't smell my betrayal. Then Monsieur Wilde raced past me up the steps, no longer barking but no less excited. He obviously assumed a treat was in his future.

When I came into the salon, I found Grand-père in his usual seat and Oncle Rafe opening a bottle of wine at the small center table. Madame X gave me and Oscar Wilde a narrow, side-eyed look from her perch on the credenza. There were two other men in the room, as well, both about the same age as my messieurs—around eighty.

One of them was still very handsome, despite his age, with dusky Mediterranean skin, a trimmed beard, and a neat mustache that was silvery gray just at the edges of the mouth. His more generously silvered dark hair was plentiful and combed straight back from a gently receding hairline. I got the sense of a regal, almost military, bearing about him, even though he was seated.

The other man had rugged features and a prominent nose that kept him from being the least bit handsome, although he certainly wasn't homely. There was something about him that suggested he wasn't French, but American—perhaps it was his blunt mannerisms emanating from his long, knobby fingers and lanky build as he shifted in his seat and adjusted the pillow on the divan.

"Ah, and there she is! Tabi, *ma chère*, please, come to say hello to our friends," said Grand-père, half rising from his chair with a pleased and proud smile.

Oncle Rafe turned and was about to hand a glass of wine to each of the guests. "Ah, Tabi, you've returned just in ti—"

"*No!*" I cried, lunging toward him, grabbing for the glasses. Oscar Wilde launched himself toward the altercation, barking madly, and barely managed to keep from being stepped on. "*Stop!*"

For I had seen on the table, next to the wine, the crumpled piece of blue and green damask silk and the jaunty red ribbon that had tied it closed around the neck of the bottle. . . .

CHAPTER 13

I MANAGED TO SNATCH ONE OF THE GLASSES FROM ONCLE RAFE'S hand, but he held the other one out of my reach.

"Now, now, *ma petite*, do not overset yourself," he said with a smile as I struggled with my emotions.

"You don't understand! That bottle of wine"—I stabbed my finger violently at the offending vessel, prompting another round of yapping from Monsieur Wilde—"is *poisoned*!"

"Oh, *oui*, but of course it is, *ma mie*," Grand-père said with a smile.

I felt as if my head was going to explode as Oncle Rafe firmly extracted the glass from my grip. All four of the men were looking at me as if I were crazy . . . while I was wondering if *they* were crazy.

"Then why were you going to *drink it*?" I cried, my arms wheeling about, which set off Oscar Wilde again. I didn't care that I was making a scene in front of their guests—this was life and death!

"We weren't going to drink it, Tabi," Grand-père said in a tone that suggested I should, somehow, have known that—all evidence to the contrary. "Now, take care so you don't knock over those other glasses and spill it on the floor for the dog to lap up—although I do not know whether that would be the worst thing," he added under his breath as Oscar Wilde continued to bark as if the world was ending. Any excitement was enough to set off the little beast—but even so, Oscar Wilde was always on the lookout for food morsels that might be dropped. Knowing him, he *would* lap up poisoned wine.

Grand-père winked at me, so I knew he was joking, then sighed and offered the excited dog a fingertip-sized biscuit from the glass canister next to him. It had the desired effect, for Oscar Wilde stopped yapping, thank heavens.

"We were only going to smell *le vin*, Tabi, and then to examine it," said Grand-père.

I looked at Grand-père suspiciously, then at Oncle Rafe, and then finally at the two guests, who seemed unaffected by the circus around them.

"Please, *ma mie*, won't you sit, and I will explain it all," Grand-père said.

"But first, we must introduce you to our guests," Oncle Rafe said. "Perhaps that will help you to understand."

I eyed the wineglasses with bald suspicion as I took a seat on the divan, next to the American visitor. He had picked up one of the glasses of wine and was examining it, ignoring the rest of us.

"Bitter almonds, *oui, c'est vrai*," he said, removing his rather large nose from the interior of the glass. His accent, though mild, was most definitely American. "Now, don't smell it too closely, or you'll poison yourself. Cyanide can kill with the gas, too . . . but go ahead and give it a little sniff. I want to know which of you can smell the bitter almonds. Not everyone can, you see."

"Tabi, meet *monsieur le docteur*," said Grand-père, gesturing to the American. "Thomas Jackson, one of the finest *médecin légistes* in all of Europe. He has been here in Paris far too many years— fifty, is it, *non?*—and is no longer working in the morgue, of course. Instead, he spends his evenings at home with his glorious wife."

"I don't come home smelling like dead bodies any longer," said Docteur Jackson casually, eyeing the contents of his glass. "Most of the time, anyway. Lucie greatly appreciates that. But to be called on a visit for something like this is a pleasure." He must have noticed my confusion, for he added in English for my benefit, "*Médicin légiste*—it means 'medical examiner.'"

I was feeling far less concerned now, and things were even beginning to make sense.

"And so you are the famous Mademoiselle Knight," said the other visitor. He looked at me with intense gray eyes that reminded me of Merveille's, and suddenly, with a rush of shock, I realized who he was.

"Monsieur Devré, is it?" I said, suddenly feeling exposed. I felt my cheeks warm a little, which annoyed me greatly. Even so, I felt the need to sit up straighter on the divan. "It is a pleasure to meet you, er, Inspecteur."

Monsieur—or Inspecteur (I wasn't certain whether the title still held)—Devré was an old friend of Grand-père's and Oncle Rafe's. He was, as my grandfather had told me, one of the finest detectives in the entire history of la Sûreté—the former name for the *police judiciaire.*

He was also Inspecteur Merveille's great-uncle.

"Ah, she is quick with the wit, as you promised, Maurice," Devré said, with a smile at my grandfather. "*Oui,* mademoiselle. It is I, Devré, and I am here to assure you that I would not allow any harm to come to your grand-père or my dear friend Rafael. They telephoned most immediately after receiving the wine, and I collected Jackson, and we came."

"Thank you," I told him very sincerely. The last bit of tension drained from my body.

During the investigation into Thérèse Lognon's murder, my grandfather and uncle had consulted with Devré to get information about the details, which Devré, of course, obtained from his grandnephew, who, fortunately for us, used him as a mentor and advisor.

"Do you smell it?" Jackson demanded, handing his glass to Devré. "The bitter almonds."

Devré put his nose inside the glass, carefully, of course, and removed it, nodding. "*Oui.*"

Oncle Rafe had poured a fifth glass and offered it to me. I put my nose carefully inside and sniffed cautiously. "Yes, I smell it, too. Bitter almonds." I felt, somehow, as if I had accomplished something. I supposed that now I did know for certain what cyanide smelled like.

"But alas," said Oncle Rafe, removing his nose from his sample, "I do not smell anything but . . . um . . . peach. There is also a bit of the . . . ah, yes, beeswax, yes . . . and some floral." He shrugged. "But none of the bitter almonds."

"You see?" said Docteur Jackson, as if we had been skeptical. "There are some who can smell the scent of cyanide and some who cannot. Maurice?"

"Ah, *oui*, I smell it," replied my grand-père. "The bitter almonds. And the delectable peach, as well, *mon cher*." He glanced at Oncle Rafe with an affectionate smile. "It would have been an excellent bottle. What a loss."

"That could explain why Monsieur Loyer did not react to the nose of the Sauternes he was tasting yesterday," I said, my eyes widening. "He couldn't smell the bitter almonds . . . but I think Chef Beauchêne could smell it. Is there ever an almond scent in wine, Oncle?"

"Ah, *oui*, there can be. Not commonly, though. But perhaps, then, Beauchêne thought only the bitter almond was part of the nose of the Volnay . . . or even perhaps he wondered whether it could have gone bad. But, of course, he would have to taste it regardless, you see? An eighteen ninety-three Volnay? It would be impossible not to taste it."

Oncle Rafe put his nose inside the glass once more, as if to make certain he couldn't smell the almonds. I resisted the urge to warn him to be careful; I hadn't realized the fumes from cyanide were poisonous, as well.

"Ah, yes, that is quite likely," said Grand-père. "If one does not smell the almonds, or even if one does, it would not seem to portend anything ill. It is only the almonds flavoring the wine."

"*Oui.* And, *vraiment*, who would throw out a bottle of such a rare wine on only a strange smell, *non*? No one," said Devré with a spread of his hands. "*No one.* But, of course, they would taste it instead. And so it was a murder certain to occur."

I looked around at the men, who were taking far too casually the fact that *someone had tried to poison my messieurs.*

The four of them seemed to have missed that part during the discussion about bitter almonds.

I stood, clearing my throat loudly, and everyone looked up at me.

"Yes, *ma mie?*" said Grand-père.

"You do realize that someone tried to *poison* you, don't you?" I said, my hands planted on my hips.

"Oh, yes, that is certainly undeniable," replied Grand-père. There was a saucy gleam in his eye that I didn't like.

I wondered if that was the same light that shined in mine when I was about to do something rash or crazy.

"We will have to tell Merveille," said Oncle Rafe. He glanced at Devré, who smiled a little and nodded. "But perhaps not immediately. And perhaps it is best if you were not here when we did so, *non?*"

Devré nodded gravely. "*Oui,* that would be best, I think."

"Yes, yes, we will definitely tell Merveille," I said, the tension inside me rising again. "But what I want to know is, *Who* would want to kill *you?*"

Grand-père and Oncle Rafe exchanged bemused glances. "Why, *ma chère,* but the list would be far too long for us to say," said my oncle.

I gaped at them, unable to find any words that wouldn't come out in a shriek, then transferred my attention to Devré.

Instead of being shocked or appalled, he merely looked at my messieurs with a sort of indulgent smile. "Ah, *oui,* perhaps we do not have all the time for that," he said.

What was wrong with these men? Just because they were in their eighth decade, they thought they were impervious to death and threats and . . . and everything?

"Now, calm yourself, Tabi," Grand-père said when he saw my

expression. "We will help to find out who sent this package of death to us."

"It is a great shame," said Oncle Rafe, picking up the bottle with a napkin in order to admire its label. His mouth flattened in disgust. "A nineteen thirty-three Armand Rousseau, now desecrated and ruined. I suppose now you know someone who *will* throw away such a fine wine over a bad smell, Guillaume." He gave Devré a saucy look, then shook his head. "Again, I say it is a *blasphemy* that someone has chosen to kill using such treasures of France!"

Restless and frustrated, I went over to the piece of blue and green damask and the red ribbon, that had been discarded on the table. "Was there a note card with it?" I asked, looking around.

"Ah, *oui*, here it is," said Oncle Rafe, pulling it out of his pocket. He wasn't wearing gloves, but he'd wrapped the gift tag in a handkerchief. "I suppose we must give it to Merveille, but perhaps you would like to look at it first, Tabi? And, Guillaume, you, as well?" This last was directed to Devré, who nodded.

I was pleasantly surprised when the former police detective didn't attempt to push in and take the tag, but allowed me to examine it first. I took the card, using Oncle Rafe's handkerchief, and laid it on the table.

The tag seemed to be made from the same material as the other two: cardstock, like one would use for posters or postcards. Plain brown, in the shape of a rectangle.

"It was cut by hand," I said, noticing that the corners weren't exactly ninety-degree angles and that there was a slight jag on one side, as if someone had hesitated when using scissors. "From a larger piece."

I read the note.

Enjoy this in honor of Saint Vincent and in memory of former days.
—*Maldon*

"Who is Maldon?" I asked, looking up. "And this is the second time—maybe even the third, but I didn't see Beauchêne's gift tag—that the killer has referenced Saint Vincent in the note. What is the significance?"

"Maldon . . . he is an old friend from before the war," said Grand-père as he lit a cigarette. "He is living now in Marseilles. We write on occasion."

I frowned. "And so there was no reason for you to wonder whether it was really from him or not? Is it his handwriting?"

Grand-père shrugged. "When the wine arrived wrapped in the silk, as you had described the others, I did not wonder for even a moment whether it was truly from Maldon. The handwriting . . . eh, it changes as one ages, you see, and it is always possible someone else wrote it for him, *non*?" He held up his knobby, arthritic hands. "But the silk wrapping and the red ribbon told me immediately that it was not from Maldon. And were it not for you, Tabi, and your involvement in the two murders, we would not have known to be suspicious about the gift at all, would we?"

"No," I said, a horrible chill running down my spine. "No, you wouldn't. No one would. The police have been mum about the details of the poisonings. I understand why, but . . ." I looked at Devré. "Maybe it's time they were more public about it. How many other bottles of wine are being delivered, poisoned with cyanide and wrapped in silk?"

"*Oui, c'est vrai*. I am certain Étienne—my nephew—will agree at once when he learns about this," said Devré. "More likely, he has already taken those steps since the second event yesterday."

"As for the mention of Saint Vincent," said Oncle Rafe. "It is very logical, for the twenty-fourth of January—yesterday—was his feast day. And he is the patron saint of the vignerons . . . so chosen, as the story goes," he added with an amused smile, "because the beginning of his name is *vin*, you see?"

"And so sending these wines, poisoned, with a reference to Saint Vincent near his feast day, makes some sense," I mused. "And gives it a sense of urgency—'Drink me right away to celebrate the feast day.' Beauchêne got his the day before, but it was delivered during a demonstration, with the urging to drink it then, and so he did as part of his class.

"Or maybe the killer thought Beauchêne would wait and drink it on the feast day—which would have been the same day Monsieur Loyer received his gift of wine, as well! That might have been his intention, that they both would drink and die on the same day. Maybe the killer doesn't even care. And even though your bottle came today, Grand-père—a day late—you would simply believe its delivery had been delayed."

"Yes, the twenty-fourth of January is a well-known date for the winemakers, and there is always much drinking to celebrate. The vintners traditionally go to the church for Saint Vincent's feast day mass. How I well remember," Oncle Rafe said, smiling fondly. "They pray for his intercession for a good upcoming crop and a bountiful harvest and then return home to drink in his honor."

"All right. So does that mean the killer is a vintner himself? Or herself?" I mused. Signs were definitely pointing toward Émelie Loyer.

"It is possible," said Devré. "But anyone could know that information. What is important, I think, is that it implies the specific timing, as you said, Mademoiselle Knight. 'Drink it now.'"

I had returned my attention to the gift tag and, turning it over, discovered a small splotch of blue ink and a printed black line on the reverse. "The gift's note could be from the back of something . . . a poster or flyer," I said, wishing now that I had more carefully examined the gift tag on Monsieur Loyer's wine.

In all three cases, the tag had been tied onto the neck of the wine bottle with the red ribbon. I handed the tag, still wrapped in the handkerchief, to Devré and then turned my attention to the piece of silk that had been the wrapping.

"He—or she—has used a piece of this same material every time," I said, picking up the silk from one of its corners. I wasn't certain whether you could get fingerprints off textured fabric like damask. It was a large irregular rectangular piece of cloth, as if whoever had cut it didn't care about the perfection of right angles or straight lines but only wanted the wrapping. "Was it convenience or purposeful?"

Grand-père suddenly sat up straight, and Madame X was jostled in her seat on his lap. She jumped down lightly and glared at him, but he ignored her as he held out a hand to me. The lines between his brows had creased more deeply. "I know that fabric. That material. I've seen it . . ."

I handed him the swath of silk, no longer worrying about fingerprints. Merveille would have the bottle and the gift tag, which would be more likely to have prints.

"But where have I seen it?" Grand-père stared down at the silk, then closed his eyes, then opened them again. "*Pouah . . .* my old brain . . ."

Oncle Rafe gave a quiet exclamation, his own eyes narrowing. "Oh. Yes, I think it is familiar, too . . ."

"From a dress? Or a vest?" I asked, mystified. It wasn't the sort of material one would use for a man's coat. Maybe a tie or a scarf . . .

"No, no, no . . ." Grand-père shook his head, his eyes still closed. "I am picturing it . . . the sheen of the fabric . . . the dark pattern . . . it is . . . Ah!" His eyes popped open, and he sat up, trailing smoke and ash with his excited movements, his cigarette forgotten. "Rafe! Maison de Verre. On the walls . . ."

"Ah!" Oncle Rafe's eyes widened, and he smiled. "*Oui, cher,* that is it."

I looked from one to the other. "Are you saying that this fabric used to hang on the walls of Monsieur Loyer's restaurant? The one he abandoned to the Germans when they came in?"

The messieurs were nodding in affirmation.

"So it *must* be purposeful that the killer is using this fabric to send the wine," I said, my mind spinning. "They wanted you to recognize it, to remember it. But why? And what's your connection to Maison de Verre and Chef Loyer and Monsieur Beauchêne?"

Grand-père shrugged. "But . . . nothing really. We patronized the restaurant quite often. It was rather close to here, in rue Las Cases, and we could walk, you see."

"Ah, but the bank financed the restaurant, too, Maurice, do you not remember?" Oncle Rafe said. "Loyer was very grateful to you for extending that loan."

My grand-père had made his fortune as the partner at the well-respected Banque Maine-Saint-Léger.

"Ah, yes, but we financed many, many businesses at the bank. I hardly think—"

"But it's a connection," I said firmly. "Not only did you go to the restaurant regularly, but your bank enabled it to exist. The killer is practically sending you a message with this wine by wrapping it in the silk from Maison de Verre. But why?"

"And who?" Devré said quietly. "Obviously, this person has some connection to Maison de Verre."

Suddenly I snapped to attention. The pieces fell into place with what felt like an audible click in my mind. "Wait. The *wine!* We've been talking about how rare the poisoned wines were . . . The question I've been asking is, How did the killer get such rare vintages? Where and how? Grand-père, Oncle Rafe, did they hide wines from the Germans at Maison de Verre?"

Grand-père paused in the process of sipping from a glass of whisky. "But . . . yes, of course they did. The wine cellar there was not as extensive—and certainly not as famous—as that at La Tour d'Argent, but it was quite magnificent and beautiful, thanks in part to Émelie Loyer."

"As I recall, they walled much of it up in the cellar," said Oncle Rafe.

"They did," said Grand-père, "but—"

"Then that must be where the killer is getting these wines!" I exclaimed, gesturing to the poisoned bottle. "From that secret cache at Maison de Verre!"

But Grand-père was shaking his head sadly. "*Non, non, petite . . .* that is a good thought, but the wines at Maison de Verre were not as fortunate as those at La Tour d'Argent and others. The hidden cache was discovered and . . ." He grimaced. "The Germans, they took or destroyed them all."

I didn't like that answer. I thought for certain I'd hit upon at least part of what was happening. But I couldn't change the facts.

"Still, even if the wines were found and destroyed, whoever it is who's sending them *has* to have a connection to Maison de Verre . . . and that's where we have to begin to find out who is doing this," I said flatly.

"*We?*" Devré said delicately, exchanging glances with Grand-père and Oncle Rafe. "I am not certain my nephew would be pleased with your involvement, mademoiselle."

I waved him off a bit more brusquely than was strictly polite, but I was incensed. "Someone tried to kill my grand-père and my oncle," I said. "It's become personal, and I am now involved. And no one is going to keep me out of it."

CHAPTER 14

"WE MUST TELEPHONE MERVEILLE," SAID ONCLE RAFE AFTER A brief silence over my outburst. "Surely, he will come immediately."

Devré rose a bit stiffly, rubbing his lower back, and offered me a wry smile. "I will take my leave, then. Please, I beg of you, do not endanger yourself, mademoiselle. My nephew—he is well able to solve this case. After all, it is *I* who trained him." He smiled, and I saw for a moment a flash of rakishness I had not expected from the serious detective.

"I have no doubt that he is," I replied firmly. "And I have no intention of endangering myself. But I am not just going to sit by and wait for someone else to get a bottle of cyanide-infused wine. Anyone could have had a glass of it with Grand-père— even you," I reminded Devré. "Not only is this killer targeting people connected to Maison de Verre, he does not care who else is poisoned."

"*Oui*. It is most unsettling, and, mademoiselle, I do understand your excitement. But once again, I implore you to allow Étienne to handle it." I looked at Devré with mute stubbornness, and he sighed, then turned his gaze to Grand-père. "The girl—the lovely rosy apple that she is—does not fall far from the tree, *non?*"

Oncle Rafe gave a dry chuckle. "As I have been saying for months, Guillaume. And now I begin to wonder over the wisdom of giving her a car." He chuckled. "Still, Tabitha is no fool, and she will not interfere." He looked at me with stern, dark eyes. "We do not want anything to happen to her, either."

"I'm not going to *do* anything," I said finally, as four pairs of eyes fixed on me. Even Docteur Jackson had looked up from the glass and bottle he'd been sniffing and examining minutely. "I promise. But I'm going to keep in touch with Inspecteur Merveille and . . . and just make sure he's not leaving any stone unturned."

Devré made a sound that was like a muttered cough, but his eyes lit with humor. "I am certain my nephew will be delighted to hear of that," he said. "And now I must go, before he arrives and learns of my perfidy." He chuckled and leaned over to kiss my grand-père and then Oncle Rafe on the cheeks.

After I escorted our two visitors to the door, returned their coats, hats, and scarves to them in the foyer, then bade them farewell and thanks, I went back up to the salon. Oncle Rafe was just hanging up the telephone, presumably having called the *police judiciaire* to notify Merveille of the latest developments.

"I'm leaving, as well," I said.

Grand-père looked at me suspiciously. "Where are you going, then? I thought you would want to stay and ensure that the good inspecteur has all the information."

"I have to go to the market," I said truthfully. "We don't have anything for dinner tonight, and I have to find something to make." Was I imagining it, or did my grandfather and my honorary uncle both wince?

"Oh, Tabi, I am certain there is something left over in the icebox that we can have to eat. Do not trouble yourself. Perhaps a bit of that veal roast from Madame Child? Or *les suprêmes?*" said Oncle Rafe hopefully.

"I'm sorry—there is nothing left but two little slices of *jambon* and a bit of cheese." This wasn't quite accurate, for there were more than two slices of ham left, but the veal and chicken were long gone. I refrained from suggesting I make croque monsieurs; that would defeat the purpose of my excuse to leave, and I could still do it when I returned.

I'd just have to ask Julia how to make the béchamel sauce that goes on top of the sandwich.

Which reminded me . . . "I'm going to call Julia and see if she can go with me."

Immediately, almost farcically, the two gentlemen brightened. "Oh, *oui*, that is an excellent idea," said Grand-père. "Madame Child could help you at the market." He was careful not to come outright and say that she could help me cook, but we all knew what he was thinking.

I chose not to comment on that. Instead, I simply replied with a smile, "I'm sure when I tell her I have new developments, she'll be straining at the bit to go with me."

I was correct. I called Julia and simply said that a bottle of silk-wrapped wine had been delivered to my grandfather, and she was halfway out the door before she hung up the phone.

"And so you left before Merveille showed up?" Julia said after I explained everything that had happened, including the fact that I had met the inspector's great-uncle.

We were walking to the market during this conversation, and by the time I finished, we'd reached the first few stalls. As we paused, I waved to Madame Marie, who looked over with a delighted smile.

"I'm surprised you didn't want to be there in order to fill Merveille in on what he should be investigating," Julia went on, giving me a sly smile.

"Well," I said, knowing I could be honest with her at least, "I thought it might be interesting to take a look at Maison de Verre." I grinned at her and lifted an impertinent eyebrow.

"You little devil," Julia replied, laughing uproariously. "You planned all of this. Merveille would be busy at your house, giving you the chance to check out the restaurant before he got there."

"Guilty as charged," I replied gleefully and did a goofy half pirouette. It was a good thing it wasn't slippery, or I might have landed on my bum.

"So, do you really think Émelie Loyer is the killer?" Julia asked.

"I don't know, but she's probably my top suspect. There are lots of reasons it makes sense—both victims were close to her, and her estranged husband comes back to the city after years, and *boom*! He's murdered. But it's the *wine* that keeps nudging me in her direction. Who better than a sommelier to know that a Frenchman would *always* drink—or at least *taste*—a rare bottle of wine, no matter what it smelled like?"

"That's true. I do believe Paul would risk his life for a glass of such wine," Julia said, shaking her head at male bravado. "And who better than a sommelier to know where to *procure* such rare vintages. Madame Loyer would certainly know how to access the building of Maison de Verre. Since her husband owned it, maybe she even still has a key."

My eyes widened, and I stopped dead. "Julia! I hadn't even thought of that! I bet she *does* have a key—or something. And it makes a lot of sense . . . except I still don't have a motive. *Why* would she want to kill her newly returned husband?"

"Maybe she didn't want him to reopen the restaurant, after all. Maybe she's got a secret hidden in there or something," Julia said. "Her younger lover, hmm?" Her eyes danced. "I wonder how much younger he is."

"Could be. I thought maybe there was a cache of wine hidden in the cellar there from when the Nazis came in, but Grand-père said that the Germans found what they had hidden, so it can't be that." I sighed, then smiled. "Now I *really* want to poke around at Maison de Verre. Grand-père said it was on rue Las Cases, which is right off Bourgogne, by Sainte Clotilde, before the market. I didn't want to ask him too much about it . . ."

"Because you didn't want him to get suspicious," Julia finished for me, as we started walking again. Her eyes were still lit with laughter, and her nose was tipped pink from the chill. A random snowflake fluttered down and landed on one of her eyelashes. "I completely understand. I'm sure Madame Marie knows where Maison de Verre is or used to be."

"I am making the assumption that the building is there, but that the place is still closed or unused. Otherwise, how would our killer be getting the fabric for his gift wrapping?"

"Right," said Julia. "That makes sense. Bonjour, Madame Marie!"

"Bonjour, Madame Child! Bonjour, Mademoiselle Knight! And thank you, *thank you* for what you did for poor Gérard!" For the first time ever, Madame Marie slid off her stool and rushed into us for an enthusiastic embrace. After she released Julia and me, she took me by the shoulders and kissed me on each cheek and then on the mouth, and then she tried to do the same with Julia, but Madame was just over half of Julia's height, and she couldn't quite reach. *"Merci, merci, merci!"* Her cheeks were flushed pink, not from the wintry air, I thought, but from excitement.

Julia bent and hugged the chubby little woman. "Tabitha is the one who noticed him stowed behind the barrels, and I'm so glad she did."

"But you were there, and you helped, and if both of you had not gone with Michel to see the mushroom farm, I do not know what would have happened to poor Gérard and his honey and mead!" Madame's eyes glistened with tears of relief, and she swiped at her red nose with her coat sleeve. "And who is it who is *doing* these things? All these years of harmony, and now all at once, these terrible things. It was not even so bad when the *Boches* were here—well, that is not true," she said, her face twisting. "That is not true. It was hell when they were here. But again, I say, Who would do this to his own people?"

"How is Monsieur Gérard doing?" I asked. I chafed a little at the delay—I wanted to get to Maison de Verre before Merveille did, and surely, that would be his first destination after leaving my house—but the niceties had to be observed. And besides, I did want to know how the mead maker was doing.

"He is recovering at home with his daughter. He is loud and angry and wants to go back into the catacombs to see about his mead—for he claims it is nearly ready—but she is very strict,

and he is not going." Madame's eyes had softened since her dia-
tribe a moment earlier. "And the fact that he is loud and angry
proves he will soon recover, *non?*" She smiled, showing irregular
teeth stained with tobacco and coffee. "Now, what is it you are in
need of today, madame and mademoiselle?"

"We are looking for Maison de Verre," I said before Julia
could launch into some rapturous conversation about food.
Normally, I wouldn't care, but I knew I had only a short while
before Merveille would be on my heels.

"Maison de Verre?" Madame Marie said, her face wrinkling.
"Do you mean the old restaurant? But it is long closed, mademoiselle, and it is much better to cook at home, is it not?" She
picked up a plump red beet by its green leaves swinging it in
front of her as if to tempt me. Since I wasn't Julia, it had very little effect.

"I know the restaurant closed. I'm only just looking for the
building, where it was located," I said smoothly.

"Well, I know that it was in rue Las Cases, but it has been so
long, and my memory is not what it was," replied Madame
Marie. She'd taken a seat back on her stool and lit a cigarette.
Then she shook a finger at me. "But, *ah! Oui*, Nanette—she
could help you. Her husband worked there, I think, many years
ago, before the Germans came."

"Nanette's husband?" I exchanged glances with Julia, trying
to hide my excitement and impatience. Finding someone who'd
worked at the restaurant could be very helpful.

"*Oui*, Nanette—her husband. She is the one who makes the
baskets, you see?" Madame gestured to the baskets that displayed her shallots, potatoes, turnips, beets, and other offerings.
"They are for sale, too, from Mademoiselle Tana, with the linens
and wooden spoons."

I thanked Madame Marie effusively and hurried off to see
Mademoiselle Tana, while Julia stayed to select some parsnips
and carrots (and probably beets) for whatever gloriousness she
was cooking tonight. I had the thought that perhaps I should
have been doing the same, but I pushed it aside.

Investigating a crime was far more interesting to me than buy-ing vegetables—or anything—to try to figure out how to cook.

I had met Mademoiselle Tana before and remembered the baskets she had for sale in her little market stall, along with em-broidered linen napkins and tea towels. I hadn't realized they were from a local weaver.

Despite my impatience, I approached Mademoiselle Tana with a casualness and warmth that implied I had all afternoon to chat with her, even though it was going to be dark soon. I ad-mired the baskets and selected one to purchase, asking about Madame Nanette.

"Oh, Nanette? Why, she is there," said Mademoiselle Tana as she took my money for a pretty oval-shaped basket that would be perfect for a French loaf. She looked over at the tall, slender woman talking with Monsieur Robert, the fishmonger. "Nanette!"

Madame Nanette looked as if she was in her late forties. Dressed in a wool coat that had seen better days, she wore newer leather gloves and a pair of warm boots. Thin light hair strag-gled from beneath the soft wool hat I was sure she wore for warmth rather than fashion, and streamed over a thick knitted scarf. She had an air of sadness about her, despite the pretty smile she offered when I complimented her on the design of the basket.

"Thank you, mademoiselle," she replied. "I have been weav-ing baskets and trivets for over thirty years, after my mother and my grandmother taught me. I don't know what else I would do if I didn't weave. Perhaps take in the mending?"

"Madame Marie told me that you might know about Maison de Verre," I said after a few more compliments and comments about her baskets. "Where it was, I mean. And that your hus-band worked there?"

"Oh, oui, of course I knew it well," replied Madame Nanette. "Jacques, he worked there for the whole time it was open. From the beginning, you see! He was promoted to the maître d' after only one year, and he was so proud. And then when the Ger-mans came"—she spat to the side, as it seemed every Parisian did at the subject—"he could no longer bring himself to go to that place and serve them . . . or work anywhere for them. Our three sons were in the army, you see." She sighed. "And so Jacques stayed home, and he carved the spoons and the cutting boards and the salad pairs." She gestured to the sets of large wooden spoons and forks that would be used to toss and serve green salads. "And some bowls, too, but they are long gone."

"They are beautiful," I replied sincerely.

"That is all we have left of the spoons, mademoiselle," said Mademoiselle Tana hopefully.

I looked at Madame Nanette, and she gave a quiet shrug, with a sigh of acceptance. "My Jacques, he died in the summer. And so now it is only me and my youngest son. The other two died in the war." She blinked rapidly and looked away.

"I'm so sorry," I said. My throat was suddenly dry. I knew many people who'd died in the war or who'd lost loved ones— or who had managed to get home but were irrevocably changed. Every mention of such losses, even four years later, brought forth those memories.

"But my son François—he is not married, and he takes care of me when he is not working, and so I am content for now." Madame Nanette shook her head briskly, as if to dismiss her sorrow. "Now, what is it about Maison de Verre that you would like to know?"

"Where it was," I said simply.

"Oh, but of course. It is only an old, quiet, dark building now. Monsieur Loyer has been gone for years, and since the Germans left, no one has reopened it."

It appeared that Madame Nanette hadn't heard about Louis Loyer's death, and possibly not even his return. I debated whether to tell her as the woman gave me the address, but ultimately decided there was no reason to do so, and it would likely only prolong the conversation.

"And what about Émelie Loyer? Has she been around the restaurant?"

Madame Nanette looked at me strangely. "Émelie? But, no, I have not seen her for many years, of course."

By that time, Julia had joined me. Her market bag sagged

with the weight of her purchases, while mine remained embarrassingly lax, containing only the bread basket from Madame Nanette.

I made brief introductions and tried not to look impatient while Julia admired Madame Nanette's baskets and the carved wooden spoons. It was after three thirty, and the sun was sinking. As curious and determined as I was, I didn't relish the idea of poking around an abandoned restaurant that could harbor a killer after dark. Besides, I just *knew* Merveille would be on his way there as soon as he left his interview with Grand-père and Oncle Rafe.

Finally, I extricated Julia from an animated conversation about how to oil wooden utensils in order to protect them from stains and splits, rather than to merely wash them with soap and water.

We walked quickly back up Bourgogne and then turned east onto Las Cases. It was a bit narrower than the market street, but the little *rue* was busy with pedestrians and bicycles. There were few cars down this road, for it ended at the Fontaine des Bois and a small *parc* I often walked through. The steeple of Sainte Clotilde's peeked over the trees.

"There," I said, pointing across the street to the dingy storefront.

We stopped, waiting for a car to trundle by, and stared. The front window of what had been Maison de Verre was dark, covered from the inside by something like a curtain or blanket. A sign that once might have proclaimed the name of the celebrated eatery sagged, splintered and weathered, above the door. The only remaining letters were *ERRE*. A remnant of cloth fluttered above it, and as Julia and I crossed the *rue*, I realized the cloth had long faded from red.

The red of the swastika flags flown by the Nazis.

My stomach heaved a little as it hit me, harder than it ever had, that many of the shops and establishments on this street—and on countless other *rues* in the city—had been cloaked with those ugly spiderlike symbols. Banners from the occupiers had obstructed French billboards, and replacement plaques in German had often hung over signs, as well. How horrific it must have been for a Parisian to see signs such as SOLDATENHEIM or GASTSTÄTTEN FÜR REICHSDEUTSCHE hanging over previously beloved French-owned establishments.

That fluttering, tattered bit of red cloth that remained was a terrible reminder of destruction, oppression, and death.

Maison de Verre was one establishment in a row of four, all built as part of the same structure out of the familiar creamy Lutetian stone, but each had a slightly different storefront. The restaurant boasted a wide, very tall bow window made from ten narrow vertical panels of glass. Every other panel was clear glass, while the others were textured glass, which added to the interest and depth of the window. From the inside, the tall, narrow decorative glass design would have given the diners the sense of being inside a crystal. Hence the name of the restaurant: House of Glass.

The large window would also have offered a tantalizing glimpse inside to passersby. And now that I was standing in front of the building, I could see that there was a strip made from pieces of clear glass, some textured, some smooth, set in an ornate iron framework at the top and bottom of each of the vertical panels. I could only imagine how beautiful the window would have looked at night with the golden lights shining from inside the restaurant. It must have been incredibly elegant and striking.

Next to the window was a door—also featuring ornate glasswork—tucked inside a small alcove up two steps from the street. I could barely make out an etching on the door's windowpane: a wide ornate *V* with an *M* inside it, the logo for Maison de Verre.

What a miracle it was that none of the glass had been broken during the Occupation and subsequent Liberation. There had been fighting and riots, but somehow Maison de Verre's window remained fully intact. The glass wasn't broken, no, but there were bullet holes in the bricks on the building next door. And someone had imprinted a large swastika in the concrete on the step leading into the restaurant.

I smelled fresh urine in the little doorway nook and saw a damp stain that had leaked over the symbol of hatred and intolerance. Apparently, I wasn't the only one revolted by the sight of it.

"Now what?" Julia asked, cupping her hands to peer into the bow window. But I'd already confirmed there was nothing to see, for the glass was completely swathed in cloth from the inside, and the windows were filthy, with more than four years of dust and dirt.

It had been too much to hope that I could simply open the door (I'd tried the latch, to no avail) and walk into the restaurant to snoop around. Now that we had gotten to this point, I realized I didn't really have any other plan.

I stepped back and assessed the situation. On one side of the former restaurant was a shoe repair shop, and on the other side, a place that sold leather goods, like belts and gloves. They appeared to be in business, and even if it wasn't a brisk business, at least they were open.

"I want to take a look around the back," I said.

"I can go into the leather shop and ask whether they've noticed any activity at the restaurant," Julia said. Her eyes glinted with enthusiasm. Was my friend going to become the George Fayne to my Nancy Drew? "I can pretend to be all gossipy about Monsieur Loyer's death and the timing of it just before he was going to reopen the restaurant."

"Perfect," I said with a grin. "You do that, and I'll check the back. There has to be an entrance for staff and deliveries and trash removal." I started to walk off, then paused. "If I'm not back in ten minutes, you'd probably better come around and check on me."

"Don't do anything stupid, Tabs." Julia took my arm, suddenly sober. "Maybe you shouldn't do that."

"I'm not going to do anything stupid. I'm just going to go around the back, like any delivery person or staff person might do. The shoe repair and the leather shop have to have back entrances, too," I replied, waving off her concern and gently pulling my arm away. "And they're obviously being used. It's not like I'm going to go into a dark, deserted area. It's a delivery road, like an alley. There's probably four people back there smoking, anyway."

Julia huffed a breath, but before she could say anything else, I turned and hurried off through the icy gray slush.

There were narrow lanes on either end of the four-part building, barely large enough for a truck. Maison de Verre was the second of the four establishments, with the shoe repair being the first, so I walked past the shoe repair and turned down that drive. As I knew there would be, a grimy little alley ran behind the building, providing access to those rear entrances. Since there were tire tracks in the little bit of snow and slush, I knew I'd been right in my assessment that the alley was accessed regularly.

Back here, the smell of urine and other unpleasantries was stronger. Scattered along the edge of the alley, as if blown or dropped up against the building, were crumpled packs of cigarettes, along with their butts, and a myriad of shoe and boot prints in the messy gray slush. More random items littered the alley: a broken Coke bottle and several wine bottles, crushed paper bags and a *métro* time schedule, someone's ratty scarf that had ended up bunched behind a trash can, and a soggy, mutilated feather that might have come from a woman's hat.

What had been the random snowflake here and there was becoming a little more like flurries, and the sky was getting heavy with dark gray clouds. I wondered if there was going to be a lot of snow. Fresh snow, I reasoned, might indicate fresh footprints at the back of the restaurant . . . so if I didn't find anything today, I could come back tomorrow and see whether anyone had gone in the back door of Maison de Verre.

I easily found the door to the old restaurant. It was conveniently tucked into a side alcove, which would help to hide anyone who accessed it.

There were footprints all over the area, including by the entrance, but it was difficult to tell whether someone had actually gone into the building or had just used the tiny covered alcove to smoke a cigarette out of the snow and wet. Several cigarette butts littered the ground, along with the streak of ashes mashed into the slush.

As I'd made my way down the alley, I'd taken care to walk as close to the building as possible, instead of in the center of the alley, in order to keep from obliterating any tire tracks or footprints—just in case. I had scrutinized all the markings as I'd walked by, and now I looked even more closely around the entrance to Maison de Verre, but nothing stood out to me as important or unique. It was a gray, slushy mess that would soon be covered by a light dusting of snow.

When I stepped onto the little brick stoop leading to the tiny alcove at the back of Maison de Verre, I looked around carefully. The footprints, as I'd already noticed, were a mess, but there were also cigarette butts collected on the stoop, and I knelt to examine them. With my gloved finger, I poked at them and noticed Lucky Strikes butts as well as Gauloises. Whether that was relevant, I had no idea.

At last, I could delay no longer. I rose from my examination and faced the back door of the old restaurant, protected from weather and view by the little alcove, and eyed the door. It was either unlocked or locked, and I hadn't (yet) learned how to pick a lock, although I'd played with my father's handcuffs and managed to get them open several times.

I decided right then that picking locks would be a skill I might find handy someday.

My insides fluttered a little as I reached for the door handle. If I went inside, I would cross the line from "just looking around" to "getting involved."

The knob didn't turn when I twisted it, and I felt a pang of disappointment and relief at the same time.

I was off the hook. I didn't have to be tempted.

But as I stepped back from the door, I looked up. I noticed the frame around the door was thick and deep. A little hum of interest buzzed in my belly, and I reached up, standing on my tiptoes, trying to slide my hand across the top of the tiny ledge.

I couldn't quite reach the top of the doorframe, but, of course, that didn't stop me. I quickly found a brick and stepped on it, which raised me just enough to slide my fingers across.

Clink.

A key tumbled from the top and landed on the stoop at my feet. I picked it up, and with that same fluttering in my stomach, I fit the key into the lock.

It worked. The knob turned. The door opened.

CHAPTER 15

I REPLACED THE KEY, THEN STEPPED INSIDE QUICKLY, BEFORE I COULD change my mind.

When I closed the door behind me—no reason to advertise my intrusion—I was enveloped in darkness. Musty, dusty, earthy darkness.

And silence.

It was cold, black, and deathly quiet in Maison de Verre.

Fortunately, I had followed through on my intention from yesterday and purchased a small flashlight, which I withdrew from my handbag. When I turned it on, the beam cut through the darkness and revealed the sprinkling of the dust motes I'd disturbed.

Since I'd come in through the back, I found myself in a short L-shaped hallway. One leg led toward the front of the restaurant, and the other led into the kitchen.

I had the presence of mind to shine my light onto the floor before I took even one step. This was not only to ensure I didn't trip on anything, but also so I could see whether there was any sign of footprints or other disturbances in a place that was supposedly abandoned and forgotten.

When I saw the array of footprints, the mosaic of oblong shapes disturbing the dirt and dust in irregular pathways along the hall, I smiled with satisfaction. Someone had definitely been here recently, definitely more than once, and had been very active with whatever they were doing. The trails of footprints led to both the kitchen and the front of the restaurant.

I opted for the front of the restaurant first—where the heavier traffic of footprints led. I had no fear that anyone would see my light, for the front window was swathed in fabric and the main entrance's window was partially obstructed by a small entrance hall and coatroom.

Having assured myself that no one could see me and that I was alone in the empty, long-neglected restaurant, I relaxed and shined my light around the dining room.

There were several tables still in place, arranged as efficiently as possible in the compact space. Most still had chairs, and there were two or three tablecloths that had once been white, but were now gray with dirt and age, still in place. Two tables were tucked into the bow of the large front window, and there were several private booths arranged along the wall, each separated by privacy barriers.

Crystal chandeliers of every size and design hung everywhere like great, complicated raindrops. House of Glass it was indeed. I could only imagine what a lovely place it must have been when the crystal was clean and the lamps were lit.

Now the space smelled like dust and mildew, along with something rotting . . . and the faint scent of cigarette smoke that had to be recent.

I smiled as I beamed the light over the walls and saw the decor there. Grand-père had been right. The same fabric used to gift wrap the three bottles of wine still hung in large framed and slightly padded sections on the interior walls. I could see where one of the pieces had been cut from its moorings and lay crumpled on a table.

When I drew closer, I found the scissors the killer had used to snip the rectangles of silk, along with a spindle of red ribbon.

There was no longer any question as to whether there was a connection between Maison de Verre and the killings.

The killer had to be someone who knew the restaurant . . . and who wanted their victims—and possibly even the police—to make the connection to Maison de Verre. The two chefs who were connected to it were dead. Victims.

The loyal maître d', Jacques, Nanette's husband, was dead.

But the wife and former lover of the two chefs, Émelie Loyer, was also a wine expert. I kept coming back to the fact that she *had* to be the prime suspect. There was no one else, was there?

But why would she—or anyone—want to kill Grand-père?

Was there anyone else who had a connection to the restaurant?

I realized I should have questioned Nanette a little more about any other people who might have worked here before the war or even during the Occupation. Maybe she even had some photographs of the restaurant and the people who worked there.

But my mind kept returning to the wines. Someone was getting rare bottles of wine from *somewhere*—and they didn't mind destroying them, despite their value.

If the killer was tying the murders to Maison de Verre, maybe they were getting the wine from somewhere here.

Grand-père had said that the Germans found the stash that had been hidden at the restaurant, but what if they didn't actually drink all of it? What if there was still a small stock somewhere? Could that be where the killer was getting the wine?

Or even if they weren't from the original wine cellar here at Maison de Verre, it made sense for the killer to keep a supply on site, anyway, since this was where he or she was preparing them to be delivered—as evidenced by the cut silk and ribbon.

The most logical place to store wine was in a *cave*. I hadn't seen any door or passage that might lead to a cellar on my way from the back to the dining room, so I turned to go back toward the kitchen.

As I did so, my flashlight beam swept over one of the private booths near the back of the dining room. Something glinted there, near the floor.

I drew closer, beaming my light over the space. My breath caught as the illumination spilled over the shiny metal.

It was the metal buckle of a woman's shoe ... which happened to be attached to a foot.

Oh no ... no, no, no ... !

My heart was in my throat as I stumbled toward the table where a leg sagged from its bench seat.

Everything else had been in shadow, protected by the private booth, except for that shoe buckle.

Whoever she was, she was obviously dead ... slumped awkwardly in the booth, one hand desperately gripping the table's edge, her feet arched back, knees recoiling, her body frozen in pain. On the table was a bottle and a glass that contained a small amount of red wine. I didn't even need to sniff at them to know they'd smell like bitter almonds.

I shined my light down into the booth, where the woman had collapsed onto the bench, partially under the table.

I could see her face now. And even with it being frozen in a contortion of pain, flushed red, and with the corners of her mouth flecked with dried foam, I recognized her from the photo on Merveille's wall.

Émelie Loyer.

CHAPTER 16

*T*HERE WAS NOTHING I COULD DO NOW FOR ÉMELIE LOYER BUT take her off my list of suspects.

I even felt a rush of guilt for having suspected the woman without ever having spoken to her . . . especially now that it was clear she'd died an unpleasant and painful death. My eyes were damp, and I blinked back my emotions, offering up a prayer of peace and Godspeed for her soul.

Because Madame Loyer was obviously well beyond help, I marshaled my emotions into calm and organization and decided I could take a moment to examine the crime scene. It was the first time I'd ever had the opportunity to do so without anyone else present or someone rushing me away.

The bottle of wine and glass were obvious clues to what had happened. Madame Loyer was still wearing her coat—likely due to the lack of heat in the abandoned building—but she had removed her gloves and hat. I didn't see any sign of a pocketbook or purse, but I didn't want to move her to look more closely.

I was wearing gloves, but I removed one before I reached over to touch the woman's hand, bracing myself for the eerie, expected chill.

Yes, she was cold.

No, her fingers wouldn't move.

From the little I knew about rigor mortis (something I confess I'd looked into after the previous murder investigation in which I'd been involved), I concluded it meant she hadn't been dead for more than a day. The body stiffens over the six to eight hours after death—the toes and fingers first, then the extremities, and so on—and then relaxes again after many more hours, another eight or ten after full rigor, I thought. The fact that Émelie Loyer was cold and stiff from fingers to arm seemed to indicate that she had died earlier today—maybe only hours ago.

I stepped back, and as I shined my light around, I saw the glitter of broken glass on the floor beneath the table.

I crouched to have a better look and found a second wineglass, this one shattered.

That was interesting. Two glasses meant Madame Loyer had been sitting here with someone else—most likely the killer—having a companionable drink.

I put my glove back on and picked up the glass sitting on the table. It smelled of bitter almonds.

But the bottle of wine, which was still half full, did not.

Interesting.

Taking care about glass splinters, I crawled under the table and managed to locate the stem and base of the broken wineglass. There was a little residue of wine in it, and I sniffed carefully.

No bitter almonds.

The scene was clear to me: two people had sat at this table, sharing a bottle of wine. One was the killer, and he (or she) had added cyanide to Émelie Loyer's glass . . . then had sat back and drunk with her.

I shivered at the cold-bloodedness of that scenario. Murderers who used poison—if one were to believe the detective novels and Hercule Poirot's emphasis on understanding the *psychology* of the killer—generally did so because they could distance themselves from the death and it didn't require any physical strength. But the person who'd killed Émelie Loyer had more than likely sat back and watched her die.

A painful, horrible death—struggling to breathe, overtaken by seizures, foaming at the mouth—albeit a relatively quick death. The agony, such as it was, would have been over in minutes.

And then, obviously, the killer had left . . . and left the body.

Were they planning to come back and move it? Or did they not care whether it was found? Or did they never *expect* it to be found?

The latter seemed improbable; after all, the killer had basically painted a trail to Maison de Verre by using the silk from the wall hangings . . . although, I had to ask myself, *Would* anyone have realized where it was from other than Grand-père? And even if he had realized it and had drunk the wine, he'd be dead before he could tell anyone.

The same thing could have been true for Loyer and Beauchêne: even if they'd recognized the silk wrapping, they wouldn't have had time to tell anyone.

Maybe the killer *wasn't* trying to be obvious about the connection to Maison de Verre. Maybe he or she was just using whatever was at hand to make the wines look attractive and special so they would be consumed. Maybe the killer was even counting on the fact that no one would recognize the wrappings as being from Maison de Verre.

I was just about to ease myself back out from beneath the table when I saw a scrap of paper.

I'm not embarrassed to admit that my heart leaped with hope and excitement as I reached for it. *A clue!*

I backed out, clutching the flashlight in one hand and the piece of paper in the other. I left the broken glass fragments on the floor—Merveille would figure it out himself.

But when I shined my light on the paper, I grimaced. It was a drawing—or part of a drawing, as the paper was torn—but I couldn't make heads or tails of what it was. It wasn't detailed, like a sketch, but it had a lot of lines that intersected and curved. A few had circles on them. There was an arrow, too, and I wondered about that, and a few Xs on some of the lines.

Could it be a crude map?

I hesitated. I wanted to keep it, but it was from a crime scene, and I knew I needed to leave it, especially since I wasn't certain I was going to report the death of Madame Loyer. I expected the dutiful Merveille to arrive at any time, and surely, he'd find her.

I'd just as soon he didn't find *me*, as well.

I quickly scrabbled in my purse and extricated a small notebook and a pencil. Quickly and very roughly, I copied the drawing on the paper as well as I could, then tossed the scrap back beneath the table.

Just then, I heard the front door rattle, then clunk in its frame.

Damn.

That had to be Merveille . . . or maybe it was Julia, wondering where I was.

Or warning me . . .

I hesitated, then bolted toward the back door, reasoning that I'd have plenty of time to get out before Merveille (or whoever) got around to the back.

I'd just stepped off the little stoop into the slush when I heard voices. Quickly, I stepped away from the back door and stood in the middle of the alley, looking at the back side of Maison de Verre as if I'd never seen it before.

When Merveille came around from the side lane, his dark coat flapping gently, hat pulled down low against the snow flurries, I gave him a little wave.

"Bonjour, Inspecteur," I said. "I see you've been speaking to my grand-père." There was no sense in pretending that I wasn't there for the same reason he was.

"Mademoiselle Knight," he said. "I wonder if there will ever be a time that I don't come upon you in the midst of a murder investigation."

I didn't even attempt to defend myself. There was no point.

"The door is locked," I said, gesturing to the entrance in question.

Merveille gave me a sharp look, then went up to the stoop. Too late, I realized I'd left the brick on the step . . . but surely he wouldn't realize I'd had to use it to replace the key, would he? It was just a brick. . . .

He looked down, likely seeing the same cigarette butts I'd seen, along with my brick riser, and then he tried the door—

only for form, I was certain. I was relieved that I'd had the presence of mind to lock it behind me when I came out, otherwise my playacting would have all been in vain.

With one more sidewise look at me, he slid his hand along the top of the door frame, just as I had done.

"Ah," he said with a complete lack of surprise. "A key."

I kept my expression composed as he eyed me. "Does it fit? May I come inside with you? Perhaps you shouldn't go in alone."

I'd added that last bit, knowing he'd refuse, but also knowing that if I hadn't already been inside, I would have asked.

Merveille looked at me in such a way that I was fairly certain my ingenuousness had not fooled him in the least. "I think it is best if you leave this to me, mademoiselle."

"Very well," I said as he slipped inside the door.

And then I made my exit, hurrying back down the alley and around to the front of the building.

Julia was there, pacing up and down the street with both of our market bags.

"Tabs! What happened? Merveille showed up, and he was *very* suspicious. I didn't know what to tell him."

"It's all right. Let's get out of here before he comes back," I said, taking my bag and slipping my arm inside the crook of her elbow. "I'll tell you everything, but the most important thing is that Émelie Loyer is dead."

I was on my own making dinner that night.

I muddled through croque monsieurs, laying thick pieces of ham and Gruyère on crusty bread and grilling the sandwiches, then adding another layer of cheese on the top and sliding them under the broiler until they were light brown and bubbly.

If Julia had been there, we would have made the béchamel sauce to go over the top of them. Grand-père and Oncle Rafe didn't complain, though, and we opened a bottle of Burgundy to go with the sandwiches.

It was nearly nine o'clock and we had just finished our dinner in the salon when the door knocker clunked loudly downstairs.

I felt the hair at the back of my neck lift. . . . There was some-thing about the peremptoriness of the sound that boded ill.

Sure enough, it was Inspecteur Merveille on our front stoop. He looked tired, bad-tempered, and frustrated.

"Come in, Inspecteur," I said warily.

"May I have a word with you, mademoiselle?" he said in a tone that made it clear it wasn't a request. We ignored Oscar Wilde, who'd, as usual, appeared at the top of the stairs to bark the alarm.

"Of course, Inspecteur. Let me speak to my grand-père first, for he will want to know who's here. I'll be right back . . . unless you'd like to join us up in the salon?"

"I think it would be best for you and I to speak alone, if you permit, mademoiselle," Merveille replied.

My heart sank even further. "All right. Just a minute."

I explained to Grand-père and Oncle Rafe that Merveille had stopped in just for a moment and that I'd be cleaning up in the kitchen. I wasn't certain they believed me; in fact, there was an unholy and interested (and very misguided) light in Oncle Rafe's gaze when he exchanged glances with Grand-père.

I could have told them not to get too excited.

When I came back down, I found Merveille examining the bottoms of my boots, which had been set on a tray near the closet to dry. He was still in his coat and hat but had removed his gloves.

"I've got coffee on the stove." I realized why he was looking at my boots and suppressed a grimace. "You look as if you could use something warm to drink."

He cast me a cold look, as if to quell any thought I might have about softening him up. "This is not a social call, mademoi-selle."

I spewed out a sigh. "I understand, but there's no need for you to stand there dripping, cold, and obviously exhausted while you grill me. Come into the kitchen, take off your hat, and sit down. I'll make you some coffee and you can interrogate me to your heart's content."

I stalked into the kitchen, knowing he'd follow me.

He took a seat at the table where Julia and I had cut up champignons last night, and I poured him a cup of coffee, then set a clean ashtray nearby. Merveille removed his hat, and I saw, for the first time, one tiny lock of hair that had curled up, out of order, from behind one ear.

So the man *wasn't* perfect, after all.

"Have you eaten?" I asked. I truly wasn't trying to delay the inevitable; he just looked exhausted and worn out.

"Mademoiselle Knight—" he began, but I talked over him.

"You might just as well call me Tabitha at this point, Inspecteur. We're a lot less formal in the States. And I'm not trying to delay our conversation, but you look as if you could use a good meal. I'm not Julia Child, but I can make a decent sandwich for you. And that will enable you to build up your strength for my interrogation."

His stony demeanor softened with a bit of crinkle at the corners of his eyes. "I suppose I will need all my strength for that, mademoiselle."

"Excellent." I turned back to the stove and prayed I wouldn't make a fool out of myself cooking. I was certain Marguerite was a whiz *en cuisine.*

"I was surprised when I arrived here today, this afternoon, to speak with your grand-père and found you were not here," Merveille said. "I expected you to be present in order to ensure that none of the finer points were missed in our discussion. But I soon realized why you were absent."

I glanced over at him as I finished layering ham and Gruyère onto bread slick with Dijon mustard. Then I slipped the sandwich into a hot buttered pan—with probably not as much butter as Julia would have wanted—to brown. "I went to the market."

"*Oui, c'est vrai,*" he replied gravely. "And how coincidental that Maison de Verre was located almost right *next* to the market."

Apparently, he wasn't going to wait to build up his strength in order to question me.

"Yes," I replied. "I was curious, as I'm certain you'd expect."

"Mademoiselle, you know what they say about the curiousness of *le chat.*"

I flipped Monsieur Croque onto his other side. He was perfectly brown and crispy on top! I wanted to do a little dance, but, of course, I didn't. "I was just going to look in the windows. And see if there was any sign of activity around it."

"But then you found the key."

I didn't respond right away. I was watching the sandwich closely. The last thing I wanted was for it to burn.

It was done—the cheese was gooey and melting everywhere, making me want another sandwich for myself!—and I carefully removed it from the pan and added another two slices of cheese on top. Then I slid the sandwich under the broiler, which I had had the forethought to turn on ahead of time. Maybe Julia was rubbing off on me.

"Yes, I found the key," I admitted. I crouched, watching through the glass door. It wouldn't take long for the cheese to melt. . . .

"Even if I had not suspected it, your footprints—they were all over the alley and inside the restaurant," he went on. "Your boots, mademoiselle . . . they are new, and they have a distinctive sole."

"My parents sent them to me for Christmas," I said, yanking open the oven door. I was just in time. The Gruyère on top was lightly brown and bubbly. Perfect. *Whew.* I slid the sandwich onto a plate and set it casually in front of Merveille, although inside I was triumphant.

I could almost feel his tension ease as he looked at the simple meal. It smelled delicious. "*Merci*, mademoiselle. It is very kind of you."

Huh. So he wouldn't fall into the informality of using my name. I wondered if that was because I was being interrogated in an investigation, or if it was just his way of keeping his distance from everyone—or just from me.

I turned away to slice up an apple that was only slightly wrinkled, giving him the opportunity to eat without feeling as if he was being watched. By the time I returned to the table with a plate of the apple and some cheddar, he'd nearly finished the sandwich, and his coffee was gone.

I refilled the coffee and sat down across from him with a cup for myself. He reached for a slice of apple. I was surprised he hadn't lit a cigarette, as many people did at the end of a meal, but then, I had never seen him smoke; nor did I smell cigarettes on him. Maybe, like drinking spirits, he didn't partake while on duty.

I propped my elbows on the table and leaned forward. "Inspecteur, let me save you some time. I found Madame Loyer, but I didn't touch her—well, except to see whether rigor mortis had set in, and then I only touched her hand and wrist to see whether they moved or not—or the crime scene."

His eyes had widened a little during this explanation. I was sure I had surprised him once again with my knowledge of crime scene investigation.

I stifled a smile and went on. "I had gloves on the whole time. I noticed the second broken glass on the floor and only smelled bitter almonds in one glass, which implies that someone was with her and probably watched her die." My lips curled in disgust at the thought. "Honestly, I really only wanted to see whether Grand-père and Oncle Rafe were right about the silk pieces coming from Maison de Verre. I didn't expect to find another dead body."

"Of course you did not, mademoiselle," he said. "But, it seems, you *do* manage to be on the scene with death more often than one would expect."

"It's certainly not intentional, Inspecteur."

"Mademoiselle, has it occurred to you that your grand-père might not have been the target for the poisoned wine that was delivered here today?"

I stiffened, and a rush of fear swept over me. "You mean Oncle Rafe. I . . . . I suppose I *did* think about the fact that he would have had it to drink, as well, since they are always together—and being a fanatic oenophile himself, he would be interested in such a rare vintage . . . but are you saying you think *he* was actually the target? And not Grand-père?" My heart was pounding, and I felt ill.

I knew that Oncle Rafe had what one might call a checkered past. I didn't know whether he'd done anything terribly illegal. I had the impression he'd been involved in the black market (which, honestly, so had everyone else during the Occupation and the first years after the Liberation), and that he'd dallied with the anarchy movement before the Great War . . . and, of course, I knew that he'd been involved with the Resistance. And by his own casual admission, he had a number of people who might want him dead. But I couldn't imagine him ever doing anything violent to anyone. He wouldn't even stomp on a spider if he saw one skittering across the floor—which was something I really didn't understand. Spiders belonged *outside*.

"Mademoiselle . . ." Merveille heaved a sigh, then pinned me with those sea-gray eyes. "The gentlemen are not the only ones who live in this house."

I stared at him for a moment, then reared back in my chair. "You mean *me*? You think someone sent that wine for *me*? Why, that's ridiculous. The bottle was from Grand-père's and Oncle Rafe's friend Maldon. No one would think it was for *me*."

"But you might very well have had some, might you not? If your grand-père or Monsieur Fautrier would have offered you some, *non*? And you are often home in the afternoon, at teatime, when the bottle was delivered, *non*?"

I flapped a hand at him. "Maybe. But I can't imagine that poisoning me would have been anything other than a happy coincidence for the killer."

He nearly laughed at that. I saw his eyes glint and his lips twitch before he caught himself, but I knew he'd almost lost it. I smiled at him to let him know I knew.

He recovered quickly, his eyes going cool again. "Mademoiselle, it is a very dangerous thing, this investigation. Here we have a killer who does not care who else might become his victim. And we do not know how many more people he has tar-

geted. Will he try again for your grand-père and Monsieur
Fautrier and yourself? We do not know."

"No, we don't, and my—uh—I mean the best suspect is now
dead," I said. "Émelie Loyer, I mean. She was the only person
who made sense, with her connections to everyone involved,
but now she's gone. And it can't have been suicide from re-
morse or anything on her part, because someone else was with
her—and that someone else wasn't poisoned." This last bit I
said in a rush because I had just thought of it. "So, now what?
We are at a dead end."

"*No*, mademoiselle, it is *not we*." He slammed his hand on the
table, making the flatware and plate jump a little. "It is *I*, not *you*,
who will be investigating this crime. It is dangerous, and this
killer—*mademoiselle, écoutez-moi!*—he *knows* you were present at
both deaths. He *knows* you saw the delivery boy—you are the
only person who saw the delivery boy at Le Cordon Bleu. The delivery boy who now cannot be found, eh? I wonder if that is an
accident . . .

"And now, thanks in part to your insatiable curiosity, *your boot
prints* are all over rue Las Cases and the back alley and inside
Maison de Verre. It is very, *very* clear that you have been nosing
about. Do you understand what I am saying to you, mademoiselle?"

The color had drained from my face, and the rest of my body
felt numb. He was making excellent points. And even though I
really, truly hadn't done anything dangerous—or even stupid—
I felt chastised.

"I understand."

His eyes held mine a moment longer. Then he gave a brisk
nod and looked down at his coffee, then once more back at me.
"Stay away from Maison de Verre, mademoiselle, and please do
not trouble yourself any further with this investigation."

"I won't. I really don't want to die, you know," I said earnestly.
"I was only . . . all right, all right." I held up a hand. "But, if you
have not, maybe you should talk to Madame Nanette. I don't
know her last name. She is the basket maker at the market, and

her husband was the maître d' at Maison de Verre. Maybe she has some information that might help."

"*Vraiment.*"

"And . . . perhaps Madame Loyer's *propriétaire* at her *hôtel* . . . she . . ." I trailed off when he speared me with his cold gaze.

"This is what I am saying to you, mademoiselle! You must stay *out* of it."

"I know. I will." I swallowed and decided I shouldn't mention my conversation with Théo about Pierre . . . at least, not yet. "And . . . apparently, Madame Loyer had a young . . . man. Um . . ." I willed him to understand what I was implying without me actually having to say it, and being French, of course, he grasped my meaning immediately.

"I see." His eyes flashed a glint of something that might have been humor, but who knew with Merveille. He finished the last of his coffee. "Thank you for that, mademoiselle." I thought he meant the lead of Madame Loyer's young man, but he might have been talking about the coffee.

"Inspecteur . . . the person who is doing this . . . they had to have been at the cooking demonstration, because they took the gift tag. Have you considered that perhaps he or she was there in disguise? And then slipped out during the confusion? And that he or she would surely also have been at the Deschampses' the other night, when Monsieur Loyer died—but not in disguise?"

He stood and pushed his chair back up to the table. "*Oui,* mademoiselle, all of that is known to me and has been considered by myself and those working with me. Now, please . . . if you would confine yourself to the tutoring lessons you give and the cooking lessons you are taking and leave the murder solving to me. I do not wish to have to deliver bad news to your grand-père." He gave an uncharacteristic grimace.

"Merveille yelled at you?" Julia goggled at me as we walked down rue de Bourgogne late the next morning on our way, once again, to the market.

"In all fairness, he probably had the right," I replied, giving Mademoiselle Fidelia, the egg seller, a little wave as Julia and I paused in the street.

"But you had just employed the first of my rules for managing men," Julia said. "You know the three-part plan. Feed them, flatter them, and f—"

"Yes, yes, I know—*fornicate* with them," I said, laughing. "I have no intention of fornicating with Inspecteur Merveille. *Any way*," I went on loudly when I saw Julia's eyes lighting up. I just knew she was going to say something silly about that was why he'd been mad at me—because he was worried about me. Because he *liked* me, and so on.

I figured he just didn't want to have another body on his hands—and, as he'd admitted, he definitely wouldn't want to have to tell Maurice Saint-Léger that his granddaughter was dead.

"Anyway," I said again, "I'm definitely going to stay out of the whole thing. I told him what we thought about maybe someone had been in disguise at the cooking demonstration. Maybe wearing a thick blond mustache?" I was thinking about what Théo had told me regarding the man who gave Pierre the wine for Chef Beauchêne. "Julia, it would be really helpful if you could think about who you saw there and whether anyone, oh, I don't know, didn't belong? Or someone you hadn't seen before? Or *maybe*," I said, my own eyes lighting up with an idea, "maybe we should go talk to the ladies you said are part of a bridge club that were at the demonstration. Maybe they noticed something."

"Tabitha, you just said you weren't going to do anything else," Julia said, putting her hands on her hips.

"That's not really doing anything. It's just talking to someone you kind of already know. They might be more open to talking to you than the police, you know," I said. "None of *them* are the murderer."

"True." Julia smiled as we started walking again. "It's a good idea. I'm going to be at the demonstration this afternoon—do you want to go with me? If they're there, and they usually are, we can try and talk to them after."

"Oh, that's all right." I really didn't want to sit through another demonstration again. "Why don't you go, and then if they want to talk, you can have them go with you after? I'll just plan to meet you at a café near the school. Besides, I'm supposed to meet Bryant Howard for a Coke this afternoon. He says he's been *dying* for one since coming over here."

"Bryant Howard?" Julia stopped dead again in the middle of the walkway. "But you said he had a baby face and was trying to grow a mustache—which made the baby face worse—and he wouldn't stop talking."

"I'm not going to date him," I said. "But I called him the other day to suggest coffee, partly because I left the party so abruptly, but also because I thought he might have some interesting information about what happened with Monsieur Loyer before the wine tasting. The bottle of poisoned wine was delivered there, you know."

"Tabitha, you just said you weren't going to do anything else!" Julia said, her usual tenor voice lifting into soprano range.

"I made this date *before* I told Merveille I was going to stay out of it," I said. "And I'm not going to cancel on Bryant. It would be rude. Besides, it's just a Coke. And there's no way he's the killer. He's American and hasn't even been here for more than a few weeks. What motive could he possibly have? Anyway, I won't even *ask* him about that night," I said—really meaning it.

"If you say so. So we can plan to meet at Au Pied de Cochon? It's just a little brasserie down the street from the school and has *stupendous* onion soup. I'll convince the bridge ladies to come no matter what." Julia sighed. "I tried to learn bridge once—when I first got here. I actually *did* learn it, and it wasn't bad, but I just couldn't see spending all my time playing cards and bidding no trump or three hearts or whatever. And I definitely didn't like making *hats.*"

I knew that story: In an effort to find something to occupy herself in Paris when she first arrived and Paul was busy with work, Julia had signed up for a hat-making class. It had not been her favorite thing.

"Thank God I found French food and *cooking*!" she finished

exuberantly as she swept up to Madame Marie and greeted her with enthusiasm.

We finished our marketing in record time. I knew Julia wouldn't have time to help me cook tonight, so I fell back on poor Madame Poulet, with the plan to roast her with a few potatoes and carrots. It had, after all, been at least five days since we'd had *roasted* chicken—even though we had eaten *les suprêmes* with the creamy mushroom sauce two nights ago. I really needed to improve my repertoire *en cuisine*. Maybe I should pick up some sausages for tonight instead and save Madame Poulet for tomorrow.

"Oh, mademoiselle!"

I turned to see Monsieur Michel waving to me. With a smile, I went over to greet him.

"And how were *les champignons?*" he asked.

"They were delicious! We cooked them up in a luscious shallot and cream sauce. Thank you for such lovely mushrooms, monsieur. I hope there haven't been any other incidents with the vandalism," I added.

"No, no, not since poor Gérard was found with his head bashed," replied Monsieur Michel. "He is ready to come back to the meadery, but his daughter won't let him, you see." He grinned, as if the thought amused him. "His daughter is quite the spitfire, she is." His smile faded. "But, mademoiselle, I was hoping to impose upon you for a little problem, could I?"

"Of course. I'm certain it would be no imposition," I replied, slightly mystified but, of course, also curious.

"You see, Gérard often assisted me—and so I assisted him— on the day that I am due to refill the lanterns in our area of *les catacombes*. It is better to have the two of us, you see, to go through all of the tunnels and refill the oils and check the wicks on all of the lanterns. And, of course, he cannot come with me because his daughter will not allow him to put even one toe onto the floor outside of his bed." He laughed, truly seeming to enjoy his friend's misfortune—which I'm certain was an indication of how relieved he was that Monsieur Gérard was on his way to recovery. "And so, I was hoping perhaps that you might be willing to assist me. It is much to ask of any of the other sellers here in the marketplace to take the time, you see?"

"Of course I will help you," I replied, immediately deciding that I would take another look at the area where Monsieur Gérard had been attacked. After all, I'd been strictly banned from doing anything related to the wine poisoning murders, so maybe I should divert my investigative curiosity to whoever was vandalizing the market. "When should we go?"

Monsieur Michel's round face lit up. "Oh, merci beaucoup, mademoiselle! I knew you would help me! And you will have all of the fresh champignons you should want, whenever you want! But when could you take the time?" He looked over me dubiously, obviously noting that I was carrying a full market bag.

"Oh, go ahead with him now, Tabs," said Julia. "I'll take your market bag back and leave it with Bet and Blythe, and then we can meet up later with the bridge ladies."

Monsieur Michel was delighted with the arrangement, and he and I walked back down the alley to the entrance to the catacombs.

"I'm glad there hasn't been any more vandalism since Monsieur Gérard's injury," I said as we prepared to climb down the ladder. "I hope it's over—whatever was prompting it."

"*Oui.* But, sadly, we are no closer to finding who has done it," he said, handing me a lantern. I had my flashlight in my purse, and I slipped it into my coat pocket just in case.

Then I began the descent into the catacombs for the second time in two days.

CHAPTER 17

*B*EING IN THE CATACOMBS LEFT ME WITH THE SAME OTHER-
worldly sensation I'd experienced before. That pervasive sense
of *presence*... of enduring sadness, discomfort, misplacement...
and yet, still, there was an inexplicable aura of peace.

The dank smell, the cool air, the uneven ground, the glistening sweat on the walls... the deathly, incredible silence, and the
unrelenting maw of dark just beyond the circle of my lantern's
glow...

I knew Monsieur Michel and I were not alone down there
among the bones and skulls... yet I didn't feel a threat. Only a
mild uneasiness.

I felt *aware*... of layers and layers, of ages and ages, of depths
and depths of *presence*. We shared the space with those who had
not chosen to be there, but who nonetheless would live eternally beneath the cobbled streets of the City of Light.

My companion must have sensed and respected the uneasy
awe I felt, for he hardly spoke at all as I followed him through
the tunnels.

It didn't take long to help Monsieur Michel with his task. We
each carried a lantern, but I held mine up to provide the light.
This gave him two free hands to fill the oil in each of the
lanterns that hung on large metal rings bored into the walls in
the tunnels, ready to be lit as needed. He checked and trimmed
the wicks and clicked his tongue with satisfaction as he finished
each one.

As I followed him through the dank, cool tunnels, I saw the occasional evidence of living human presence (as opposed to the bones and skulls around which the walls had been built): cigarette butts and empty, crumpled packs; a wine bottle; a few ratty newspapers someone might have tried to build a fire with; matchbooks; and more.

We went farther into the tunnels than I remembered from before, passing by the barrels of mead and the mushroom farm I'd seen previously to a second mushroom farm another fifteen minutes' walk past eyeless skulls, stacked femurs, and ripple-patterned vertebrae.

There was a portion of the natural wall that had strange, pale, waxlike protrusions growing from it that I wanted to touch, but didn't have the chance, as my companion trudged on.

"Only one more stop, mademoiselle," Monsieur Michel said as we finished at the second mushroom farm. "There is one more lantern from the other entrance I sometimes use, see?"

"It's no worry," I replied. I truly didn't mind at all. It was fascinating—even while being depressing and sobering—moving unseen and unhampered beneath the city streets. Every so often, someone would step on a manhole cover, making a jarring *clank* or *clunk* that echoed a little in the tunnels or clanged over my head.

I wondered how many of the passersby realized that just under their feet was a warren of tunnels with living beings— myself and Michel—making our way through them . . . even tracing some of the exact same routes below as above.

"How do you know your way through all these tunnels?" I said as we came to yet another intersection and he unhesitatingly chose a direction.

"Ah, mademoiselle, it is decades I've been going about down here," he said with an easy smile. "Although there are many parts of *les catacombes* that I have not seen, of course. No one has been through it all, you see?"

"But there must be a map of all the tunnels and passageways," I replied, wondering how to get my hands on one. "There are street plaques and markings carved and painted onto the walls for direction."

"There is no complete map of the catacombs. No one has ever made one—at least one that is known. But there was René Suttel . . . He worked at a hospital, and he began to create a map of *le grand réseau sud*, here, the tunnels in the Left Bank. He meant to give it to the Resistance, you see, but he never finished. It was far too difficult and dangerous, and he came upon a hidden German bunker more than once—ah, *oui, c'est vrai!*" he said when I made a sound of surprise and horror. "And so he found it impossible to finish. It is so many intertwining tunnels, and they go all over beneath the city. But even so, they're not all connected, for there were many different and separate quarries that were dug under the city. And there are passages that dead-end, and some that are caved in, and some that are too narrow or too low . . . It is impossible. And it is not necessary, you see? We know where we must go . . . and where we do not *want* to go."

He stopped suddenly at a four-way-intersection and, his voice suddenly hard and bitter, said, "Do you see?"

I raised my lantern to join his in spilling a mellow glow over the wall in front of us. There was a white patch painted on the right side of the wall. Three arrows—one brown, one red, one blue—were painted on the white patch, all pointing in the same direction. I read the words painted next to them:

HINTERHOF

S. MICHEL

N. DAME-BONAPARTE

"What does it lead to?"

"It is the bunker for the *Boches*. The Nazis," he spat. "It is where they planned to hide when the Resistance took over—ah, they knew it would happen, that we Parisians would say, '*Enough!*' They knew it was a possibility. And the cowards, they took *our* catacombs, *our* bomb shelters, for their own."

"That leads to a German bunker?" I immediately—despite

my loathing for everything the Nazis stood for—wanted to see it. "Down that way?" I shined my lantern into the tunnel where the arrows pointed. I could see a door at the end of my spill of light. It looked old and metallic and rusty, but there was a ship's captain–wheel on the front of it.

"It was, *oui.* In the yard behind the Montaigne school, near boulevard Saint-Michel." He gestured vaguely above.

I was practically jumping out of my skin, wanting to go look at the bunker—to see what was there, what mysteries and remains had been left behind—but Monsieur Michel had no interest. He made that clicking sound with his tongue and led me down a different tunnel.

I followed reluctantly, since I certainly wasn't going to stay and poke around by myself. There was a reason Monsieur Michel, who knew these tunnels—at least, this area of them—like the back of his hand, wouldn't come into the catacombs alone. I was curious, but I wasn't stupid.

We finished with the last lantern and started back the way we had come. As we passed those arrows pointing to the bunker, I almost asked him to take me down that tunnel . . . but I didn't.

I could only imagine the horrors he and his fellow Parisians had endured at the hands of the Germans during their Occupation—the demeaning of their pride, the ruination of their national identity—the torture, the disappearances, the conflicts and mistrust and loathing between those who resisted and those who collaborated.

Instead, I just followed him back, looking at the walls—at the altars that had been carved into stone, the designs made with bones and bricks and even rotting timbers, the strange natural formations of earth and stone that glistened and seemed to *breathe* with the lives of those interred there—until something made me stop suddenly.

It was carved into the wall near a tunnel that branched off. I wouldn't have thought anything of it if I hadn't seen the same symbol only yesterday.

It was a crude but recognizable carving: a broad *V* with an *M* set inside it.

The logo for Maison de Verre.

"That is a dead end, mademoiselle," said Monsieur Michel, who realized I'd halted. He came back around with his lantern, which both lit and shadowed his bulbous nose and round, protruding chin, giving him a clownish look.

But I was already peering into the tunnel with the help of my own lantern. It didn't look like a dead end to me.

"I just want to look," I said, glancing back at him from over my shoulder. I did *not* want to be left alone, but curiosity impelled me to edge into the tunnel. "May I?"

He sighed, then threw up his hands, sending the light bouncing around erratically. "Of course, mademoiselle. But I tell you, it goes to nowhere. There is a wall at the end."

I held my lantern high as I edged farther into the tunnel. There was a weird prickling over the back of my neck, as if something was about to happen . . . and even though I had a suspicion about what it might be, I didn't allow the thoughts to manifest.

I was maybe ten feet into the tunnel—happily, it was easily wide and tall enough for me or even a man of average size to walk through without stooping or having to maneuver—when I saw something that made those prickles over my nape leap to attention.

A cigarette butt, there on the ground. Someone had been along here recently, for when I stooped to shine my light on the smoke, I could see that it was fresh. I poked at it with my gloved finger to try and determine what brand of cigarette it was. Gauloise, I thought, but it was difficult to tell for certain, for the dampness had affected the ink on the stub.

Now my heart was beating harder, and I went on, expecting at any moment to encounter the dead end that Monsieur Michel had warned me about.

But when I came to a large pile of rubble—bricks, stones, all sorts of masonry detritus—and could see the tunnel yawning past it, I knew.

What had once been a dead-end tunnel was no longer.

CHAPTER 18

I CALLED TO MONSIEUR MICHEL, AND MOMENTS LATER I COULD SEE his light bobbing through the tunnel.

I didn't have to say anything; he made a sound of surprise and curiosity when he saw the rubble.

"So someone has opened it."

"When was the last time you saw that it was blocked off?" I asked. My whole body felt as if I'd been plunged into an icy stream: my hair was standing up everywhere, and my skin prickled. Somehow, this was related to the murders.

"Oh, ah, mademoiselle, I cannot say . . . perhaps a year? Maybe it is less. But I have had no reason to come this way, so I would not know." He sounded far less interested in the mystery of the missing wall than I would have hoped.

"Will you come with me, monsieur?" I asked. "I want to see where this tunnel leads."

The expression on his face said, *Ugh*, but he shrugged. "But, of course, mademoiselle, although I do not know what it is you expect to see."

"Merci beaucoup," I told him and led the way down the tunnel. "I won't take long, monsieur. I promise."

If he was grumbling as he followed me, I didn't hear him. I was too busy looking around for anything that might be a clue.

We didn't have to go far before we came to a door. An actual metal door, embedded in the tunnel, blocking any further passage. My heart leaped. I suspected I knew what was on the other side of that door.

But there my luck evaporated. There didn't seem to be any way to open the door from this side. I pulled my trusty Swiss Army knife from my pocket, hoping for inspiration from the tools there. Monsieur Michel watched me silently as I felt around, trying to locate a release or a latch or *something*, but I could find nothing.

At last, he cleared his throat and said, "Is it enough, mademoiselle?"

I'd been crouching near the ground, trying in vain to figure out if I could *pry* the door open from the bottom using one of the tools on my knife.

Defeated, I rose. *"Oui."*

There was nothing more I could do but follow him back out the tunnel and through the catacombs.

I knew I had to tell Merveille about this new development, but to be honest, I was a little nervous about doing so. After all, he'd been very vehement and adamant about me not being involved. Not that I was afraid of him, but I found I didn't care for his disappointed and irritated expression when he lectured me.

And even though my discovery of a catacombs tunnel that *surely* (although I hadn't actually confirmed it) somehow led into Maison de Verre had been purely innocent and accidental, I suspected the inspecteur would not see it that way.

But, I told myself as I walked home from the market, having left Monsieur Michel happily at his mushroom stall, there was a good likelihood that the inspecteur had already discovered an entrance to the catacombs from the restaurant. I was certain he'd done a thorough search of Maison de Verre for clues.

So perhaps I didn't really need to rush to fill in the inspecteur.

At least, that was what I continued to tell myself as I climbed into the Renault to drive over to the Right Bank and meet Bryant Howard.

He'd chosen Fouquet's, a well-known brasserie on a corner of the Champs-Élysées. It had long slanted awnings along both street sides, under which tables, with the quintessential curved rattan wicker chairs you saw everywhere in Paris, were clustered, even during the winter.

Tall, narrow mirrors hung on the exterior walls between broad windows, which were embellished with wrought-iron decorations. Large neon signs above the overhangs were emblazoned with FOUQUET'S, with another neon ad for Bière Tuborg flashing above them. I was surprised to find that the establishment, which was located in a fancy hotel, actually offered bottles of Coca-Cola, along with beer and wine.

This was surprising because there was an ongoing struggle between Coke and a good portion of France's natives about what had been dubbed "Coca-Colonization." The drink had been unofficially available in France for years, but now, partly because of the Marshall Plan—which was a financial effort by the American government to familiarize the French with our culture as we helped Europe rebuild after the war—Coca-Cola was instituting a far-reaching marketing and production campaign. This included adding a number of bottling plants in France in order to grow the company's market share there. But many Parisians and their countrymen feared that Coke would overtake the local beverage industry—particularly their beloved wine—and that soda pop was far too addictive and capitalistic for a nation with such large Socialist and Communist movements.

I, who'd grown up drinking Faygo pop in the Detroit area, enjoyed an icy Coke once in a while, but I didn't crave it like Bryant obviously did, and he'd obviously sought out a place to satisfy his yen for the drink.

When I slid into my seat across from him, I grinned when I saw that he had finished one bottle of Coke and was working his way through another. In deference to the wintry weather, we sat inside, in a circular booth, but there were a few brave souls who were bundled up and sipping coffee or beer at tables just outside our window. There was even a nicely dressed woman in a stylish wool hat sitting at a table with her dog—a fairly large chocolate Labrador—sitting on a chair next to her. I smothered a smile. I was used to seeing dogs in restaurants here—something that would never happen back home—but I hadn't seen one actually sitting at a table until now.

The cat perched on a long shelf near the ceiling was not quite as rare.

"I sure do miss this," Bryant said, grinning, as he toasted me with the little curvy bottle as I settled into my chair. "Wine is good and all—after all, that's how I make my living—but there's nothing like a cold Coke."

"Maybe you should start working for Coca-Cola," I teased after I ordered a kir—which was white wine to which cassis syrup had been added—instead of a pop.

"If I actually thought Coke would make it as a success here, I probably would," he replied, still smiling beneath his sparse mustache. In my opinion, he would look much better if he just gave up on it. "My dad would flip his lid, though. He and Uncle Roger have worked hard to build the business back up since the war."

I hoped he wouldn't be too vocal about his love for Coca-Cola, for that could very well rattle the cage of some of his suppliers.

I mentioned that, and he grimaced, then grinned, with a happy-go-lucky shrug. "Why do you think I invited *you* for a Coke and not anyone else?" His expression dimmed. "Seriously, I just wanted to make sure you were all right after everything that happened the other night. I didn't realize you had also been there when the other man died. Was it only the day before?"

With that, I could honestly say to Merveille and Julia and anyone else that I hadn't brought up the murders to Bryant. But since *he* had . . .

"It was awful seeing it happen twice," I said, smiling at the garçon who brought my drink, then sobering. "It felt like déjà vu when Monsieur Loyer read from the note and opened that bottle wrapped in silk. I wanted to say something, but I didn't. I *should* have spoken up."

"It was a good thing you didn't," Bryant said firmly. "I don't mean it was a good thing Louis Loyer died, but even if you had said something, no one would have believed you. They're so snooty about their wine here," he said, leaning over the table and lowering his voice, even though we were speaking in English. "They never would have listened to you."

Merveille had said the same thing, and so had Julia and my grand-père. But I still couldn't quite put away that lingering guilt. "Thanks," I said, sipping my drink. I considered whether I should mention that Grand-père had also received a poisoned bottle of wine.

Before I could decide, Bryant said, "The Deschampses—Fréderick and Sadie—are so upset about what happened. The police have been over there every day, questioning all of us, since the wine-tasting party. Mostly that inspector and his sidekick." He drained the rest of his Coke, and I wondered if he was going to have a third one. "I don't know how much longer I should stay with all of this happening. Or if I should move to a hotel. I was supposed to be here until the middle of February, but I wouldn't mind going home early. I sure could go for a hamburger." He flashed a smile, and it had the effect of making his freckled, juvenile features seem even softer.

"It must be really creepy knowing that someone delivered a bottle of cyanide-laced wine to the house you're living in," I said with a shiver that wasn't the least bit faked, since the same thing had happened to me. "Did anyone see who brought the wine for Monsieur Loyer?"

"I didn't. I heard the butler talking—it's very strange living in a house with an actual butler," he said, with another grin, as the waiter approached. This time, Bryant ordered a glass of Chablis, but without the cassis I had opted for. "Anyway, I heard the butler saying that the package was just left on the front porch, and they found it when they opened the door. It had Monsieur Loyer's name on it, and so they gave it to him."

"I wonder why anyone would want to kill him," I said. "And the other chef."

"It seems like a trend, doesn't it? But it's a trend I don't like." He ran a hand through his hair, ruffling it like messy corn silk.

"Did Monsieur Loyer have any visitors when he was staying there?" I realized I had moved beyond the bounds of not getting involved, but after all, Bryant had brought up the subject. "Hadn't he just returned from many years in London?"

"I didn't see him with any visitors, but I did hear him on the telephone the day he arrived," he said as the server brought us a small bowl of peanuts with the Chablis. "He didn't sound very happy."

"I wonder who he was talking to," I said casually, sipping my kir.

"It sounded like a woman's voice through the line," he replied. "He was talking about houses of glass, whatever that is. My French isn't nearly as good as yours." He grinned and lifted his wine to salute me, then stuck his nose inside the glass to sniff.

"Houses of glass? Wasn't that the name of his famous restaurant? I wonder if he was going to reopen it now that he was back in Paris. Maybe that was his wife he was talking to."

"His wife?" He took his nose out of the glass. "I didn't know he had a wife. Is she still back in London?"

"No, I think she lives here." I had to catch myself from saying "lived."

Bryant shrugged as he took a sip. "Well, it doesn't matter now, does it?"

"No." I mulled for a minute, then decided in for a penny, in for a pound, and said, "It's so strange that someone was putting cyanide in such rare wines. Why would they waste something so valuable by ruining them? And where did they *get* them?"

"That," said Bryant, leaning across the table again, "is a very good question. Those wines—they were worth a lot of green. Not only because they were old, but because they survived the Occupation. Forty or fifty bucks or more apiece."

I nearly dropped my glass. "Are you serious? *Forty or fifty* dollars? For a bottle of *wine*?" I barely remembered to keep my voice down. You could buy a pretty good bottle of wine, *plus* a meal for two at a two-fork restaurant, for four hundred francs, which was about five dollars.

"Some bottles like that might even be worth more to a collector," Bryant went on, his eyes gleaming.

"And someone *ruined* them? Used them as a murder weapon? That would almost be like—like painting over a Monet or the *Mona Lisa*, or, no—more like setting a bomb to go off in the Louvre in order to kill someone. Why would someone do that?"

"It is nuts, isn't it? When you think about it." He shook his head. "Whoever poisoned those wines must have one hell of a wine cellar not to care about wasting them."

"Wow." I didn't have to feign confusion and shock.

We talked for a little longer, with most of the conversation being Bryant comparing (usually negatively) living in Paris to living in New London, Connecticut, where he was from. I was glad he didn't seem to be interested in me in a romantic way; I certainly felt no attraction to him other than that of a casual friendship.

But when we finished our drinks and the peanuts we'd nibbled on, he insisted on paying the bill instead of splitting it with me. "Business expense," he said, giving me a wink.

I thanked him, and we left Fouquet's together, then parted at the street corner to go our separate ways. I was still thinking about the fact that someone had wasted 120 dollars' worth—at least—of wine in order to kill (or, in the case of my grand-père, to *try* to kill) three people.

Whoever did that must have one hell of a wine cellar. . . .

Bryant had said that, and that got me to thinking. Who *did* have an extensive cellar of rare wine? It had to be someone connected to Maison de Verre.

I couldn't think of anyone with such a wine collection other than Grand-père and Oncle Rafe and the famous Tour d'Argent restaurant, which had succeeded in hiding its best wines from the Germans. I wondered if the Deschampses had an extensive wine cellar. I should have asked Bryant. He would know. It was his business, even if he'd rather drink a Coke.

But I also knew someone else who might have an idea about an extensive and special wine collection where those vintages might be found. Ignoring the fact that I wasn't supposed to be investigating or following up on leads or doing *anything* related to the cyanide wine killings, I decided it couldn't hurt to ask Monsieur Nicolas if he had any ideas. Maybe there was a rival restaurant owner who still had a stash of exemplary wine.

I could even ask Oncle Rafe, as well, although that might get me into trouble with him and Grand-père if they thought I was poking around.

I wondered whether Merveille knew how much those poisoned wines had been worth. Oncle Rafe surely did, and so maybe he'd told him during their interview . . . but even so, now I had two things I'd found out that I should make the inspecteur aware of.

I still didn't want to face him with the information.

As I walked to where my car was parked, I checked my watch. It was only four o'clock; I didn't have to meet Julia until five thirty, after the cooking demonstration was over. I sighed.

It was the right thing to do, I told myself, to drive over to Île de la Cité and give a report. I wasn't far away, and I had the time.

Maybe I'd be lucky, and Merveille wouldn't be in, and I wouldn't have to see his disapproving face.

I *was* lucky. Merveille wasn't in, and as I was finishing a note for the agent at the front desk to give to him, I got even luckier.

"Bonjour, Mademoiselle Knight! What brings you to the 36?" It was Agent Grisart, greeting me with surprise and delight.

"Oh, bonjour, *monsieur l'agent*," I said with a smile as I handed my note to the man behind the desk. "I was just leaving a note for the inspecteur. But maybe I could just tell you about it. It has to do with the cyanide wine murders."

"But, of course, mademoiselle," Grisart replied with a smile. "Perhaps you would like to sit down and tell me?" He gestured in the direction of the room we'd spoken in before.

"And how is the investigation coming about the attacks at the market on Bourgogne?" I asked as we settled into the same chairs in the same room as before.

It felt very formal for a situation where I only had some small information to share, but I didn't mind, because I hoped Grisart might spill the beans about anything else going on with the investigation. I was merely warming him up by asking about the vandalism problem.

"Ah, mademoiselle, I have not made many leads in that investigation, unfortunately. I have been helping Inspecteur Merveille. It seems more important to keep people from dying while drinking *le vin* than to worry about some broken shelves and torn awnings, *non*?" He gave me a rueful smile.

I didn't smile back. Both were important concerns, and while I certainly didn't want to see anyone else dead from drinking cyanide-laced wine, I also felt great sympathy for the market vendors. I'd meant to look around again where Monsieur Gérard had been attacked, but I'd been so excited about finding the Maison de Verre tunnel that I hadn't taken the time—and I hadn't wanted to delay Monsieur Michel any longer, either.

"I'm sure it's very challenging to be working on two different cases at one time. Are you any closer to finding out who's poisoning the wine?" I asked, then smiled, for I remembered I wanted to butter him up so I could find out what Merveille wouldn't tell me.

"Ah, *non*, mademoiselle, I don't believe so. In fact"—his face sobered—"*l'inspecteur* is not here right now, because he has been called to the scene of the body of a boy." He heaved a sigh. "A messenger boy, you see?"

"Oh *no*!" My heart plummeted. I hoped it wasn't Pierre. And if it was, that likely meant a fourth death could now be laid at the feet of this terrible and cunning killer . . . "Are you certain it was Pierre?"

He looked at me in surprise. "Pierre? Do you already know the messenger boy?"

I'd forgotten that Grisart hadn't been there when I told Merveille about it last night. "No, no, I don't know him at all. But, of course, I met him when he gave me the wine to deliver to Chef Beauchêne. And yesterday I spoke to a friend of his, who said they'd been told to work in a different area by the police, that no one wanted them loitering around, and so they went away and lost track of each other. He did tell me that the person who gave the wine to Pierre—that's the messenger boy's name—had a very large, bristly mustache and was wearing sunglasses and a very large, bulky coat. But no hat. Isn't that strange? No hat. And the mustache was probably fake."

Agent Grisart had been listening to me intently, and then with a start, he obviously realized he should be making notes, and so he began to jot them down. "And did you tell all of this to Inspecteur Merveille, mademoiselle?"

"N-no . . . I didn't." I gritted my teeth, thinking of the disapproving look on the inspecteur's face. "Not yet. That's part of what I came here to tell him today."

"*Ah, bien*. Very good. Then I won't be wasting his time to tell him what he already knows. Is there anything else, mademoiselle? This boy you spoke to, the friend . . . What was his name? Where did you find him? It is possible we might need him to identify whether the dead boy is this Pierre."

I gave him all the details from my conversation with Théo. "There's something else the inspecteur might want to know."

His brows rose. "And what is this, mademoiselle? Are you investigating these crimes, too?" He didn't look any more pleased about it than Merveille had, and I hesitated.

But I told him. I had to—they needed all the help they could get to find this murderer. "There is a tunnel in the catacombs that I think leads into Maison de Verre."

He was so astonished he forgot to write down my information. "*Qu'est-ce que c'est?* What are you saying, mademoiselle? That you have been roaming *les catacombes* by yourself?" His eyes had turned dark with concerned fury.

Suddenly reluctant, I nevertheless went on and told him what I'd discovered earlier in the catacombs. "I don't know for certain, but I think the tunnel leads to the restaurant. That could be how the killer is getting in and out of Maison de Verre."

At that, he sat back in his seat and folded his arms. I could see the skepticism and some irritation in his expression now. "Eh. And even if there is a connecting tunnel, I fail to see how that would be important, mademoiselle. It means nothing, I am sure." He must have read the stubbornness rising in my face, because he sat up and instantly became more polite, throwing up his hands. "But, of course, I will tell the inspecteur all of this. And he will determine whether it is of importance. He may see a point that I do not, you see? I am very new to this, eh? Before now I was only *un gardien de la paix*, patrolling the streets for the peace, you see. Now I have become the assistant to *l'inspecteur*." Was he actually *preening*?

"Thank you, *monsieur l'agent*," I said and rose. I had meant to also give the information for Merveille about the high cost of the wine, but I no longer felt impelled to do so in the face of Grisart's disinterest. I had written it out in the note that I left at the front desk, so Merveille would probably see it at some point.

I left the *police judiciaire* quickly and drove over to Faubourg Saint-Honoré, somehow feeling less than satisfied. But I had done my duty, and if the authorities didn't give my information any credence, then there was nothing more I could do about it.

The sky was heavy with stone-gray clouds, and snow had begun to fall. I wondered how much snow we were going to get. Most of what had fallen overnight had begun to melt, turning to slush, and every bicycle or car that sped by sent up a little biting spray of icy yuck. But now the wind had stirred up all of a sudden, and I almost lost my hat at one point. The backs of my legs—protected only by tights and boots, because even in Paris women still mostly wore skirts—became cold and damp. I was certain my nose was red, and it was definitely running a little. The sun had sunk far enough that it was only peeking through the chimneys and their pots, like a child hiding behind their fingers. It would soon be even colder.

I got to the place where I was meeting Julia early, and since it was near where I had spoken with Théo yesterday, I walked around a few blocks and looked for him. I thought I might tell him of my fears about Pierre and warn him that he might actually have to talk to *les flics*, but I didn't see Théo. At last, I made my way back to Au Pied de Cochon, ready to sit down somewhere warm. Onion soup sounded wonderful.

Moments after my *café* was served—I'd waited to order soup—Julia burst into the brasserie, scarf trailing, hat askew, with all her normal enthusiasm and energy. She was alone.

"One of them saw him," she said, waving desperately at the server for a cup of coffee. We also ordered the onion soup, of course. "And, oh, Tabs, the demonstration today was *magnifique*! I am going to make Paul and you and your messieurs the most spectacular meal tonight! The chef cooked us *rissolettes de foie gras* and a magnificent *sole à la normande* and *petites charlottes de pommes*, and I'm going to make it all again for you! We'll have to go to the market for supplies. You don't have anything planned for dinner, do you? You will come tonight, won't you? Paul and I won't be able to eat it all, and he'll want to hear everything about what you've been doing for this investigation.

"And if Maurice and Rafe don't want to leave the house . . . Who would on a night like tonight? All at once, it's *freezing* out there! I wonder how much snow we're going to get. I'll just send some of it over for them, okay? I promise you, these *rissolettes* and the sole are going to be the two best things you've *ever* put in your mouth, Tabs!"

My head was spinning, and by the time she stopped for breath and to slurp up a gulp of steaming coffee, I had agreed to come to dinner and to go to the market with her first to get the sole and see about some apples for the charlotte dish. I wasn't certain what a *rissolette* was—although I was familiar with *foie gras*—but I knew whatever it was, it would be delicious.

I did know what a charlotte was—a creamy, frothy molded cake sort of thing—and I was already imagining them topped with apples, accompanied by a cup of coffee after the meal.

"What did you say about one of them seeing him? Who saw *who*?" I demanded when Julia was just about to go off on another gushing, glorious description of what we were going to eat. Honestly, my mouth *was* already watering, and I was ecstatic that I wouldn't have to make dinner. Madame Poulet would surely wait another day, and if she wouldn't, I'd have Bet (or Blythe) make a stew with her in the morning.

Thank goodness our *soupe à l'oignon* arrived at that moment.

"Oh, right! That was the most important thing, wasn't it?" Julia said with her bubbly laugh. Her eyes were bright, and her cheeks still red from the cold. It was moments like this that I realized how lucky I was to have her as a friend.

"And where are the bridge ladies?" I asked, before taking my first sip of soup. It was the perfect treat on a snowy, blustery afternoon. I sighed with pleasure.

"Didn't I tell you?" Julia said, gesturing with her own spoon to mine. "Anyhow, the bridge ladies have a tournament tonight, and they couldn't come here with me, but I quizzed them before the demonstration started. One of them said she saw the man who gave the messenger boy the bottle of wine. She noticed him—listen to this—because *he wasn't wearing a hat*! And because his mustache was just *too* much. Too big and bristly— too big for his face or something. It was all she saw, she said. This big, bushy mustache!"

"I *knew* it was a fake. It *has* to be. Where did she see him? What else did she say? Did she notice anything about him?"

"He was light haired and bulky—but probably from his coat. She said it was big and flappy. And he was in a hurry. That's how she noticed him—she was coming down the street to the school, and he ran into her, practically knocked her over! And he didn't really apologize—he just sort of muttered, '*Excuse-moi*,' and kept going. He didn't even stop to see if she was all right, and he knocked the handbag right out of her hand!"

I felt both a pang of frustration that the woman hadn't seen more and a rush of satisfaction. This was confirmation of what

Théo had told me, and that was helpful. Now that Pierre was possibly dead (I sent up a little desperate prayer that he wasn't), there wouldn't be any chance of getting more information from him.

We finished up quickly at the brasserie, for Julia was straining at the bit to get back to her tiny *cuisine*, where she could rattle around and produce miracles, and I was more than happy to help her eat them.

We parked our cars at home, then walked to the market together. It was just after six o'clock, but that was early for Paris! It would be the perfect opportunity to ask Monsieur Nicolas if he knew of any large and rare wine collections that had made it through the Occupation.

Unfortunately, the wind had not calmed down any more here on the Left Bank, and both Julia and I were in no mood to be outside any longer than necessary. We hurried to the market, distracting ourselves with conversation as I told her about my meeting with Bryant and my conversation with Agent Grisart at the station.

By the time we got to the market, we were regretting walking instead of driving, even though it was impossible to find a place to park. But we whipped down Bourgogne's line of vendors and stalls, hardly conversing with anyone except for the required "Bonjour, madame!" or "Bonsoir, monsieur!" and the obligatory lamentations about the weather. Fortunately, most of the vendors were still open, despite the stinging cold and swirling spate of snow.

Julia had just finished with all her purchases when I heard someone calling me.

"Mademoiselle Knight! Oh, mademoiselle!"

I turned to see Madame Nanette waving at me from across the street.

"You should go on home," I said to Julia when she hesitated. She had two market bags, and they were both full. "I'll talk to her. Maybe she remembered something about the restaurant.

After, I'll go to Monsieur Nicolas's and get some wine, then bring it straight to your house. Ten, maybe fifteen minutes behind you."

It was a logical arrangement. It made sense, as it was more efficient for us to split up and for me to go on by myself.

It was an honest mistake.

CHAPTER 19

"OH, MADEMOISELLE KNIGHT, I HAVE ONLY JUST HEARD ABOUT poor Émelie Loyer!" cried Madame Nanette as I approached. "But . . . she was *murdered*! How is that possible? And her husband, too?"

She wrung her slender gloved hands and looked at me as if I had all the answers. Unfortunately, I had none of them.

"Yes, it's true," I replied. "I think she was found inside Maison de Verre."

"And so I have heard! My son, he told me all of it. He knows about it all, of course. *Ach*, I cannot believe it is true! There in rue Las Cases, where we had so many meals and so many nice times, and Jacques was so very happy there, and he was friends with Louis and Émelie . . ."

Because she seemed so upset, I felt as if I couldn't just walk away, even though I had things I had to do.

Things might have turned out differently if I had.

"Maybe you remember something that might help the authorities find out who is doing this. Someone who might have wanted everyone who owned or worked at Maison de Verre dead? Someone who is still here in Paris, who was connected to the restaurant? Maybe," I said, as a thought struck me, "you even have some old photographs of the restaurant, with the people who worked there?"

"Oh . . ." She looked at me with sudden interest, her sad eyes lifting. "I might have something like that, mademoiselle. There were some photographs from the opening, and when Colette came to dine one night . . . and I think when Édith Piaf visited, and there was once Gertrude Stein . . . Do you think that might be helpful?"

"It might," I told her, quelling a little prickle of hope. Just because the killer had a connection to Maison de Verre, that didn't mean he'd worked there. Or would be in the photos. "Would you show me?"

"Oh, *oui,* I could do that. I think. I don't know whether I can find them, but I—I know where to look. In Jacques's old trunk."

She seemed so frail and fragile that I was compelled to slip my arm through hers as we trudged off through the slush. It was getting colder, and the snow that had been portended by the stony-gray clouds was beginning to fall, blanketing the gray iciness.

Madame Nanette, it turned out, lived three blocks from the market, in a little flat on the ground floor. Its entrance led from a narrow alley peppered with other doors, garbage cans, cigarette butts and empty bottles, a bicycle with a crushed tire rim, and a tawny cat that sat on a window ledge, eyeing us distrustfully. The alley smelled faintly of garbage but more strongly of boiled cabbage and sausages—the latter of which made my stomach want to growl. I couldn't wait for Julia's *sole à la normande.*

Once inside, Madame Nanette and I brushed the snow from our boots and hats, and my hostess gestured to a small round table near the stove. The place was small, and there was no delineation between kitchen, living room, and dining area; they all spilled into one L-shaped space. There was a short hall with two doors. A bedroom and bathroom? I wondered where her son slept. Was there an upstairs?

I left my hat on and slung my coat over the back of my chair as Madame Nanette hung hers on the coatrack, which I—as was my habit—had ignored.

When she turned back, I saw that her expression had tightened into a worried mask. "What if they come for *me*, mademoiselle? What if they want to kill *me*?"

"Why would anyone want to kill you?" I asked, my attention sharpening. Did she know something after all?

"I was there—we were all there, all the time. At the restaurant, you see . . . I should sit down, mademoiselle. I am not feeling so well." She felt for a chair and plunked into it without looking. Her eyes seemed to have sunken into her face . . . or maybe it was just the shadows in the dimly lit kitchen.

"Did something happen when you were all there at the restaurant?" I asked, wondering how I was going to encourage her to get up and look for those photos now that she seemed to be breaking down.

"No . . . no . . . I don't know. It's just that they're all dead—Beauchêne too!—and I, I am not. Even my husband . . ."

I sat up straight. "What happened to your husband?"

"He died. In August, it was. It was a lump in his neck, you see," she said, gesturing weakly to her own throat. "Cancer. They couldn't save him."

I sagged back a little. "*He* wasn't murdered."

"No, no, no, of course not," Madame Nanette said. "But now everyone else is gone. Why?"

I felt a tug of impatience. This roundabout conversation wasn't doing either of us any good. I wanted to look at some photographs or leave, but I still felt a little badly about abandoning her while she was upset. She seemed genuinely frightened. "Will your son be home soon?" Maybe he could attend to her.

"No. Oh, I don't know. He works the unusual hours, you see. Of course you know." She smiled weakly. "Maybe some coffee, yes? Would you like some coffee?"

"Yes, thank you," I said. "Would you like me to help you look for the photographs?"

"Ah, *oui* . . . but let me put the kettle on." She turned on an overhead light. It was dim, but it took away some of the dreariness in the little flat.

As she fussed with a kettle, filling it from a slowly trickling faucet that at least *did* spit out water, I looked around the flat. There were two framed photographs sitting on the fireplace mantel, and I rose to take a better look. In mystery novels, the detective would often find a clue in pictures, recognizing a suspect or seeing a new face that would lead them off on a trail of clues. Regardless, I was feeling antsy and reasoned that if I was standing, I could leave more easily than if I wasn't, coffee or no coffee.

It was getting late, and I still had to get the wine from Monsieur Nicolas.

The photographs were pictures of Nanette's family—she and her husband on their wedding day in one, and the two of them with three young boys in the other. No help there, even though I scrutinized the photo of Nanette and her deceased Jacques. There was something about him that seemed familiar.

But as I turned to go back into the kitchen, my attention fell on the rack where Madame Nanette had hung her coat.

There was another coat hanging there—a heavy, bulky, dark men's coat. That in itself was unremarkable, but it was the pair of shades sticking up out of the breast pocket that caught my attention. A little skitter rushed over my shoulders, and my belly did a funny little flip.

A lot of people had sunglasses.

And then, as I let my attention slide down over the dark, heavy coat, I noticed something else that made my hair stand on end.

It was poking from a side pocket, where one might stuff a pair of gloves: a pale, bristly sort of item that looked almost like part of the fur trim on a glove.

But it wasn't a glove.

It was a false mustache.

My heart surged into my throat as my belly did that weird, nauseating flip when something awful happens.

I glanced toward the kitchen, where Madame Nanette was busy grinding coffee beans. Her back was to me, and I took note of how tall she was. Slender, but tall.

Tall enough to be mistaken for a man—especially if she were wrapped in a bulky coat.

And she was making *coffee.*

Something for me to drink . . . something that could easily deliver cyanide.

Now my hands went numb.

Madame Nanette? A killer?

My brain scrambled, trying to make sense of everything, but it couldn't. I didn't understand.

All I knew was that I was in the flat of a possible murderer and she was making coffee for me.

Had she exaggerated her weakness, her fears, in order to manipulate me here so she could poison me, too?

I needed to leave.

"Ah, madame, I've just realized how late it is," I said, already shrugging into my coat. I kept my eyes fastened on her. She couldn't poison me now, but she was in the kitchen, and surely, there were knives about. "Madame Child is expecting me. Thank you for the coffee, but I'm going to have to be leaving now."

She turned from the stove. "But, *non*, mademoiselle! I've just made the coffee, and I was going to find those photographs for you." She seemed genuinely disappointed.

If I were stupid—which I was not—I would have said something casual about the coat hanging there, to try and see what her reaction would be that I had noticed it.

But I was not stupid.

I was leaving, and I would call Merveille's office the minute I got home.

I pulled on my gloves as I started toward the door. My heart was racing; my knees shook. . . . Was she going to try to stop me?

She didn't. "Ah, well, mademoiselle," she said, looking at me with confusion and a little sadness. "Bonsoir. I will—I will look for those photographs, then, and perhaps I will see you at the market tomorrow. Anyway, my son will, I hope, be home soon."

"*Oui, oui,* of course," I said, reaching for the doorknob. "*Merci. Bonne nuit, madame.*"

I didn't breathe until I stepped out into the snowy evening.

My hands were still shaky, but now that I was outside in the little alley, my heart rate was getting back to normal. Had I completely overreacted?

No.

I hunched against a sudden swirl of snow that had been caught up in a little vortex in the narrow alley, and soon came out onto rue de Grenelle. Here it wasn't so windy and blustery, and even though it wasn't quite dark, the streetlights had come on, and hardly anyone was left on the sidewalks. I didn't mind the little kisses of snowflakes on my cheeks as I hurried along the street, passing only a few stragglers—one with a dog, who was clearly out only to do his business—on their way to their warm and dry homes.

As I turned onto Bourgogne, I heaved a sigh of relief. I was safe, and I was pretty sure I'd solved the murders. I felt as if I was floating on air as I tramped through the fallen snow. I couldn't wait to tell Merveille. I only had to get to Monsieur Nicolas's before he closed for the evening, and then—

"Mademoiselle Knight!"

I heard my name and looked over, suddenly even more relieved. "Agent Grisart! Bonsoir! What are you doing over here?" What *excellent* timing.

Grisart crossed the *rue* to meet me, dodging between the only two cars on the road. His eyes smiled from beneath the brim of his képi hat as he reached my side. "Why, I'm going home, of course. And what are you doing out so late in this snow, mademoiselle?"

"I've just come from the home of a woman named Nanette, the woman whose husband worked at Maison de Verre. She lives in rue de Martignac." I didn't know whether Agent Grisart had gotten that information from Merveille or not. "And now I have more information for *monsieur l'inspecteur.* I've learned something very interesting. I saw that she has a coat hanging there, with a f-false . . ."

My voice trailed off. Just as the words were coming from my mouth, I understood what a grave mistake I'd made.

For all at once—and far too late—I realized something very important.

Agent Grisart had been at both Le Cordon Bleu and at the Deschampses' house.

And he was Madame Nanette's son.

CHAPTER 20

"WHAT IS THIS, MADEMOISELLE?" GRISART ASKED. "YOU HAVE found what?"

It was getting too dark for me to really see his eyes, but his voice had changed to something less . . . friendly.

"Oh, it is nothing," I said, stepping back. "I . . . I was on my way to Monsieur Nicolas's *cave*—"

But Grisart was too fast for me. One moment I was edging away, and the next, I slipped—due to a sudden, sharp, and well-placed shove—and fell to the ground. I landed on my butt in the fresh snow as my purse slipped off my arm.

The wind was knocked out of me, and my palm ached where I'd tried to catch myself, but before I could do or say anything, Grisart yanked me to my feet. His hand was surprisingly strong on my wrist, and before I could try and spin away, an arm came tightly around my middle and he pulled me up against his side. Something nudged me, then slipped across my middle and through the opening of my coat, nosing between two buttons.

"I would not move or cry out, mademoiselle," he said. "It may be a small blade, but it is sharp, and I am strong, you see?" To punctuate this warning, he prodded me with the weapon right in my belly.

My mind went blank for a moment, and my vision closed around me into only a pinprick of light. I felt as if I was suddenly in a dark tunnel.

I was helpless. And in mortal danger.

There were very few people around, and the ones who might see us would only notice an innocent couple walking down the street, his arm around her, both huddled together against the falling snow.

"What . . . ?" I began before my voice dried up.

"Come along, mademoiselle. I want to show you something."

I didn't like the sound of that.

By now my brain had unfrozen a little. I thought about pretending to slip and fall again, hoping I could extricate myself that way. I even thought about trying to pull away suddenly, hoping the knife would slip free and be unable to penetrate my coat.

But he must have felt me tense up, for he poked me again with the knife tip. This time, I felt the sting as it cut my skin through my blouse. My belly trembled.

"No, mademoiselle, that is not a good idea. You will come with me, and then I will decide what to do so that the good inspecteur does not discover what has been happening, understand? Now, walk with me, or I will cut you again."

The man I had thought of as young and too gregarious to be a good police officer—and honestly, he *wasn't* that good of a police officer if he was going around killing people—had metamorphosed into a hard-faced, implacable individual. Most of his change of demeanor was probably due to the knife beneath my coat, but it didn't matter. He meant business, and I was at his mercy.

But the reminder of Merveille gave me a thought . . . and a bit of hope.

Surely, when I didn't arrive at Julia's house—she was probably already wondering where I was, at least, if she wasn't too wrapped up in making *sole à la normande* and *charlottes de pommes*—she'd begin to worry. We both knew that the killer was frequenting Maison de Verre, which was right near the market. If I didn't show, Julia would put two and two together, wouldn't she? Especially since she'd last seen me going off with Madame Nanette, someone who we both knew was connected to Maison de Verre.

And then, hopefully, Julia would call Merveille. And—if Merveille even got the message—surely, he'd come storming over to rue de Bourgogne in order to lecture me about getting involved in a murder investigation.

There were a lot of maybes and ifs in that stream of thought, but that was all I had right now. It was all I could cling to as Grisart propelled me through the growing darkness toward rue Las Cases.

But, as we'd said back home, it was time to listen to Johnny Mercer and "Ac-Cent-Tchu-Ate the Positive."

Because what else did I have besides hope and my own ingenuity?

I had plenty of both, but would they be enough when faced with a man who'd killed four people? I'd never been in a situation like this before—well, not since the recent murder investigation I'd been caught up in, but that had been completely different.

Once he got the message, how would Merveille know what to do? Where to find me?

Your boots, mademoiselle. They have a distinctive sole.

A new surge of hope washed over me as I remembered his dry comment in the kitchen.

There was fresh snow, and if I left some good prints, maybe he'd be able to use them to trail me. The snow had mostly stopped. As long as it didn't start up again . . .

And, of course, that depended on where Grisart was taking me.

"Where are you taking me?" I tried to think of a way to delay the inevitable, even as I started to pay attention to where I put my feet, looking for untouched snow near the edge of the sidewalk.

Grisart had lost his képi during our little altercation, so his eyes were unshadowed, and with the aid of a streetlight, I could see an unpleasant glitter in them. "You seemed so interested in the catacombs, mademoiselle, I thought you might like to see them again." His breath was hot against my cheek, and he sounded a little out of breath. Was it from nerves or excitement or merely from the effort of rushing me along while gripping me in such an uncomfortable position?

A new wave of fear swept over me as his words sank in. He was taking me to the catacombs? Those winding, eerie, death-filled, *endless* ink-black passages . . .

No one would ever find me down there. He could hide me anywhere and—

I stopped that thought dead in its tracks. I couldn't allow myself to freeze with terror; I had to think of a way out of this situation. But as we started down rue Las Cases, approaching the narrow alley that led to the back door of Maison de Verre, I became a little breathless with fear. Once we went inside, there would be no one to hear me scream. No one to see me.

This was serious.

There was a very good chance I was going to die.

I thought about screaming then, but that knife was so close to my belly, I didn't want to chance it. One plunge into my abdomen, and I'd be dead before any help could come. Everyone was in their homes; I doubted anyone would even hear me.

There *would* be another chance, I told myself, even as he maneuvered me into the alley. I watched my footsteps, still trying to make clear prints for Merveille.

Maybe when Grisart retrieved the key from the ledge over the door, I could twist away and make my escape.

But when we got to the stoop that led to the old restaurant's back door, he didn't have to reach up or otherwise contort himself to get the key. He pulled it from his pocket.

He kept his knife hand tightly across my abdomen and my body pulled up against his torso as he unlocked the door. He propelled me inside.

The door closed behind us, and we were in the silent, musty darkness.

In the same place he'd killed Émelie Loyer.

My hands were clammy, and I'd gone light-headed. My heart thudded up in my throat. I felt as if I were choking.

Grisart used my momentary paralysis to take me by surprise with smooth, sudden moves: he pulled the knife free from my coat and at the same time spun and tripped me. I fell forward, landing full on my hands on the dusty, dirty floor of Maison de Verre as my hat tumbled to the ground. I left it there and rolled over just as he yanked me to my feet. This time, he was holding a pair of handcuffs.

As he briskly fitted them onto my wrists in front of me, I realized that he probably wasn't going to kill me quite yet, for why handcuff me if he was going to stab me? And I felt a little glimmer of optimism laced with desperation.

"What now, Grisart?" I asked, trying not to sound too provoking.

"Sit," he said and shoved me toward one of the booths.

A cloud of dust poofed up when I landed on it, and I bumped my elbow on the table. He sat down across from me, and I was mollified to see that he was panting a little himself. He extricated a pack of Gauloises from his pocket. With what looked like a slightly unsteady hand, he lit one and took a deep drag.

"How did you know?" he asked, spewing smoke at me.

So we were going to have a conversation? I liked that idea for a number of reasons: first, I had questions I wanted answers to, and second, it implied he had questions, too, and he probably wouldn't kill me until he had his answers as well.

Delay, delay, delay, I told myself and tried not to cough at the smoke he was blowing toward me.

"About which part?" I asked.

"The wine in the tunnels."

I managed to hide my surprise, but barely. That was the missing piece . . . the part I had been on the cusp of realizing when I discovered the tunnel to Maison de Verre.

The wine in the tunnels.

I shrugged in Grisart's direction as I scrambled for a way to respond without revealing my ignorance. "It was obvious, really," I said. "You were using wine as a murder weapon. You had to get it from somewhere."

"Merveille hasn't put it together," he said with a sneer, sucking on his cigarette. "He's touted as the most accomplished detective at the 36—the modern Vidocq, the French Sherlock, the heir apparent to Devré—and here I am, his new assistant, always one step ahead of him, making a *fool* of him . . . and a *girl* putting the pieces in place before he does. *L'idiot.*"

"How did you know about it? The wine," I said, ignoring his backhanded compliment and blatant disregard for his superior's intelligence. I suspected Merveille knew far more than Grisart was giving him credit for.

At least, I hoped he did.

"You were very clever to use such a tool to deliver the cyanide. Who could resist an eighteen seventy-one Chateau d'Yquem? Or an eighteen ninety-three Clos de la Rougeotte?"

Grisart nodded. "I knew it would work . . . although it didn't every time, did it? Why didn't Maurice Saint-Léger die?" His brows drew together. "He and his disgusting *fairy* friend were meant to die together."

"Along with me," I said suggestively, pushing away the haze of red that threatened my vision. I could have punched him—or worse—for that sneering "fairy" comment alone. "You wouldn't have minded if I had joined them."

"Ah, well, you dying would have been a definite loss," he replied with a leer that made the blood in my veins go icy. "But I was willing to risk it. And since it didn't work, and here we are . . ." He shrugged easily and blew more smoke at me.

My stomach roiled in a way it hadn't when I thought he was only going to kill me. Swallowing hard, I rallied, reasoning that the longer I could keep him talking, the longer it would be until . . . he did something else. I hoped. "How did *you* know about the wine?"

I still wasn't completely clear on the details of what we were talking about, but I was starting to have an inkling. If there was wine in the catacombs, then either it had been hidden *from* the Nazis or it had been hidden *by* the Nazis. And somehow Grisart had found it.

Grisart pulled a crinkled piece of paper from his pocket. I recognized it right away: it was the larger part from the scrap I'd found on the floor beneath the table where Émelie Loyer had died here in Maison de Verre. I suppressed a shudder. I didn't want mine to be the second body found here in less than two days. Suddenly, the dusty, musty expanse of the restaurant felt cloying and tomblike.

"My father," he replied. "The loyal and misguided maître d' of Maison de Verre. He drew this for me before he died."

"A map of some of the catacombs," I said, reaching for it with my manacled hands. The metal scraped over the top of the table as I laid out the paper. Yesterday I had sketched a rudimentary copy of what was on the scrap and stuffed it in my purse, which was currently lying on the street, where Grisart attacked me tonight. But I could see where the two pieces of paper connected, and remembered the part that was missing now that I looked at the larger piece.

"But it's wrong," he said, snatching the paper away from me before I had a good look. "It took me *months* to realize it was wrong. He was ill when he drew it—dying—and he remembered it wrong! And I wanted to make certain he didn't tell Maman about it. I should have waited until I found it before I—" Our eyes met, and I felt another squiggle of ugliness. He shrugged. "I wasn't certain whether the cyanide was still potent."

"You killed your father?"

He spread his hands, smoke following the gesture in an S curve, and grimaced. "He was already dying, mademoiselle. I only helped him on his way. Put him out of his pain, you see?"

Grisart was lucky my hands were manacled, or I might have struck out at him. What a horribly evil person he was. "Your *mère*—Nanette—she didn't know about the wine?"

"She didn't know," he replied. "Papa never told her about it.

He claimed she couldn't keep a secret, that she would gossip about it all, and then the Nazis would hear about it and punish them all."

So the wine had been hidden *from* the Nazis? But Grand-père had told me the cache from Maison de Verre had been found by the Germans . . .

Was this a different cache of wine? Where was it from?

"How did you get your father to tell you, then?" I asked. "How did you even know about it?"

"I overheard Papa one day talking to Beauchêne. He'd telephoned when he heard Papa was dying. I didn't realize what it meant at the time. '*La deuxième cave,*' he'd called it." Grisart shrugged. He seemed relaxed—almost enjoying our conversation. I wasn't certain what to make of that.

Why were we just sitting here? Was he waiting for something?

I realized I shouldn't be impatient for whatever was to come next. "So you asked your father about the second wine cellar, and he drew you a map to it."

"*Oui.* And as I said, I couldn't find it at first. The map was— *pouah!* It was very wrong. I didn't know there was a connection between the restaurant and the catacombs. He didn't *tell* me about that. I wasted much time wandering around down there over the months."

Suddenly I sat up straight. "Are you the one who attacked Monsieur Gérard? The mead maker?"

Grisart shrugged. "He might see something. I didn't want him to notice me, you see. Or any of them. There are some who go down into *les catacombes* . . . I thought I might dissuade them from doing so, you see?"

"So you were causing the vandalism, ruining their carts, trying to keep the merchants from going around down there while you were . . . what? Moving the wine?"

"*Oui.* Once I found it, I couldn't have anyone see it, or me, you understand."

"And you pretended to investigate and even helped us with

Monsieur Gérard," I said, my anger rising. What a horrible person he was, in so many ways.

"But of course. It helped me, you see, so that I knew what was happening. I didn't *hurt* the merchants . . . well, not so very much, except for the mead maker. But he is not *dead*, so . . ." He spread his hands, projecting his innocence.

It was all I could do to hide my loathing for him. "Why did you have to kill Beauchêne and Loyer?"

"Do you have any idea how much money that wine is worth?" Grisart said, leaning across the table so I felt the heat of his breath. "I don't want to live in a hovel like my maman the rest of my life. I *won't*. And I won't be a *flic*. I will be a rich man when I sell all that wine—very carefully, of course. But it is *mine*. There is no one else left, you see? Do you have any idea how much those bottles are worth? *Thousands* of francs. Tens of thousands, perhaps, when the story is told about how the Germans were outwitted to save *le vin*."

"So Beauchêne and Loyer were killed so you didn't have to share it with them?"

"*Mais bien sûr.*"

"What about Émelie Loyer?" I asked.

Grisart's expression changed, and he moved, sitting back in his chair, as he stabbed out the last of his cigarette on the table. A little smile played beneath his sparse mustache that, I realized, must have been hidden beneath the bushy false one he'd worn when he gave the wine to Pierre to deliver. "Ah, yes, you were the one who found *pauvre* Émelie, weren't you? Snooping around here, as you were. It was good for me that you reported it, you see, because I did not realize how close you'd come to finding out everything.

"But then, after we talked, I knew I must watch you, mademoiselle. Until that time, I thought you were only a silly girl who had the bad luck of seeing both deaths as they happened. But then I began to see. And it helped me that you kept running to Merveille to tell him everything you knew."

With a sick feeling, I realized how well he'd played his role. "And so you didn't tell Merveille everything I told you, did you? Perhaps parts of it, but not anything important." My mind was racing as I tried to remember what I'd told the inspecteur and what I had told Grisart . . . and what I'd written on the note I left at the front desk of the *police judiciaire*.

With a horrid drop of my stomach, I realized that I had told Grisart, not Merveille, about my conversation with Théo regarding Pierre . . . about how the original messenger boy had been chased out of his area and had gone to find work over by la Vendôme. Had Grisart hunted him down there, too?

"Did you kill Pierre, too?—the messenger boy—because I told you about him working at la Vendôme?" I asked before I realized he was probably already dead before I told Grisart, for Merveille had already been called out to see the body while I was speaking with Grisart.

My heart stopped. Théo . . . he knew everything, too, and I had told Grisart about him, as well.

Grisart shrugged, a little smile playing over his face. "What do you mean? A street urchin was found dead? There is much violence and death on the streets, *non*?"

"Did you use cyanide on him, too?" I could see it easily—a young boy lured to his death when a man offered him a beer or even a hot chocolate.

Laced with cyanide.

He traced a finger through the dust on the table, still smiling to himself.

"Thé—" I caught myself. "The other boy said a policeman had chased them away from the corner where they waited for work. You did that, didn't you? And when you found out where he'd gone, you found him yourself . . . and made certain he couldn't talk."

Now I felt like I was going to vomit, for surely Théo would be next.

Grisart shrugged. He seemed far too pleased with himself. His hubris made me even more nervous, especially since we were just sitting here talking. Was he waiting for something? *Someone?*

But who? I was pretty sure he wasn't working with anyone else, now that Madame Loyer was dead.

He seemed to read my mind. "She was helping me, you see. Émelie. She was here at the restaurant when they devised the plan to hide the expensive and rare wines—and some that were only just excellent or even good, you see—in the two places. One place for the Germans to find—not too difficult, you see? But not too easy, also, of course, or they wouldn't be fooled. And then the second cache—the larger one, with the better wines, *bien sûr*. But it would be a complete collection—for the restaurant when she was reopened. Émelie decided which wines were to go in which *cave*. Of course, Maison de Verre was not as renowned for its *cave à vins* as d'Argent, and so it was much easier for them to hide most of the very good ones."

I nodded internally. Things were making sense now. "And you and Émelie—you were lovers, and so she trusted you, *non?*"

"But of course. I went to see her after my papa died—she came to the funeral, you see. And then we became the very close *friends*. I was a policeman, you see, and she liked that very much." He leered again. "She thought it was very helpful—and, of course, it was. She remembered me from when I was young, and I . . . well, Émelie Loyer is a difficult woman to forget. Even when one is so young as fourteen or fifteen." He smiled at the memory.

"I made certain I would be there on the street nearby, in my uniform, of course, when Beauchêne died so I could be called to the scene." His eyes gleamed. "But Èmilie . . . she was not so happy when her husband announced he would come back here to Paris, and so it was decided he and Beauchêne . . . Ah, well, we didn't need them, and we didn't want to share the wine with them. Émelie, she knew that the first thing Loyer would do was to get the wine and use it for the reopening of the restaurant. And so." He shrugged with the insouciance of a man who readily justified murder.

"And so you killed both of them—Beauchêne and Loyer."

"Ah, but I did not say that, mademoiselle, did I?" His eyes fairly twinkled at me, and for a moment, I almost believed him. But then I remembered I'd accused him earlier, and he hadn't denied it.

He went on, "Perhaps it was Madame Loyer who sent the wines poisoned with the cyanide, *non?*"

"But you poisoned *her*," I said.

"Ah, but no, no, no, mademoiselle. Not intentionally! It was she who poured *le vin*—it was over there, you see, *non?*" He gestured lazily behind him toward another table. "And when I lifted the glass to sip, did I perhaps smell the scent of the almonds? And then did I know of her betrayal? And then did I exchange the glasses so that she was the one to drink of the poison?"

I watched him closely. He could be telling the truth . . . but I didn't believe him for one moment. No, I did not.

But I could see how he would explain it to Merveille. His innocence . . . getting caught up with an attractive woman whom he'd known since he was younger, being lured into such a plot . . . and then saving himself when he realized at the last minute what was happening.

Merveille could easily believe him. Especially if Grisart explained how he hadn't known that Madame Loyer had put cyanide in the wine, and when he confronted her, she tried to kill him, here in the restaurant, and he managed to switch glasses.

It was very believable. Especially since I was the only person who knew of the connection between Émelie Loyer and François Grisart.

"And now, mademoiselle, I have one more question for you . . ." He leaned on the table, looking sharply at me. "What does Maurice Saint-Léger know about all of this, hmm? What does he remember about *le vin* from Maison de Verre? Surely, he is the one who has told you about it."

I shook my head vehemently. "The only thing he told me about Maison de Verre was that the Germans found the wine that had been hidden."

Grisart pursed his lips and eyed me closely. "Is that so?"

"Yes. It's true. He doesn't know anything about the second wine collection."

"You are lying to me, mademoiselle. I don't believe you. Saint-Léger, he was there all of the time. Even I remember seeing him and his fairy friend draped all over each other in the booths, laughing and talking with my father. And Loyer, too—going into the kitchen, even, to speak to him or waiting until the last have gone and Loyer coming out to sit with him and Fautrier to drink. He must have known. And that, I think, is how *you* have known all of this."

A cold, cold fear began to work its way down my spine.

If he thought Grand-père and Oncle Rafe knew about the second cache of wine, he'd need to kill them, too.

"I tell you, they don't know about it," I said, hating that I was pleading. "They *don't* know. I swear it. They—they recognized the silk wrappings on the wine bottles," I went on, gesturing wildly with my cuffed hands toward the walls, "but that is it . . . and they have never mentioned you, the son of Jacques."

He looked at me for a long moment as my eyes filled with desperate tears.

"I think that it is time to go, *non?*" He rose, and it was all I could do not to keep begging. I *knew* what was next. It wasn't me so much I was worried about—it was what he would do to Grand-père and Oncle Rafe.

"Please," I said. "They don't know anything. I swear it. Don't . . . don't hurt them."

His mouth was set in a cruel line. "How devoted you are, mademoiselle. It's too bad you are such a poor liar. Now come."

My hair stood on end all over my body, and despite my heavy winter coat, I felt an ugly chill sweep over me. "Where are we going? What are you doing to do?"

He yanked me from my seat and shoved me ahead of him. I managed to keep my balance this time, but my knees nearly gave way when he answered me.

"Why, mademoiselle, as I have already told you, we are going to *les catacombes*. I believe you will be most comfortable there until . . ."

He never finished the sentence.

But he didn't need to.

CHAPTER 21

*T*HROUGH A FOG OF PARALYZING TERROR, I SOMEHOW MADE MY LEGS move as Grisart maneuvered me out of the main area of the restaurant toward the back. I was vaguely aware that we were going toward the kitchen, where I had not had the opportunity to look around when I was here previously.

It was small comfort to me to realize that I'd been right about there being a connection between the restaurant and the catacombs. All I could think about was what Grisart was going to do about Grand-père and Oncle Rafe.

I could hardly force my body to move; I was so frozen with fear and nausea.

If only I'd never gone to Madame Nanette's and seen that coat . . .

But it was too late for regrets.

All I had left was my brain. . . .

And the Swiss Army knife in my pocket.

That, and the fact that Grisart had foolishly handcuffed me in the front (just another example of what a poor cop he was), gave me a little flare of hope.

I didn't know what he had planned for me, but I didn't think—or at least I hoped—he would take the time to kill me now and then go back to my grandfather and uncle's house.

What was he going to do to *them*?

Would he just kill them right there at home? He couldn't use cyanide; Grand-père would smell it (thank goodness).

Should I tell Grisart all of this or let him make the mistake on his own? If I told him, would he just go prepared with another way to kill them—a gun? A knife? His police-issued billy club?

My elderly messieurs would be no match for this desperate young man if he was intent on hurting them.

My heart squeezed in my chest, and I fought to remain calm. The best thing that could happen, I thought, was for me to delay Grisart as long as possible . . . hoping that Merveille would put everything together and somehow find us.

I shook myself out of my fear and forced myself to pay attention to my surroundings. If I somehow made an escape, I needed to know how to get back out of here.

There was a door in the restaurant's kitchen, and it led into a pantry. Inside the pantry was a set of shelves and their dusty, grimy cans and canisters that all had been moved out of the way—previously a camouflage to trick the Germans, I was sure.

Now where a wall had been behind the shelves was an opening in the brickwork that led to unrelieved darkness.

Grisart gave me a knowing look as he turned on his flashlight—

Flashlight! With a start, I suddenly remembered I'd put my own little flashlight into my coat pocket earlier today, when I went into the catacombs with Monsieur Michel!

Sure enough, when I bumped one of my arms against my side, I felt the shape of the small metal cylinder in my pocket.

That was *something.* At least I wouldn't be left in the dark if the worst happened. . . .

Grisart propelled me none too gently through the opening in the back of the pantry, and I saw a rat skitter out of the way.

"I see you don't mind the rodents, do you, mademoiselle? That is quite convenient, as they will be your only companions for a time," Grisart said with a chuckle, unknowingly giving me another burst of hope.

So he wasn't planning to kill me right away.

That was probably good.

"You were wearing a disguise when you gave the bottle of wine to Pierre to deliver," I said as we tramped into a tunnel that was comfortably high enough that neither of us had to duck. I drew in the moist, cool air in long, deep breaths. It made me feel less anxious when I breathed that way. "A heavy coat, a pair of sunglasses, and a big, bristly mustache. But no hat? That made you more memorable to the people who saw you."

He made a sound of disgust. "*Oui*. It was my fault—the hat I meant to bring fell away, and I didn't have it with the coat, after all. I certainly couldn't wear my képi hat, now could I?" He chuckled, and the sound echoed a little in the tunnel. "But there is no one else who remembers that besides you and the friend of the delivery boy. And I will find him, too."

"That will be a lot of dead bodies for a cache of wine," I said dryly. My paralyzing fear had begun to ebb, and my mind was working.

"Ah, well, one must do what one must. If you had not been so nosy, mademoiselle, perhaps there would not be quite so many corpses, *non*?"

We'd reached the heavy metal door that I'd seen from the other side in the catacombs.

"Was this door always here, before the Germans came? Or did your father and Loyer put it in place?" I asked, thinking what fast work that must have been.

"It was here. A bomb shelter, you see, for during the other war. But when they thought it was certain the Germans were coming, Papa and the others quickly moved the wine and built the shelves over the new brick wall to hide the entrance. And there was some dust—*much* dust—that was put on the cans and the shelves to make them camouflaged. You see, the Germans, they were not so smart. And now I will be very rich, because no one knows about it."

We were well into the catacombs by now. I can't say that it looked exactly *familiar* to me, but having been down there twice in the last two days, I felt less unsettled than if I had never been. And the knowledge that I wasn't without resources—my multi-tool knife, my flashlight, my brain—made me even more . . . well, not exactly confident, but hopeful, at least.

"Why did you take the gift tag from the bottle at Le Cordon Bleu?" I said. "That was what made me realize it was you." It was a very tardy realization, to be fair, but I *had* realized it . . . just a little too late not to have gotten myself into this situation. "You were the only person who was at both murders."

"Ah," he said, sounding proud of himself, and likely not realizing he had just confirmed for me that he *was* the one to kill Beauchêne. "Yes, of course. I took off the mustache and the heavy coat and put my uniform hat back on, and made certain I was there when Madame Brassart came out to look for a police agent. It was simple to slip the tag into my pocket."

"What was on it that you didn't want someone to see? Fingerprints?"

"Ah, no, I was not worried about that at all, for I would be looking at any fingerprints that might be taken," he replied loftily. "But the note . . . I made it seem that it was written from Émelie Loyer, you see, so that Beauchêne would drink the wine, and I didn't want Merveille to make the connection to Maison de Verre or to Émelie. And so I had to take the tag."

"The bottle you sent to Monsieur Loyer—that was with a tag supposedly written by Beauchêne. That was awfully risky—what if he had realized Chef Beauchêne had been poisoned by a bottle of wine the day before?"

"That," said Grisart with glee in his voice, "was a lightning bolt of an idea for me. It was I who spoke with Louis Loyer after the death of his friend the day before . . . a routine interview, you see, one of many that Merveille and I did with all of Beauchêne's friends and family. But, of course, I did not tell him of the details of his friend's death, knowing that he would soon receive the same gift.

"It was very convenient that I was able to convince Merveille to allow me to assist him with this investigation," he went on. "But I have been *un très bon flic* since returning here to Paris from Vichy. I didn't know that I was going to stumble upon a fortune in wine instead."

"Your mother never mentioned that you were a police agent," I said.

"Oh, no, that she would not do, I think," he replied, pushing me to the right at an intersection, the fourth. I'd been chanting in my head, *Left, left, right*, in order to remember the way. Now I would think, *Left, left, right, right*. Of course, I would have to reverse it on the way out. . . .

"Maman is perhaps a bit embarrassed that I have become a police officer. I was in Vichy, you see, during the war. And it was there I became trained as a police officer."

I understood. The Vichy government, led by Marshal Pétain, was the one that had allowed the Germans to occupy France and had insisted that their countrymen collaborate with them. It seemed that Grisart had never truly been a loyal Parisian, and so it was maybe no surprise he didn't mind destroying such rare and beautiful wine in an effort to become rich.

For was that not what the collaborators had done? Destroyed their own countrymen and nation—and its pride—in order to improve their lot?

It was no wonder Nanette chose not to mention any details about her son other than that he took care of her. I wondered if she had any idea what kind of man he really was.

"And here we are, mademoiselle."

My breath caught when I saw the painted arrows on the wall.

And when Grisart shoved me in the direction in which they pointed, I realized I was about to get my wish.

I was going to see the German bunker.

CHAPTER 22

I DIDN'T SAY ANYTHING AS GRISART MANEUVERED ME THROUGH THE doorway into a bomb shelter that had been created by Parisians, then taken over by the Germans—the very people the French had meant the bomb shelter to protect them from.

Grisart had easily opened the heavy metal door, leading me to believe he'd been through here many times. It hadn't so much as creaked or squeaked, even when he'd turned the heavy metal wheel in the center of it.

"In we go, now, m'moiselle," Grisart said and shoved me hard— just as he'd done the previous two times we'd gone through a doorway.

Thus, I'd been expecting it, and I managed to catch myself before falling—a lucky thing, as it would have been very painful, if not fatal to my hope for escape, to land on two handcuffed wrists. As it was, I stumbled several steps in my heavy boots and ended up bumping into the stone wall, just below the stenciled sign that read: RAUCHEN VERBOTEN.

I recovered quickly, however, and looked around, leaning against the wall to catch my breath, as Grisart pushed a light switch.

I was shocked when electric light from several naked bulbs filled the room. How was it possible there was still electricity flowing here?

The illumination revealed a large, clean room with white-washed walls. Its furnishings were ruthlessly organized: a long table with a number of chairs around it sat in the middle, as if meant as a meeting place. Other chairs lined a wall. I saw a doorway that led to what appeared to be other rooms beyond, and caught a glimpse of at least two beds lined up in one of them.

In the room we were in, there were cabinets, some with sagging doors that revealed old, dusty linens, plates, cups, and other items that would be common in a home economics class. Some of the cabinets had large medical crosses painted on them. And, of course, there were swastikas everywhere.

Electrical boxes were mounted on the wall, and I could see the thick cords of wiring projecting from them. The wires climbed up and overhead, crawling across the stone ceiling like black snakes. Some of them looked newer than others—which I deduced Grisart was responsible for. They were likely a connection to the city's electrical system.

In a corner was an opening in the floor, and I realized it was an open well. Beyond, in a tiny alcove, with no privacy to speak of, was a chemical toilet. The bunker must be below the city's sewage system.

Then I saw the wine.

It had been stacked neatly along one wall, below a sign with an arrow that read NOTAUSGANG. Next to the collection of bottles was a small wheelbarrow that would fit through some, but not all, of the tunnels we'd traversed.

Grisart noticed my attention. "It will be a very arduous task to bring all of that wine to the surface, m'moiselle . . . but it will be worth it all in the end."

Inside, I was furious. If I had convinced Monsieur Michel to go with me to look at the bunker when I saw the sign earlier—was it only this morning?—I might have avoided my entire predicament. Surely, I would have figured out the plot (or most of it) when I saw the bottles—there had to be at least two thousand of them—lined up on the wall.

"Was it all hidden here in the bunker the whole time?" I asked in wonder.

"*Non*, of course not," Grisart said. "I had to bring the wine to this place in order to do an inventory, and to have Émelie do an assessment of it, you see. It was too dark and cramped where it was hidden away in the tunnel from the restaurant to see to it there, and I did not want to bring it to the restaurant. Someone might have found it. No one comes down here," he said with a nasty smile. "No one wants to be reminded of the Nazis. Only the mead maker and the mushroom grower, and they . . . they do not come *here*."

I had seen evidence of that myself with Monsieur Michel, and so I couldn't disagree. Still, Grisart had been taking a chance, leaving the wine out in the open.

"It was hidden not so far from here," he went on, pleased, I think, to have someone to whom he could brag about his accomplishments. "And I moved it. It took many days. But from here, it will be no difficulty to move it to the aboveground. There is an emergency exit from the bunker that opens beneath a bridge near Notre-Dame. It is close and only through a cellar. I will build a small lift."

I nodded absently, my eyes trailing around the room. The wine was of the least bit of interest to me, quite honestly. I was looking for an opportunity to escape . . . and for a weapon.

But when I saw the medical supplies laid out on one of the counters near the cabinets, I drew in a deep breath. *Of course.*

"That was how you put the poison into the bottles," I said, walking over to the pile of syringes, bandages, and other first aid items. "Through the cork, with a needle. As we suspected. But where did you get the cyanide—*oh*."

I'd remembered something Grisart had said earlier, when we were sitting in Maison de Verre.

I wasn't certain whether the cyanide was still potent.

"It was here—you found it here, in the bunker."

I'd mentioned it to Merveille, too. *Potassium cyanide was also in the suicide pills they gave to spies during the war. They bit down on them, released the poison, and* boom. *Instant death.*

Of course there would be a supply of potassium cyanide here, along with all the Germans' other supplies. In the event things did not go the way the Germans expected, they could do what Hitler did: fatally poison themselves, instead of allowing themselves to be captured.

"Ah, *oui*. This is an excellent hideaway with many benefits," Grisart said. "Even a generator powered by a bicycle. It still works, of course." He gestured to the lights that illuminated the space. "But I only needed that at first, until I was able to reconnect the electrical wires."

It seemed he'd thought of everything. Or, at least, the Germans had, and Grisart had simply taken advantage of their survival preparations.

"But," he said, giving me a strange smile, "you'll have no need of any such things."

My stomach lurched with nausea. I could tell this was *it*. Something was going to happen.

He advanced toward me. I thought about striking out at him; I even looked for something I could use to hit him with, but there was nothing nearby.

He had the knife in his hand again, and when he reached for me, I tried to spin out of the way, hoping to make a dash for the doorway, but I wasn't fast enough—and I was sensitive to the wicked blade he wielded.

In the end, I didn't put up much of a fight as he grabbed the chain between my two manacles and propelled me over to the long, heavy table. There was a length of rope on it, and Grisart used it to tie the chain on my handcuffs to one of the legs.

He stepped back and looked down at me. "I believe that will hold you for a time. But even if it doesn't . . ." He shrugged. "*Les catacombes* are dark and endless . . . Perhaps you would like to join the others who have been here?"

He gave me one last look—one that made my hair stand on end and my mouth go dry. "If only I had a bit more time right now, but, no, I have a call to make. You see, Agent Grisart must speak with Monsieur Saint-Léger on a follow-up interview about the special wine he was sent." His smile was a hot leer, but I didn't care. I almost wished he'd stay and do whatever . . . instead of going to Grand-père's house.

"Please," I begged, knowing he'd expect it. I had already sagged to the floor, with my knees crunched up near my wrists. I wasn't acting when I pleaded. "Please . . . Grand-père doesn't know anything. I swear it!"

"Ah, so you would rather I stay?" He licked his lips and assessed me, then abruptly pushed the light switch. The bulbs went dark, and all that was left was the glow of the flashlight he held and the sounds of his heavy breathing. An icy chill swept over me, and I felt faint. Somehow the idea of him assaulting me in the dark was worse. . . .

"I am tempted, I confess, m'moiselle . . . but time is of the essence. I must attend to your grandfather and his friend before they begin to wonder where you are and telephone Merveille."

He shined the light directly at me, blinding me for a second, then turned. The door scuffed over the floor, making the softest metal groan, and then closed behind him, and he was gone . . . leaving me in the most complete, enveloping darkness I'd ever known.

CHAPTER 23

*F*OR A MOMENT, I WAS PARALYZED. THERE IS NOTHING LIKE BEING IN utter darkness, without even the slightest gray or shadow relief.

It's beyond terrifying.

It feels as if the inky world is sucking you inside of it and smothering you at the same time. It was as quiet and dark as death.

I *was* terrified, even though I knew I had a flashlight in my pocket. My breathing became shallow and quick, and my limbs felt completely numb. Every breath I drew in—shallow and quick—was damp and cool and cutting. I could feel the cold metal of the table leg against my cheek, and I could hear *nothing*.

Nothing except my own breathing filling my ears. When I stopped for a moment, holding my breath, there was no other sound but the thudding of my heart in my ears.

Silence.

Impenetrable darkness.

Grand-père.

My paralysis snapped. I whooshed out a breath and began to work to extricate the flashlight from my coat pocket. I couldn't allow myself to delay, to freeze in terror. I had to get home to Grand-père and Oncle Rafe. I had no idea how quickly Grisart would go there—would he stop at home to see his mother first? Maybe to find out if I'd said anything to her? Would he kill her, as well? Or would he go immediately to rue de l'Université and pound on Grand-père's door?

He was a police agent; of course, my grandfather and uncle would invite him in, bring him up to the salon, offer him something to eat or drink. . . .

My body erupted with prickles of fear. I had to get out of here.

First, I tried to lift the corner of the table, using my head and shoulders, in hopes of just slipping my bound hands down and off the leg. It almost worked, but my arms weren't long enough to get under the table leg when I had it lifted.

Frustrated, I sank back to my butt on the floor and shook my head, bumping my temple against the table. I shifted my hips so I could try and get my fingers into the side pocket of my coat.

It was an awkward movement, and the pocket was large and deep, but I was eventually able to use my thigh to lift my coat, and then I shifted my hips up and to the side, and at last, I felt the flashlight slip out. It fell onto the floor next to me; I felt it land near my leg. By now, I was sweating and panting from the effort of those desperate contortions while wearing a heavy wool coat.

With the movement of my hands restricted, it took me a minute to maneuver around so I could grasp the flashlight, but at last, my fingers closed over the slender metal cylinder. Moments later, a soft, small beam of light filled the room, and I heaved a little sigh of relief.

Somehow, the light made things better, even though I'd done nothing yet to actually free myself. The next task was to get the multi-tool knife out of my skirt pocket—a difficult maneuver similar to removing my flashlight, but even worse because I was wearing the heavy coat over my skirt. But the light made me feel more optimistic, and the fact that time was ticking away made me determined.

I forced myself to go slowly . . . to think about how to move, how to shift my coat out of the way so I could get to my skirt pocket. I ended up inching my feet up the table leg, hoisting them up and onto the table, boots on the surface for leverage, as I twisted, turned, and upended my hips (all the while connected to the table leg by my handcuffs) until I felt the weight of the knife slide free from my side pocket. It got caught in the folds of my coat, but once I got back on my knees and shook it out, the knife fell to the ground. And because the flashlight was on, I saw where it fell.

Whew.

Flashlight on. Tool knife in hand. I was making progress.

I focused, trying not to imagine what was happening—where Grisart was, how quickly he would get to my house, how he would sit down with Grand-père and Oncle Rafe in the salon and join them for a cup of coffee or a whisky, and how the cyanide would get into their drinks. . . .

But Grand-père would smell it, surely, wouldn't he? And then if he smelled the bitter almonds and made any sort of indication of suspicion, then Grisart would be forced to do something more violent. . . .

I had to shove away those thoughts. I had to focus on the *now*, or there was no chance of getting there in time to save them.

Julia? Have you noticed I'm missing yet?

I thought really hard, hoping she would somehow hear me . . . even as I picked up the knife with my shackled hands and worked to pull out the little reamer tool. It was sort of like an awl—long and slender, with a slightly tapered tip.

It was an awkward movement, with my hands restricted as they were, but I finally got it free. When I held that knife in my hand, tool extended, I took a moment to be thankful for my father, who'd sometimes let me play with his handcuffs.

And being the sort of person I was—interested in how things worked and what mechanisms did, how pieces fit together—I already knew how to open a pair of handcuffs. You don't even need a key; it's really a fairly simple mechanism. And the key itself is really just a long pin, not dissimilar to the reamer on my knife. The fact that Grisart had made the fatal error of cuffing my hands in front was a gift of fate, but I probably could have freed myself if he hadn't. After all, Houdini had done it, and he wasn't trying to save his grand-père.

But with my hands in front, it didn't take much for me to fit that reamer into the tiny keyhole on one of my manacles. I had to maneuver it so that I pushed my cuffed wrist against the table leg, tightening the cuff one more notch painfully over my wrist—but I knew the feel, I knew how it worked . . . and when the moveable part of the cuff slipped out of its notch in order to go tighter, the little reamer caught the loosened mechanism, dislodged it, and *click*.

One wrist was free.

I breathed a sigh of relief. I'd been confident I could do it, but until it was actually accomplished, deep inside I'd had a lot of worries—the least of which was, What if French handcuffs were different from American handcuffs?

But they weren't. And even as I felt that rush of relief, I was already working my other wrist free.

Click.

I lurched to my feet, dropping the flashlight and knife in the process, but I quickly scooped them up. The knife went back into my skirt pocket (this entire event underscored that I would never get dressed without putting my Swiss Army knife in my pocket), and I shined the flashlight around the room. I was still looking for a weapon. When I caught up with Grisart—and I *would*! I *had* to!—I wanted to be able to hurt him, at least a little.

My attention lit on the rows of wine bottles. Hardly giving it another thought, I rushed over and snatched one up, then dashed for the door . . . suddenly terrified that I wouldn't be able to open it and I would be trapped here after all.

My heart was in my throat as I shined the flashlight over the door. There was the same ship's wheel sort of handle on this side as there was on the other. But when I tried to turn it, *it didn't move.*

My heart surged into my throat, and a wave of panic threatened to wash over me, but I drew in a deep breath. I was going to figure this out.

Keeping my panic—mostly driven by terror for Grand-père and Oncle Rafe—at bay, I carefully scrutinized the mechanism.

I heaved a sigh of relief and felt the feeling rush back into my body when I figured it out. There was a latch. I found it, lifted it, turned the wheel.

And the door opened.

I was out of the bunker and into the plain, dark, damp, twisty tunnels of the catacombs, a relief after being in the stark white, organized world of the Nazis.

I ran down the tunnel from the bunker, the bottle of wine, which I'd thrust into my pocket, bumping heavily against me. I had almost left it behind but had decided to keep it, just in case. I held it in place against my body as I rushed down the stone tunnel.

When I came to the intersection where the painted arrows were, I hesitated for a moment. I knew where I was. To the right was back to the tunnel leading to Maison de Verre. To the left was the way out via the mushroom farm and the meadery.

I took the left turn, and although every fiber of my being wanted me to *run, run, run*, I couldn't. I had to take my time to make sure I didn't make a wrong turn and get lost.

Thankfully, I'd been through here several times over the past few days, and my insatiable curiosity had had me looking at everything around me: the markings, the street plaques, the alcoves, the decorative bones. I remembered many of these landmarks, so to speak, very well.

By the time I reached the vast chamber just past the mushroom farm, I *was* running. And when I got to the silo-like shaft with its metal ladder in the wall, I was nearly sobbing with relief.

I turned off my flashlight and shoved it in the pocket without the wine and clambered up those rungs like a nimble sailor. It took some effort to push the manhole cover away, but I wasn't going to let *that* stop me now that I'd gotten this far. Once I got it slightly ajar, I was able to use my head and shoulders to heave it aside.

When I pulled myself up and I saw the film of moonlight over the floor of the crude little shack, I *did* start crying.

I'm coming, Grand-père! Oncle Rafe, I'm coming!

I stumbled out of the shack, then pelted down the alley

toward Bourgogne. It was dark except for the moon and streetlights—which were enough to light my way. The wine bumped heavily against my side, and I again thought about tossing it aside, but I didn't. I knew it would be proof of what I'd learned, for Grisart's fingerprints (and mine now) would be on it.

I ran down Bourgogne, nearly the only one on the street. I passed a man on the opposite side, but he was too tall to be Grisart, and so I kept going. The snow had stopped, and it tossed up behind me as I flew, hoping I wouldn't hit a patch of ice buried under the snow and crash.

I thought I heard someone shouting, "Mademoiselle!" but I ignored them. I *had* to get home. It was the only thing I could think. *Get home. Get home.* I chanted that in my head as I kept running up Bourgogne, nearly to the end of the market, even as I began to slow and tire, even as I knew I had more than a mile to go . . . I had to press on.

I had to get there.

"Mademoiselle!"

It was a man, and he was shouting at me, but I wasn't going to stop. My chest heaved, tears stung my eyes, I had a stitch in my side, and that stupid wine kept banging into my hip, but I didn't stop.

"Tabitha!"

That made me hitch, and I glanced over my shoulder. He was running after me.

It was Merveille.

The hitch in my stride and the fact that I'd turned to look— plus a poorly timed car driving down a cross street at the corner—slowed me enough that Merveille caught up.

"Mademoiselle! What—"

"Grand-père," I sobbed, gasping for breath, as I dashed into the street on the tail end of the car. "Oncle . . . Rafe. Gris . . . art. I . . . have to—" I couldn't breathe, could hardly form the words around my tears and desperation.

"Mademoiselle!" A strong hand grabbed me by the arm and spun me around. I tried to whip away, but he held firm and said, "This way! Come!"

The next thing I knew, he was directing me to a car sitting, thank God, thank God, right there on the street.

I dove in and tossed that stupid wine bottle to the floor. To his credit, Merveille didn't even wait for me to close the door before he started the engine and the car leaped into the street.

I sat there, leaning forward, eyes peeled out the windshield, gripping the dashboard as if it would make the car go faster, gasping and half sobbing, silently urging him to go faster, to *fly*, to *get me there in time! Please get me there in time!*

Merveille didn't speak; he navigated the car smoothly and with frightening speed around the loop at Palais Bourbon, then onto Université.

He hadn't even hit the brakes when I was opening the door, half tumbling onto the street as he shouted, "Mademoiselle!" followed by some healthy curses.

But I was already running up the steps to the house. The few minutes in the car—thank God for the car, for I would still be running up Bourgogne without it—had given me a breather.

Now I reached the front door and caught myself just before I burst in. With heaving breaths, I realized I should be more careful . . . take more care.

All I wanted to do was rush in, pound up to the salon, make certain Grand-père and Oncle Rafe were safe, but if I burst in, I would give myself away to Grisart, and who knew what he would do.

All of this went through my head at lightning speed, and so when I opened the door, I was quiet. I don't think anyone heard me, but the fact that Oscar Wilde—who heard everything—didn't rush to the top of the stairs, yapping his head off, sent a cold shiver down my spine.

Was I too late?

Oh, God, was I too late?

Had something happened to Monsieur Wilde and—

I couldn't think it.

Panting, trying to keep my sobs at bay, I realized I'd left my only weapon—the bottle of wine—in Merveille's car. I wasn't going to look for another one.

As I started up the steps, quickly and quietly, I pulled out my Swiss Army knife and opened it to the corkscrew. That could do some damage.

I heard a car door slam out front and a voice from upstairs.

"Ah, that was quick." It sounded like my grand-père. He didn't sound as if he was under any duress. . . .

My heart leaped, and I rushed the rest of the way up to the salon.

"Grand-père! Oncle Rafe!" I cried when I saw that they were alive and well.

And then I saw Grisart, sitting there in a chair across from them. He wasn't moving and seemed to be making no threat, but his eyes shot wide open when he saw me, an exclamation strangling in his throat.

My heart surged up, choking me, and I cried, "He's a killer! Grand-père, don't drink anything! He's the one who—"

"But of course, *ma mie*," said Grand-père, with an easy gesture of his cigarette. "We already know that."

I heard the pounding of feet coming up the stairs just as I looked over and saw Oncle Rafe. He was smiling at me, holding a whisky casually in one hand and a pistol in the other.

. . . And it was pointed at Agent Grisart.

CHAPTER 24

*I*COLLAPSED ONTO THE SOFA AND BURST INTO TEARS . . . JUST AS MER-veille made his appearance from the top of the stairs.

But I didn't care. I was shaking and sobbing and smiling, nearly laughing, through my tears. And I could finally shrug out of my heavy coat.

They were safe. My messieurs were safe.

The next few minutes were a blur of voices and activity. Every-one was talking. Grisart was handcuffed (with his hands in the back, of course). Someone—Merveille—pressed a generous glass of whisky into my still-shaking hand. And Madame X had some-how swallowed her pride enough to come and sit in my lap.

I found I needed that most of all.

I needed to feel the warmth and life of something beautiful and comforting, and I knew if I hugged my grandfather or uncle, I'd just start bawling and sniveling again. When Madame began to purr under my hand, I was finally able to fully relax.

"Where's Oscar Wilde?" I said, suddenly anxious again.

It was the first time I'd spoken since my shrieked accusation as I burst into the salon, and Grand-père, Oncle Rafe, Merveille, and even Grisart all turned to look at me.

I was vaguely aware that Merveille had called for the French equivalent of the paddy wagon to come and retrieve *le blaireau* Grisart and take him off to jail, but for now, the murderer was sitting on a chair, cuffed and silent and looking very subdued.

"Ah, but Monsieur Wilde was getting his teeth cleaned today," explained Oncle Rafe. "And so he stayed at the veterinarian's surgery overnight. They have to put him to sleep, of course, for he does not like it so much."

Thank goodness. "I was frightened when he didn't bark," I said, stroking Madame X down her long, silky ink-black back. "I thought . . ." I shook my head as my throat closed up.

"You're unhurt, mademoiselle?" said Merveille. He'd taken a seat on the sofa next to me—the only place available—even while leaving a generous space between us. He gestured to my wrist.

"Tabi! What did he do to you?" demanded Grand-père, his blue eyes warm with concern. He had almost completely ig-nored me before now, except for many worried sidelong looks. I suspected he, too, was more emotional than he let on and had been holding back his feelings until the situation was under control. "What did that bast—"

"Oh," I said, noticing for the first time the ugly red marks on my wrist. Now that I noticed them, I realized they did hurt. "He handcuffed me, and I had to tighten the manacle too much in order to . . . um . . . get free." I realized too late that maybe I shouldn't be admitting to a police officer that I knew how to get out of handcuffs.

Grand-père choked off a triumphant cry, the whisky in his glass sloshing a little. "Do you see, Rafe? She even knows how to escape the handcuffs!"

Ah . . . thanks, Grand-père, for emphasizing that fact in front of a cop.

I glanced at Merveille, but to my surprise, he didn't seem an-noyed or appalled. If anything, his expression was amused . . . which was difficult to believe. I had to be reading him wrong.

Grisart was the one who expressed the most astonishment. "But . . . how?"

"Partly because you cuffed me in the front," I said. "That just made it easier. But also because I've had some practice." I didn't look at Merveille when I said that; I wanted him to wonder what exactly that meant.

The inspecteur murmured something that sounded like "*Bien sûr.*"

"You are certain he did not hurt you, *chérie?*" Oncle Rafe's eyes flashed dark in Grisart's direction, and for a moment, *I* was almost afraid of my honorary uncle. He looked lethal.

"Only a few bruises, I think," I said. "But how did you come to . . . well, *this?*" I gestured to the pistol, which now sat innocently on the table next to him.

"Ah." Grand-père smiled as he settled back into his seat, his glass of whisky fully refreshed. He'd offered some to Merveille, and as expected, he'd refused. Instead, the inspecteur sipped coffee. "*Monsieur l'agent* arrived here and asked to speak with us about the poisoned wine that had been delivered to this house. We had, of course, already spoken with *monsieur l'inspecteur*, but, of course, we invited Agent Grisart to join us here in the salon. And, of course, we are the hosts most excellent and considerate, and so we offered him the cognac or the whisky or the coffee."

"When he agreed to the whisky," Oncle Rafe said, with a meaningful look at Merveille, "it was wrong, *hein?* There is no police agent *consciencieux* who will drink when he is on his duty, *non?* But, of course, I then thought perhaps it was because it was so late and it was so cold outside."

"And then . . . ah, but *then,*" Grand-père said, lifting a pale, wrinkled finger in emphasis, "he talked of you, *ma mie*, and how he'd driven you home that first night, and how terrible it was that you should have seen two deaths, and so and so and so—"

"And I remembered that you were looking for someone who had been at *both* deaths, *non?*" Oncle Rafe seamlessly picked up the story. "And I looked at Maurice, and I could see that he was thinking of the same thing, you see? But, of course, that was still not enough . . . and then—"

"He mentioned Maison de Verre, and that was when I saw it. It took me far too long, eh, *mon cher* Rafe, did it not? Ah, this old brain . . ." Grand-père heaved a sigh and lit another cigarette. "It is old and feeble, but it still works . . . yet a bit slowly, *non?*"

"What do you mean?" I asked. "What did you see?"

"But he looks very much like his father, Jacques. Jacques Grisart, *le maître d'* at Maison de Verre," said Grand-père. "I remembered him well. It is the smile. It is the same."

I slumped a little on the sofa. "Don't feel bad, Grand-père . . . I didn't realize it until it was too late. I saw a picture of Jacques Grisart at his home with Madame Nanette, and I thought he looked familiar, but I didn't see the resemblance until . . . until it was too late. And Grisart—he made certain never to mention his mother's name or any details about her, so that we wouldn't make the connection."

"Ah, *pauvre petite*," Grand-père said. He reached over to pat my arm for the third or fourth time, and I realized that he needed to touch me just as much as I needed to feel the touch after all that had happened. I looked up at Oncle Rafe, who was watching us with somber eyes, and I gave him a look of love.

He blinked rapidly and looked away, then smiled a little. "And so, of course, we were becoming suspicious, *non*? But it was when Agent Grisart was so very conscientious and offered to refill our whisky glasses that we knew for certain. 'Ah, please, do not bother yourself, messieurs,' he said. 'Let me fill our glasses.' And he took our glasses to the counter, you see?" Oncle Rafe gestured to the ornate maple bar cabinet. "His sleight of hand . . . well, it is not so good, *hein*? He would not fool anyone who was looking—and I was looking."

"And then when *monsieur l'agent* sat back down with our glasses, well, he was met with quite the surprise." Grand-père chortled.

Oncle Rafe picked up the pistol and demonstrated. "He sat down, glanced up, *et voilà*! Down the front of the barrel he was looking." He chuckled.

"And so then we had a little discussion, *non*?" Grand-père said, looking meaningfully at Grisart. "But, of course, we did not know that he had *left* you in the catacombs!" His expression tightened into a cold mask. "*Bâtard.*"

"And, of course, we did not drink the whiskies he so kindly poured for us," my uncle added, reaching over to pat Grand-père's hand. "But we have saved them for you, Inspecteur, to take to the laboratory. I believe Maurice will confirm that both of them—the glasses—they smell of the bitter almonds."

"*Merci*," replied Merveille. There was a gravity in his expression that seemed overdone. Was he *enjoying* himself?

"And so while I sat so cozy with Agent Grisart, Maurice telephoned to your office, Inspecteur," Oncle Rafe said. "We were quite surprised at how quickly you arrived after that telephone call."

"But it was Tabi instead—and you as well, Inspecteur," added Grand-père.

Merveille shifted a little in his seat and sipped from his coffee. "Ah, yes, well . . . as it happens, I didn't yet receive your message at the 36. I was . . . I was on rue de Bourgogne, and I saw Mademoiselle Knight running down the street."

So much for me leaving my footprints and my purse and hoping that Merveille would find Grisart's képi hat and put the pieces together.

"You see, I knew it was you," Merveille said, looking at his assistant.

Former assistant now, I assumed.

"Only this morning, unfortunately, did the pieces fall into place for certain, but they did," Merveille went on. "The missing gift tag from the first death, of course, was most important. It was curious to me, you see, that you were in the area of Faubourg Saint-Honoré and were called in to Le Cordon Bleu.

"It wasn't a thing that made me suspicious so much—at least then—but I did notice it. For that was not your patrol area, *non*? But you were there, and then you made yourself so helpful to the investigation that I agreed you could assist. And then, of course, I was curious as to why you were so insistent . . . but I thought perhaps it was only that you wished to work with the protégé of Devré." That bit of immodesty from the normally restrained Merveille had me stifling a smile.

"And then when mademoiselle told me about the man who gave the wine to Pierre for Chef Beauchêne . . . how he was without a hat . . . why, that made me curious too. Why not a hat on a winter's day on the street? And the large mustache . . . well, that was patently obvious.

"And so I remembered that, and it was interesting. But it was the death of Émelie Loyer that told me all of it. I went to speak to her *propriétaire* at her *hôtel*"—he glanced at me, almost as if to acknowledge what I'd told him last night—"and that's when I learned about her young lover. The man with *la moustache négligeable* who is not so very tall." There was a definite dryness to his voice at the insult to Grisart's pathetic facial hair. "When I showed a photograph of you to her—Ah, but I also showed the photograph of Monsieur Bryant Howard, too, for he is of the same age and had been at the second murder. But *la propriétaire,* she agreed that you, Agent Grisart, were the same man as the lover of Madame Loyer.

"And then I remembered the missing hat. You could not have worn your képi to give the wine, *non? La moustache fausse, oui,* but not the cap. And so then I *knew.* But I needed more of the evidence, and then I was called out to the scene of the body of the young boy." Here Merveille's expression turned completely arctic. Even I had never been faced with one that cold, and certainly not one filled with such unmitigated loathing and disgust.

"And you were seen, you see, François. Giving the hot chocolate to the boy. You were not so careful that time, for who would have thought the death of a street urchin to be a problem, *non?* In fact, you offered to go instead of me, did you not, when the notice came into the 36? Likely to attempt to throw my scent off."

By now I had realized the inspecteur was a master at demonstrating thorough disgust in a cool, devastating manner without even lifting his voice or even twitching a brow.

"And so I was going to Maison de Verre tonight to see what I could find, and then I saw the mademoiselle's handbag . . . and the scuffle in the snow. *Oui,* mademoiselle, and your boot prints, too." He nodded in my direction. "And the discarded képi hat . . ."

Merveille spread his hands. "It is my great failure and deeper regret, mademoiselle, that I did not find all of this sooner . . .

before you were subjected to such . . . ugliness." He gave Grisart a look that would have curdled stone.

I didn't know what to say, so I lifted my glass in a toast to Merveille. "Agent Grisart didn't give you enough credit."

"Ah, no, of course. I took care to make certain he thought I was only the ignorant fool. But . . . I nearly made a mistake, waiting too long to expose him, and for that, my grave apologies, mademoiselle. I should not have delayed, for it put you—and others—at risk." His apology, as pretty as it was, was a little stiff and reserved. Almost as if he were embarrassed to have to deliver it.

"Well, everything has turned out all right, then, hasn't it?" I said, smiling at my grandfather and uncle.

Before they could answer, the sharp *brrrilll* of the telephone cut through the room.

I bolted to my feet, wondering who would be telephoning after eight at night.

"Hello?" I said.

"Oh, good, Tabitha, you're there!" Julia's voice rang through the wire. "Did you get the wine?"

CHAPTER 25

"*T*HAT SETTLES IT," SAID JULIA AS SHE SPUN FROM THE STOVE, A wooden spoon in one hand, her apron splattered with stains. "I'm going to have to start carrying my own Swiss Army knife. This is the second time it's saved your skin, Tabs!"

"Well, it certainly helped," I said with a laugh, after taking a healthy sip of Sancerre. I was still a little wobbly from everything that had happened tonight, but I was finally about to find out just what *rissolettes* were.

The three of us—Grand-père, Oncle Rafe, and I—had all hurried across the street to Julia and Paul's apartment as soon as I hung up from the phone call, for according to Julia, dinner was nearly ready!

When I say, "Hurry," and "As soon as," I mean that Grand-père carefully wrapped himself up in a thick wool coat and cashmere muffler. Then he took his time to rakishly position a fedora over his shock of white hair—which he had just combed—and draw on a pair of dark blue leather gloves.

Oncle Rafe wore a similar style of elegantly tailored coat, but his had a bit of fur trim at the collar and cuffs, and so he disdained the need for a muffler, although he replaced his normal knit cap with a fedora of his own.

In crossing the street (once I had herded my messieurs down the stairs and outside), Grand-père did more of a spirited hobble than a hurried walk, with Oncle Rafe's arm slipped through his as he paced jauntily but circumspectly next to my grandfather, while brandishing an unnecessary but very stylish walking stick. I walked behind the two of them in an effort to make certain no one slipped and that I didn't rush too fast for their more sedate pace.

Now the three of us, plus Paul Child, crowded at the table in the tiny kitchen on the upper level of the Childs' apartment at 81 rue de l'Université along with a busy Julia and an amazing fusion of smells.

And she, the goddess of the kitchen, took up the space and energy of four more people in that very small area, where, with her grand height, Julia fairly stooped over the low counters and tiny stove and *never stopped moving*.

Watching Julia cook a meal was like watching a single person play every instrument in a jazz quintet . . . and in perfect time. She swept from task to task with hardly a pause: stirring, poking, peeking, flipping, measuring, pouring, chopping, sprinkling, sniffing and, of course . . . tasting.

"*Ye gods*," she moaned as she sampled the sauce for the sole fillets. "This is going to be one of the best things you've *ever* tasted, I promise. It's just so . . . so . . . *voluptuous*. And you know what they say about oysters!" She winked at Paul, who gave her a provocative look in return.

"What a wonder," he murmured, his eyes warm as they followed her. "Best thing I ever did was marry that woman—and the second best thing was bringing her here. I only wish I were learning to cook along with her. It would be so much *fun!*"

"Madame Child is indeed *la déesse* in the kitchen," Oncle Rafe said, pouring more wine into everyone's glasses.

I hadn't actually brought the wine over to Julia's apartment (it was still in Merveille's car), but Oncle Rafe had selected two bottles from his own collection . . . along with three bottles of the mead he had, apparently, purchased from Monsieur Gérard.

"Of course we will bring this, if Madame Child is to feed us," my uncle said when I balked at raiding his *cave*. "It will be my pleasure. And . . . what else will I do with two entire cases of mead, *hein*?" He chuckled wryly.

And so we were sipping a clean and slightly acidic Sancerre

from Fautrier et Fils and were just about to be served *les rissolettes de foie gras.*

What a way to end an evening.

A killer had been apprehended, along with an amazing cache of fine wine.

My beloved messieurs were safe and, from the look of it, enjoying themselves immensely discussing fine paintings with Paul as we watched the symphony of gastronomy unfold before us.

And we were about to eat a magnificent meal that included a "voluptuous" sauce made—or so we'd heard—from steeped and simmered fish bones, cream, wine, butter, and mushrooms, poured over delicate fillets of sole, with mussels and oysters tucked in next to them. I moaned inside my head at the very thought of it.

And then there would be the little moist, cake-like *charlottes de pommes* for dessert.

I couldn't be more content.

I smiled and sipped again. It was almost impossible to believe that less than three hours ago, I had been sitting in Maison de Verre, talking to a murderer, fearing for my life and that of the men I loved.

What had seemed like hours and hours of fear and desperation, determination and craftiness, had really taken place only during a short time. It was hardly believable.

"So, Tabitha," said Paul, suddenly looking at me from over the top of his wineglass. He was an intensely intellectual man with an extremely creative side—he painted, sculpted, carved—but he sometimes came across as overly serious and even a little intimidating.

I knew he'd worked for the US spy agency during the war, and that made me wonder about what he might have done and seen . . . which gave him an even more interesting aura in my mind—obviously.

And since I'd seen him and Julia together many times and enjoyed the way their two personalities mixed—not to mention the obvious love between them—I had come to thoroughly like Paul Child.

"Now that you've solved two murder investigations, do you think you've found your calling?" he said with a little smile from beneath his neat dark mustache. His eyes twinkled. "Julia has her cooking, and you have your crime solving?"

I felt heat rush into my face, and, thankfully, before I could think how to respond to that (because, well, if the thought *hadn't* crossed my mind, I wouldn't be *me*), the doorbell buzzed.

Paul rose to answer it, his expression quizzical and intrigued. He left through the door that would take him down the stairs to the lower level of their flat.

I could feel my grandfather and uncle looking at me assessingly—clearly wondering about the answer to Paul's question—but before I could think of how to respond, Julia saved the day.

"I suspected Bryant Howard for a while, you know, Tabs," she said as she surged to the table with a stack of clattering plates and a basket balancing a loaf of crusty bread.

"I thought he was a good candidate—he knew all about wine, but he wasn't French, so maybe he didn't care too much about spoiling those rare vintages. And he really likes his Coca-Cola— and I kept seeing empty bottles of Coke in the catacombs and in the alley behind Maison de Verre, and it made me wonder about him," Julia explained.

"Yes, I thought about that, too," I said. "And he, of all people, would have known how to sell off that wine and make a fortune. But in the end, I concluded it wasn't him. He hadn't been in Paris long enough to know about the wine, or to know his way around . . . Besides, Madame Loyer's landlady would probably have mentioned if the young lover was an American. So I just didn't see him as a serious suspect."

"Well, that's why *you're* the private investigator and *I'm* the cook," said Julia as she set down a platter with about a dozen small grayish patties on it.

"*Et voilà! Les rissolettes de foie gras Carisse!*" she announced.

We were sampling the soft, herby little patties made from duck liver and heaven knew what else—smearing them over the bread, then crunching into the crusts; *divine!*—when the door opened and Merveille walked in, followed by Paul.

"Inspecteur," I said in surprise as he looked around, seemingly taken aback by the sight of all of us.

"Ah . . . I don't mean to interrupt, but you left this in the car, mademoiselle," he said, holding up the wine I'd swiped from the bunker. He seemed very ill at ease. "I'll only leave this and be off—"

"No you won't!" said Julia firmly. "There's plenty of food and room at the table"—the latter of which was not quite true, but no one cared—"and *surely*, you're off duty by now and can have something to eat and drink."

"An eighteen ninety-three Volnay?" Oncle Rafe breathed reverently. He was holding the bottle Merveille had put on the table, and now he looked around at us, clutching it to his chest. "I beg you to tell me that it doesn't have cyanide in it."

Merveille and I laughed, catching each other's eyes briefly. I felt an unexpected rush of warmth, which unsettled me for a moment, but then it was gone.

"No, I don't believe so," replied Merveille, sitting with an air of reluctance after Julia fairly glowered him into a chair.

"*Ah, merci, le bon Dieu,*" Oncle Rage said. I swore his eyes glistened with tears. "May I?"

"Why not?" I said, glancing at Merveille. "Thank you for bringing that, Inspecteur."

"But of course, mademoiselle. I do not wish to interrupt—"

"Inspecteur, you're not interrupting anything but a *magnificent, voluptuous* meal!" Julia told him, sliding a plate and a wineglass in front of him. "Now, eat and drink—the *sole à la normande* is going to be the best thing that's ever passed between your lips—I promise you!"

Oncle Rafe had opened the Volnay, and his face was a vision of bliss as he tasted it. I almost wanted to tease and ask him if he needed a moment alone in order to get his emotions under control.

Instead, I asked, "What will happen to all that wine in the

bunker, Inspecteur?" I'd just taken my own first sip of the Volnay. It was, incredibly, the best wine I'd ever tasted—and it didn't smell like bitter almonds. I could see why Oncle Rafe was in a state of bliss.

"Ah, but that will be for the courts to decide, mademoiselle," said Merveille.

"*Berk*," said Grand-père as Oncle Rafe made a similar sound of disgust. I understood their reactions, for from what I knew, the Parisian judicial system wasn't quite as logical—or equitable—as it could be.

"It will be a shame if something happened to all of that wine secreted away in the bunker," Oncle Rafe said. "Before it is decided, *non?*"

Merveille gave him a measured look. "It certainly would. Quite criminal, in fact."

Oncle Rafe merely smiled and lifted his glass to sip again.

"But you have plenty of mead now, Oncle," I teased, reaching over to pat him on the arm. "Surely, that's something."

"Ah. Mead. I have nothing against it, you see," Oncle Rafe said, "but it is made from *honey*, not *le raisin*." He tried, and failed, to keep the underlying disdain from his voice.

"And that is why you have brought some as a gift to Madame Child, *non, cher?*" said Grand-père, smiling. "Surely, she will find something delightful to do with it."

"Mead?" said Julia, turning from the stove. She had a long, deep platter in her hands. I could see the delicate fillets of sole partly submerged in the glorious creamy sauce. Mushrooms, oysters, and sassy little mussels—looking like yawning mouths—swam in the lusciousness, as well.

"Oh, I'm certain I could do wonders with mead. It's like cooking with any other wine or spirits—you just need to take into account its flavor and how it will *marry* with the others. Why, I could use it in a braising glaze over a pork loin," she said, still standing there with the platter as her eyes looked off into the distance. She seemed to have forgotten she was about to set it on the table. "Or it would be *delightful* for a marinade for chicken, I think, most definitely. And then for desserts . . . *oh la la!* Sauces and soaked cakes and glazes . . ."

"Delicious! All of it would be delicious!" exclaimed Oncle Rafe, probably enthusiastic about the idea of getting use from the mead that didn't involve actually drinking it.

"And perhaps, then, Madame Child, you will be so kind as to help our dear Tabi with it *en cuisine, non?*" said Grand-père hopefully.

"Ah, yes, that would be most appreciated," Oncle Rafe said with a teasing smile at me.

"But Mademoiselle Knight is not so very poor in the kitchen," said Merveille.

Everyone stilled and looked at him and then looked at me. I felt a rush of heat swarm up over my cheeks under their very curious and *very* interested regard.

And then Julia, thank heavens, once again saved me from replying. She remembered she was holding the platter, and she set it on the table with a flourish.

"And now for *sole à la normande!* Bon appétit!"

And she winked at me.

AUTHOR'S NOTE

I had the most delightful time writing and researching the second An American in Paris Mystery. Some of the things I learned were so fascinating that I had to include them in the story, and I want to take a few paragraphs to clarify which nuggets of historical detail are true and which ones are figments of my imagination.

But first, I'd like to say that I am not a French speaker, and although I have had resources who've helped me with some of the French and I've done my very best, any errors are most definitely my own. I must give big shout-outs to Marty Lewis, Aurélie Filiol, and Miriam Miller for answering questions and helping me to keep any French errors to a minimum.

I'd also like to take a moment to thank the entire amazing team at Kensington Books for all the love and effort they've put behind the An American in Paris Mystery series.

On a daily basis, I am blown away by the attention to detail, the creativity, the enthusiasm, and the sheer energy that has been invested in these books. *Thank you* from the bottom of my heart, especially to my unflagging agent, Maura Kye-Casella, along with my brilliant editor, Wendy McCurdy, and her on-top-of-everything assistant Elizabeth Trout. Larissa Ackerman, Matt Johnson, Vida Engstrand, and the entire publicity, marketing, and social media team are consistently hitting things out of the park. You all blow my mind, and I'm very grateful to you for your support for this series. A shout-out to Seth Lerner, who has created two of the most stunning and appropriate covers (so far) for the Tabitha and Julia books. . . . I couldn't have imagined anything more perfect for them. Thank you.

I want to extend special gratitude to the Julia Child Foundation, and Todd Schulkin in particular, for your steadfast commitment to honoring Julia Child's legacy and advancing the culinary arts. I very much appreciate your work in all forms of media (television shows, museum exhibits, etc.) to that end, as well as the time you've taken to personally share your stories and knowledge of Julia with me.

I am additionally thankful for Kate Miller Spencer and Kate Leder from *Cherry Bombe* and Donna Yen from the Santa Barbara Culinary Experience for embracing "The American in Paris Mysteries" and sharing *Mastering the Art of French Murder* with your wonderful community. Now, to those historical details that may or may not have been fabricated . . .

First, Julia Child did live at 81 rue de l'Université, and she did attend the Cordon Bleu. But, as far as I know, she was never involved in any murder investigations.

Her schedule as portrayed in the book is accurate: early morning classes with Chef Bugnard (whom she eventually hired to give her private cooking lessons) and a group of American GIs, followed by a trip to the market so she could make at home what she'd learned in class . . . Paul home for lunch from the office to test it out . . . then Julia back to the school for the afternoon demonstrations with what we might call today "celebrity chefs." The depiction of Chef Beauchêne's demonstration in the small auditorium is accurate (with the exception of the poisoned wine, of course), and Julia would, on most days, do exactly as she does in the book: head to the market a second time in order to buy the supplies so she could make whatever had been prepared during the demonstration.

It was no wonder Paul Child had to keep moving the hole on his belt. . . .

Regarding the Germans and their control of the wine industry in France—most everything I've written about relative to that is true and accurate. The French did their best to combat this element of the Occupation by doing everything from hiding wines in mountain caves, behind armoires, and in secret cellars behind new walls, to mislabeling them, to secretly draining barrels on trains when they came into the station, to adding the very old dust that—yes—was saved at Chevalier & Son's carpet cleaning company for that very reason. Vintners who combatted or resisted the *Weinführer* were often imprisoned and beaten and sometimes were even killed. La Tour d'Argent is a real restaurant, still operating today, and is renowned for its wine cellar. Unfortunately, some of its wines were lost to the Germans, as described in *A Murder Most French*.

I don't know for a fact whether any wines were hidden in the Paris catacombs, but it seems logical that they could have been. And the spiders brought in to spin their webs in front of newly constructed brick walls to hide wine caches were my own invention—but, again, seemed logical given the fake walls and the antiquated dust.

Tabitha's adventures in the catacombs and the descriptions of them are also realistic. And although today the catacombs are officially off-limits (except for a small area for tourists), there were no restrictions until 1955—five years after Tabitha's adventures therein.

That's not to say that there aren't people, known as cataphiles, roaming the catacombs illegally today. They certainly are, and they just take care not to get caught when they set up bars, film theaters, and other underground (literally!) activities. There still is a man who ferments mead in the catacombs, in fact, and there were more who did so previously, like my fictional Monsieur Gérard. The mushroom farmers, as described by my invented Monsieur Michel, have mostly moved to Lyon and parts of Asia, but there were many of them farming what we call "button mushrooms" throughout the catacombs for centuries for the reasons described here, as well. It was the building of the *métro* that began to affect the usage of the catacombs for farming, and the lack of maintenance by the quarriers.

The German bunker, which had been co-opted by the Nazis during the Occupation, is as described herein, as well, and it really is located very near (within a mile or so) to the rue de Bourgogne and the fictional restaurant Maison de Verre.

And, finally, the ongoing culture war against Coca-Cola was a real thing for the reasons described in the story.

Dear Reader, thank you for picking up *A Murder Most French*. I hope you enjoyed the read and perhaps learned something in the process.

I love to hear from readers and can be reached at my website, colleencambridge.com.

—Colleen Cambridge, May 2024